OUTFOXED

Books by Melinda Metz

Outfoxed
Crazy Like a Fox
Fox Crossing
Talk to the Paw
The Secret Life of Mac
Mac on a Hot Tin Roof

OUTFOXED

MELINDA METZ

KENSINGTON
PUBLISHING CORP.

www.kensingtonbooks.com

KENSINGTON BOOKS are published by

Kensington Publishing Corp.
119 West 40th Street
New York, NY 10018

ISBN: 978-1-4967-3778-6 (ebook)

ISBN: 978-1-4967-3777-9

First Kensington Trade Paperback Printing: December 2022

10 9 8 7 6 5 4 3 2 1

Printed in the United States of America

For Carrie Enders and Chessa Metz—
Fox Crossing wouldn't be the same place without you

PROLOGUE

Tonight, The Fox was drawn to the town. It wasn't often she craved the presence of humans, but tonight she wanted to walk among the cords of light connecting them. In her woods, there were cords everywhere, between mated pairs, between hunter and prey, between trees in a grove. There was beauty in each of these connections, but tonight she wanted to experience the cords between humans, the way they tangled and frayed, the way they flared and dimmed, not always beautiful, but always surging with energy.

The cords between the creatures of the woods gave a constant, steady glow that soothed her. But tonight, she did not want to be soothed. She was restless and wanted the diversion the changeable cords of humankind offered. And so, she entered their world.

CHAPTER 1

"It's so unusual." And by *unusual* Victoria Michaud meant "unusually ugly." Truth? She wasn't a hundred percent sure exactly what *it* was. It weighed about ten pounds and was about two feet tall. It was painted gold and liberally dusted with rainbow glitter. It didn't seem to have a function, so she'd have to classify it as a . . . sculpture, a sculpture of something with eyes. At least she was about ninety percent sure the large faux emeralds were eyes. But were they the eyes of a camel? Or a swan? There was a curve that could be a hump or a neck, but the eyes didn't seem in the correct position for either creature. "I could give you . . ." She hesitated, taking in Mrs. Haggerty's bouclé coat, nice and cozy for fall, but not nearly heavy enough for Maine in March. At least she was layering. It looked like she had at least two sweaters on underneath. "I could give you twenty-five for it." Which would probably mean a loss of $24.50.

"Wonderful! I hope someone gets as much pleasure out of it as I did." Mrs. Haggerty set the . . . the swamel on the counter and gave it an affectionate pat. As soon as she was out the door, Bonnie came over and picked up the statue. "When you said twenty-five, I was hoping you were talking cents. Even then you might take a loss. I'm not sure this would even go on the ten-cent-Tuesday table."

"I know." Vic sighed. "I know, I know, I know."

Bonnie raised her eyebrows. "And yet?"

"The store's called Junk and Disorderly. There needs to be some fun junk on the shelves. That's part of the appeal, seeing some crazy ugly."

"I think we've got that covered." Bonnie put the swamel on top of a low mahogany dresser between a lovely brass comb, brush, and mirror set, and a Barbie Fashion Head that had, unfortunately, been given a makeover with Magic Markers, permanent Magic Markers. She used both hands to brush rainbow glitter off her black overalls. "Herpes of craft supplies," Bonnie muttered, glaring at the glitter that had been left behind.

"Gives you a little pizzazz."

"I don't do pizzazz."

True. Vic's assistant liked straight lines and solid colors, especially black, set off by a sleek blunt bob. Vic's own style was eclectic. Bonnie sometimes accused her of dressing in all the pieces that didn't sell at the shop, but not true. Mostly not true.

"I never thought I'd say this, but Barbie is looking almost pretty next to the thing." Bonnie fluffed Barbie's hair. "Maybe we can use that. We'll just put it next to whatever we're hoping to sell."

"Once we hit hiking season, all this will go. The trail widows are always ready to shop." Bonnie looked dubious. Time for a new topic. "How's Addison doing?" A question about Bonnie's thirteen-year-old daughter was always an easy way to change the subject. Besides, Vic wanted to know. "She still missing Rose as much?"

"As much as if she just moved yesterday. Addison and Rose were so tight, and I always thought it was great. But maybe it kept her from connecting with the other girls enough. Last night, I asked if she wanted to invite a friend to come to the movies with us, but she said no."

"You could bring her the swamel. I bet that would cheer her up."

Bonnie snorted. "As in 'swan-camel'?"

"Exactly." Vic loved how she and Bonnie were almost always on the same wavelength. She looped her arm around Bonnie's shoulders and gave her a squeeze. "I know it's got to be so hard watching Addison feeling sad and not being able to fix it."

"I keep telling myself to give it time, and that Addison will eventually get close to some of the other girls. But I remember seventh grade. I remember how cliquey it could be, even though now it feels like they are way too young for all that. What if she never makes a friend ever? Which is how I know she thinks of it. Never ever."

"I remember how a school year felt so long back then. Summer vacation went on forever. Now—" Vic snapped her fingers. "But there's no way she won't eventually find another bestie. Addison's too—" Vic was interrupted by her brother coming in the door. "Henry!" She rushed over and got one of his patented Henry hugs, so hard it felt like it dented her ribs. "Are you hungry? Have you eaten? Are you tired? Do you want a nap? The drive was long, I know. Or maybe you want coffee? Or something cold? Or—"

He held up one hand. "Research shows people are only able to hold three or four things at a time in their working memory. I've reached capacity." He grinned at her. "But I appreciate the welcome."

"It's how she greets me almost every afternoon." Bonnie smiled at him. "I'm Bonnie, the assistant."

"I can't believe you two haven't met. Bonnie's been working here for three years. It's been too long since you've been home, brother of mine."

"Only because we've been doing the annual beach trip," Henry answered.

The beach trip where Henry, Vic, and their mom and dad visited both sets of grandparents, who'd made the move from Maine to Florida together and gotten side-by-side condos. That trip was never going to happen again.

"Well, it's good to finally meet the big-shot doctor brother," Bonnie said.

"Brother, yes. Doctor, kind of. A PhD, not an MD. Big shot, not so much." He walked over and shook Bonnie's hand.

Vic's brother always acted like his accomplishments were nothing. Not like he should walk around bragging all the time, but Vic wished he would just take a compliment without deflecting. Okay, a PhD wasn't an MD, but he'd worked hard for that degree.

"I say heading up the community health-needs assessment qualifies as big shot." Bonnie winked at him. "Your sister talks about you once in a while."

"Vic's always been my cheerleader." He sucked at taking a compliment, but he was always generous about giving one.

"She just paid twenty-five bucks for this." Bonnie patted the swamel on the hump. "I think she may be in need of a health assessment."

"I know, okay? I know, I know, I know." Vic ran her fingers through her long hair, accidentally pulling one of her sparkly butterfly barrettes free. "But it was Mrs. Haggerty selling it." She slid the barrette back in place so it would hold her wavy hair, same dark brown as Henry's, away from her face.

"I don't remember— Oh, wait. Cafeteria lady, elementary school."

"Yep."

"Always gave me extra, which I didn't need." Henry pulled his parka off. "Was coffee one of the hundred things you offered me?"

"In my office. Come on." Vic led the way to the back room. She filled up a YOU'RE FOXY mug for him, and one with a little ceramic fox in the bottom for her. She doubted there was anyone in Fox Crossing who didn't have at least one fox mug. She gestured Henry to the overstuffed armchair on one side of her desk, keeping the wooden one with the wobbly leg for herself.

"Should I ask if you're turning a profit?" He eyed the pair of clown dolls dressed as a bride and groom propped on one of the half dozen bookshelves she used for storage.

"With my eye for hidden gems?" She laughed. "I do okay. Especially in the summer."

"Summer is, by my calculations, a quarter of the year."

"I don't need much. Pop-Tarts and Diet Coke."

"I hope you're kidding."

"Diet Coke has no calories, so that takes away some of the calories of the Pop-Tarts, if you average the two together." Vic realized she had half a Diet Coke sitting on the desk and took a swig. Warm and flat. But still not bad.

"You do realize you have a cup of coffee in your other hand?"

Vic laughed and downed the rest of the soda. She picked up the wonderfully ornate footed bowl she used for sugar, then looked around for the spoon. She didn't see it, so she shook some sugar into her mug—and a little onto the desk—then grabbed a pen as a stirrer.

"You drink Diet Coke, but put sugar in your coffee?"

"I'm not having Pop-Tarts, so it's okay."

Henry shook his head. "I'm having Mom flashbacks."

"Yeah." Their mom had constantly been on a diet. She'd also constantly made food that had been on no diet ever— fettuccine Alfredo, chocolate pecan pie, mashed potatoes with butter, butter, and more butter. Usually, she'd just sit and watch them eat, drinking a Diet Coke. But Vic had caught her downing the leftovers straight out of the fridge more than once. Vic's mother always said whatever you eat standing up didn't count.

She was the queen of rationalizations when it came to food, and Vic was still using her calorie math. "She kept her weight at—"

"One-thirteen." Henry sent the pitch of his voice higher. "'Same weight as I was when I won Junior Miss Georgia Peach.'"

"Exactly. And she thought I should be the same. I guess it did leave me with some messed-up eating habits. But that's all going to change when I turn thirty. I'm going to become disgustingly healthy."

"Only one day left." Henry pulled the lumpy pillow out from behind his back, shook his head as he read the I LOVE WEIRD embroidered on it, then tossed it on the floor.

"Right. Except, I have to have birthday cake. So maybe I'll take two days. Although, according to Mom, cake with writing on it doesn't have calories." Vic took a sip of coffee. "I forgot to ask if you wanted sugar for yours. I can find a real spoon if you don't want the pen."

"Don't bother. I'm doing the Whole30. No sugar. No MSG. No—"

"No, no, no. I'm not sure if I can live with you."

"It's only until I find my own place. You could do the 30 with me. You said you wanted to get healthy, disgustingly healthy."

"I said disgustingly healthy, not revulsingly. And I told you, you should stay with me the whole year. We hardly ever get to see each other. It will be fun. Unless you try to make me give up sugar entirely, then we'd have to throw down."

"If I do stay, I'm paying you rent."

"Don't be stupid. I really am fine. I told you, I've got everything I need."

"Everything you need, plus whatever those things are on your legs."

"These, brother of mine, are spats, short for 'spatterdashes.' Mine are brocade, and before you say anything, I know they don't match. I prefer that they don't match. People used to wear them to keep rain and mud from spattering on their shoes and socks. I just think they're purdy." She stretched her legs out in front of her to admire them. The motion almost dumped her on the floor, but Henry caught her arm and held it until she got the wobbly chair steady again.

Vic noticed a worry line forming between her brother's eyebrows as he took in more of her inventory. He blinked several times as he studied one of her latest acquisitions, a Fiji mermaid.

"Isn't she cool?" Vic said. "I like the shape of the skull. Sometimes artists make it look too human. The real Fiji mermaid had the skull of a juvenile monkey."

"That has to be the ugliest thing I've ever seen, and I had to dissect a cow's eye in one of my bio classes."

"I'm not sure I believe you, considering you puked when Buddy Dyer showed you his toenail-clipping collection."

"Because I had the flu."

"So you say." Vic grinned at Henry. It was so great having her brother home. "Anyway, ugly or not, there's a market for those mermaids. I have to remember to spell Fiji *f-e-e-j-e-e* on the tag. More authentic. That's how Barnum did it in his sideshow." The frown line on Henry's face didn't go away. "Dude, seriously, I'm fine, just like I am every time you ask. Do I need to remind you the shop is paid for, as is the apartment above it?"

"I'm still paying rent."

"Don't be stupid. I always make a few good estate-sale finds, and Bonnie made us a website." Henry was looking stubborn. Vic knew he was never going to agree to stay if he didn't pay something. "I guess you could split utilities with me, if you really want to."

"I pay it all, or no deal."

Vic considered the offer. "Whoever can hold their breath the longest decides."

"I know you used to cheat."

"No, you didn't."

"Yeah, I did. You'd puff up your cheeks real big, then breathe through your nose." He did a demo to remind her.

"Why'd you let me win all those times then?"

"It's a big-brother thing."

"Little brother," Vic corrected.

"I'm much bigger than you."

True. He was a six-one tower of muscle. He'd always called himself her big brother back in the day too, although back then they were about the same height and he probably weighed fifty or sixty pounds more. At least their mom hadn't expected *him* to be the weight she was when she'd been crowned Junior Miss Georgia Peach. He'd gotten a growth spurt the summer after his senior year and lost the rest of the excess weight in college, but by then the damage had been done. Years of being fat-bullied had left him with scars.

"Just let me pay the whole utility bill. Like your friend said, I'm a big-shot doctor."

"I suppose, if you insist, you can pay the entire thing." She gave an elaborate, put-upon sigh.

"Why, thank you." Henry took a swallow of coffee. "I'm not sure if I should ask, but how are Mom and Dad?"

With the mention of their parents, Vic felt a familiar surge of sadness. It'd been more than a year since they'd split, and the divorce would be final in less than a month. She should have dealt with it by now. She wasn't a child. But a part of her that still needed them, needed them together. "We have a system." She'd never admitted this to Henry when they'd talked on the phone. But now that he was going to be living in town, he was going to find out.

"A system," he repeated.

Vic picked up a calendar—she had a separate one just for their parents—and handed it to him.

His eyebrows went up as he studied it. "I'm assuming *M* for 'Mom' and *D* for 'Dad.'"

"Brainpower of a PhD at work," she teased.

"I wanted to be sure, because this seems like craziness. Why are you keeping track of their appointments?"

He didn't get it. Well, why would he? "It's more than that. They refuse to be in the same room, so I make a schedule that shows when each is allowed to be at one of their usual places—Banana's, Flappy's, the BBQ, every place."

"They can't even sit at different tables and ignore each other?"

Vic shook her head. "A trivia tournament is coming up, and I live in fear that both their teams will end up in the final round. I guess maybe I could ask Banana to set up a table outside his pub and one team could yell their answers though the window. But it's pretty cold for that."

"How did you decide which one of them had to leave the Quiz Pro Quos?"

"Oh, that wasn't even an option. The only way I could make it work was to have them both quit Quos and join other teams. The trivia world was rocked. Rocked, I tell you."

Henry scrubbed his face with his fingertips. "I can't believe Mom and Dad . . . just never saw it coming."

"Me either." They were both silent a moment.

"What would happen if you just refused to mediate?" Henry tossed the calendar back on her desk.

"I didn't at first, but every time they ended up in the same place, which happened a lot because, Fox Crossing, there would be shouting and tears. I'm talking about from me." She forced a laugh. "It just got too stressful. And now you know why I am having two birthday parties tomorrow night. You are required to attend both. One, because they are your sister's birthday parties. Two, because if you choose the one Dad is organizing, Mom would never forgive you, and vice versa. Mom's is at

Wit's Beginning because, of course, Banana insisted on his pub being used for at least one of the parties. Dad's is at Shoo Fly's because, Dad claims—now he claims—that Shoo Fly's cakes are better than Mom's."

"Being back is going to be an adjustment. A part of me feels like if I go to the house, it will just be like every other time I've come to visit. Mom and Dad waiting for me."

"Sometimes I feel the same way. Pretty soon the house will be sold." It shouldn't matter. Vic hadn't lived there for years. But it felt like such a loss.

"And they've still never said why they're getting divorced?"

"They grew apart. That's all either of them will say." Her eyes suddenly stung with unshed tears, and she blinked them away before Henry could notice. She needed a subject change. "So, tell me more about the job."

"I saw what you did there," Henry said, but went along with the new topic. "The study covers all of Piscataquis County. The first thing I need to do is make some community contacts in each town, people who can help me get information from every resident. If the study is going to end up getting funds to the people who need it most, I can't miss anybody."

She could hear the enthusiasm in his voice and knew it would be infectious. He was going to be able to get everyone he needed involved.

"I'm going to start with Fox Crossing, since the local-boy factor will give me an in. That's what got me the job, really."

There he went again. Downplaying. "Yeah, I heard it was between you and the Duck of Justice. It has more than two hundred and fifty thousand Facebook followers." The DOJ was the mascot of the Bangor Police Department, a duck illegally killed that had been taxidermied.

"And it's dead. Which maybe gave me an advantage." He picked Vic's letter opener off her desk—Lucite with samples of horse estrogen pills inside, some kind of veterinary pharmaceutical giveaway, she guessed. He frowned at it, then put it down without commenting on its fabulousness. Her brother had no appreciation for the finer things. "Never thought I'd be living in Fox Crossing again. But it's right in the study area—"

"And allows spending time with your fabulous sister."

"And allows spending time with my fabulous sister." He stretched. "I might take you up on that nap."

Vic pulled out a set of keys with a miniature Sorry! game on the ring and handed them over. "I made you a set. Guest room's all made up." Henry opened the miniature Sorry! box and twirled the tiny spinner. "There's a little side drawer that has magnetic game pieces." As soon as she'd spotted the key ring on one of her garage-sale sweeps, she'd thought of Henry. They'd played many a game back in the day.

"I let you win at Sorry! too."

"No way. I earned every moment of sweet, sweet revenge." Every time she'd sent him back, she'd done a victory dance and yelled "Sorry!" as loud as she could. She might have been a tad obnoxious.

"That's it. Rematch at dinner."

"You're on." They both stood. Vic put her hand on his arm as he started for the narrow staircase that led from the back room to her apartment. "There's something you should know. Not a big thing. Just— Maybe it doesn't even matter."

"Obviously it matters. You're getting all twitchy."

Vic realized she'd been twisting one of her rings around and around and forced herself to stop. "Okay. Here it is. Cassian Gower died last week."

"That's too bad. I didn't ever really know him. I mean, he was the mayor, so I knew him that way. He wasn't a family friend or anything. Or did that change?"

"No. It's just that . . . his estate has to be dealt with, and that means—" She realized she'd started fiddling with her ring again and made herself stop and meet her brother's gaze. "Bowen Gower is back in town."

* * *

Bowen Gower stared at his grandfather's house, his home for his last two years of high school. His hand closed around the door handle of the rental, still somewhat annoyed that he'd reserved an Audi TT, but gotten a Hyundai Kona. He tightened his grip on the handle, but didn't open the door, just sat there looking at the massive house, every window, balcony, and gable familiar.

Just do it, he told himself. It's not like he could keep sitting out here on the driveway, not in Maine in March. He shoved the door open, popped the trunk, grabbed his bag, the Lotuff No. 12 *GQ* said was the best duffel, and strode to the front door. He fumbled a little with the locks, the bottom one sticking, then stepped inside. The house was warm, too warm. Or maybe it only felt that way because he'd been sitting in the cold car. He shrugged off his coat, a Kingsman Shackleton, a *GQ* pick for one of the best winter jackets. Not that he really cared. But some of his associates and clients would. He'd learned that from his granddad, who'd taken him shopping for interview suits when Bowen graduated from college. When Bowen needed clothes, he usually checked a *GQ* list, then used the link to order online. No fuss, no muss.

As he hung the jacket in the corner coatrack, the grandfather clock began to chime the quarter hour. The same chimes that played in St. Michael's Church in Charleston. The British had taken the bells back to England after they took over the city during the Revolutionary War. His grandfather had told him that story many times. The man loved history. He'd had a story about that compass-rose inlay on the floor too. The compass rose had once been called a wind rose, and—

"I cranked the clock." Bowen looked up and saw his sister coming down the staircase. "I always wanted to, but he'd never let me. Only you."

"Because I was older."

"Yeah, let's go with that, so my feelings don't get hurt. Anyway, brown furniture is dead, at least according to my last boyfriend, who, it turned out, shared our dear departed grandfather's opinion of me."

That was a lot to parse. Bowen decided not to ask any questions. When she reached the foyer, he took a step toward her, then hesitated. Was he supposed to hug her? They weren't a huggy family, but it had been a couple years since he'd seen her.

"I took the guest room on the second floor. Hope that's okay." She hadn't moved toward him.

No hug then. "Whatever you want is fine." His eyes moved over her, assessing. Smudges under her eyes, her sandy-blond hair in need of cutting, cuticle on one thumb gnawed on until it had bled, sole coming away from the upper on one sneaker. She looked like hell. He didn't think it could be grief over their grandfather. It's not like the two of them had been close. He doubted she'd even seen him more than once or twice since the family left Fox Crossing.

Bowen saw him at least once a year. Granddad would come into the city, and Bowen would take him to Keens. *Time Out New York* listed it as one of the ten best steak houses, and as soon as he'd seen it, with all those pipes on the ceiling belonging to old Keens' Pipe Club members like Babe Ruth and Teddy Roosevelt, he'd known he had to bring his grandfather there. The bow ties on the waiters cinched it. And he'd been right. Granddad did like the place, although the first time they'd gone, it had been disappointing to discover his grandfather had been there before. Bowen should have realized that his grandfather would know the best places in every major city. Still, that night Bowen had gotten the Nod of Approval, and the Nod did not come easily.

The silence was stretching out between Bowen and his sister, about to get awkward. "When did you arrive?" he asked.

"Just a few hours ago."

"I didn't realize you were here. I didn't see a car in the drive."

"I left the driving to Greyhound. At least to Bangor. Then I had to take a taxi."

He raised his eyebrows. She'd taken the bus all the way from El Paso? She didn't even have a car? Or plane fare? "I could have picked you up in Bangor if you'd let me know. Or I could have gotten you a plane ticket."

"Not necessary. And anyway, the bus has free internet access now. Well, enough to get thirty-five emails or post four pictures to social media, then you have to pay. I wanted to post a lot more pictures of the trip than that, but . . ." She shrugged.

What was he supposed to say to that? Was he supposed to laugh? She'd sounded sarcastic when she'd said that thing about the pictures, but he wasn't sure. Hard to read her, even though he was usually good at reading people.

"Kidding," she told him.

There was nothing to say to that. "I talked to the funeral director. We won't be able to have the burial until the first or second week of May."

"Yeah, that's what you said in your email."

Right. He'd already given all the details to her and their parents. He searched his brain for another topic of conversation, but couldn't come up with one, although he usually had several conversation starters at the ready. "I think I'll go unpack."

On their own his feet took him up the stairs and down the hall to his old bedroom. He opened the door and pulled in a long breath, the air thick, smelling faintly of linseed oil and beeswax from the furniture polish and the dusty burning smell the heat got when it was first turned on.

The trophies were still there. All those trophies. Catching the light, as if they'd been newly polished. The room was immaculate. The foyer had been too, the hardwood floor gleaming. His grandfather had had a live-in housekeeper and aide the last few years. The clock probably hadn't needed cranking, and Tegan probably didn't know how to do it properly. He could almost hear his grandfather's voice, telling him to turn the crank slowly, only one-half turn at a time, and never to force it.

He dropped his bag on the bed and walked over to the built-in display shelves, running one finger over the player in a three-point stance on the Maine State Champions award. Usually, the school would have kept that one in the trophy case, but his coach had given it to Bowen because he was the team MVP. He'd even been chosen one of the three finalists for the Fitzy award for best player in the state. He'd hardly been able to choke down his steak that night, knowing his grandfather was one table over, waiting to hear who won.

"Glory days, huh?" Tegan lounged in the doorway of the room.

"Not the way I think of them." He hadn't won.

"Come on. MVP of the football team twice, and once you were MVP of the baseball team in the same year." Bowen was surprised she remembered. She hadn't been especially interested in sports. "Grandfather ate it all up. Mayor Gower's grandson crapping out awards all over the place."

It was twelve years since they'd lived in Fox Crossing, and she still sounded resentful. It wasn't his fault that their granddad had been a sports guy more than a . . . whatever she was into back then. "You were the mayor's granddaughter. People paid attention to you too."

"Oh, right. I remember all those Sunday breakfasts at Flappy's with everyone coming to congratulate me for— What was it? Oh, right. Nothing."

It took Bowen a moment, but he came up with something. "You won that art contest that time."

She walked over to the bookshelf, not bothering to reply, and tapped the three trophies on the top shelf. "He kept everything in here the same. My room got made into a gift-wrapping center."

"Granddad had a gift-wrapping room?" His ex, Alexandra,

had had one, with rows of wrapping paper for all occasions mounted on the wall, scissors in a vintage letter holder, and rolls of ribbon on a three-tiered pastry stand, but he couldn't see his—

"Kidding."

Missed another cue. Damn it.

"Nothing's the same in there, though. My collection of My Pocket puppies wasn't enshrined, not even the glitter-sparkle Jazzy Chihuahua. But the guest room has its own balcony. I always wanted one of the balcony rooms. She looked pointedly at the doors leading to the balcony off Bowen's room.

Her voice had a bitter edge. Bowen couldn't come up with a reply that seemed appropriate, so he made a noncommittal sound and busied himself putting away the few things he'd packed.

Tegan plopped down on his bed. "Nice bag." She patted the duffel. "Expensive, I bet. What'd it run you?"

What kind of question was that? She'd come rolling in with a lot of attitude. Bowen hadn't been expecting that. Actually, he hadn't thought about it one way or the other. He and Tegan didn't have much of a relationship. He'd headed to college, Wharton, his grandfather's alma mater, a few months after he and his family had left town. He'd visited them in Oregon every couple Christmases for a couple days, and Tegan had usually been there, but now he was realizing they hadn't talked much, not about anything personal anyway. The time together had been spent at group dinners and group gift-openings and group viewings of Christmas movies.

"I don't remember. I've had it for years," Bowen answered. Lie and lie, but he wasn't going there with her, not when she'd arrived on Greyhound with sneakers about to fall off her feet.

"Mine was eleven seventy-nine, partly because it had Skunk Fu on it, and Skunk Fu, sadly, just never got close to Kung Fu Panda in popularity. Also, I used my ten percent employee discount."

"It could turn out to be a collector's item someday, if not that many were made."

"Hey, maybe." Tegan widened her eyes with exaggerated excitement. "We could trade if you want." She patted his duffel again.

Bowen forced a laugh, then retrieved his laptop. "The sleeve's made of recycled fire hoses," he said to stave off another stretch of uncomfortable silence. "The company that makes them is a client. It's lined with reclaimed parachute fabric."

"Why do things made from recycled stuff always cost more? Shouldn't it be the opposite?"

"In the case of FireOptics, meeting the third-party eco-friendly standards adds to the production costs, as does using renewable energy sources and minimal waste containers. The nontoxic ink on the packaging costs almost twice as much per gallon. Then there is—"

Tegan held up one hand. "I get it."

"It's going to change as there's more demand. Gen Z and millennials are continuing to represent a larger demographic share, and there are going to be long-term consequences for companies that don't include sustainability as part of their core value proposition." That was something he wanted to emphasize in his presentation on Feathered Nest. One source of their feathers was free-range birds. In the past, the feathers had been waste products, but now Feathered Nest purchased them from farmers, giving them a new revenue stream.

"I get it." Obviously, Tegan wasn't interested.

He set the laptop on the desk. "I should probably check in with work." True. But also lie. He needed to do a few tweaks on the Feathered Nest financial template, but he didn't have to do it right that moment.

"I can take a hint." Tegan shoved herself off the bed.

"That's not what I meant. I was just thinking out loud. You don't have to leave."

"I should unpack anyway." Tegan started for the door, then turned back. "Um, I was thinking maybe I'd just stay here until we're done going through everything in the house." She wasn't quite meeting his eye. "There's a ton of stuff. I could handle packing it up and selling it or whatever. After you decide what you want to keep," she added quickly. That attitude of hers had disappeared, at least temporarily.

"Don't you have to get back to your job?" He wasn't sure why she'd come now, instead of waiting for the service in the spring. He was the executor. He didn't need her to handle anything.

"My jobs are kind of like Kleenex."

"Kleenex?"

"Disposable. Easy to replace. I was getting tired of folding clothes anyway. People are unable to take a T-shirt out of the middle of the stack without messing up the whole thing. I could use a change of scene. And some snow. It's been too many no-snow winters. El Paso got some sometimes, but before that I was in Tuscaloosa, and no. So, is it cool with you? If I stay. Like I said, I can work on getting things organized here."

"I'm planning to come every weekend until I have things settled." The estate was his responsibility. He wasn't going to pass it on to her. "But if you want to stay, you should stay. This place is as much yours as mine."

Tegan gave a snort of laughter. "We both know that's not true."

He did know it wasn't true. His grandfather had set up a trust for Tegan that gave her $25,000 a year, a trust administered by Bowen. Same arrangement for Bowen's dad. Other than a few minor bequests, mostly to charities, Bowen had been given everything else. It didn't feel right, but it was what it was. "What I meant was, this used to be your home too, same as mine."

"I wouldn't say same, exactly." She stood. "So, I guess I'll be here a couple months, helping out." He nodded, and she left, shutting the door behind her.

Bowen sat down at the desk and powered up the laptop, then looked over at the shelves of trophies. His grandfather had kept them all these years, even though Bowen hadn't managed to win the Fitzy or Mr. Baseball. It felt like he'd just gotten the Nod of Approval.

CHAPTER 2

Tegan ran both hands over the sheep that sat by the fireplace in her grandfather's study, digging her fingers into the wool. It felt real, at least from what she remembered from a petting-zoo visit when she was little. Bowen had given her his bag of pellets so she could keep feeding the lambs. The memory just zapped into her brain. Long time ago, pre–Fox Crossing by many years.

Grandfather would have a complete fit if he could see me right now, she thought, giving the sheep a pat. It was big enough for a stool, and she'd sat on it once. Grandfather had come in and— He hadn't yelled. He wasn't a yeller. But he'd given her a look that made her insides shrivel up. Never did that again.

She didn't think Bowen would want it. She'd never seen his NYC apartment, but a large sheep with possibly real wool couldn't possibly match the decor. Tegan definitely didn't want it. Even if she did, it was so big it would need its own Grey-hound seat, and she wouldn't be paying for that. She'd started three piles—donate, sell, and keep—and shoved the sheep over with the donate stuff.

Bowen would need to look at everything. It was pretty much all his, except for the allowance he'd be doling out to her and Dad every year. But she'd figured she could give him a head start. She'd gotten up extra early so she could get something done before he came downstairs. She didn't need to be here living in the house, and they both knew it. She needed to make herself useful.

Next, the mechanical bank with William Tell shooting an apple off his kid's head that sat on one end of the mantel. She'd always wanted to try it out, but never had. She hadn't wanted to earn another of those looks. What you did was put a penny in William's crossbow, then press his foot. He'd shoot the penny over his son's head and into a slot in the bank. If she had a penny, she'd try it now, but, nope, only a quarter and a nickel in the pocket of her jeans.

She picked the bank up. Hefty. She was pretty sure it would be worth something, but was it something Bowen would want? It was antique-y looking, so maybe he'd think it was cool for a desk toy in his office. She pictured it as big, with floor-to-ceiling windows on two sides, because Bowen, being Bowen, would have a corner office at age thirty.

She wasn't sure exactly what he did. Some finance-y thing. To her, he was kind of like Chandler on *Friends*, where none of the friends could explain what his job actually involved. Whatever Bowen did, she knew it made him a lot of money. All it took was looking at him to know that. They didn't sell those shoes of his anyplace she'd ever worked, and his nails had been manicured, unlike hers. She bet he spent a ton on his hair too. It's not like he'd be seen at a Supercuts, even though they could probably do that classic Don Draper side part as well as some salon.

She pictured Bowen at one of those salons that served you coffee. She'd never even passed by one, but she knew they existed. His monthly hair-product budget would probably pay her monthly grocery bill. He had to use styling wax or pomade to keep it that perfect, at least from what she'd seen on *Queer Eye*. Did she watch too much TV? Everything made her think of something she'd seen on TV, maybe because TV was a cheap form of entertainment.

Tegan looked from the possibly sell pile to the possibly keep pile. Probably Bowen's office was way too sleek for the toy bank, which was vintage, but clunky. She put it in keep anyway. She didn't want to annoy Bowen by assuming he wouldn't want it. She didn't know what would have sentimental value for him.

There wasn't anything in the house that she felt an emotional attachment to. Living here had sucked. Mostly sucked. Her parents were always fighting, and her grandfather pretty much ignored her, which at least was better than the way he'd treated her dad. No unrefined yelling, but with these mean little digs that might even have been worse. Even though the meanness hadn't been directed at her, it had still given her that shrivel-y feeling inside. At least she'd had Henry. If she hadn't had him, she might have lost it.

Those pipes on the mantel should definitely go in the throwaway pile. No one was going to want to put their mouth on somebody's old pipe.

"You're up early," Bowen said as he came into the room. He glanced down, taking in her piles.

"Just thought I'd do a little organizing. That one is to donate. Possibly to donate," she corrected herself. "And that one is to sell, possibly. And that one to throw away, possibly."

"My plan was to do an inventory and take pictures before I started making any decisions."

His tone was neutral. So was his expression. But Tegan could tell she'd screwed up. So much for earning her keep. "I should have waited for you. I didn't know what things you might want to keep for yourself."

"I'm not planning to take much. Maybe one of his watches, some small memento. What about you?"

Even if transporting things wasn't an issue, even if there was something in the place that had a good memory attached to it, Tegan didn't have an apartment. She'd been renting a room back in El Paso and had given it up before she'd gotten on the bus. She wasn't sure where she'd end up next, but it wasn't back there. She'd done a lot of bouncing around the last few years, trying to find a place that felt right. Whatever that meant. Whatever it meant, El Paso wasn't it. Or Tuscaloosa. Or Butte. Or Newburgh. She'd only ended up in Newburgh for those few months because she'd followed a guy, who was not worth following. "There's nothing special I want."

"Do you think there's anything we should keep for Dad? Possibly he'd want one of Granddad's watches. He had several. There's the Omega Seamaster he always wore, and a couple others that I want to get estimates on."

What was Bowen thinking? "We can ask, but it's hard to picture Dad wearing something of Grandfather's. They weren't exactly close."

"True. But it's his father. He might want something."

There was that. Her dad and grandfather had enough of a relationship that Grandfather had let the whole family live with him for a couple years. That meant something. "I'll probably talk to him and Mom tonight. I'll ask."

"Let me know what he says."

Silence stretched out between them. It had been so long since she'd spent any time with Bowen, not since they lived together in this house. Talking to him felt awkward, so awkward, she'd skipped dinner last night, saying she was tired after the trip. Had it always been like this? Maybe not when they were really little. She flashed on Bowen giving her the extra feed at the petting zoo. That had been a nice big-brother thing to do. She wondered if he'd remember that day, but didn't ask.

He had to think she was such a loser. He had what she was sure was a gorgeous apartment in Manhattan, and she'd had to beg him to stay in a place she'd always hated, just to have some place to sleep.

"Do you want to go get breakfast? We could go to Flappy's the way we used to."

Breakfast at Flappy's. Not something she wanted to relive. She could still remember how endless those breakfasts had felt, with Grandfather holding court, enjoying everybody stopping by and sucking up to him. Sucking up to him and congratulating Bowen on whatever great play he'd made in whatever sport was in season, which was just a more subtle way of sucking up to Grandfather. "I'll just grab some cereal in a while," Tegan answered. Bowen had brought a few groceries with him when he'd arrived on Friday. It felt kind of weird eating his food when she hadn't contributed, but she needed to conserve cash.

"Oh. If that's what you'd prefer."

"I'm not a big breakfast person is all." Tegan added, realizing that he'd been being nice and she'd shut him down.

"I'm not either. I usually just have a smoothie at the gym."

Of course, he had a gym membership. "Me too," she lied. Why was she bothering to lie to him about her life? He already knew she didn't have a car. Or a job. At least he didn't call her on it.

The silence descended again. Say something, she urged herself. But what? What could the two of them possibly talk about?

"Think I'll go for a run," Bowen said.

"Okay, have a good one."

"Why don't you wait on dealing with all this. I made a checklist. I want to go through Granddad's papers first, then start on the inventory. You should just get settled in."

Translation: you don't know what you're doing. "I promise not to touch anything."

"That's not what— It's just that I want to take pictures first."

He stood. "I was thinking, since you don't have a car, maybe you'd want to use Granddad's while you're here. The keys were in the things the lawyer picked up from the hospital." Bowen pulled them out of his pocket and set them on the end table.

He hadn't been able to hide his pity when she'd told him she took the bus. She had the crazy impulse to tell him to shove the car and his pity, but that would be stupid. "Sure. Yes. Thanks."

Vic ran her fingers over the buttery-smooth cover of her brand-new journal. A thirtieth birthday present to her from her. Starting a new decade felt like a good time for a little reflection, a little planning, and the prompts in this journal were designed to help her "discover her deepest truths." She picked up the fountain pen she'd found in a box of stuff from the last estate sale she'd gone to and carefully filled it with purple ink. No, amethyst. This ink was way too special, or pretentious, to call itself purple. Whatever it was called, it was beautiful.

She opened the journal to the first page. "Five dreams that haven't come true—yet" was written across the top in loopy script. The *i* in *five* was dotted with a tiny butterfly. Which made Vic want to forget the whole thing, but, no, her birthday called for self-discovery, and she was going to get some, damn it.

Okay, so five dreams that hadn't come true yet. The first thing that popped into her head was her dream to have a monkey, back when she was around six. She'd drawn probably a hundred pictures of her, Henry, and the monkey because, of course, she'd planned to share. It would sleep on her bed, but she would let Henry play with it sometimes. She decided not to write the monkey dream down, even though the thought of it on her list amused her.

The next dream that popped into her head, accompanied by the remembered scent of grape Hubba Bubba, was her dream to be in *The Guinness Book of World Records* for blowing the biggest bubble-gum bubble. She'd spent weeks attempting it, back when she was about ten. Henry had had the job of holding a string in front of the bubble to measure the diameter. And it was then she'd learned that peanut butter worked surprisingly well for getting gum out of your hair. She didn't write that down either. Get serious, Vic, she ordered herself.

Okay, dreams. Adult-type dreams, suitable dreams for a thirty-year-old, not dreams from elementary school. This time her brain brought up the image of a wedding dress; not any wedding dress, *her* wedding dress. Her supposed-to-be wedding dress. She could almost feel the cool satin sliding across her skin. Was that supposed to mean getting married was a dream that hadn't come true yet? Did she even want to get married?

Six years ago, she had. But now? Uhhh, well, maybe. But just maybe. And it's not like she had a lot of opportunities. She'd met every single guy in Fox Crossing, at least it felt that way. Bonnie was always trying to get her to "expand her horizons" and put herself on Plenty of Fish, or at least go with Bonnie to a bar in Bangor, but it didn't appeal. She'd feel like everyone was evaluating her. Bonnie said that Vic was the one who would be evaluating, but that didn't appeal much either. She'd rather just meet someone in normal life, a free-range kind of meeting where she and a man maybe laughed at the same thing at the same moment or reached for the same book while browsing at Foxy Loxy's.

She stared at the blank space where she was supposed to be writing her unfulfilled dreams. She wasn't putting getting married on there. She just wasn't. Because she wasn't sure if it even was a dream of hers now. Vic started feeling twitchy, and when Persephone pounced on her toes, she realized she'd been tapping them. Even missing one eye, Persephone was an excellent hunter. Vic reached down to give her kitty a scratch under the chin. A second later, Pemberley butted Persephone out of the way, so Vic could give her ears some attention.

Years ago, Vic had gone to the animal shelter looking for a kitten. Instead, she'd come home with two adults. Miss Violet, owner of the boardinghouse, who volunteered at the shelter, insisted they couldn't live without each other. She'd then sung a song, in a register as high as the yowls the cats were producing, about how they'd been waiting for someone like Vic, someone who could see that beauty didn't require two eyes, or, in Pemberley's case, hair in all the usual places, someone who could appreciate a deep bond of friendship. After Vic finished applauding, which was until her hands were stinging because Miss Violet expected due appreciation after a performance, Vic filled out the adoption application, and that was that.

Vic returned her attention to the journal. If marriage wasn't one of her dreams anymore, what did that mean about kids? Was having kids an unfulfilled dream? Vic liked kids. Bonnie's thirteen-year-old daughter, Addison, had regular sleepovers at Vic's, and they always had a blast. And Vic was psyched when she found out Annie Hatherley, one of Vic's besties, was pregnant. Vic was ready to have tea parties with unicorns or go on road trips to construction sites, whatever the kiddo turned out to be into. No matter what, she'd always have kids in her life. Maybe Henry would make her an aunt someday, although he'd never gotten serious with anyone, claiming he was too busy, working and going to school at the same time.

But would not having kids of her own leave a black hole in her life? She was thirty now. Wasn't thirty-five when pregnancies started being high risk? Should she start thinking about freezing her eggs, or—

She turned the page. She'd go back to the dreams one later. Okay. "What impact do I want to have had on the world when I'm gone?" Unfair. That should not be a page-two question. That was a question you needed to build up to.

She turned the page. "What do I need most right now?" Okay. She could do this one. What did she need most right now? A doughnut popped into her mind, pink icing, rainbow sprinkles. "Can we go a little deeper, please?" she muttered. She pulled in a long breath, then gave a gasp as she felt two sets of claws dig into her toes. They must have been tapping again. She forced herself to be still. "What do I need? What do I need?" More time would help. Both her parents had become insanely high-maintenance after they split. There was always something one of them needed. And it's not as if Vic had had a lot of free time to begin with. After she'd adopted her cats, Miss Violet had convinced her to spend a few hours each Sunday afternoon at the shelter, and Vic put in a few hours a week at the food bank. If she had more time though, what would she do with it? Which basically went back to the question of what she needed, and what her dreams were. And she didn't know. She just didn't know.

That twitchy feeling got stronger. Vic shut the journal and pressed both palms against the cover. All due respect, Socrates, but sometimes the unexamined life is just fine. She stood up. A walk. That's what she needed right now, a walk. That would get rid of the twitches. She pulled on her boots, hat, jacket, and gloves and headed out. In less than fifteen minutes, she was on the trail that ran around the lake, the snow packed down by enough hikers that she didn't need her snowshoes. The noise in her brain grew quiet as she focused on the creaking of the snow-laden pine boughs, the crunch of the snow under her boots, and the chickadees singing *hey, sweetie.* At least that's how her dad described their three-note whistle.

Vic rounded a curve in the trail and froze, disbelieving. The Fox sat in the center of the trail less than six feet from her. Its amber eyes met hers, and Vic felt the little hairs on the back of her neck prickle. She was looking at The Fox.

"Wow," a male voice said, low and soft.

Vic jerked her head up and saw a man standing on the other side of The Fox, about as close to it as she was. He must have rounded the curve in the trail just as she spotted the vixen. His face could have come off the Solidi Medallion of Constantine the Great, with that aquiline nose and chiseled jaw. Chiseled jaw? Had she actually just thought the words *chiseled jaw*? Yes, she had, because that's what it was. She continued to take in the details—blond hair cut short, broad shoulders, eyes the blue-gray of a winter sky. It took a moment for all her quick impressions to snap into the realization of who was standing in front of her.

"Oh, hell no." Vic turned and strode away.

The Fox considered the cord connecting the male and the female humans. It had been formed years before, and it had dimmed, in the way some cords between humans did with time and distance. In her woods, the cords were constant, but not in the human world.

Yet, though the cord was dim, The Fox could feel strength in it. It reminded her of the connection between predator and prey, yet that was not how the humans had behaved in their encounter. There was the faint scent of fear mixed with aggression from the female, but no attack.

"I can't believe you saw The Fox."

Vic stared at her brother. "That's your takeaway? What about the part where I saw Bowen Gower? Freaking Bowen Gower."

Henry shrugged. "You said he was in town."

"How can you be so casual? Are you telling me you'd be fine if you came face-to-face with that guy?" When she'd seen him, adrenaline had flooded her body, kicking her heart into overdrive.

"It's a small town. And in winter, without all the hikers, not so many people around, I accepted that it was probably going to happen."

Henry sounded so calm. Well, he had amazing self-control. He'd eaten zoodles last night, as in noodles made of zucchini. That was barely human. But that didn't mean that underneath all that calm and self-control there wasn't a volcano of emotion spewing inside him. "And you're really okay with that?"

"It would be kind of pathetic if I wasn't okay. It's been a lot of years." Again, with the calm.

"You're more forgiving than I am."

"You're a good big sister, you know that? Still looking out for me."

"I wish I did a better job back then." Henry might be willing to forget, if not forgive, the unadulterated hell Bowen Gower and his buddies had put him through back in school, but Vic never would. Just thinking about it made her want to smash something.

"Let it go," Henry sang in a falsetto, and Vic laughed. "That's better. Come on, it's your birthday. Time to get to celebrating." He led the way out the door. They'd decided to walk the few blocks to Wit's, where party number one was about to start. A cheer went up as soon as they opened the bar's door, followed by a loud, somewhat off-key version of "Happy Birthday."

Their mom got up and wrapped Vic in a Charlie-scented hug. The woman had been wearing the same perfume as long as Vic could remember. When her mother's Jetta wagon finally conked out, she'd replaced it with another Jetta wagon. She ordered the same thing every time they came to Wit's Beginning, Katahdin Dreams, named for the peak at the northern end of the Appalachian Trail.

Same perfume, car, and drink for decades. But here she was, without her husband of forty-two years. How'd that happen? For God's sake, their names were Claude and Claudette. What were the odds? The belonged together. They just did. Vic just wished they'd give her more details. Something to help her make sense of the split

"My baby. Happy birthday." Her mother pulled at the sides of her velvet blazer, but it didn't come close to closing. She needed new clothes, probably two sizes bigger. She'd gained maybe ten pounds when she was going through menopause, but after she and Dad split, she'd gained maybe fifteen more.

Vic kissed her cheek. "Thanks for having me."

"You're very welcome. Although it's impossible that was thirty years ago. I saved you a seat right next to me. And one for my boy on the other side." She gave Henry a hug.

Her mom and dad had both wanted to see Henry last night, his first night in town, and Vic hadn't been able to negotiate an arrangement that worked for both parents. She'd ended up saying that she was keeping Henry to herself, and that they would both have to wait until the birthday parties.

She wondered what Henry thought of their mom's appearance. It had been more than a year since he'd seen her. Besides the weight gain, her mother had let her hair go gray, start to go gray. It was about half-gray and half a faded brown. Before the breakup—*breakup* sounded like the wrong word, too inconsequential—her mother had always had a standing appointment at Vulpini to keep her hair that Junior Miss Peach dark brown.

Vic's heart started to feel a little achy when she sat down at the table. Her dad should be here. She should be able to have a party with everybody she loved in one place. You'll be seeing him in a few hours, she reminded herself. Get over it. Lots of her favorite people were at the table, ready to celebrate with her—Annie and her husband, Nick; Honey, Vic's godmother; Honey's husband, Charlie; Maggie, who owned the Foxy Loxy bookshop across the street from Vic's place; and Bonnie and Addison.

"Addy, I love that sweater." The chunky cherry-red sweater had a cutout over one shoulder. Not exactly practical winter wear, but cute. Cute hair tonight too. She'd braided a small section and looped it over the top of her head like a hair band. She's growing up. Vic knew it had been happening, but it's like Addy had flipped a switch and turned from little girl to teen all at once.

"Mom took me shopping on Thursday."

"Nice, Mom." Vic smiled at Bonnie. Vic knew that her assistant didn't have a lot of spare cash. She must have saved up to give Addy a special treat. Vic hoped the shopping trip took Addy's mind off missing Rose. "Thanks for coming tonight!"

Banana, another of Vic's favorite people, came over and set a drink in front of her. "A new concoction in your honor, with chocolate, peanut butter, caramel, and raspberries."

"Girlie beer," Nick teased.

"Girlie is always better," Annie shot back, giving him an elbow jab in the ribs.

Vic smiled at Banana. "You're too good to me."

"Impossible." Banana gave her a kiss on the top of the head, before heading back to his spot behind the bar. He'd been giving her a special birthday drink forever. The first she could remember was a peanut-butter-and-jelly-infused chocolate milk, which tasted a little like tonight's birthday brew.

Annie raised her glass. "To Vic, always there when you need her."

Charlie raised his glass. "To Vic, best whistler in the county."

"To Vic, who gives every unwanted, ugly thing a home," Bonnie called.

"Not just things. Have you seen her cats?" Maggie asked.

Henry joined the chorus. "To Vic, the kindhearted, especially when it comes to cats and brothers, and as of this morning, Vic the lucky." He leaned across their mom to clink mugs with Vic. "You're not going to believe what happened to Vic this morning. She saw The Fox!"

"You saw The Fox?" Bonnie exclaimed. "The actual fox?"

"Saw the white ear, saw the white sock, and the black tail tip. It was The Fox. Or a descendant of The Fox, depending on your personal beliefs."

"Hallelujah!" Honey exclaimed. "Finally, you'll get your true love." She took her husband's hand and kissed it.

"Seeing The Fox just means luck," Vic protested. "There are

other kinds of luck. Like when The Fox led Nogan to those comic books." Logan and Noah, such constant companions that they were known as Nogan, had scored enough cash from selling the comics that their college educations were now covered with enough left over for a summer at space camp.

"No, you have love coming your way," Honey said. "The Fox found someone for Annie, and you know we all thought she was way too temperamental for any man to tolerate."

"My Annie isn't temperamental." Nick took Annie's hand and kissed it. "Temperamental suggests change. She's pigheaded every hour of every day of every week."

"Whatever you call it, I was starting to fear she'd never get married until—"

Annie interrupted her grandmother. "Nothing wrong with never getting married. Women do not need men to be happy." She flexed her arm, like Rosie the Riveter in the poster, and made a *harrh* sound, the way she always did when she wanted to remind everyone that she was an independent woman who didn't need any help from anyone. Which was true. Annie was the strongest woman, person, Vic knew, except possibly Annie's mother, Belle, the mayor of the town, who had taught Annie to go *harrh* and flex. Still, Vic thought even Annie would admit that, though a woman didn't need a man to be happy, she was happier now that she was with Nick. And now the two of them were about to have a baby.

"And The Fox brought me Charlie." Honey smiled at him like he'd hung not only the moon, but every single star. Vic flashed on the first question in that journal—What dreams haven't come true yet? Having someone look at her the way Charlie was looking back at Honey or the way Nick was looking at Annie . . . Maybe that should be on her list. It's the way Dad always looked at Mom, a little voice whispered from deep inside her.

"It's your turn, Victoria Ruth Michaud." Ruth Allis was

Honey's name, although no one ever called her that, and she pulled out Vic's middle name when she wanted to remind her of the bond between them. "I feel it in my heart."

Vic was getting that same twitchy feeling she'd had staring at that empty journal page that asked for her unfulfilled dreams. She realized she was twisting one of her rings around and around and forced herself to stop. "Henry, I'm sure everyone wants to hear all about what brought you back to town," Vic said, not wanting any more love talk. She took a swallow of her beer. Chocolate, peanut butter, caramel, raspberry—now that was something she could love.

Henry gave the rundown on the community health survey, and she loved hearing the passion in his voice and seeing how attentively everyone listened. He was going to do so good.

Almost as soon as she took the last swallow of her drink, Jilly, one of the barmaids, came over with another. "From a guy at the bar."

"What guy?" Vic looked over her shoulder, expecting to see a friend who'd decided to send her a birthday drink. Instead, she locked eyes with Bowen Gower. Freaking Bowen Gower. Oh, hell no.

He raised his glass to her and smiled. Like he thought she'd forgotten everything he'd done when they were in school. Or maybe he didn't even remember, which was equally bad. No, which was worse. She jerked her head back around.

"See? It's happening already!" Honey exclaimed.

"Nothing is ever going to happen with that man."

"She's not having it." The barmaid put the drink in front of Bowen. He stared at it. What was the woman's problem? He shot another fast glance over his shoulder. She'd come in with a guy, but they weren't sitting next to each other. Were they together? They didn't have that vibe.

He'd sent over the drink the way his grandfather had taught

him. He'd waited until she'd finished the drink she had. When she looked over, he smiled and nodded and did a small raise of his glass. If she'd smiled back, he would have gone over and introduced himself, but that was not going to be necessary.

"Doesn't happen to you often, does it?" the woman a few barstools over asked, flicking her long silver braid over one shoulder.

"No." Actually, it had never happened. "I mean, objectively, I'm decent looking. And, objectively, I have good shoes." He shook his head and laughed, not wanting to show that the rejection had stung.

"Shoes?" the bartender asked.

"I read an article once that claimed women made a lot of judgments based on a man's shoes." His Chelsea boots had been on a *GQ* list of best winter footwear, so they couldn't be the issue. Bowen shrugged. "I don't exactly understand it, but shoes carry more weight with women than you might expect."

"I don't care much one way or the other," the woman said. "I'm okay with anything except sandals on a first date. I don't need to be shown toes, that's all I'm saying."

The bartender gave a deep *haw-haw-haw*. "A woman wants to see my piggies, she has to put a ring on it."

"I'll remember that," the woman told Banana, then turned to Bowen. "Don't take it personally. It's not like she knows you." The woman stood. "Right back." She headed for the bathrooms.

Bowen didn't know why he'd even bothered sending the drink. Some impulse to turn the situation around. Make it right. Not that he'd done anything wrong. He hadn't done anything at all back on the trail, just stood there. But she'd looked at him with shock and, although it made no sense, disgust.

Before she'd realized he was on the trail with her, when she'd locked eyes with that fox, she'd had an expression of . . . of wonderment on her face that had pulled him in, made him wish anything could make him feel what she seemed to be feeling.

"Bowen Gower," the bartender said. "Just realized it's you. I heard you were back in town." He reached out his hand, and they shook. "Don't know if you remember me. Banana Jones."

Banana. Bowen had forgotten how people who ended up in town after hiking the AT usually went by their trail names. He wondered if anyone in town knew the name Banana was born with. "I should have remembered." His grandfather had known the name of every single person in town and had introduced Bowen to most of them. And it's not like there were a lot of African American guys in town.

"No reason. Most adults are basically indistinguishable to teenagers." Banana ran one hand over his bald head. "I'm sorry for your loss. If there's anything I can do for you while you're in town, let me know."

"Thank you." The man's words had felt genuine, more than just basic good manners, and Bowen had a talent for reading people. Well, except maybe his sister. Also, that woman over there. He shot another fast look at her. Her head was tossed back, and she was laughing so hard her whole face was crinkled up. He had no idea what her issue with him was.

"He was really proud of you. Not just from back in the day, all those games you won. He used to talk about you all the time and what a success you made of yourself."

Bowen's grandfather had been talking about him. Bragging about him. Warm pride filled him, just the way it had back in the day when Granddad had given him the Nod of Approval after he'd made a good play. "Thanks for letting me know."

The woman was laughing again. He already recognized the sound. The memory of her disgusted expression kept flicking at him. He didn't understand it. Banana had recognized him. Had she recognized him too? She looked around his age. Maybe she knew him from back in high school. But, objectively, he'd been popular back then, so that wouldn't explain her attitude.

"That woman who sent back the drink and I both saw The Fox out on the trail this morning. If the town legend is true, we should be falling in love, and I don't think that's going to happen."

Banana's eyes widened. "You saw The Fox?"

"What is it with this town and foxes?" the woman with the silver braid asked, as she returned to her barstool. "Your place is one of the only ones that doesn't have one in its name," she said to Banana. "There's Vixen's and Vulpini and the Foxy Loxy bookshop. Plus, I'm assuming the Hen House ice cream shop is named for the one the fox is always said to be in."

"Do you want to tell it?" Banana asked Bowen. Banana looked over at the woman. "His grandfather loved to tell the tale of our fox."

"You go ahead," Bowen said.

"Before I tell the story, I need your name," Banana told the woman.

"Maisie Bauer."

"Well, Maisie, the story begins long ago, before Fox Crossing was even Fox Crossing, back when it was just a settlement, a settlement that seemed unlikely to survive a particularly harsh winter, harsh even for Maine. A woman named Annabelle Hatherley—"

"Of Hatherley's Outfitters?" Maisie asked.

Banana touched his nose and pointed at her. "Exactly. Annabelle's namesake Annie Hatherley is right over there with the birthday girl who turned down this young man's drink." Banana jerked his chin toward Bowen, and Bowen gave a half bow.

"Annie co-owns the Outfitters, along with Annabelle's other namesake, Annie's mother, Belle, who is our mayor. Probably neither one of them would be here if Annabelle Hatherley hadn't come across a fox with its leg in a trap and decided to save its life. Maybe she was struck by its strange markings, one white sock, one white ear, and a black-tipped tail," Banana continued. "Maybe when she looked into the vixen's eyes, she saw pain that mirrored hers. Whatever her reason, Annabelle took The Fox back home with her and literally nursed her back to health."

Maisie tsked. "Oh, you're one of those people who misuses *literally*. I barely know you, and, yet I expected better."

"When I say *literally*, I mean *literally*. She nursed The Fox the same way she nursed her little boy. My theory is Annabelle had seen so much death, including her husband's, that she couldn't bear one more, even that of a fox."

"I apologize for doubting your grammatical expertise." Maisie flicked her braid over her shoulder.

"I accept."

If Bowen wasn't mistaken, some flirting was going on. Banana clearly had better game than Bowen did.

"Once The Fox was healed, Annabelle set it free, and not long after that, a fellow by the name of Celyn Hanmer, recently immigrated from Wales, was out on his horse, Mud, a remarkably skittish animal. Our fox crossed the trail in front of Mud, and Mud reared up and dumped Celyn on the ground, leaving Celyn to chase after him. Before he caught up to his ride, Celyn noticed something glittering in the side of a cliff."

As Banana spoke, Bowen was flooded with memories of his grandfather spinning the same tale, drawing it out the way Banana was. Granddad never got tired of it. Bowen bet that back in the day almost every tourist coming through town had heard the story of The Fox from Mayor Gower. The Fox was still bringing luck to the town because most of those tourists ended up buying a foxy souvenir. Some people even came to town— staying at the inn or the boardinghouse, eating at Flappy's or the BBQ or right here at Wit's, shopping up and down Main Street—just because they wanted a chance to see the magical fox and get some good luck of their own.

"Celyn knew what that gleam meant—mica," Bowen continued. "And where there's mica, there might be slate, which in this case there was. And our Celyn knew what to do with slate once The Fox led him to it. He'd mined slate back in Wales. That's how the mine, the mine that ended up saving the settlement, came to be. The land where he found the slate was owned by Annabelle's deceased husband, and the money from the mine allowed her to start Hatherley's Outfitters."

"But why did people think the fox that spooked Mud was the one Annabelle saved?" Maisie asked, then immediately answered her own question. "Those strange markings."

Banana did the nose touching and pointing thing again. "And that's why you'll find so many establishments named for foxes, and how the town came be called Fox Crossing."

"I do love a good story well told. Thank you." Maisie took a sip of her ale, then put it down. "Wait." She looked at Bowen. "You said that you and the woman who refused your drink should be falling in love because you both saw the town fox at the same time. Which raises several questions. The settlement was formed back in?"

"The year 1803," Banana supplied.

"And the fox from the story is still supposed to be alive?"

"Well, that's a matter still in dispute," Banana said. "Some in town, and I'm one of them, say yes, that very same fox is still living in our woods. But some say that those strange markings have been passed down through generations, and The Fox people have seen hereabouts is one in a long line of descendants from that first vixen."

"That answers one of my questions. What's the connection between The Fox and falling in love?" Maisie took a sip of her drink.

Banana waved to a couple coming in the door. "Everyone who sees The Fox gets luck. For some, that luck is falling in love, especially when two people see The Fox at the same time. When I saw The Fox a few years ago, I assumed it meant I'd finally have the luck I needed to get through the Hundred-Mile Wilderness, the section of the Appalachian Trail that starts right outside town. I'd done almost the whole trail, but I couldn't get through those last hundred miles. Something always happened. Somebody needed help, I broke something, you name it. I was planning to head out to finally conquer the Wilderness the day after I saw The Fox. Instead, I got a call from my daughter. We didn't have the best of relationships back then, but she was in a bind, and she was desperate for a place to leave her daughter. That's a story for another time. But to cut to the chase, I now have a wonderful relationship with my daughter, my son-in-law, and my granddaughter. The Fox didn't bring me the luck I thought I wanted, but what it did bring transformed my life."

"I do love a good story well told," Maisie said again, the crinkles at the corners of her eyes deepening as she smiled at Banana.

Banana gave a tip of an imaginary hat, then turned his attention to Bowen. "I wouldn't discount love too fast. Annie pretty much detested Nick, who is sitting over there right beside her, at first sight, or at least she hoped that she'd never see him again. Then our fox made an appearance. Now they're going to have a baby. I promise you this, Bowen, love or not, somehow, some way, your life is about to change."

Bowen didn't want his life to change. He and his grandfather had come up with a ten-year plan the day Bowen graduated from Wharton. In January, just a few months behind schedule, Bowen had gotten promoted to VP at the boutique private equity firm his grandfather had guaranteed was on the rise.

"If you want a change, you don't have to wait for a fox, you can just change it yourself. I did." Maisie put a ten down on the bar. "Hope to see you again," she said to them both, but her eyes lingered on Banana a moment longer.

"You don't have to hope. I'm here most nights," Banana called after her.

"Banana, hey, man! Good to see you." The guy who'd come in with the woman from the trail, the woman who'd loathed Bowen at first sight, paused in front of the bar and shook Banana's hand.

"Good to have you back, Henry. That study of yours is going to help a lot of people."

"I didn't mean any offense when I sent that drink over," Bowen told the guy, Henry. "I was just trying to be friendly."

The smile disappeared from Henry's face, his expression turning hard. "Guess she didn't feel like being friends." With that, he left, presumably heading for the bathroom.

What the hell?

"Guess he didn't feel like being friends either," Banana commented.

"Guess not."

Bowen reached for his wallet, but Banana waved him off. "On me. A welcome home. And when that luck comes your way, stop in and tell me about it. I also love a good story."

CHAPTER 3

Henry finished up the second round of "Happy Birthday" for his sister. Shoo Fly had kept the bakery open late for the private party. Although private didn't mean that much in Fox Crossing. Vic knew everybody, and pretty much everybody who knew her loved her, which meant pretty much everybody was welcome. Except their mother and any of their mother's friends who would feel it was disloyal to be at a party with Henry and Vic's father.

Last time Henry had seen his parents, they'd been together. Last time he'd seen them, they'd been happy. At least he thought they'd been happy. He looked over at his dad, who was smiling as he watched Vic blow out the candles on an enormous cake decorated to look like the Junk & Disorderly sign. He was acting as if everything was all good. Back at party one, Henry's mom had been acting the same way.

He hadn't liked the way she looked though. Not because her hair was gray on top, and faded brown on the bottom, or because she'd gained a few more pounds. It's just that his mom was one of those women who got up, got dressed, put on makeup, and blew out her hair before she left her bedroom. Tonight, he didn't think she'd had any makeup on and her bangs had gotten so long that she'd pinned them out of her face with bobby pins. Which, who cared? He didn't. Except that his mother would usually have cared. And he was concerned about what her appearance said about her mental health.

"What did you wish for, Vic?" Flappy asked, and Henry turned his attention back to his sister. He'd have lots of time to check up on his mom now that he was back in town. "I hope it was a year's free breakfasts at my place, because that's what you're getting."

Vic rubbed her hands together, grinning. "Did you take into consideration the number of blueberry pancakes I'm able to consume on any given day? I don't want to bankrupt you."

"I've got you covered. Extra whipped cream included."

"I actually wished for a million wishes. But I just blew it. I wasn't supposed to say." Vic looked over at her dad, and they exchanged a smile.

Henry knew they were remembering the first time Vic had given that answer. She'd been eight or nine and had been heartbroken when she messed up and said her wish out loud. Her dad had finally gotten her to stop crying by promising she could have the wish when it was his birthday.

"You can have mine," their father told Vic, just the way Henry knew he would. His dad and sister had had the same exchange every year since that first time.

Henry took a moment to study their dad. His appearance hadn't changed the way Henry's mom's had. He was maybe a little grayer, a little thinner, and the cuff of his flannel shirt was missing a button. Mom wouldn't have let him out of the house in it. But the way he looked didn't set off alarm bells.

Vic started cutting the cake and handing out pieces to the group. Henry'd already had cake at party number one, but he wasn't going to pass by anything baked by Shoo Fly. Henry took a bite, the thick fondant causing a sweet explosion on his tongue. Tomorrow, back to the Whole30.

He forked up another bite and noticed a large dog trotting toward Vic, a package held lightly in its mouth, his stubby tail wagging so fast it looked like it was vibrating. He stopped in front of Vic, stretched out his front legs in a low bow, then dropped the package, somewhat drool stained, in front of her.

"From me and Clarence," Shoo Fly said.

Ah, the famous Clarence. Henry should have known. Vic had told him that Shoo Fly had gotten a dog. Well, *gotten* might not be the right word. Shoo Fly had basically had the dog foisted on him by The Fox, who had led the beast directly to Shoo Fly. Lucky for both of them. Clarence had been starving after being abandoned in the woods. And Shoo Fly had been, well, much different from the smiling guy standing with his arm around Belle Hatherley, Annie's mother.

The Shoo Fly Henry remembered barely talked. He rarely came out of the bakery's kitchen. He'd never have taken on hosting a party. But Vic had said that Clarence was extremely people-shy at first, and Shoo Fly had decided the dog needed to be socialized if Shoo Fly was going to find him a home, because Shoo Fly definitely wasn't keeping him. Socializing Clarence had pretty much socialized Shoo Fly, according to Vic. And Clarence had found his forever home.

There were so many stories like that. Stories of people whose lives had been changed, always for the better, after a sighting of the town's legendary fox. Henry hoped Vic had something good coming. Obviously, it wouldn't be with Bowen Gower. Nothing involving him could be considered good. But Henry hoped something, or someone, great would turn up in his sister's life. She deserved it. She'd never quite bounced back after what happened with Leo. At least, she'd never gotten into another relationship, just some dates now and then. Not that he should talk.

Vic unwrapped the package, revealing a bag of little fish-shaped nuggets.

"Some are salmon and some are tuna," Shoo Fly said. "My first time making cat treats, but maybe I should add them to the menu."

"Definitely. Why should dogs get all the love? Although Clarence is very lovable." Vic leaned down—didn't have to lean too far—and gave the dog a hug, then gave a double hug to Shoo Fly and Belle. Belle started to hand her a gift, but Miss Violet loudly cried, "Do mine next!" and thrust a small package into Vic's hands. Henry didn't think he'd ever heard Miss Violet speak in what would be called a normal tone of voice.

Vic ripped open the purple wrapping paper. Vic was a ripper. She held up a CD. "It's the Broadway cast recording of my show." Miss Violet sang the words, and the crowd applauded. Miss Violet gave a low curtsy, her dozens of strings of purple beads swinging. "I meant our show, of course," she corrected herself, taking the hand of the man with the longish white hair standing next to her. He didn't seem to mind letting Miss Violet have the spotlight. Henry knew the man was her new husband, Simon, from the wedding pictures Vic had texted him. And the pics from when the musical, based on The Fox and the luck it brought, was performed in town. Vic had been in the chorus, playing a chipmunk. "There's talk of a London production. We're going to be an international sensation," Miss Violet trilled. Married or not, she would always be Miss Violet to Henry.

Vic gave out hugs to both of them. "Thank you. I love it. I can't wait to hear the interpretation of the role I created, Chipmunk Number Two."

"This is from me and Mama." Yvette Martin handed a lavish bouquet to Vic.

"Yvette's mother is in assisted living now. Your sister goes over there to Dwell Dell at least once a week," his father told

Henry. "She sets up a little table with things from the shop and sells them for ten cents a pop. They love it." Her father looked over at Vic and smiled. "They love her."

"Like Clarence, she's pretty lovable." Henry watched as Vic tore open another present.

"Lovable, but alone," his father said, echoing Henry's earlier thoughts. "I hate to see it."

"How are you doing with that? Being alone?"

"Look what Buddy gave Vic. A Pisces pillow. I bet he embroidered it himself. He heard something on NPR about embroidering being a stress reliever and took it up."

"Nice." Henry took a bite of cake, deciding not to push his father on the being-alone issue. He'd try again another time.

When Vic had opened her last gift, their dad waved her over. "I want to go to the BBQ on Wednesday night."

"You know Mom and her book group are going to be there. What's wrong with Thursday? Or, really, any other day this week other than Wednesday?"

"Jake's getting out of the hospital. He says all he's been thinking about for weeks is a pulled-pork sandwich, and the guys and I want to treat him."

"And he can't think about it for one more day? Or maybe you could order in."

"My place is too small. I don't even have enough chairs." His father looked at Henry. "That reminds me. You need to stop by the house and look at what you still have stored in the garage. It's about to go on the market. Vic has a key."

"I'll stop by." It might be the last time Henry'd be able to go in his childhood home. The thought hurt more than he had expected it to.

"So, Wednesday, Vic?" her dad asked.

She sighed. "I'll talk to Mom and get back to you."

"Thanks, baby. I'm going to go grab another drink." Shoo Fly had set up a bar on top of the pastry counter. "Either of you want one?"

Vic shook her head.

"Still good," Henry told him. Once their dad was out of earshot, Henry turned to his sister. "Maybe you shouldn't be doing that."

"Doing what?"

"Making it so easy for him and Mom not to see each other. If you didn't run interference, they'd have to deal with each other."

"And you think that if they did, they'd remember they were in love, renew their vows, and live happily ever after?"

"I hadn't gotten that far. But it would be . . . It would be great if they could actually manage to speak to each other.

"It would, but I don't see it happening. I ended up managing their schedules because Mom told me she wasn't even sure she could keep living in town if it meant seeing Dad, and then he told me pretty much the same thing about her. I couldn't stand the thought of either of them moving. They have all their friends here, and they've each managed to keep half of them."

"Maybe after some more time they'll be able to at least be in the same building and their friends won't have to choose between them." Henry took another bite of cake and realized he'd finished the piece.

"One can hope. Oh, I need to talk to Buddy for a sec. There was a stork-shaped pair of embroidery scissors in a box I picked up at a storage-unit auction, and I thought he might want them."

If he did want them, Henry thought, she'd probably give them to him. At least Vic had Bonnie around to help keep Vic solvent. Henry wandered back to the center table and put another slice of cake on his plate. Nobody else made chocolate-cherry cake as good as Shoo Fly's. Henry had taken two bites before he realized that, not only wasn't he hungry, he was actually kind of nauseous. And why wouldn't he be? He was working on his third piece of cake in just a couple of hours. He never ate like that. Not anymore. Back when he was a kid, yeah. It had gotten to be this horrible cycle. Get teased for being fat, go home, and eat something good, get fatter, then repeat. Every day. For years.

Hot shame flooded him. He'd told Vic seeing Bowen Gower wouldn't be any big deal. But it had obviously gotten to him. And just like in the old days, he'd turned to food to stuff the feelings down. His mom did the same thing, except after she had an episode of binge eating, she'd go on her cereal diet, where she'd eat cereal and skim milk for every meal until she got back to her 113. He tossed the rest of the cake. He wasn't that fat kid anymore, and Bowen Gower had no power over him.

"Not that I don't want you to achieve your goals, but I'm so glad you already ditched the Whole30." Vic took another bite of the breakfast casserole her brother had made.

"I didn't," Henry answered.

"But yummy, yummy cheese." She pointed at the casserole.

"Yummy, yummy nutritional yeast giving the illusion of cheese."

Vic poked suspiciously at the casserole. "I don't even know exactly what that is."

"It's basically the same as the yeast you use to make beer or bread, but that yeast is alive, and nutritional yeast is killed off during manufacturing," Henry explained. "And I don't know exactly what that utensil you're using is."

"It's a pie fork. They never should have gone out of fashion, in my opinion. They should be rebranded as knirks, because they're really a knife and fork in one, and there's no reason to limit them to pie." She held the knirk up so Henry could admire its geniusness. "You can cut with the one extra-thick, extra-sharp tine and pick up food with the other four. I thought someone would snatch it up the first time I put it on the ten-cent table, but, no, which means now it's all mine. But you may use it while you're here."

"Why, thank you, although sticking something with a blade into your mouth seems a little risky." Henry yawned, and Vic realized he looked tired.

"Sleep okay?"

"Great." He blinked twice.

"Liar." Henry always double-blinked when he was lying.

He blinked twice. "I'm not lying. Why would I lie about how I slept?"

"Exactly what I was thinking. But you did, then you lied about lying. And you know I always know. Are you going to keep lying, or are you just going to tell me?"

He hesitated.

"Come on. You know I'll get it out of you eventually."

"No big. Just a bad dream." He stood up and refilled his water glass, even though it had been half-full.

"You still have those?" she asked when he sat back down. They talked pretty often, but he'd never mentioned nightmares. Henry was always more about talking through her problems than his own, though.

"Not often."

Just regular blinking. Good. There was a time when Henry was waking up yelling every couple weeks. Sleepwalking too. "Remember when Mom and Dad used to tie the handles of the double front doors together?"

"So I wouldn't wake up in the middle of the street. Yeah." Henry drained his water glass in two long swallows.

"Freaking Bowen Gower."

Henry laughed. "*Freaking?* What are you, ten?"

"I've given up swearing since I hang out with Addison pretty often."

"She's what, thirteen?"

Vic nodded.

"She's probably heard it all then."

"But not from the mouth of a role model, which is what I

am, thank you very much." Vic took another bite of the casserole, then asked the question that she was pretty sure she already knew the answer to. "It was a Gower dream, right?" Back in the day, they almost always had been.

"Guess seeing him yesterday stirred some stuff up."

"I should have done something."

"What exactly do you think you could have done?" Henry asked. "Walked up to him at the bar and punched his face in?"

"More like walked up to him in the cafeteria the day he first called you names and punched his face in."

"Vic, come on. That's nutso. There was nothing you could have done that would have changed anything."

"I could have told the principal what was going on. I could have told Mom and Dad." Her voice trembled a little, the frustration and helplessness feeling almost as fresh as they had back in high school.

"If anyone was going to do that, it should have been me. But going up against him would have been social suicide for you. And if I'd done it, it would only have made things worse. Anyway, long time ago."

"Yeah." Long time ago, but . . . she'd still been his big sister. She'd known how bad it was for Henry at school. She'd heard him wake up screaming so many nights. She should have done something, but she hadn't even tried. She'd been too scared. "Freaking Bowen Gower," she said softly.

"Hey. Stop twisting your ring and look at me."

Vic hadn't even realized she'd been turning her ring around and around on her finger. She made herself stop, then raised her eyes to Henry's.

"Long time ago, okay? Seeing him brought up some old crap in my unconscious and it came out in a dream, but that's nothing. I'm fine. Bowen Gower doesn't have the power to hurt me anymore."

She nodded, then quickly finished her casserole. "Thanks

for cooking. I've got to head down to the shop." She dumped her dishes in the sink, then pointed at him. "Leave those. If you cook, you don't do the dishes. Maybe you can catch a nap later."

"I'm not that tired." He blinked a couple times, but she didn't call him on it. "I want to go to Buddy's Gym and get a membership."

Vic groaned. "You're going to exercise regularly too? If you don't have any bad habits left, I'm really not sure I can live with you."

He laughed. "Don't worry. I'll pick up some meth while I'm out."

"Good. You know what, though? Maybe I'll get a membership too. I told myself I'd start doing some healthy stuff when I turned thirty. I haven't done more than take a walk since the days of PE class." Vic headed out the door and took the five-second commute down the stairs. Bonnie had already opened up.

"Vic, seriously?" Bonnie picked up a heart-shaped vase, an anatomically correct heart, not a Valentine's heart. It had holes in some of the arteries sticking out the top for flowers. Vic had hidden it in the drawer of a nice lingerie chest to avoid the conversation she was now about to have. "Seriously? What, did your second cousin's best friend's substitute first-grade teacher come in barefoot, her feet blue with cold, one toe about to succumb to frostbite?"

"I know, I know."

Bonnie waggled the heart vase at her.

"I know. But there's a lid for every pot, at least according to Honey Hatherley, and that means somewhere out there is someone who would love that."

"I'm not sure that is a person I would want to meet, especially in a dark alley." Bonnie put the heart vase down.

"Okay, but the lingerie chest you found it in? You know it's lovely and that we'll make a nice profit on it. There are actually many lovely things in the shop."

Bonnie shook her head at Vic. "Agreed. But wouldn't it be nice if all the loveliness wasn't so often hidden by all the atrociousness?"

"Addison was looking so grown-up last night at the party," Vic said, because she'd heard enough of Bonnie's lecture, and Bonnie could always be distracted with talk about Addy. "It's like she went from the gawky girl I met three years ago to someone who should be on the cover of *Teen Vogue* just like that." Vic snapped her fingers.

"A little too fast. I really wasn't sure about that sweater we got when we went shopping. She loves it, though. She couldn't decide if she should wear it to school on Friday or save it for your party, then decided to wear it both times."

"I thought it looked adorable on her. Was it too pricey?"

"Well, that, yes, but I didn't mind splurging. It just seemed kind of sexy with that cutout."

"The cutout that showed a portion of one shoulder? It's not like she wears one of those old neck-to-toe bathing costumes when she's at the pool."

Bonnie considered that for a moment, and Vic realized that this was something she shouldn't have been joking about. It was important to Bonnie.

"It's the context that's different. Of course, her bathing suit shows more skin than the sweater, but it's just your basic one-piece," Bonnie answered. "It's not saying, 'Hey, look at me, boys.'"

"And you think the sweater is? Do you think there's a boy she's crushing on?"

"I don't know. And I hate that. I feel like I used to know everything that was going on with her."

"Momming has got to be so hard."

"I've started thinking back to how I was with my mother when I hit puberty, and I'm terrified," Bonnie admitted.

"My mom and I definitely went at it a bunch of times during those years, usually over my complete lack of interest in being beauty-pageant ready. Not that she ever tried to get me in a pageant after the Baby Miss North-Central Maine debacle. There was projectile vomiting from both ends, and it was captured on video. But we have a great relationship now. And you're close to your mom. You and Addison are going to be fine."

"Thanks." Bonnie smoothed her already perfectly smooth bob. "I suppose I should check the rest of the dresser drawers for more surprises."

"That's not necessary." Vic moved to step in front of the lingerie chest. Too slow. Bonnie had already pulled out the plastic head with the bulging eyes and the exposed brain. "Someone is absolutely going to want that."

"For what exactly?" Bonnie stared into the bulging eyes.

"Didn't you ever play with a Gooey Louie?" Bonnie shook her head, and Vic patted her on the shoulder. "Poor thing. You were a deprived child. What you had to do was pull plastic snot out of a plastic nose—"

"Without making the brain pop out," a man said.

Vic turned and saw that, of course, who else, freaking Bowen Gower, had just come through her door. "Right, the brain, pop, yeah." She felt like her own brain was about to burst out of her head. It was a small town, but running into Bowen Gower three times in two days? Had she accidentally opened a portal to one of the circles of hell? "When it would pop, I'd always scream, *Ahhh!*" Why had she decided she needed to demonstrate the scream? She rushed on. "Remember the slogan? 'Pick a good one.' As in pick your nose." As in you're babbling, Vic, babbling in front of freaking Bowen Gower, and you need to stop.

She pulled in a deep breath while Bowen stood there looking at her with a little smile on his face. No, not a smile. A smirk. A smirk on those thin lips with their perfectly carved cupid's bow. A cruel mouth, that's how it would have been described in an old novel.

"You're the guy who sent Vic a drink last night," Bonnie said.

Oh, thank you, Bonnie, Vic thought. She'd been planning to pretend that she had no idea who he was and hoped he'd do the same.

"I was." His smile widened, showing perfect teeth, probably professionally whitened, and causing dimples to form on either side of his face. Not the little-dent kind of dimples, the long ones that were almost like creases and were definitely sexier than dimples. Limples? Not that they were sexy on him. Bowen Gower's personality negated everything sexy in his appearance. She'd almost forgotten about those limples. Almost. "Since the two of us are destined to fall in love, I thought it was appropriate."

Three responses, all snarky, came to mind, but Vic reminded herself that Bowen was in town to settle his grandfather's estate, his wealthy grandfather's estate, which meant he probably had some very nice things he'd like to sell, things that she could assist him in selling, which would bring her a very nice profit, allowing her to buy some more very ugly items from very deserving people.

"She told us you saw The Fox together. There's not a better person to be fated to fall in love with than Vic," Bonnie answered.

Thanks again, Bonnie. Thanks for that. Go ahead and encourage him, why don't you. Vic hadn't told Bonnie about what Bowen had done to Henry in high school, but it had to have been obvious last night that Vic had no interest in the man. "Is there something I can help you with?" That was abrupt, if not outright rude, and it was the best she'd been able to do. At least it wasn't babbling. She realized she was both twisting her ring and tapping her toes and made herself stop.

"I'm here handling my grandfather's estate. I had a few things I was interested in getting appraised." He looked around the shop, expression dubious. The Louie head Bonnie still held probably wasn't helping give the impression that this was a serious place of business. Vic took it and set it next to the Barbie head.

"Cute couple," Bowen commented.

Vic could hear the condescension in his voice, and her face flushed. She knew he was living in New York and had some big, fancy job. His grandfather had made sure to tell everyone that. Clearly, Bowen didn't find her shop—or her—up to his standards. "I've handled many estates. I'm sure I can assist you."

"I'm sorry for your loss," Bonnie said.

Damn. Vic should have said that. She wasn't thinking straight. "I am too. Your grandfather did so much for Fox Crossing."

"Thank you." Bowen pulled a Tamponato watch case out of his leather satchel, and Vic gestured for him to set it on the counter. When he opened it, she saw it held five beauties. Now she'd have the chance to show him that he was dealing with an experienced professional, even if her shop was a little . . . eclectic. "That one in the center is a real collector's item. Patek Philippe Gondolo. The blue dial is rare." She leaned closer. "Looks like there is a little glue residue near the twelve, probably from a crystal replacement. Still has the original Patek crown with Calatrava cross."

"You lost me," Bowen told her.

See, Mr. New York City, you aren't dealing with some small-town hick, she thought. Well, maybe he was. She hadn't even left town to go to college. She hadn't needed college to run the shop, and that's all she'd ever wanted to do. She'd been working there since she was old enough to have a job, eventually running it when it got to be too much for Mrs. Libby.

"The crown is the little knob you use to set the time. That piece gets the most wear and tear, and you see a lot of watches where it's been replaced. But not here. If I put it up on my site—

I sell online, not just in the shop—I would start the bidding at four thousand dollars." Even if she was a small-town hick, she knew her stuff.

Vic moved on to the next watch, a lovely Universal Genève Polerouter, with eighteen-karat rose gold. A little slight scratching, like the Patek. "Your grandfather wore these. He didn't just collect them," she murmured.

Bowen nodded. "He had this one on the night of the Fitzy banquet."

"What's a Fitzy?"

"She's not a down-easter." Vic turned to Bonnie. "A Fitzy is the Fitzpatrick Trophy. They give it to the best high school football player in Maine. Bowen was a finalist." It figured he'd bring up that up. "The town gave him a parade." A *parade*.

"Probably just because my granddad was mayor."

And let's be sure to keep reminding us who your grandfather was, Vic thought. "He was also Mr. Baseball." He wanted to show off, well, she'd help him out.

"Did you get a sash?" Bonnie teased

Bowen laughed. "Yes, but the tiara wouldn't fit. My head had gotten too big after that parade. And it wasn't the real Mr. Baseball. That's for the best player in the state. I was just Central Maine's Mr. B."

Vic rolled her eyes. His aw-shucks act might be working on Bonnie, who was halfway to having hearts for eyes as she looked at him, but it wasn't working on Vic.

"What year did you graduate?" Bowen asked Vic. "Only a fellow Splitter would know that sports stuff."

"I still can't believe the high school mascot is a splitter," Bonnie said.

"Splitting slabs of slate is what Fox Crossing was built on," Vic told her. "And I graduated in 2011, same as you," she told Bowen.

"Sorry I didn't recognize you at first."

At first, right. He still hadn't recognized her. He just knew they were at school together because she clearly knew about all those athletic triumphs of his. "I wasn't the school MVP in a multitude of sports, so what's to remember?" Before he could respond, she rattled off the details about the Polerouter, then moved on to the next watch. Sooner she finished, the sooner she could get him out of here, and she wanted him out. But not until she got his business.

"Are you this good with other types of collectibles?" Bowen asked, when she'd finished giving the rundown on the last watch.

"She is," Bonnie answered for her. "I keep telling her she needs to change the name from Junk and Disorderly. That makes it sound like this is an indoor rummage sale."

Bowen glanced around the shop, clearly trying to decide how the shop differed from said indoor rummage sale. Truth? It didn't. And, for Vic, that was the best thing about the shop. Even before she'd worked here, she'd loved spending Saturday afternoons poking around, never knowing what she'd find. It had been like going on a treasure hunt, and Vic wanted to keep it that way.

"The name of a business has a powerful impact. Branding sells. Your online business might—"

Vic cut Bowen off. "Mrs. Libby named this place, and she left it to me. Maybe because she felt sorry for me after the wedding that wasn't, but I think it's because she knew I loved it as much as she did." Vic wished she could suck that part about the non-wedding back into her mouth, but too late.

Bowen opened his mouth, probably to give her some more unwanted advice. Vic didn't give him that chance. "Despite the name, despite appearances, I know collectors all over the country. I can think of three right off the top of my head who'd love to get an exclusive look at the watches and possibly make an offer on them as a set. If that's something you'd be interested in."

"I'll think it over." Like he was doing her a favor. Except it would kind of be doing her a favor.

"If you have any questions, just let me know." She handed him one of her business cards.

"Actually, would you consider coming out to the house at some point? I'm in need of an appraisal on a lot of my grandfather's things."

"Of course."

"I'm only going to be in town on the weekends. Would next Saturday be possible?"

"Absolutely."

"How about lunch this afternoon?"

"No." The word came out flat and hard. Yikes. She should have found a softer way to turn him down. Possibly she shouldn't have turned him down at all, but the *no* had just come blasting out of her mouth.

"Go on," Bonnie urged. "Your tuna salad will keep, and I can watch the shop."

"I . . . I'm sorry. I'm not available." She knew the words sounded stiff, but they were the best she could do. She could handle having a professional exchange with Bowen Gower, but that was it.

He didn't respond for a moment, and Vic thought she'd blown the chance of handling the estate, but then he said, "I'll see you Saturday at three. I assume you know the house."

Vic nodded. "I'll be there."

As soon as Bowen left, Bonnie exploded. "Why didn't you go? Forget about him being someone who could put thousands of lovely dollars in your pocket. The guy was hot. Like, ouch-I-touched-the-stove hot."

"You know what, it's crazy, but I don't actually find the idea of touching a hot stove appealing."

Bowen sat down at the breakfast bar—the dining room was too big for one person—and pulled his sandwich, applewood-smoked chicken, out of the bag. It was his favorite item on the BBQ menu. Just as he brought it to his mouth, he realized he hadn't brought anything for Tegan. He should have texted and asked if she wanted anything. He could offer her half, but it would be clear she'd been an afterthought. She would probably have turned him down anyway, like she'd done when he offered to take her to Flappy's for breakfast. And when he'd offered to take her to the BBQ their first night.

He realized that he'd taken a couple bites of his sandwich without even registering the taste. What a waste. He took another, savoring. Best BBQ sauce he'd ever tasted. His thoughts returned to Tegan. It's like she wanted to spend as little time with him as possible, even though he'd tried to be friendly. They hadn't been close when they were kids, but they hadn't had the kind of fights some brothers and sisters did. He didn't get her attitude.

And Victoria Michaud—he now knew her name, thanks to her card, but he still didn't remember her from school—was just as baffling. He'd gone out of his way to be nice, even asked her out to lunch, and she'd acted like she'd just seen him kick a puppy.

He wondered how much she'd changed since high school. He didn't think he'd have forgotten her if she looked mostly the same. She was definitely his type—dark eyes; long dark hair he could imagine tangling his fingers in; wide, generous mouth made for kissing; great body, at least what he could see of it. She'd covered it with a truly atrocious ensemble. Her skirt, which went down to her toes, looked like it belonged on an Amish hausfrau, or it would have if it hadn't been a chartreuse so bright it almost made his eyes water. On top, she'd worn a baseball shirt with Frida Kahlo on it—which existed why? The shirt, while appalling, at least had the benefit of showing off some nice curves. Very nice curves.

Too bad her dislike of him radiated off her. Whatever her problem, it wasn't on him. The other woman was friendly and flirty. If he'd asked, he was sure she'd have taken him up on the lunch offer. Her boss should have. She had the potential to earn a fat commission on the items from the estate. She could have been a little nicer to a client who was bringing so much business her way. She could have been a little nicer to a man who'd sent her a drink too. Last night, she hadn't even bothered with a nod or an apologetic smile. The only reason he'd even gone into her place was that's what his grandfather would have wanted. He'd always supported local businesses.

Bowen knew he could win Victoria over. His boss called him "the people guy" because he could get anyone to like him. Which reminded him. He pulled out his cell and checked his calendar. He had a lunch opening on Tuesday. He shot a text to Brian. He wanted to keep that relationship going. There might be a coinvest opportunity at some point. He sent a text to Ray, reminding him that Bowen needed the latest Nest P&L first thing tomorrow. Ray was probably on it, but it didn't hurt to be sure. Bowen didn't want to be caught with his pants down.

He took the last bite of his sandwich and ate the last of the slaw, then tossed the trash and wiped down the counter. He glanced at his phone. Still a couple hours before he needed to leave for the airport. His grandfather's paperwork had been meticulously organized, no surprise, and Bowen had already emailed the lawyer about next steps. Bowen needed to get pictures of the paintings in the upstairs hall, and he should do an inventory of the china in the dining room sideboard. Not his area of expertise, but he could notate the markings and take photos. He should do the silverware too, at least what they'd used on what his granddad had called "occasions."

As he started for his bedroom to get his laptop, he caught sight of his sister through the open study door. The piles she'd started yesterday morning seemed to have gotten bigger. What was she doing? Hadn't he made it clear he didn't want her messing with things?

"I figured since you photographed everything in here, it was okay to go back to sorting," she said when he stepped inside. He'd told her before he left that morning that he was going to the antiques store to start the process of getting things appraised. He didn't think he'd needed to explain that meant she should leave everything alone.

He winced as she picked up a rack of pipes from one pile and put it in a box that looked like it had been found behind the Mercantile. It had a stain on one side that looked moist. He made a mental note to order some proper packing materials. "I think we should just leave everything out for now. Victoria Michaud, she owns the antiques place"—he couldn't bring himself to use the shop's ridiculous, bad-for-business name—"is going to come over when I'm here next weekend. Sometimes it takes a trained eye to be able to tell junk from collectible," he said, trying to be diplomatic. Tegan could be touchy. "Like those pipes. I have a colleague who collects them. They might be worth a couple bucks, or they might be worth a couple hundred." He noticed that the box she'd put them in had DONATE scrawled on the side.

Tegan returned the rack to the mantel, then jammed her hands in her pockets. "Why wait until next weekend? I'm here. I can show her everything."

Bowen hesitated. He didn't have any reason to think Victoria wouldn't give a solid appraisal. She'd come up with an evaluation of each watch without hesitation. He was planning to do some research though, just to be sure she'd known as much as she'd seemed to. But that didn't mean there wasn't some room to negotiate. Maybe a lower commission would be appropriate for such a large estate. There could be a sliding scale. He needed to research that too.

"You don't think I can do it."

Definitely touchy. "No. That's not what I was thinking. It would be good for both of us to hear what she has to say is all." He made sure he didn't let annoyance creep into his tone.

"Like we did today at her shop," Tegan shot back.

It hadn't even occurred to him to ask Tegan to go with him. She could have if she'd simply said she wanted to. When people didn't say what they wanted, they shouldn't complain when they didn't get whatever it was.

"I really just went in to see if there was a person with the necessary experience in town. We didn't have a long discussion. When she comes next weekend, you'll be here, and she can tell us both what she thinks."

"Forget it. I don't need to. You're in charge of it all."

He took a moment to frame a response. "Having two executors would have complicated things. I think each one would be legally responsible for the actions of the other. It made sense for Granddad to go with one. He probably just chose me because I'm the oldest." That sounded plausible, although they both knew that even if she'd been older, their grandfather would have given Bowen the responsibility.

"Not the oldest if you count Dad."

True. And until she brought it up, Bowen hadn't even thought about it. Had Bowen being chosen as executor felt like a slight to his dad? Worse than a slight? Bowen's grandfather didn't respect Bowen's father. Bowen and his grandfather hadn't discussed Bowen's dad often, but it had been clear. His grandfather had sent Bowen's dad to Wharton too, wanted Bowen's dad to have a career like, well, Bowen's. But his dad couldn't hack it. "I have more business experience than Dad is all. That must have been the thinking," Bowen said, carefully choosing his words.

"I'm sure it didn't take much thinking. He made his mind up about all of us a long time ago. He valued . . . what was it? 'Outstanding achievement.' And you delivered."

Was Bowen supposed to see that as a bad thing? Because that was absurd. Achievement was . . . achievement. Empirically good. But that wasn't a conversation he wanted to have with Tegan, queen of the Kleenex jobs. "Did you ask Dad if there was anything of Granddad's he wanted?" Bowen asked instead.

"The blue china bird on the bedside table in Grandfather's bedroom. Dad gave it to Grandmother when he was a kid."

"Nothing else?"

"Nothing else." Tegan gave a short laugh. "Except the allowance you'll be doling out. Both of us will be taking that."

Doling out an allowance? What the hell? That made it sound like Bowen would be making the decisions about how much they got and when. "I'm just administering the estate. Granddad is the one who made all the decisions."

"Just following orders. I get it."

She looked around the room. "Since there's nothing else I'm allowed to do in here, I guess I'll go upstairs."

Bowen stared after her. He was the people guy, but he had no idea how to finesse the situation with Tegan. He clasped his hands behind his neck, tilted his head back, and stared up at the ceiling for a few long moments. At least he was going home in a couple hours. He went upstairs and checked email, then sent one to Ray reminding him that Bowen needed the Nest P&L for Monday's meeting. As soon as he hit send, he realized he'd already sent Ray a text saying the same thing. Well, now he'd be sure and get it done.

Bowen thought about packing, but decided to leave everything but the laptop. He'd be back next weekend. Maybe he didn't have to be commuting back and forth every weekend for months. The lawyer could handle the paperwork. Bowen could e-sign documents when necessary. He could come back long enough to show Victoria Michaud the items he was looking to sell, then she could take it from there. If it didn't appear that she could handle it, he'd hire someone else.

And Tegan? He could give her a few little errands to do, since she obviously wanted to stay for a while. He thought about her taking the bus here, clearly with no job worth going back to. If she wasn't staying here, would she even have a place to live? Did she have enough even to buy groceries?

He did a time check. He could make a run to the Mercantile and buy enough to fully stock the fridge and pantry. He'd only bought necessities on his way in. He stepped out into the hall. Her door was closed. He hesitated, then walked over and knocked.

"What?" Tegan sounded annoyed at the interruption.

He was trying to do her a favor, and she had him wondering why. He thought about walking away, then pictured that falling-apart sneaker of hers. She needed taking care of, whether she liked it or not. "I'm going to the store. Do you want anything?"

"No."

He didn't even get a "Thanks for asking." Fine. Perfect. He was going to the store anyway. Somehow, she'd ended up as his responsibility, at least for now. He bet she'd eat what he brought.

A few hours from now, he'd be home, and tomorrow he'd be back at work, he reminded himself. And he'd have almost a week when he didn't have to see Tegan or Victoria Michaud.

CHAPTER 4

"Our first step is to get together a community group, somewhere between fifteen and twenty people, who will be responsible for deciding which health needs are the most important in Fox Crossing," Henry explained, once he'd given Mayor Hatherley the basics of what a community health assessment involved.

"So local doctors and nurses?" Belle asked.

"Some of those, but they should only be part of the mix."

"Who else?" Belle pulled a yellow legal pad out of her top desk drawer and grabbed a pen from the dozens stuck in a lump of clay. "Annie is always on me for not using the laptop, but I'm of the ain't-broke-don't-fix-it school."

"I should write longhand more myself. It's good for your brain." Henry shifted in his seat. Belle's office above the Mercantile was big enough for a desk, two chairs, and a filing cabinet, without much left over for legroom. "It creates communication between different parts of the brain, and that improves learning and memory."

"Huh. I'll make a longhand note to remind myself to tell

Annie that." Belle frowned as the pen she'd chosen wouldn't write. She selected another from the lump. "In case you're wondering, that pencil holder is supposed to be a hedgehog. Annie made it in the third grade. She claims those two minuscule dots are eyes."

"Don't let my sister see it or she'll want to put it in her shop."

Belle laughed. "It's a little like the Island of Misfit Toys in there, but she has some good stuff too." She drew a few circles on the pad to test the new pen. "Local doctors and nurses and who else?"

"We need people from local businesses, the schools, the churches. We should definitely have someone from the mine, the Recreation Department, the American Legion."

"The library? The Town Council?"

"Yes, to both of those, if we can get people to sign on."

"We'll get people. I guarantee it," Belle said firmly. "There's the Economic Development Council. It serves the whole county, but the offices are over in Dover-Foxcroft."

"I'm going to be getting together groups all over the county. They're on my list of places I want to reach out to. The Y over there too. I want to get in touch with the Maine Community Coalition. They're doing some great work on equity."

"Virgil Escobar was able to get his mobile dog-grooming business going with some money from one of their Equal Opportunity Grants. He gives out the dog biscuits Shoo Fly makes. You've never seen dogs so eager for a bath."

"If he'd be willing to join the group, that would be awesome. Shoo Fly too."

"They'll both be willing. I guarantee it."

Henry believed her. He imagined it would be a rare person who could say no to Mayor Hatherley. "What I want to do is hold an informational meeting, maybe at Banana's if he'd be up for it."

"He'll be up for it. I—"

"Guarantee it." She was going to make Henry's job easy. "At

the first meeting, I'll explain what a community health assessment is and what the benefits for Fox Crossing would be, then I'll lay out the levels of participation. One way of participating would be joining the core group we've been talking about, but we'll also need people to help gather feedback from the community, and then we'll want to get as many people as possible to take surveys and come to focus groups."

"If they live in this town, they'll participate. I want to be part of that core group myself."

He hadn't thought it would be hard to get Mayor Hatherley on board. The assessment could only be good for the town. But he'd gotten more than her approval. She was all in, and he didn't doubt that she would use all her considerable influence, and charm, to make sure his first meeting was packed.

"I'll set up a date and time with Banana and start pulling together preliminary population data—insurance stats, income, education, veteran status, anything that's out there that will give us a head start."

"Let me know as soon as it's scheduled and I'll start getting the word out." Belle reached across the desk and shook his hand. "It's good to have you back in town, Henry."

"Good to be here." And it was. He hadn't been sure how it would feel to be back in Fox Crossing, but he was glad he'd come. Partly because heading up a study like this one was his dream job, but also because he'd come to realize Vic could use a break. Whether she knew it or not, wrangling their parents was wearing on her. He got it. He didn't think he'd ever completely accept that they weren't together anymore, that they couldn't even stand the sight of each other.

He decided to wait until that night to get started on the research he needed to do before the meeting and stop by the house to go through the things he'd left behind when he left for college. He wanted to get it over with. Until he did, it was going to be this weight he was carrying around.

When he arrived, he went straight into the garage. His dad

had said the boxes would be in there, and Henry didn't want to walk through the empty rooms. Too sad.

He left the garage door open to give himself more light, then hunted around until he found some garbage bags on one of the shelves. He could use one for what he wanted to toss, one for what he wanted to keep.

Here goes. He opened one of the boxes with HENRY written on it in his dad's blocky printing. A lot of the decisions were easy. No need for old textbooks and binders. His old magic set made him smile, but he didn't want to keep it, and too many of the pieces were missing to give it to Vic for the shop. Maybe she'd want his collection of Bionicles though. Man, he'd loved those things. As he looked at them, every name came back— Uxar, Creature of the Jungle; Icarax; Toa Kopaka. He decided he also needed a bag for things Vic might want. But maybe he'd keep one of the Bionicles. Or two. Von Nebula, for sure.

He reached back into the box and pulled out a little puppet, the strings tangled. He gave a snort of laughter as he recognized it—an NSYNC marionette. He had no idea which guy it was. The toy should have been in Vic's box, not his. She'd get a kick out of seeing it again. He suspected she wouldn't add it to the Junk & Disorderly merch. She'd keep it, same way he was keeping Von Nebula.

And that was one box down. He ripped the duct tape off the second one and pulled it open. Yearbooks. Toss. Definitely. There was nothing he wanted to remember from back then. He shoved them into the bag of trash. Next, he pulled out a battered copy of *Altered Carbon*. He must have read that twenty times. Probably because the idea of transferring consciousness appealed to that fat kid he used to be, a kid who hated his body.

Loved the book then, didn't want to read it now. It was almost falling apart, so he put it in the toss bag. A pair of Heelys, a skinny black tie, and a *Guitar Hero* guitar all went with the stuff for Vic to go through. All the clothes went directly into the trash. He didn't care if there was anything Vic might want to try to sell. He didn't even like to think about how he felt when he was that size.

That was one toss bag filled. He started to tie it closed, hesitated, then dug through it until he came to one of the yearbooks. He pulled it free. Sophomore year. He hesitated again, then opened it and flipped forward a few pages. There it was. Tegan's message:

"Always remember, grasshopper bean hot chocolate, the Fortress of Solitude, tree pee, artsy fartsy, Mr. Noball, getting kicked out of Miss Dibble's class, moose boots, Von Ultra vs. Jazzy Chihuahua, getting kicked out of Miss Violet's play (on purpose), voting everyone off the island, star pow-ah. Running out of room. Most of all, remember illegitimi non carborundum! Love, Tegan"

Her words brought a rush of memories. He tended to think of high school as an unending stretch of humiliation and pain, and a lot of it had been, but then there'd been Tegan. She'd gotten him through. More than that, she'd somehow gotten him to laugh, laugh a lot.

Illegitimi non carborundum. That had been their catchphrase. Latin, well Latin sounding, for "Don't let the bastards get you down." Henry had come across the motto in a book about World War II, and Tegan had loved it. They'd said it to each other pretty much every day when they had to go their separate ways after walking to school together. He'd repeated it to himself over and over until, finally, the last bell rang, and he and Tegan would meet up for the walk home.

He turned to the section of sophomore pictures and found hers. She was smiling that shy smile of hers, lips pressed together, one side of her mouth curving a little higher than the other. "Thank you, Tegan," he said softly.

"Hey. Just thought I'd come over and say hello." Henry

looked up and saw a guy around his age, red hair in a brush cut, standing in the driveway. "You moving in?"

"Going through stuff I left in my parents' garage when I left for college. They're getting ready to sell, so . . ."

"Ah. I just moved in next door a couple months ago. My cousin lives in town, said it was a good place. Your folks were already gone. I was hoping I was getting a neighbor. A neighbor of my generation, I mean. The Osbornes on the other side are great, but they have to be in their seventies."

Henry stood up and walked over to him, since it was turning out to be more than a hi. "Yeah. They were living there when I was a kid. My sister used to dog-sit for them. They had a schnauzer named Mr. Bones."

"They still do!"

"They were on, I think, their third Mr. Bones when I moved out."

"I gotta tell you, Mr. Osborne scares me. Twice I caught him on a ladder, once looking at my gutters, another time repairing a loose shutter. I can't just say, 'Mr. O., you're just too damn old to be doing that.' And yet he is."

"He always was a man who couldn't sit still. There were Saturday mornings when my dad would roust me out of bed because Mr. Osborne had decided to shovel our driveway, which was my job."

"Already caught him shoveling mine multiple times. He and his wife help me out big-time with Kenzie, my daughter. She's thirteen and insisted she was too old for a babysitter, which she probably is, but I'm still getting used to being a single dad. My wife and I—" He made an explosion sound and waved his arms around in frantic circles. "Thinking of her home alone scared me more than Mr. O. on the ladder, but I agreed she didn't need supervision. Then what I did, and I'm not proud of it, because it's basically lying to my kid, is ask the Osbornes if they'd keep an eye on her from when she gets home from school until I get home from work. I was planning to pay them back by doing chores, but Mr. O. is too fast." He shook his head. "Sorry. You didn't need to hear all that. Any of that actually. It's just I mainly only have a thirteen-year-old girl to talk to, and you have to be veeerrry careful what you say around a thirteen-year-old girl. One wrong word and—" He did the explosion sound and arm-waving thing again. "Sorry."

"Nothing to be sorry for. I'm new in town too, in a way. I haven't lived here in more than ten years. We should hang out sometime. I'm Henry."

"Samuel."

Henry handed Samuel his phone. "Give me your number, and we can meet up."

"I'll let you get back to it." Samuel returned the phone. "Sorry again for the spew."

"Not a problem." Henry returned to the boxes and garbage bags. He picked up the yearbook, carefully tore out the page with Tegan's note and the page with her picture, then folded them and put them in his wallet.

He jammed the yearbook back in the trash. Tegan was all he wanted to remember from high school.

Amazon Prime immediately started the next episode of *House*, and Tegan got sucked in, trying to figure out which person was going to be the patient. Usually, it wasn't the obvious one. Like now. It wasn't going to be the fat guy running the bleachers. Gonna be the personal trainer, for the ironic twist, she decided. And, yeah, she was going down. Tegan gave a self high-five, slapping her hands together over her head, something one of her exes had done all the time, then clicked the remote to skip over the opening credits. She reached for another handful of nuts, remembered that Bowen had bought them, and froze with her hand hovering over the bowl. This was probably exactly how her brother thought she was spending her time, watching TV and eating his food. She didn't want him to be right. She didn't want to be that person.

She forced herself to click off the TV. It was already almost three, and here she was, still in her pajamas, having watched, she wasn't even sure how many eps. Four? Five?

"Okay, Tegan, what are we going to do today? We're going to go out there and get ourselves a job!" she said in her peppiest cheerleader voice as she sprang off the sofa. "Oh, joy," she added in her regular voice. She made herself walk directly to the bathroom, then got in the shower, no passing go, no collecting two hundred dollars. She knew herself, and she knew if she didn't get herself dressed and on the move, then somehow it would end up being dark. And when it was dark in the winter in Maine, you just wanted to cozy up under an afghan with maybe another episode or three of *House*. She didn't know why, but *House* was her TV equivalent of comfort food. Maybe because House was more screwed up than she was. Also, a little voice in her head added, he's a bitter, friendless bastard, so you have that in common. Except he was also way more brilliant than she was. And a doctor, so with a way better job then she had. When she had a job.

After the shower, she studied her limited wardrobe choices and decided on her navy wool pants and the sweater her parents had given her for Christmas. She put on her ankle boots. They were still in decent shape. She'd been trying not to wear them too much to keep them nice. She plaited her hair in a French braid and put on her at-work makeup. If she was going to be asking around for places that were hiring, she needed to look like a person. That's always how she thought of it—looking like a person. As opposed to whatever she was in her natural state, some kind of part-person, part . . . creature.

Tegan grabbed her coat and headed out. After a couple-block walk, she was on Fox Crossing's main drag, what there was of it. It hadn't changed much. Shoo Fly's bakery had added

a big patio and was selling dog biscuits in addition to the yum-
mies, according to the chalkboard out front.

Flappy's looked the same. Exactly the same. It was almost
freaky, like she'd had a time slip and gone back twelve or fifteen years. She thought she could see the back of Flappy's head
through the serving hatch behind the counter. And that might
even be Mr. Osborne sitting on one of the stools. Grayer, back
a little stooped, but that maroon sweater with the leather elbow
patches could have been the same one from back in the day.

She'd eaten at Flappy's every Sunday of the two-plus years
her family had lived in Fox Crossing. Her grandfather insisted.
He said as the mayor he had to support local businesses, but
it always seemed like the breakfasts were so he could get his
weekly ass-kissing. Every person who came in stopped by their
booth. She jammed her hands deep in her jacket pockets and
kept walking.

Vixen's big front window still looked like a foxplosion had
just happened. Today's mix included fox tea towels, knit hats
with fox ears, and a trio of fox music boxes. Tegan wondered
what they'd play. She laughed imagining them playing "The
Foxy Song" from *Five Nights at Freddy's*. She'd done a little
babysitting back in El Paso, and the kid had loved *Five Nights
at Freddy's*. Even though it gave him nightmares every damn
time. They'd have to watch a couple *Beat Bugs* vids before he
could go back to sleep. Sometimes after he was back in bed,
Tegan would watch a couple more because, come on, they were
bugs singing the Beatles. Genius.

She crossed the street, passed the Hen House ice cream
place, more of a hot-chocolate place in winter. They had more
than ten kinds. She and Henry would try mixing them up in
his kitchen, inventing crazy ones, like Peppermint Pepperoni
Mocha and Grasshopper Bean. They never went into the Hen
House. Never knew who would be in there.

Tegan wondered if Henry still lived in town. Maybe she'd

run into him. She wondered if they'd still click, the way they used to. He'd been able to make her laugh so hard she'd forget about her parents fighting, and her grandfather disapproving of pretty much her whole existence, so hard that once she'd snorted Peppermint Pepperoni Mocha out of her nose. Burned like crazy, but she hadn't cared.

She paused outside Wit's Beginning, the microbrewery. She had bartending experience, waitressing too. She should go in and ask if any shifts needed filling. Yep, she should go in. It took her a few more moments, but she managed to get herself though the door. She might have been there a few times with her family, but she didn't have any real memories of the place. It had a nice vibe though. Vintage outdoor kerosene lanterns on the tables gave off a warm glow, and the mellow ska was just right to encourage the early-evening patrons to hang out and maybe stay for dinner.

A stool near the taps would be the best spot for chatting with the bartender. She'd order a drink, make a little small talk, show she could act like a person, then casually ask if they needed anybody. A black guy, maybe sixtysomething, came over as soon as she sat down. She thought she remembered seeing him around when she was a kid.

"New customer's first drink is always on the house. What'll you have?"

"What do you have in a cream ale?"

"I've been playing around with a pistachio, and I always have St. Joseph's."

"St. Joseph's, like the baby aspirin?"

He touched his nose, then pointed at her.

"I've got to have that. Although it always seemed strange that they made them taste so good. As a kid, I could have eaten them like candy. Do you have it on nitro? I love all the extra bubbles," she added, just to show him she knew what was what.

"Coming up."

He turned, grabbed a mug, filled it, and put it in front of her. No matter what it tasted like, she'd been prepared to do a little gushing. But it was amazing. "Smooth. Great balance. I can pick out individual flavors if I focus, but with this blend, all the flavors become one." She hoped that hadn't been overkill. She'd wanted to show she knew her brew, but not sound like an annoying beer snob.

"You're Tegan Gower, am I right?"

"I can't believe you recognized me." She liked to think she looked a lot different from what she had at sixteen. She'd had an awkward stage that lasted the whole time she lived here.

"I recognize those eyes of yours. Unusual shade. Gunmetal blue, I'd call it, same as your brother, your grandfather too. Bowen was in here a few nights ago, so I knew you might be in town. I'm sorry for your loss."

Tegan nodded, struggling to come up with the right thing to say. She settled on "I appreciate it." Which was true. She appreciated the genuine sympathy she'd heard in his voice and seen on his face. Her feelings about her grandfather were such a tangle. It's not like she was happy he was dead. She hadn't packed her dancing shoes for a visit to his grave. But she wasn't sad. She wasn't feeling much of anything, probably because they hadn't had much of a relationship. He'd been all about Bowen, loving having one of the most popular kids in school as his grandson. Tegan hadn't given him much to be proud of, but he hadn't even tried to get to know her. Maybe he'd get out a polite question once in a while during a meal, but he was on to the next topic before she'd gotten the answer all the way out of her mouth.

And the way he'd treated her dad . . . Tegan couldn't forgive him that. This man—she couldn't remember his name— probably had no idea beloved Mayor Gower could be such a bastard. She'd never seen that part of him come out in public. "I know I should remember your—"

"Name's Banana."

"Banana. So do I get the story?" Banana had to be a trail name, and trail names always came with a story.

"Nope. I have lots of other stories I can tell you though, stories of heroism, romance, terror."

"Hmmm. I'll take terror for a thousand, Alex."

Banana gave a *haw-haw-haw* and rubbed his hands together. "Terror it is. Just talking about what happened to me one night out on the trail out in Tennessee is enough to set me shivering. I'd decided I needed some solitude and found a place to pitch my tent. It was one of those nights where the moon is as thin as a fingernail clipping, so it was dark, dark in the way it can only be out away from civilization. I was just about to crack open a can of refried beans when I heard it, the sound of stone against stone. Getting louder. Getting closer. *Scrrich, scrrich, scrrich.*"

He paused until Tegan said, "What was it?"

Then he continued with a satisfied grin. "I knew what that sound meant. Spearfinger was near. I could almost feel that stone finger of hers, sharper than any knife, jabbing into my liver. There's nothing Spearfinger enjoys more than a fresh, juicy liver. And my liver was the only one nearby, since I'd decided to strike out on my own."

He gave another of those dramatic pauses, and Tegan obliged by begging him to tell her what happened next. She wanted a job, but she was also having fun, something she hadn't expected when she walked in.

"There was only one thing I could think to do. I'd been gifted a bottle of trail moonshine, and I doused myself with it. Then she was on me, gravel raining down on my head from her stone mouth." Banana ran his hand over his bald head, as if he were feeling that gravel again. "Her finger sliced though my parka like it was nothing. It pierced my flesh, a few drops of blood oozing out. She gave an ecstatic moan in anticipation of her meal, then I figure she must have gotten a good whiff, be-cause, next thing I knew, *scrrich, scrrich, scrrich*, she was moving away. She must have figured anyone who smelled like me must have a liver destroyed by alcohol."

"Is that why you decided to open a pub?. Because alcohol saved your life?"

He slapped both hands on the bar. "Precisely."

Okay, this was good. They'd gotten a little rapport going. Now was the time to segue. "I, um, I'm going to be in town for a while, a few months at least. I'm hoping to get some work, at least part-time. I've done some bartending, waitressing too. Any chance—"

He didn't make her finish. "I can give you a couple weeknights and a Saturday. I just had one of my guys head off for Georgia to start a northbounder a couple weeks ago. I get it. In February, you can feel like you're the first person ever to set foot on the trail."

Tegan felt muscles from her neck to her shoulders and all the way down her spine relax. She needed this. "Thanks so much."

Mayor Gower's granddaughter serving up beers and burgers to the townsfolk. Good thing he was already dead, or this would probably kill him.

CHAPTER 5

"Bowen, how goes it?" Jana, one of the directors, a mentor to Bowen since almost day one, dropped into one of the chairs opposite his desk and took a swig from the enormous water bottle she always carried.

"Not bad." He tilted his head to stretch out his neck, then glanced at the time on his laptop. A few minutes to nine. It felt like only a half an hour ago it had been seven. He'd been in the zone, deep in the zone, where he had no awareness of time passing, no awareness of anything but the task in front of him. The zone was one of the things he loved best about his job.

"I'm just taking a look at a teaser for a company that has to be Jumbie, since the teaser says the company accounts for forty-three percent of all the apps on Google Play," he told her. "Compound multiple growth of thirty percent. They're planning to expand internationally and are expecting the EBITDA margin to increase ten percent by fiscal year 2024. That seems a bit optimistic to me, but I think it's worth digging into."

"Agreed." She took another swig.

"You got this."

Jana raised an eyebrow, and he nodded toward the water bottle, which had a line for every hour of the day. That last swig had taken her to the 9:00 p.m. line, right on schedule.

"So, I'm healthier because of the water intake, but now I'll have to get up to pee at least twice during the night, causing interrupted sleep, which makes me less healthy."

"You need to factor in how getting up increases your daily step count."

She laughed. "I'm going to step count my way out of here. It's getting late. You coming?"

"I need to hit the data room for a few first." The few turned into almost another hour. He decided to stop off at the Dead Rabbit on the way home. One of their shepherd's pies sounded good for a late dinner, and Mitchell Sayer could be found in the downstairs taproom at least a few nights a week. Bowen liked to "run into" him periodically. Bowen thought if he had the right opportunity, the endowment would partner up, but it hadn't happened yet.

There was no sign of Sayer when Bowen walked in. He could still show, but if not, it would happen another night. Bowen took a seat at the bar and ordered a Guinness. The Rabbit had an extensive drinks menu, but his grandfather had taught him that it was wrong to order anything other than Guinness at an Irish pub. He did a phone check. Nothing in the messages or email needed immediate attention, so he put the cell away. A woman with light red hair sitting near the other end of the bar caught his eye. She wore a well-fitting wool dress in a flattering shade of blue. No eye-piercing chartreuse for her.

She was almost finished with her drink. The timing was right. . . . Impulsively, Bowen asked the bartender to send her another. When she received it, she looked over, raised her glass to him, and smiled. That's the way it worked. The way it was *supposed* to work, he corrected himself.

He picked up his drink and walked over to her. They

launched into the usual getting-to-know-you chat. It was a nice end to a long day, a little pleasant conversation with an attractive woman who looked at him as if she liked what she saw.

That wasn't much to ask for, and that was all he wanted, wanted or needed. Much more than that was a distraction. He had to keep his head in the game. Next step of the ten-year plan was director by age thirty-three, and that would take all his focus.

Get over there, Tegan ordered herself. With Banana behind the bar, she had waitress duty unless he got swamped. But those three women who'd just come in . . . she knew them. Kind of. She'd gone to high school with them, but they hadn't been friends or anything. One of them had gone to the junior prom with Bowen. She probably had a real job. She was dressed like she had a real job, the other women too. She probably had a family. A kid. She probably had a life. All three of them probably did. If you were a person, by their age—Tegan's age—you had a life.

Jilly was finishing up serving nachos—it was unlimited-nachos night—to the group in the big back booth. She could take the women's order. Banana glanced in Tegan's direction, and she knew he had to be wondering why he'd hired her when all she was doing was standing around. She was already screwing up. So, get over there, she thought. Maybe they wouldn't even remember her. She wiped her clammy hands on the sides of her pants and walked to the table.

"Hi, what can I get you?" She made sure to smile.

"The wheat one with chamomile. I can't remember the name. Banana knows," the woman who'd gone to the junior prom with Bowen—Cameron, Tegan thought her name was—said.

"Same," said the woman with the newly waxed eyebrows, going by the little red bumps around them. The third woman, who wore a huge sunflower pendant, ordered a Spirited Banana. Didn't seem like any of them recognized Tegan, so she was spared that horror.

Banana was already working on the order when she returned to the bar, so way too soon she was back at their table. "What else can I get you?" she asked after she put down their drinks.

"It's bottomless nachos night, so bottomless nachos," said Cameron, clearly the alpha of the group. "With no jalapeños on them, but with a little dish of jalapeños, because I don't like them, but they do."

Tegan nodded as she took it down.

"I'll have the house salad with ranch," Statement Necklace said.

"Same," Unfortunate Eyebrows said. That was her second *same*, first the beer, then the salad. The nachos were kind of a "same," so that brought the total to two and a half.

Tegan looked at Cameron.

"Nothing else for me."

Why had she even worried they'd recognize her? Back in high school, she mostly just wanted to be invisible. Maybe because at home, getting attention from Grandfather was usually the shrivel-y kind.

She'd taken one step away from the table when Cameron said, "You're Bowen Gower's sister, aren't you? Teresa, right?"

"Tegan."

"I heard about your grandfather." Of course, she had. Everyone in town would have known when Cassian Gower, former mayor, possibly richest guy in Fox Crossing, died.

"I'm sorry for your loss," Statement Necklace said.

"Me too," Unfortunate Eyebrows chimed in.

"Thanks," Tegan answered.

"Is Bowen back in town too?" Cameron asked, doing a minor hair flip, as if Bowen was there to admire her perfect highlights.

"Off and on, until we have the estate settled." Maybe curiosity about Bowen would keep Cameron and the other women from asking anything about Tegan.

"I'd love to see him. Can I give you my number?"

"Sure, yeah." Although what Cameron expected to happen, Tegan had no idea. They'd fall in love and Bowen would move back to Fox Crossing, and Cameron and Bowen would live happily ever after? Not likely.

Cameron handed Tegan a card, showing Tegan that, yes, Cameron had a real job. She was a bank manager. Definitely not a Bowen-worthy job, but way out of Tegan's league. "Remember, I went to the junior prom with him."

"I went with Parker Clark. You set it up for me, Cam, remember?" Unfortunate Eyebrows asked. "Because Parker and Bowen were on the football team together."

"I didn't go at all. Josette and I went to some movie. *The Day After Tomorrow* maybe." Statement Necklace shook her head, then smiled. "In a way, that makes Jake Gyllenhaal my prom date. That might top Bowen."

Still standing here, Tegan thought, but tried to keep her expression open and friendly. She was on the clock.

"So, what are you doing working here?" Cameron's tone was pleasant, but that question sucked.

Tegan smiled. Still on the clock. "Long story. I won the lottery and then, although I was so sure it wouldn't happen to me, I did that thing where I blew it all—Lamborghini roadster, world cruise, Gucci bags, way too many Gucci bags—and then got hit with this enormous tax bill. I ended up totally broke. With my grandfather's house just sitting empty, at least until Bowen decides to sell, I figured I'd move back to Fox Crossing. Bowen isn't making me pay rent, and Banana was decent enough to give me a job, so here I am."

She'd buried the truth in that mass of words, but she could tell from Cameron and company's wide eyes—Unfortunate Eyebrows' mouth was even hanging open a little—that they were having trouble deciding if any of her bullshit was true. "Kidding," Tegan finally said.

Cameron gave a forced laugh. Before she or the other two could ask any more questions, Tegan said, "Let me get those bottomless nachos going." She gave a little wave and bolted.

After she put in their order, she let out a long, shaky breath. Toughen up, she told herself. This was Fox Crossing. She was going to see people she used to know. And they were going to see her. Maybe they'd think she was a loser for working as a waitress at her age. But what did that matter? Who cared what anybody thought? Anyway, it was Bowen voted Most Likely to Succeed, not Tegan. If it was Bowen back and working at Wit's, well, that would be something worth talking about.

A tall woman with a long silver braid took a seat at the bar. Banana was already serving a couple guys at the other end, so Tegan headed over to her. "What can I get you?"

"Last time I was here, Banana did some kind of aura analysis and selected the optimal brew for the state of my chakras."

"I haven't gotten my beerstrology degree yet, but, hmm, are you in the mood for light and refreshing or"—Tegan lowered her voice to a growl—"hefty and strong?"

The woman laughed. "Light."

"Tart or sweet?" Tegan drew out the *ee*'s in *sweet*.

"Tart."

"I'd suggest the Maine Squeeze. It's a blond ale with lemon and lime."

"Sounds perfect."

"Be right back." See? Tegan was good at this. No matter what Cameron and crew thought, that was a skill.

She returned with the drink and watched as the woman took the first sip. "You've got the magic." She took another sip. "What's with the dead donkey?"

Tegan should know this. She should have thought someone might ask about the bar's logo. The donkey—all four legs in the air—was on her T-shirt, and had she even bothered to ask what the story was? No.

"I'm afraid it's a tragic tale, Maisie," Banana said as he joined Tegan in front of the woman. "My beloved donkey, Bucky, died shortly before I bought the bar, and I decided to honor his memory by putting him on my mugs, napkins, T-shirts, and the like. This way, a day doesn't go by when I don't think of him."

"May I ask how he passed? If it's not too painful." Tegan could see a smile tugging at one corner of Maisie's mouth, but she managed to keep her expression mostly serious.

"I'd like to know too." Tegan wanted to be able to answer any donkey questions that came up. Wasn't there something about a donkey's grave behind the bar? She had a vague memory of Bowen and his friends stealing a tombstone. Probably it was something almost everybody at school knew about, but Tegan hadn't done a lot of talking to other kids, part of the invisibility strategy.

Banana pressed his hand to his heart. "I've made it my life's work to share the tale of Bucky. He deserves to be celebrated because there never was another donkey as talented as he was. There was a horse about a century ago who, people believed, could add and subtract, even divide."

"Clever Hans," Maisie said. "Turned out he was responding to his owner's body language. The owner's body would get tense when Hans got to the right answer, and Hans would stop tapping his foot. There's even a psychological term, the *Clever Hans effect*, for when an animal, or a person, senses what someone wants them to do."

Banana touched his nose and pointed to Maisie. "Hans was a rare creature, but Bucky was even more so. He learned to dance a polka, and you should have seen him skurfing behind my boat out on Lake Hebron. I'd started teaching him to survive without food. Every day, I gave him a little less, and every day, he kept going. Then, suddenly—" Banana pointed to the legs-up donkey on his shirt.

Maisie's eyes widened and she slapped both hands on the bar. "You know what this means? Time travel is possible! I always thought it was, but this is proof! Somebody who knew Bucky's story traveled back to Rome more than twenty-five hundred years ago. Had to be, because Bucky's story ended up in *Philogelos*."

"You're right! Many a night I've been kept awake trying to puzzle out how Bucky's story ended up in the world's oldest joke book when it was written centuries before he was born. I never considered time travel."

Banana turned to Tegan. "No charge for her drink. Finally, I'll be able to sleep at night."

"Got it," Tegan answered. "I think I might need to apologize for my brother. I think he might have stolen Bucky's gravestone back when he was in high school."

"Bucky's marker does tend to wander, especially around Halloween, but I've always believed that was the work of Bucky's spirit, sending me a message that he's still with me. His headstone always returns to its spot out back."

"Ahh. Good to know," Tegan said. "I was hoping I wasn't related to someone who would desecrate a grave."

"Order up," Big Matt called.

Tegan loaded a tray, then served Cameron and her friends.

"We were just talking about how Bowen got that parade for the football award," Statement Necklace said.

"Yep. Glory days." Tegan realized her tone had gone bitter. Not work appropriate. "Go, Splitters!" she added, getting a smile from Cameron.

A dad and a daughter—same red hair, a section of hers braided and wrapped over her head as a hair band—came in. The girl managed to walk to a two-top by the window without looking up from her phone. Jilly headed toward them, so Tegan returned to her spot behind the bar.

A guy was grabbing a seat a few barstools down from Maisie. "Tegan," he said as soon as she stepped up to take his order.

She wasn't wearing a name tag. Probably he was someone else she went to school with. He looked right around her age, but she didn't recognize him. Not until he smiled. That smile was all it took. "Henry."

"You can say it. You almost didn't recognize me without the blubber."

It was true. When they'd been friends, he'd been heavier, a lot heavier. "Same smile," she told him. Same eyes, brown with flecks of deeper brown. Same way of looking at her like she mattered more than anything.

"I'd heard Bowen was in town. I was hoping you'd be here too."

Tegan felt something open in her chest, warmth radiating from that spot until it reached her toes, her fingertips, everywhere. Henry. Henry was sitting there, right in front of her.

"Being back in town made me think about you. About us being friends." It was hard for her to find the words for what he'd meant to her. Maybe that was good. Maybe he just sort of remembered her, while he still pretty much lived inside her. Sometimes, when things got bad, she heard his voice, telling her not to let the bastards get her down.

Tegan realized a new couple was sitting at a table, and that Jilly was heading toward the back booth with another round of drinks. "I need to go take an order. Oh, wait. I didn't take yours yet."

"Do them first. I'm not going anywhere." He touched her arm lightly. "It's good to see you."

Tegan made herself take the time to be friendly to the couple, and to offer detailed descriptions of Banana's latest brews when she was asked for recommendations. She even asked a few questions when they told her they were on a microbrewery road trip. But all she wanted was to get back to Henry.

When she returned to him, he was in the middle of a conversation with Banana, who'd already served him his drink. Did

Banana have to be so fast? As she got the couple's drinks, she heard a snatch of conversation. Henry was wanting to hold a meeting at the pub.

Her thoughts were spinning as she delivered the drinks. What would it be like if she stayed here? Even after Bowen sold the house, she could get an apartment. She'd only worked here part of a shift, but she was already loving Banana, and having a good boss was the most important part of a job. She'd found that out a bunch of times. More like found out the reverse—bad boss, bad job.

Banana was still chatting to Henry. Maybe she was loving Banana a little less right this minute. Did he have to be so friendly? She'd been hoping for one-on-one time with Henry. Should she go over and join them? Or just wait until they were done? The decision was made when Banana gestured her over. Okay, back to loving him again. Actually, loving him even a little more now. "Everybody's coming home. You remember Henry Michaud?" he asked.

"He looks sort of familiar." Tegan smiled at Henry. It sounded like he'd just gotten back to town too.

Henry smiled back. That smile, wow. "We were neighbors. She was my best friend when she lived here, and not just because she was my only friend."

"You were my best friend too." Tegan caught sight of Statement Necklace waving at her. "Sorry. Gotta go."

Statement Necklace ordered another drink, then said, "Who's the guy you were talking to at the bar? I feel like I know him, but I can't, because that's not somebody you forget."

"Truth." Cameron's eyes were on Henry.

"I didn't get his name." Tegan didn't want to listen to these women go on about how much Henry had changed and, ooh, how he was gorgeous under all that fat. "Anybody else need a refill?"

When she joined Banana at the taps, he said, "Henry's going

to have a meeting here next week. We should be packed. He's heading up a community health assessment, and I know Belle will make sure everyone shows up. That's Belle Hatherley, the mayor. When she wants something done, you do it, or you regret it."

Tegan shot a quick look at Henry and found him looking back at her. "What does that involve, a health assessment?" she asked Banana, keeping her voice low, not wanting to sound ignorant in front of Henry.

"I don't have all the details, but it involves figuring out if there are any gaps in the area's health care, and figuring out ways to improve health in general. Not just Fox Crossing, the whole county."

"And Henry's heading it up?"

"Dr. Michaud is in charge."

"Henry's a doctor?" That warmth that had filled her when she'd seen him started to drain away.

"Local boy makes good." Banana headed off to the other end of the bar with the drinks he'd poured, and Tegan delivered Statement Necklace's refill, thoughts spinning again, spinning like crazy. Henry was a doctor? He was in charge of some huge project? He would probably tell her all about it when she went back over. And when it was her turn to play catch-up? *Oh, my life is swell, Henry, can't you tell? Working serving up drinks and chow. But pretty soon my brother is going to start giving me an allowance. Twenty-five thou a year, so, yeah, swell, swell, swell.*

Tegan didn't want to have that conversation, but she couldn't just ignore Henry. She had to stop back by. Maybe it would get busy, super-busy, so a few minutes would be all she'd have time for. She could handle a few minutes. It would take him longer than that to tell her about all his accomplishments. Not that that would keep him from finding out the truth about her, because, duh, here she was, obviously working here.

She returned to him. "Banana told me you're a doctor. Henry, that's so great. I'm not surprised though. You were always great at science."

"I'm not an actual doctor. Well, no, I am an actual doctor." Henry shoved his hair off his forehead, a gesture she'd seen him make a thousand times. "I have a PhD, which makes it actual, but I'm not an MD, and that's what *doctor* means to pretty much everyone."

PhD. And Tegan had, wait for it, a high school diploma. Woo! Plus some years at junior college. Woo! Woo! "That's great," she said again. Because she had a limited vocabulary, unlike a PhD.

"Thanks, Teg."

Before he could ask her anything about herself, Tegan rushed in with another question. "And Banana said that you're here for a job. What are you going to be doing?"

"The Greenville hospital was looking for someone who knew the area to head up a health study of the county. I wasn't sure how it would feel to be back. It's feeling better than I thought." Henry met her gaze.

Wham! That warmth again. "I'm sure it's good to see your family," Tegan said, to keep the conversation on the not-her.

"Yeah. Vic's the best. I'm going to be staying with—"

Tegan noticed four people coming in. "I need to go take an order." Another group came in. "Looks like it's going to get busy."

Henry nodded. "I want to catch up. Can I take you out sometime, Tegan?"

She didn't think she could survive even a few hours alone with Henry, not this Henry, Dr. Henry. She'd end up feeling like a raisin, small and shriveled. "Uh, I have a lot to do to settle my grandfather's estate, and then working here . . ."

"Oh. Right. Of course." He looked down, not meeting her eyes anymore. "Well, I'll see you around, maybe."

"Good to see you." She hurried away, the warmth draining out of her again.

Henry finished his drink. He had to finish the drink. He was an adult. He could handle a little rejection without running away. Except, it was Tegan. Tegan had always been there for him. Always. Yes, it had been a lot of years, but they'd been tight. That didn't go away, not completely, no matter how long it had been. And she'd even said he was her best friend. She'd meant it too. He'd felt it, felt it deep.

Maybe it was because he'd asked if he could take her out, instead of asking to meet up for coffee or something. Maybe it had sounded romantic or at least sounded like it had the potential to get romantic. Clearly, she wasn't interested in that. At all. She'd been a breath away from saying she was too busy because she had to wash her hair.

Probably when she looked at him, she still saw the blubber. Probably she'd never be able to see him as anything but that fat kid. Fine for a friend, but anything else—no, thank you. "Can I get an order of the nachos to go?" he called to Banana. Tegan was still at one of her tables, thankfully. "Make it a double. I'm sure Vic will want in."

"For you, Doc? A triple."

"Henry, hey."

Henry turned and saw Samuel, the guy who'd moved in next to Henry's parents' place, at a corner table with a girl who had to be his daughter. "I see someone I know. I'll just be over there." Henry was relieved he wouldn't still be at the bar when Tegan got back. She'd try to make polite conversation, and that would almost be worse than if she'd forgotten him entirely.

"How's it going?" Henry asked when he got to Samuel's table.

"Livin' the dream. Please don't wake me up."

Henry noticed Samuel's daughter mouthing the last few

words along with her dad, without looking up from her phone. She was wearing the same kind of sweater Bonnie's daughter had had on at Vic's birthday party, party number one, except hers had a narrow cutout a couple inches below the throat. It didn't come anywhere close to showing cleavage, but to Henry it seemed like the style was kind of . . . mature for both girls. Gettin' old, he told himself.

"Kenzie, this is Henry. His family used to live next door to us."

"Hey." She shot him a quick glance, then it was back to the phone.

"How are you liking Fox Crossing so far?" Henry asked.

Kenzie gave an eye roll, which Henry thought he completely deserved for the typical grown-up question. "It's okay."

"Maybe you could elaborate on that a little, Kenz." Samuel reached across the table and covered her phone with his hand. "A few details."

"I don't know what you want me to say. It's okay. Just okay." She pulled her phone free and stood up. "Be right back."

"Kenz, you—"

"I have to poop, okay?" She strode off, her red curls bouncing.

Henry bit back a laugh. What an exit line.

Samuel didn't seem to find it amusing. "Sorry. She's, let's call it sensitive, lately."

Henry sat down. "Raging hormones in teenagers aren't a myth. There's a reason for the sensitive."

"And that lasts for how many years?"

"They should even out sometime in the early twenties."

Samuel groaned. "I wish I knew how she was actually doing, you know? When I ask her something like 'How's school?,' she gives me the 'Okay,' just like she did to you. And what does that mean? Does it mean everything is fine? Or does it mean things are so horrible that she can't even talk about it? Or does it mean things are great because she's smoking weed out behind the bleachers with her new boyfriend every day?"

"Little cold for meeting up behind the bleachers." Realizing Samuel was way too worried about his daughter for a smart-ass remark, Henry added, "It's got to be tough."

"A few months before we moved here, my wife, well, she'll be my ex-wife soon, we were already separated at the time, got called to Kenzie's school. It turned out there had been a 'bullying incident.' That's what the vice principal called it, a 'bullying incident.' Some girls took Kenzie's lunch. They said they were just trying to help her with her weight issue. I don't even see a weight issue."

Henry felt his gut clench. He knew exactly how Kenzie must have felt—furious, hopeless, helpless, and full of shame. The shame was the worst. It left him feeling like what Bowen Gower and his friends did to him was in some way Henry's fault, because being the fat kid was his fault.

"I don't see a weight issue either." Kenzie was maybe a little pudgy, but if girls were bullying her about her size, she was probably feeling like she belonged in a freak show.

"And I didn't even know anything was wrong. Kenzie was going through hell, and I didn't even realize it. I was so caught up in all the drama with her mother. . . . I'm trying to do better now. I'm trying to pay attention." Samuel scrubbed the back of his neck with one hand. "But I can't tell. I really can't tell how she is. And here I am, spewing at you again."

"It's okay." Henry shook his head at his word choice. "And that *okay* means it's absolutely fine. I had some 'bullying incidents' when I was a kid, and I didn't talk to my parents about them. I was sure it would just make things worse. So, you shouldn't think it means—"

Samuel interrupted, "She's coming back."

Henry stood up, and Kenzie returned to her seat across from her dad. Henry wished he could tell her he'd been there, that he understood, and that— And that what? It got better?

It had, but when you were in hell, someone telling you things would change in college was worthless. It's not like he could say anything anyway. If Kenzie knew her dad had been talking about her with Henry, it would feel like a betrayal.

She seemed to sense it anyway, shooting a suspicious glance between Henry and her father, before returning her attention to her phone.

"Do you want to eat with us?" Samuel asked.

Before Henry could answer, Tegan came over with his order. "Here you go." She smiled at him like he was just some customer she barely knew, then headed back to the bar without giving him time to say more than "Thanks." Signal sent, signal received, Henry thought. Tegan didn't want him to think there was even the possibility of something romantic starting up between them.

"Gotta get this home." Henry held up the bag of food. "Good to see you both."

The moment he walked out the door, Henry dipped his hand into the sack and pulled out a tortilla chip dripping with melted cheese. He stuffed it into his mouth, but not without landing a clump of the cheese on his coat. He grabbed another chip as he walked toward Vic's.

No point in trying to protect the coat now. Already stained.

A couple turned the corner just as he was cramming chips four through seven in his mouth. He tried to smile and chew at the same time. He had a sudden picture of himself drinking vodka straight from a bottle, the bottle hidden by a paper sack. Because what was the difference?

He spotted a trash can up ahead and trotted over, then dumped the nachos, feeling a pang at wasting food. But it's not like there was someone around to give it to. He could have brought it to Vic's, but he knew himself, knew if the nachos were anywhere near him when he was feeling like crap, he'd eat them. Every last one.

Better in the trash than in his belly. Because he wasn't going back there. He wasn't going to be the fat kid. Not again. Never again.

From the shadows, The Fox watched the human. She hadn't seen him for several years, but she remembered him. She remembered everything beginning with the night The Woman found her. The memories of her first life, the life before she tasted death, were dim. But beginning with the snap, everything was clear. Sometimes she could almost feel the snap again, the agony, and, later, the warm liquid bringing her spirit back into her body.

She could smell this human's pain. The scent was familiar. So often, this one had been wounded in ways she could not understand. A wound without blood. She did not smell blood tonight, but the pain was there again.

CHAPTER 6

"Next Sunday, we have to have breakfast here with Dad," Vic said as she and Henry walked into Flappy's. "Otherwise, there will be badness."

"Badness?" Henry asked as they grabbed a table. "Can you give me more? Stubbed-toe-level badness? Or call nine-one-one?"

Vic sighed. "Hurt feelings, guilt trips, jealousy . . . Easier just to keep things even. If I do something with Mom, I give Dad equal time. Sometimes, like with breakfast here, we do the same thing with the time. Sometimes, I'll do something like a movie with Mom and bowling with Dad."

"How do they even know if you're keeping things even?"

"You've been in Boston too long if you've forgotten the speed of Fox Crossing's gossip network."

Nell came by and filled their coffee cups. Vic took a sip, then made sure to put the cup back in exactly the same spot.

"Got everybody you asked for committed to coming to the meeting, Henry," Belle called from the counter.

He gave her a double thumbs-up. "I never doubted it."

"You getting excited for the assessment kickoff?" Vic asked.

"Yeah. A little nervous too. A lot of the people there are going to remember me as a kid. I wonder if they'll have trouble taking me seriously."

"Not going to be a problem. Everybody's so proud of you. They're going to do whatever they can to make the assessment a success." Vic took another sip of coffee, then carefully returned the cup to its place.

"What's with the—" Henry picked up his cup, then set it down, made a few minor adjustments, then picked it up again and repeated the whole process.

Vic moved her cup. "Picture of Mom and Dad." Under the glass tabletop were dozens of photographs of townsfolk who'd lived in Fox Crossing for generations, and hikers who had only passed through once. "Outside that cabin by the lake they lived in when they were first married. Looking at it makes me kind of sad, so I'd think it would be worse for Mom. Or Dad. I always cover it up if I end up at this table with one of them."

"The cabin's one of the places she lost her wedding ring, right?"

"Yeah. There, somewhere on the Maine Turnpike, and Fort De Soto Beach." Their mother had the habit of pulling off her wedding ring and throwing it when she and their dad were in the middle of a fight. Once it had gone straight out the car window. Usually, they'd been able to find the ring after it was thrown, but not those three times.

"They used to fight a lot. Maybe I shouldn't have been so shocked when they decided to split." Henry moved Vic's cup so it was covering the picture again.

"But the fights were mostly about little things, like how Dad would dry his hands on the guest towels or how Mom didn't use the dishwasher space efficiently. They never lasted long. Usually by the time the ring was found and back on Mom's finger, the fight was over."

"I keep trying to figure out what happened. It feels like it must have been something huge. I know they said they'd grown apart, and I know it happens to couples, especially after their kids are grown-up, but . . ." Henry shook his head.

"But it didn't seem possible with Mom and Dad. They were still doing all kinds of things together. Trivia, bowling league, fishing, movies . . ."

"Yeah. Whenever I talked to them, they were— She's coming." Henry nodded toward the door.

A moment later their mom was taking a seat at the table. "What were you talking about, looking so serious?"

"Henry was trying to decide if he was hungry enough for the Trail Buster." As in three pancakes—three pancakes, plus three scrambled eggs, three pieces of bacon, three sausages, three pieces of toast, and a mountain of hash browns.

"The Buster?" Their mom shot a worried look at Henry. "That's enough to get you through a day on the trail. Most of us don't need that much on a regular day. But if you want it, you should have it." She patted his hand.

Both parents had been careful about criticizing what Henry ate. Vic had heard them discussing his weight once. Mom had said that Henry clearly felt bad about his size, and she was afraid of making him feel worse by talking to him about dieting.

"I woke up starving. I think I'm going to order it myself." A little devil in Vic had made her say it. She knew it would make her mom crazy. Junior Miss Peach didn't have the same tolerant attitude about excess weight on females.

"Don't you dare!" their mother exclaimed.

"Actually, we weren't talking about whether or not to order the Trail Buster." Henry sucked in a deep breath.

Don't do it, Henry, Vic thought. Don't do it.

But he did it.

"We were talking about why you and Dad split up. Neither of us really understand what happened. We're just trying to understand. . . ."

Their mother's face flushed, a deep, painful-looking red. Vic almost expected to feel heat radiating off it.

"If you don't want to talk about it, it's okay," Vic said quickly. "We're your kids, but that doesn't mean we have the right to know everything." Vic shot a look at Henry. His eyes were locked on their mother.

"I—I—" Suddenly tears were in their mom's eyes. She stumbled to her feet and rushed toward the bathroom.

"Why'd you do that, Henry? If she'd wanted to talk about it, she'd have talked about it."

"I just wanted to understand. I—"

Vic didn't wait to hear what else he had to say. She hurried after their mother. She found her with both hands braced against the closest sink, staring at her reflection.

"I'm sorry, Mom. Henry shouldn't have done that. It's your decision what you tell and what you don't."

Her mom pushed herself away from the sink and turned to Vic. The tears were spilling down her face now. "I cheated on your father." She used the heels of both hands to roughly wipe the tears away, but they kept coming.

Vic felt like her knees had gone liquid, like she was about to go down. Get a grip, she ordered herself. Questions were spinning in her brain. Who? Why? How many times? Does Dad know? But Vic wasn't sure she wanted the answer to any of them. What she really wanted to do was reverse time and unhear what she'd heard.

"I told your father he could tell you. You should know that everything was my fault. But he wouldn't do it, and he didn't want me to do it. But now you know, so you can go ahead and hate me now."

"Mom, I don't hate you. I could never hate you." That had to be true. She could never hate her mother. But right that second, she didn't know how she felt, not about anything. It was like she was drowning, and all she could focus on was getting air.

"I just— When I looked in the mirror, I— I think I just

wanted to feel—" Vic's mom shook her head, hard. "I don't want to do this. I don't want to come up with explanations, try to make you see my side. There are no good explanations. I don't have a side. I have to go. I can't— I'll call you later."

Vic let herself slump against the wall, needing the support. This was— Never in a thousand years would she have thought her mother would cheat on her father. Or that he'd cheat on her. Their faithfulness was a given. Like gravity.

Vic thought she was all grown-up. Even so, her parents' split had gutted her. But this . . . It felt like a betrayal of *her*. Which she knew made no sense. It had nothing to do with her. But all those feelings that had come up when Leo—

Don't go there, Vic told herself. Do not go there. It had taken her years to get to where she could block out thoughts of Leo almost as soon as they came up, and they came up way too often, even after so many years. She'd be having a bad day, feeling bad about herself for some reason, and suddenly she was back there, hearing him say the words again, and coming up with all the things she should have said.

Today, nothing had happened to her. She was fine. Everyone was fine. Her parents were fine. Maybe not *fine* fine, but they were alive, they were functioning. So was she. She was fine, fine enough. She had the shop. She had friends. She had Henry. She was fine. But her chest felt so tight, like there wasn't room for her lungs to expand.

You're getting plenty of air. Everything is okay. She closed her eyes and forced herself to take a few deep, slow breaths. See, air coming in, air going out. You're breathing. Now she had to get back out there. Henry had to be freaking out.

Vic took a moment to look at herself in the mirror. "You're fine. Now go."

She went. As soon as she sat down, Henry started firing questions. "What did she say? Is she okay? I saw her go out the back. Should I have gone after her?"

It took her brain a few moments longer than usual to process words. Finally, she said, "Mom's okay. She just got a little emo-tional, thinking about, you know, everything." Henry didn't need to know details. He thought understanding their parents' reasons would help him. It wouldn't. If one of them decided to tell him, that would be soon enough for him and Vic to talk about it. "It was better that you didn't go after her. She said she needed time to pull herself together."

"I shouldn't have done that. If she'd wanted to tell me why they split, she would have. I just have such a hard time accept-ing it. I know I'm acting like I'm seven or something."

"If you are, so am I. Maybe you're always a kid when it comes to your parents."

"Are you okay? Should we go?"

"I'm fine. Let's order. Skipping breakfast isn't going to help anything."

Henry ordered the chocolate-chip pancakes. But after Vic ordered and Nell started away from the table, he called her back and switched his order to an egg-white omelet with a side of tomatoes.

"Now I feel like I should order something healthy," Vic said.

"You want to switch it up?" Nell asked.

"I guess not."

Nell nodded and started for the kitchen.

Maybe Vic should change her order. The way she was feel-ing, blueberry pancakes with whipped cream would probably taste like sawdust with whipped sawdust on top, and if every-thing was going to taste like sawdust, she might as well eat healthy sawdust. She didn't bother calling Nell back.

"Aren't you glad I'm home?" Henry asked with a rueful smile. "Isn't everything so much better now that big brother's back?"

"Little brother. And I'm so glad you're home. I really am. I've wanted to ask her, both of them, the same thing you did."

"But you didn't. And, obviously, that was the right call."

"It's okay. She got a little emotional is all."

"You want to go into Bangor and see a movie? A loud one. With at least one explosion for every two lines of dialogue."

Vic laughed. "Perfect. But we might need to make it a double feature, because after this, I have to go over to the Gower place so I can talk to Bowen about the estate. Woo-hoo!"

Vic rang the doorbell at exactly three o'clock. She was a professional, and professionals arrived on time. Even when said professional was still trying to process that her mother had cheated on her father. Had her mom told her father about the affair? Or had her father— Stop. Just stop, she told herself. She needed to be on her game, and that meant focus.

Bowen opened the door and smiled at her, showing off his limples. Everything about him—those shoes, that cologne, the haircut—signaled wealth, success, power. But that was it. Vic believed clothes were for self-expression, and she bet she could find a hundred guys dressed exactly like him, even smelling like him, within fifty feet of his fancy New York City office. Maybe none of those hundred guys would have eyes that shade of blue-gray or those dang limples, but that wasn't the point.

"Thank you for coming. Let me take your coat." He moved to help her with it, but she shrugged it off before he could. She'd dressed carefully for the appointment. She'd borrowed the coat and a black blazer from Bonnie and dug out a black skirt she'd bought for a funeral several years ago. She didn't have on a single item that would make her mother wince and go on about how Vic could be so pretty if she would only put in a little effort.

When she'd done a mirror check at home, she'd felt that she looked crisp and professional, but now, standing in front of Bowen, she just felt like a wannabe and wished she'd worn her favorite sweater dress. She'd bought it because it reminded her of one of Picasso's cubist portraits, with the rich colors, geometric shapes, and the large eye that wrapped from the front to the back. He'd probably have slammed the door in her face if she'd worn it. Make that shut the door with a refined *click*. But at least Vic would have felt like herself.

"It's cold out. Would you like some coffee? I picked up some beans at Porto Rico Importing before I left town. The Jamaican Blue Mountain is something to experience."

"A hundred bucks a pound, and it doesn't even come with a light-up saber spoon," Tegan said as she came down the stairs.

"I ate a lot of Frosted Flakes trying to get all three colors," Vic answered, her brain trying to process that Bowen had paid a hundred dollars a pound for coffee. He probably couldn't even tell the difference between it and what was sold at the Mercantile. He seemed like a guy who wanted the best just so he could tell you it was the best.

"I'm Tegan. I don't know if you remember." She joined Vic and Bowen.

"Of course, I remember. How could I not? You were Henry's best friend. You were over all the time." Vic gave her a quick hug.

Tegan shrugged. "I can be easy to forget. Once I got an arrest warrant for failure to appear in court. And I was there."

Bowen's posture stiffened. Vic would have thought it was already at maximum. "Why were you supposed to be in court?" he asked.

"Uh, kidding."

The guy might have the mohair cardigan and the hand-sewn loafers, but he hadn't been able to buy himself a sense of humor, Vic thought.

"Would you like to try a few bucks' worth of coffee?" Bowen sounded like he was annoyed, but trying to hide it. "Either of you?"

"Why don't we go ahead and get started?" Vic realized she was twisting her ring. Big surprise. He made her nervous.

Maybe it was a holdover from high school, when she would probably have managed only a squeak if he'd spoken to her.

Bowen nodded and led the way down the hall and into his grandfather's study. "Tegan made a few piles—donate, sell, keep—but I told her to hold off on the rest until we heard your opinion."

"He didn't think I could handle it. Although, I once stopped a Black Friday stampede with only a mop and a jumbo can of Hormel's chili."

Vic laughed. Bowen didn't look amused. Hard to get amused when you had no sense of humor. There was definitely tension between him and his sister. "Impressive," Vic told Tegan.

"True, but not the skill set needed here." Tegan flopped down on the leather—full-grain Italian leather, Vic noted—sofa

"I didn't think you specifically couldn't handle it," Bowen told Tegan. "I don't think anybody who isn't an expert should be making decisions on what's of value."

"There's this thing called Google," Tegan commented.

Bowen sat down at the desk and opened his laptop. Go time. "Let's start with the Phillippe Sheep Sculpture." It was the one thing in the room Vic wished she owned. It would look adorable in that little jester hat she'd bought a few weeks ago. "New, it would cost approximately five thousand five hundred." Which is why it wouldn't ever be wearing the jester hat.

Bowen nodded and made a note on the spreadsheet he'd pulled up. She wondered if he was even a little impressed that she'd recognized the sculpture and known its value off the top of her head. It wasn't exactly a common item, but Vic had looked at every image she could find of the interior of Cassian Gower's home to prep for today.

It took hours for them to go through the contents of the study with Bowen and Tegan. There'd only been a few items, including an ostrich egg with bronze and malachite details on an iron stand and what she thought was a French fireplace fender, that hadn't been in the photos she'd studied, and on those she'd had to admit she needed to do some research. But no one in her field would be able to come up with a value for every piece in the room. The one thing she knew was that everything Cassian Gower had owned had been the best of its type. She wondered if he'd appreciated the beauty and craftsmanship of his possessions, or if he'd only wanted the best because it was the best.

"I think we need to stop for the day." Bowen closed the laptop. "Can I offer you a drink before you go?"

Say yes, Vic told herself. Don't be stupid. Be nice. Say yes. But she didn't have it in her. She could handle a business relationship with Bowen Gower, but nothing else. Not even a drink. "I'm sorry. I have another engagement."

"Her commission on the estate sale, if I—we—decide to use her, would probably be more than she brings in, in an entire year, and she can't sit down and have a drink? That's no way to treat a client."

Tegan picked up the bronze cigar lighter with the dragon embellishment and turned it over in her hands. "She knew what things were worth. Isn't that what you care about?"

And there was his sister's attitude. Her emotional range seemed to go from apathetic to angry, with nothing in between. Although, there had been one moment with Vic, when Vic had mentioned her brother, that had gotten a smile out of Tegan, a smile that went all the way up to her eyes.

"Getting an accurate appraisal is the most important thing, yes, but when you do business, it's usual to observe a few niceties."

"I thought her niceties were fine." Tegan propped one foot on the coffee table.

She was baiting him. But she was right. Vic hadn't shown any of that attitude when she'd been interacting with Tegan. "Are you're saying it's personal? That it's me in particular that

brings out the"—he paused to choose an appropriate word—
"the incivility in her?"

"Uh, yeah."

"Uh, yeah. Care to elaborate?"

"What do you expect? You made her brother's life hell."
Tegan shoved herself to her feet.

"Am I supposed to know her brother?"

"Henry Michaud. He was my best friend. His sister managed to remember me. But, then, I always went over there.
Henry wouldn't have wanted to be in the same house with
you."

Henry. Henry. Bowen tried to remember someone named
Henry from back when Bowen lived here. "Whatever it is I did,
it had to have been at least twelve years ago. And she's still
pissed about it?"

"For starters, it wasn't one thing you did one time." Tegan
stared at him. "I can't believe you have no memory of any of it.
Here's a little hint—mooobs."

Bowen remembered making that mooing call at a heavy kid,
teasing him about his man boobs. "Henry was the fat guy?"

"Wow. You're smart. No wonder they pay you the big
bucks."

"Okay, so I wasn't that nice to Vic's brother. Again, more
than a decade ago. And everybody had stupid nicknames. We
used to call my friend Adam 'Shobbit,' for 'short hobbit,' because he was the smallest kid on the basketball team."

"That's different."

"I don't see it that way."

"He was on the basketball team. He was your friend. He
was popular." Tegan spoke slowly and deliberately, like Bowen
was a little kid.

"If she has that big a problem with me, maybe I should find
someone else to handle selling everything."

"Seriously? You said it could be a huge commission, and

you're going to snatch it away from her? You did something shitty in the past, and your response is to do something shitty now?"

Tegan had a point. "Fine. We'll keep her on."

"We. I don't think there's actually a *we* in this situation."

"Tegan, you just gave me feedback, and I listened. I said we'd use Vic."

"You really don't remember her or Henry?"

"I don't spend a lot of time thinking about high school. I'm going upstairs. I need to check up on a few work things, make some calls."

"Of course you do."

He didn't have anything that needed his immediate attention, but he could take a look at the financial model he'd asked Leslie to tweak.

When he sat down in front of his laptop and started going over the numbers, he couldn't focus. He clicked over to the Abnormal Returns website. He hadn't checked the links of the day, and there was usually something useful. The first link led him to an Institutional Investor article about larger PE firms growing AUM at a faster rate than smaller ones. It didn't reference his firm, but it could have. It definitely applied. The article could give him some good elevator talk. He liked to have some tidbit ready if he ended up riding with one of the higher-ups. But halfway through the article, he realized that although he was reading the words, he wasn't retaining the information.

Twelve years. Tegan—and Victoria Michaud—expected him to remember details of his life from twelve years ago? That was ridiculous. He pinched the bridge of his nose with his fingers, then returned to the article. He had to scroll up almost to the top before he got to a paragraph he recalled reading and started again from there. A few minutes later, he realized that he wasn't taking anything in. Again.

They thought he should remember? Fine. His yearbooks

were on the bottom shelf of his bookcase. He grabbed the one for his senior year and looked up Henry Michaud. He was a sophomore when Bowen was a senior. That explained why Bowen didn't remember him that well. He wasn't even in Bowen's class.

He was the fat kid. That's all Bowen remembered. The same way he remembered there was that goth kid with the dreads and no eyebrows. Had Bowen given the fat kid, Henry, shit about his weight? Sometimes. Had he given the goth kid shit about his missing eyebrows? Bowen was sure sometimes he had. Was he proud of it? No. But it was pretty typical high school behavior. He didn't think he should be expected to feel bad about it after more than ten years. Who cared about what happened in high school? It was high school.

He took another look at the picture. Was that the guy who'd been with Victoria at the bar that night? If he'd lost a lot of weight, definitely possible. So, he was still living in Fox Crossing. Maybe living here kept those high school memories fresher. You'd still be seeing people from then all the time.

Bowen started to close the book, then flipped to Victoria Michaud's picture. She was in his year and didn't look all that different. Same dark eyes and ripe lips. Someone had scrawled a message on the opposite page. It started off, "To Bowen, Fitzy god, Mr. Baseball, King Chirpz, and President of the Titty Committee—You may be great, but I still grabbed the Glorious Mooobs more times—"

Mooobs had been enough of a thing that one of his friends had referenced it. Bowen felt a little jab of shame. But what was he supposed to do about it now?

He studied Victoria's photo for another moment. She looked like she'd just heard the best joke and was about to tell it to you. Nothing like the woman who'd been in the house this afternoon, Miss All-Business, except she didn't realize that business included people skills. Usually, Bowen would have been able to charm her. Objectively, he could be charming. But the combination of Vic's prickliness and Tegan's hostility had gotten him off his game.

He flipped to Tegan's picture. She wasn't showing any attitude. She was barely smiling, but not in a screw-you kind of way, more as if she didn't want to attract any attention. Curious, Bowen found his own yearbook picture. He'd gone for a "serious" look, but he found another picture of himself with the basketball team where his grin was so big it should have cracked his face. In the background, in the first row of the bleachers, sat his grandfather. Bowen's parents were one row behind him. They went to almost every game. Tegan was nowhere to be seen.

"Glory days."

Of course, Tegan had shown up just in time to see Bowen looking at a picture of himself. "Long time ago." He closed the book and returned it to the shelf. "Is there something I've done recently that's pissed you off? *Recently*, as in 'not in high school.' And me, personally, not Granddad. Because he's the one who laid out who gets what money when."

She stared at him. "Actually, no," she finally said.

Well, that was something. "I'm going to go to the BBQ and get some dinner in a while. Do you want to come?"

"No."

What did she want from him? He had done nothing to her. Even back when they were kids, he thought he'd been decent enough to her. They weren't close back then, but she was his little sister. He was sure a lot of brothers didn't spend much time with their little sisters.

"It's not that I—" Tegan stopped, then started again. "I know that you don't have any control over the terms of the will, and I appreciate the invitation, but I can't go because I'm picking up some shifts at Wit's, bartending some, waitressing some."

"Oh." Bowen realized he didn't even know what the last job

Tegan had was. She'd said it was "disposable," but hadn't given specifics. He hadn't gone home last Christmas. He'd spent it with Alexandra's family. Could it have been more than a year since he'd even spoken to his sister? Phone works both ways, he reminded himself.

"I know. A Gower serving beer at Wit's."

"I didn't say anything," he protested.

"You're right. You didn't. I'm sorry."

An apology. He hadn't been expecting that. "It's okay. Maybe we can do dinner another night."

"Sure. Well, I gotta go do some work stuff, make some calls," she said, echoing Bowen's usual exit line, but her tone was light, and she actually smiled.

Bowen laughed, and a second later Tegan joined in. He had not been expecting that.

"Gower!" somebody called as soon as he stepped into the BBQ. "Heard you were back. Get over here!"

Bowen grinned. Tommy Ballard. Bowen hadn't even thought about getting in touch with people from high school, but seeing Tommy came with a rush of good memories. Bowen headed over to the table and gave the top of Tommy's head a double knock, the way Bowen always had before a game.

Tommy stood and gave him a bro hug. "You by yourself?"

"Yep."

"Not anymore. You're eating with us."

Bowen shook hands with Parker and Adam. Bowen had played football with Parker, basketball with Adam. "Great to see you," he said as he sat down at their table.

They all gave him their condolences on his grandfather. "I still remember how he came to almost every football practice." Tommy picked up one of the crayons and made a rough drawing of their school mascot on the butcher paper covering the table.

"Basketball too," Adam said.

"He was a fan." Bowen could still remember feeling his granddad's eyes on him, watching every move, then breaking it down with Bowen afterward.

"More like a second coach." Tommy drew a circle around the Splitter, then put the crayon down. "He'd keep me updated on what you were doing. Last time I talked to him, he said he was expecting you to be vice president within the year."

His granddad had made VP at twenty-nine and didn't see any reason Bowen shouldn't. That was part of the plan they'd made together. Bowen had been off schedule, but not by much. He'd gotten the promotion at thirty. His granddad had gotten director at thirty-three, and that was the goal he'd set for Bowen. No one at his firm had made director that young. Jana had been almost forty. But Granddad had said that he was proof it was possible, which meant there was no reason Bowen couldn't do the same thing. And he would. Whatever it took.

"Vice president of what?" Parker asked.

"Parker moved to Bangor. If he was around more, your grandfather would have told him too," Tommy said.

"I work at Garm . . . it's a boutique private equity firm," Bowen added, when he saw the name meant nothing to Parker.

"Can I say, 'Huh?'"

"What they do is like flipping houses, except they do it with companies," Tommy explained. "Got that right?" he asked Bowen.

"Got it. Great explanation." Bowen would use it next time he had to explain what he did to someone outside the business. The waitress came by and handed Bowen a menu. "Thanks, Piper."

"You remembered my name."

"You're wearing a name tag, Piper," Adam told her. It could have been a little joke, but his tone gave it a nasty spin.

"But I would have remembered anyway," Bowen told her. It had only been a week, and he made a point of remembering names. It showed people they were important to you, and that was part of the job. "I also remember your dog's name—Jazz." He made a point of remembering as much as possible, part of what made him the "people guy."

She smiled, then started for another table. Adam snapped his fingers, calling her back. "I need a refill," he said when she turned around. They'd just been talking about her name, and he couldn't even be bothered to use it.

"What have you guys been up to since graduation?" Bowen asked.

"I have two daughters, twins. They're five and a half," Parker answered. "And they're about to get a baby brother in a couple months."

"Congratulations." Bowen noticed Parker had mentioned the kids first, not his job.

"No kids for me. Not married," Tommy said. "I'm an orthodontist. Finally. I just got a spot at a practice in Dover-Foxcroft. If Parker's kids end up with his teeth, I'll be getting some new patients."

"Yep," Parker said cheerfully. "And when that happens, you'll be buying my beer every time we go out."

"Done," Tommy answered.

"I'm head of the county's IT department." Adam stood. "I'm hitting the head." He snapped his fingers at Piper as he passed her and pointed to his half-empty glass.

"I call seven twenty-five," Parker said.

"Oh, no, my friend. With Bowen here? It'll be seven ten." Tommy turned to Bowen. "We have this thing where we bet on what time Adam will bring up how he almost made the UMaine team."

"Which, by the way, is bull. Senior year a recruiter for EMCC came to one game."

Bowen didn't even remember that. Maybe because, even though he pushed himself as hard as he could, he and his grandfather both knew there was not even the possibility Bowen could go pro. That time he'd made the finals for the Fitzy? He suspected his granddad had pulled some strings, pulled them hard. Then Bowen had to ride in the lead car in that parade, knowing he didn't deserve it. His grandfather had ridden with him, waving to everybody.

"Did you guys see that UMaine qualified for March Madness?" Adam asked as soon as he sat back down. He turned to Bowen. "I was this close to making the team." Adam held his fingers a fraction of an inch apart.

Tommy made a gimme gesture at Parker, and Parker pulled out his wallet and slapped a ten into Tommy's palm.

"I still remember that game against Penquis Valley. Remember, Bowen, that buzzer beater I got?"

"Glory days," Bowen said, thinking of Tegan.

"Glory days," Adam repeated.

Bowen thought maybe Adam did think those were the best days of his life. What would it be like to think the best days were already behind you? Adam didn't seem to mind. Bowen couldn't wrap his brain around that.

"Bowen, Adam, check out that guy picking up the to-go order. Do you recognize him? I bet you won't even recognize him," Parker said. "Hint. Someone we went to high school with. I doubt either of you have seen him since then, but the two of us ended up at the same college."

Bowen glanced over, but already knew who he was going to see—Henry Michaud.

"You give up?" Parker asked. Adam nodded. So did Bowen, just to save time. If he said he'd recognized Henry, they'd ask how, and he'd rather move on to another topic. "It's Henry Michaud."

"You've got to be shitting me," Adam said.

"Nope. He lost all that weight when he went off to college," Parker said. "He's back in town heading up something where you study how to improve health in the county. It's going to take about a year. My mom was very impressed."

"I can't believe I'll never feel those big, soft titties again," Adam said. "I got I think a hundred and twenty points off him. My little bro only got eighty. He and his buds kept it going after we graduated."

Like a punch in the gut, it came back to Bowen. The Titty Committee had given out points every time you grabbed Henry's man boobs. Heat surged through Bowen, and the bite of chicken he'd just swallowed felt like it was stuck in his throat.

"We were such little bastards," Parker said cheerfully.

"We were." Tommy's tone was serious.

"Come on. It's like Bowen used to say: 'He wouldn't have grown those titties if he didn't want guys to touch them.'" Adam took a swig of beer.

Bowen had said that?

Adam slapped Parker on the shoulder. "This guy wouldn't have gotten any action if it wasn't for Henry."

Parker grinned. "Pretty much true."

"How did we even come up with the whole game?" Bowen didn't want to know, but he needed to know.

"It was your genius idea," Adam answered.

That's why Victoria had left the moment she'd wrapped up business today. That's why she'd sent back the drink. That's why she looked disgusted when she saw him on the trail.

Bowen didn't blame her.

Bowen got to Junk & Disorderly as soon as it opened the next morning. "I need to talk to you."

"I did some research on that ostrich egg," Vic told him. "It's an Anthony Redmile, and—"

"Not about that. About your brother."

"My brother."

"I regret my part in—" He stopped, trying to remember what he'd finally decided on as an apology. Bowen was good with words. He was good with people. He was the people guy. But he had no idea how to navigate this conversation. He'd come up with a dozen different scenarios. He'd had the time, since he hadn't been able to sleep. He'd finally gotten on his granddad's treadmill and run until he was exhausted.

"Your part in? Like you just— Are you going to act like you, like you—" Victoria pulled in a breath, started again. "What you did to my brother wasn't something you had a *part in*. You made it happen. You."

"You're right."

She looked surprised he'd admitted it.

"You're right. I was thoughtless."

"Thoughtless? You sound like you're talking about forgetting to send your great-aunt a birthday card." Her eyes blazed into his. "You made my brother's life complete misery. And so you know, it didn't stop when you graduated and moved away. That game you made up kept going the whole time Henry was at school."

"I didn't realize how— I was just messing around." Those were the words of a little boy. He felt his face flushing, his gut starting to churn. "It was cruel." He corrected himself, "*I* was cruel."

"You were."

"I'm deeply sorry." There was nothing else to say. No way to repair the damage he'd done. All he could do was stand there and let her say whatever she needed to say.

Her eyes scanned his face, assessing. "I'm not the one you should be apologizing to."

He nodded. "Can I get your brother's number?"

"It's not something you can do over the phone."

"Give me his number, and I'll call and arrange to meet him in person. If he'll agree to see me."

"Wait here." She strode across the store and into the back room.

Bowen braced his hands on the long glass case that served as the front counter and stared down at the contents, the nausea roiling. He'd felt this way before, when his grandfather had looked at him after the fumble that almost cost them the game against Cape Elizabeth in the finals, and when he'd had to tell his grandfather that another associate had gotten promoted to VP before him, for starters.

"Bowen." The way she said it made him think it was the second time Vic had called his name. He hadn't heard her. Just like he hadn't seen any of the things in the case he'd been staring at. He straightened up and turned to face her. "Henry's staying with me. He said you can go up if you want to talk to him. My apartment's through the back and up the staircase."

He wished he'd had some time to prepare what to say. But it probably wouldn't have helped. He'd prepared before he came over to talk to Victoria, and everything he'd planned had gone out of his head when he opened his mouth.

Bowen was halfway across the shop before he realized he hadn't replied to Victoria. It didn't matter. He was sure she had no desire to spend even a few more seconds with him. He realized he was letting self-pity rise up inside him and slammed it down. Victoria had stood there and heard his apology. That's all he should have expected from her.

When he reached the top of the stairs, Henry swung open the apartment door. Bowen hadn't had time to knock, to get ready. Henry didn't say anything, just waited, face neutral.

"I want to apologize for the way I treated you in high school. I have no excuse for it. I just said whatever smart-ass thing I thought would make my friends laugh." Bowen could have ended it there, but Henry deserved the whole truth. "I didn't even think about how it would affect you. I didn't care enough to bother, and that may even be worse than what I did. I'm sorry."

Now it was Bowen's turn to wait.

"You want to come in?" Henry finally asked.

The last thing Bowen wanted to do was prolong this, but that wasn't his call. "Sure."

Henry led the way into the kitchen. "Coffee?"

"Thanks." Bowen sat down at the table.

"Anything in it?"

"No."

"Me either." Henry put a mug down in front of Bowen, then sat down across from him.

"Something in common, then." Part of being a people guy was finding something in common with whoever he was dealing with. But his strategies for a good business lunch weren't going to cut it here.

Henry didn't smile. "For a while, for years, I would have these conversations with you in my head. No conversations actually. You didn't get to say anything. I'd get to say all the things I never could, things that would make you feel like dirt. Not that anything I'd have said back then would have meant anything to you."

"Back then, probably not." Bowen had acted as if Henry weren't even completely human back then, not even considering how he might feel. It wasn't that Bowen had wanted to hurt him, exactly. Bowen just hadn't thought beyond getting a laugh from his friends. "But I want to hear what you have to say now."

"I don't know what I want to say. I could rub your nose in it, try to make you walk out of here feeling like crap."

Bowen already felt like crap, but he wasn't going to say it. This was about Henry, not about him.

"But what's the point? I'm not the same as I was back in high school, and I'm assuming you're not, or you wouldn't be sitting there." Henry took a swallow of his coffee. "The prefrontal cortex is still developing when you're a teenager, so emotion and aggression are running a lot of the show."

Was Henry actually giving him an out? "You're saying I shouldn't be tried as an adult?"

This time Henry did smile. "I guess that's what I'm saying."

"But I've been of age for a bunch of years. I could have gotten in touch, apologized before now."

"True."

"It didn't even occur to me." That was hard to acknowledge, as much to himself as to Henry. "My sister thinks I'm all about my 'glory days,' as if I spend my nights rerunning old games in my head, but I hardly ever think about high school." Bowen forced himself to add, "Even when Tegan told me I'd made your life hell, I didn't really remember right off."

"I'm never going to be able to forget it," Henry said matter-of-factly, but not like he was trying to, as he'd put it, rub Bowen's nose in it.

"If there's anything I can do to make up for it . . ."

"There isn't."

Of course, there wasn't.

"Unless you want to reimburse me for years of therapy."

"Give me the total." Bowen would feel at least a little better if he could actually do something to make amends.

"Forget it. You get to a certain age, you got to take responsibility for yourself, not look around to find someone to blame."

"How about letting me take you to dinner?"

"Haven't we already covered everything? It's not like now we're going to be friends."

Bowen wanted this. Henry had been more than decent. Bowen wanted to do something in return, even if it was only treating him to a meal.

What do you know about him? What's important to him? That's what Bowen would be asking himself if he were in a business negotiation with Henry. "You and Tegan used to be close. She's in town. We could all go together. Your sister too."

Bowen could almost see Henry trying to come up with a

reason to refuse. Instead, he hesitated, but ended up saying, "Sure. Why not."

"I'll be back in town next weekend. Saturday night?" Bowen wanted to lock it in.

Henry nodded. "Saturday night."

Bowen had brought up Tegan because he thought that would get a yes from Henry. But maybe the dinner would show Tegan Bowen wasn't an asshole, at least not anymore. Maybe it would even convince Victoria of that.

CHAPTER 7

"How much is this?" Addison called as she came out of the back room wearing a knee-length cape that had been bedazzled until it probably weighed fifteen pounds.

"That is just so fabulous!" Vic exclaimed. She turned to Bonnie. "See? There's always good stuff in those storage-locker sales."

"It would only be good if we're expecting a busload of Elvis impersonators," Bonnie answered. "Which we are not."

"How much?" Addison asked again when she joined them.

"You can have it if you want it." Vic adjusted the cape's collar.

"Really? That's so great." Addison's expression was serious, which didn't match her words or that sparkling cape.

Vic shot a quick look at Bonnie, who hadn't offered a comment. "It's yours, if it's okay with your mom. I should have said that the first time."

Bonnie shook her head. "I just have to figure out how to wash it with all that bling."

"Thanks." Addison turned, cape swishing behind her, and headed toward the back room.

"Remember you're getting paid to sort through the stuff in those boxes, not shop," Bonnie called after her.

"I can sort and shop at the same time, no problem." Addison shut the door to the back room behind her.

"I want to pay you back whatever you pay Addy. I know you only gave her the job because I told you she needed to earn some of the money to replace her smashed phone."

"Nuh-uh. Those boxes won't sort themselves."

"But you're already paying me to sort them."

"True. But your daughter has more of an appreciation for the finer things than you do. You might have tried to toss that cape."

"That cape! Why?" Bonnie moaned. "What could she possibly want it for?"

"Maybe Wacky Tacky Tuesday is coming up." The kids always hit Vic's shop for crazy things to wear to school for Wacky Tacky. Although Vic thought that was in September, a Spirit Week thing. "And say what you will about the cape, did you notice, not a single cutout?" Vic knocked her shoulder against Bonnie's.

"I have whiplash. First she's wearing an outfit that I could wear to a bar, then she's playing dress-up."

"Hormones are miraculous things."

"At least Addy snagging that cape means you can't wear it out to dinner." Bonnie frowned at Vic. "You're planning to change, aren't you?"

"You think this is too cutting-edge for the 380 Grill?" Today Vic had paired an oversize rainbow cardigan with pleather pants and platform sneakers.

"Not exactly the words I would have chosen, but let's go with that. It's just too cutting-edge. You should wear the dress with the cherry print. It looks gorgeous on you, and it's funky enough that you won't feel like you're not yourself."

Vic eyed Bonnie suspiciously. "You're not thinking of this

as a date, are you? Because it's an apology dinner for Henry, or as I like to think of it, a revenge dinner. I'm going to run up the tab as much as I possibly can."

"You have to run up the tab as much as possible, too," Vic told Henry. "You'll have to abandon your healthy eating for the night because you have to order dessert. And appetizers. What else? Will they have a cheese plate? I've heard tell these fancy joints have cheese plates."

"Even if you stuff yourself, then vomit and stuff yourself again, like a Roman emperor, Bowen Gower isn't going to even blink at the bill. You know what kind of money finance guys make?"

"It's the principle of the thing." Vic hit scan on the car radio. Henry had terrible taste in music.

"Same as driving in separate cars." Henry hit pause on something techno. Vic preferred something she could sing to, but this was Henry's night, so she decided to let him keep it.

"I want to be able to leave in a huff. I can't leave in a huff if I don't have a car." She pulled into the parking lot of the 380 Grill. "Figures he'd choose the most expensive place in fifty miles. He has to be sure we know he's all wealthy and powerful."

"You know you're not making sense, right? First you're plotting to stick him with a huge bill, then you're complaining that he's taking us to a place that's expensive."

"Why are you defending him?"

"Not defending him, just giving you a sanity check. Let's just go eat, with no drama, then we'll be done with Bowen Gower."

"Except for the part where I'm handling his estate." Bowen had officially given her the job. Maybe it was guilt. Maybe it was pity. Maybe it was that he'd accepted she knew her stuff better than anybody.

"Right, except for the part where you'll be making a fat commission for handling his estate." Henry got out of the car, so Vic had to get out too. They walked across the parking lot arm in arm.

"You should work into conversation about how you're heading up the health assessment. You have doctors reporting to you. Get that in."

"I'm getting information from them. They aren't reporting to me."

"He doesn't have to know that." Vic's hand tightened on Henry's arm. "Wait. If you aren't going to brag about your job, what are we going to talk about? Dinner's going to be an hour, minimum. It's going to be a disaster. I have nothing in common with Bowen Gower. We're going to have to talk about the weather the whole time."

"There's no turning back now." Henry started walking again, towing Vic along with him.

When they stepped inside, she immediately spotted Bowen at the big booth in the corner farthest from the kitchen. "Of course, he got the best table."

"That bastard," Henry answered, then told the host they'd be joining the Gower party.

"I don't understand why you aren't still hating him right now," Vic whispered as they started toward the table.

Bowen stood up, showing off his manners.

"You have to shut up now," Henry whispered back, then shook hands with Bowen and slid into the booth next to Tegan, leaving Vic to sit next to Bowen.

"Thank you for coming," Bowen said. "Should we order a bottle of wine?"

Vic gave a bark of laughter, and he looked at her questioningly. "You clearly think we're going to need to start drinking immediately to get through this."

"Couldn't hurt," Bowen admitted.

"I'm down for wine," Henry said.

Tegan raised her hand. "Yes, please."

Once the wine had been ordered, Bowen said, "Would anyone like to see a cute puppy picture?"

Vic had not been expecting that. Bowen Gower and cute puppy. One of these things is not like the other.

"You have a puppy?" Tegan asked.

"No, but I read about a psychological study where married people were shown pictures of cute puppies and other happy things interspersed with pictures of their spouse. It increased the level of satisfaction they felt with their marriage."

"And you think if we associate you with cute puppies, we'll get all warm and fuzzy when we look at you?" Vic asked. Actually, looking at pictures of Bowen would make a lot of people happy. He was that good-looking. Although showing married people pictures of a hot guy might cause the level of marital satisfaction to go down.

"I'm willing to explore a variety of methods," he answered. "I'm open to suggestions."

"A time machine," Vic shot back.

Henry gave her a little kick under the table. "Too risky. There's no way of knowing what the butterfly effect would do to the future," he said before Bowen could answer. Her brother was a much nicer person than Vic was.

The waiter came back with the wine and waited for Bowen's approval. Why did Bowen get to be the one to approve or disapprove? Vic thought. Henry would give her another kick if he could read her thoughts. Vic would deserve it. The waiter had Bowen taste the wine because Bowen had ordered the wine. She had to check her attitude and accept that freaking Bowen Gower was doing something nice.

"The butterfly effect isn't an issue," Tegan said. "Time travel is impossible because you go back in time to fix something, but then back in the present, you have no motivation to time travel because whatever you wanted to fix is fixed."

"If it's fixed, it's fixed though," Henry countered.

"But it was only fixed because you went back and fixed it," which you won't do," Tegan said. "It's the time travel paradox, which is why time travel doesn't work."

Henry had told Vic that Tegan had no interest in going out with him, but Vic didn't buy it. Tegan was leaning toward him as she spoke, and her eyes were on his face. That's not how disinterested looked.

"You've forgotten Einstein's theory of general relativity predicts time travel because something can be in the past and the present at the same time," Bowen said. "Don't ask me to explain. My head is already hurting."

Henry grinned. "This is the kind of conversation Tegan and I would have all the time up in the tree house."

"Best time travel movie of all time?" Vic asked, doing her part to keep the conversation going. "Never mind. The answer is obvious."

"She's going to say *Hot Tub Time Machine*," Henry told Bowen and Tegan. "Vic always roots for the underdog."

"Hey, *Hot Tub Time Machine* is nobody's underdog," Vic said. "But that isn't my pick."

"Has to be *Looper* or *Primer*," Tegan said.

"No." Vic held up one finger. "I can say with absolute certainty that the best time travel movie ever is—"

"*Groundhog Day*," Vic and Bowen said together.

Henry kicked her again. This was a see-you-were-wrong kick instead of a stop-being-a-brat kick.

And she had been wrong. Turned out she did have something in common with Bowen Gower.

"I wasn't sure how it was going to go tonight," Bowen said when he and Tegan got in the car. "But it was fun. And I finally got to take you out for a meal."

"Thank you." Tegan turned and looked out the window, then added softly, "And I'm sorry I've been such a brat. I really do know that Grandfather made the decisions about who gets what, and who administers the trusts."

"You're welcome."

He didn't comment on the "brat" part, which she appreciated.

"Henry is a class act. When I invited him to dinner, I don't think he really wanted to go, but I think he could see that I . . ." Bowen's words trailed off.

"That you needed to do something to make it up to him."

"Yes."

"Henry was always a good guy. He could always tell when something was bugging me, and he'd either talk it through with me or make me laugh." The way he'd made her laugh at dinner. It had been so easy to talk to him, as if they'd been hanging out a few days ago, instead of more than ten years.

To her relief, she'd got through the night without talking about what she'd been doing during those ten-plus years. The conversation hadn't gone that way. But that didn't mean that the huge differences between her and Henry had gone away. He was still this successful man with a prestige job, while Tegan was . . . Tegan. She barely felt like a person half the time.

"Now that we've made it through one meal, what do you say we go to Flappy's for breakfast tomorrow? For old times' sake."

Bowen didn't get what life was like for her when they'd lived in Fox Crossing. At least he'd finally admitted what he'd done to Henry and apologized. "Do you think we could go somewhere else?"

"But Flappy's is the family tradition."

"It's just that it was different for me. People would come over and say great things about you, about whatever sport thing you'd done that week, and basically kiss Grandfather's ass. And nobody said anything to me."

"Sports have spectators. Art doesn't, at least not until there is a show."

He was trying to make her feel better, and she appreciated that. But he still didn't get it. "I guess I was jealous of the attention you got. It's true I wasn't doing much for people to talk about. But in my own family . . . It felt like no one was interested, not Grandfather, for sure, but most of the time it felt like Mom and Dad didn't care either."

"Come on. You know Mom and Dad love you."

"I know. But they didn't pay much attention, not when we lived here. They were too busy fighting all the time."

"I don't even remember that. I know Mom didn't like it here. I know she and Dad argued about that sometimes, but the way I remember it, it was only once in a while."

"You had all this stuff going on, practice, games, parties, friends, and Grandfather was always there for you. Maybe that's why you don't remember it like I do." She wondered if it was worth saying more. Did he really want to hear it?

"What do you remember them fighting about?"

Okay, he was willing to hear more. "Mom wanted us to move, but we didn't really have enough money to get started somewhere else. The big thing, though, was she kept wanting Dad to stand up to Grandfather."

Bowen pulled into the driveway and parked. "But stand up to him why? He was letting us live with him. He helped Dad get a job here."

"And he never let Dad forget it." The words came out harsher than she'd meant them to. She continued more calmly, wanting Bowen to really hear her. "He was constantly reminding him in all kinds of little ways that he wasn't good enough, that he couldn't take care of his own family. I could see it grinding him down, more every day. I was so happy when we could finally move. Except for leaving Henry."

"I don't know what to say. All I know is that's not how I remember it."

"Think about it though. He's dead, but Grandfather is still

making Dad feel small." Her father hadn't come out and told her that, but she'd been able to hear it in his voice when they'd had the conversation about what he might want from the house.

Bowen shook his head. "I don't see it that way. I truly believe Granddad chose me because I have the finance background."

He might never understand, not with the way he idolized their grandfather, but it was worth trying. "Think about what you've had to do as trustee. Is there really anything Dad couldn't have handled just as well? He could have hired someone to appraise everything. He could have dealt with the paperwork with the lawyer's help."

"Everything is feeling slippery. I don't know what to think about anything right now."

Bowen sounded beat. Tegan decided to focus on the positive. Not her usual style, but it seemed appropriate. "Think this, Bowen. Think tonight you did the right thing by taking Henry Michaud out to dinner."

CHAPTER 8

Bowen stretched and checked the time. He'd been in the zone, and two hours had gone by. Productive hours. It was going to take a little massaging on the conference call with Stellar, but he thought his strategy would work. He had some good numbers, but he also had a good story about one farmer who'd been about to go under before Feathered Nest started buying the feathers that used to go to the trash. Liz Kaur wouldn't go for anything that wasn't backed by the numbers, but whether she knew it or not, a good story could get her to yes.

He checked his calendar to make a plan for the next few days and realized his father's birthday was coming up. Usually, he just went with a bottle of Pappy Van Winkle's because his dad was a bourbon drinker, and Jana, also a bourbon fan, said it was the best.

Had Tegan been right about how his dad felt when Bowen was chosen as the executor for the estate? Possibly, but his father might have seen it as a burden he didn't have to take on. If Tegan was right about how miserable Dad had been—Dad and Mom—living at Granddad's, then maybe Bowen was sparing his dad a painful experience. This way, his dad didn't have to spend time back in the house, deciding what to do with all Granddad's possessions. Even to Bowen, the volume of items he had to make decisions about was a bit daunting.

But Bowen knew the feeling of not measuring up to Grand-dad's expectations. Bowen knew the amount of displeasure his grandfather could show in one look or a few carefully chosen words.

Getting chosen as the county's Mr. Baseball should have been great, but Bowen remembered being handed that trophy, feeling his grandfather's eyes on him, knowing that his grand-father had wanted—expected—him to get the statewide Mr. Baseball award, even though guys who got that went on to play college ball. A few even went pro. Bowen didn't have it in him to be that good. He could practice until he had heat exhaustion. Once he'd even passed out at practice. But practice only took you so far, something Granddad never seemed to understand.

When Bowen hadn't made VP by twenty-nine, he felt the sting of his grandfather's disappointment in him. Bowen was determined to make director by thirty-three, right on sched-ule, but his grandfather wouldn't be there to see it, to give the Nod, and Bowen had to admit that the promotion wouldn't mean as much without that.

Bowen picked up the phone and called his parents' number. His dad answered, and Bowen realized he had no idea what to say, and he almost always knew what to say. "Hey, Dad. I thought I'd give you an update on the estate. I got the EIN number, and the ad notifying potential creditors of his death is running, not that there are any creditors who will come for-ward."

"If your grandfather couldn't pay cash, he didn't buy. He even paid for his cars up front. The house is the only thing he ever paid for over time, and he got the mortgage paid off six years ahead of schedule."

Was that admiration in his dad's tone? Maybe.

"I've also got a local antiques dealer to appraise pretty much everything. That sheep that was over by the fireplace, it's worth more than five thou."

His dad let out a low whistle. "We shouldn't be surprised. He was all about buying the best. Of course, his ridiculous sheep footstool would be the most expensive sheep footstool. I'm assuming it was a footstool. He didn't use it as one, but it was the right size. I never got him to admit that being the most expensive didn't always mean best. I have a footstool from Big Lots. Seventy-five bucks, on sale. It supports my feet just fine, and it's a lot better looking than the sheep."

"I bet. I've been thinking about your trust." Bowen definitely wasn't going to call it an "allowance" the way Tegan did. "I could invest it for you, if that's something you'd be interested in." He could make his parents a nice profit investing $25,000 a year.

"That's a possibility." Bowen's father sounded reluctant. Didn't he know what Bowen did for a living and how good he was at it? "Although, probably the best thing for me to do with the money, at least the first year, is pay off credit card debt. One late payment, and they gouge you on the interest."

"Getting out of debt is absolutely your priority." Bowen hadn't even considered his parents had credit card debt. How much? Would it take the whole $25,000 to pay it off? His dad probably wouldn't see any money from the trust for at least six more months. That meant six more months of interest, probably at 18.26 percent. He did a quick calculation. If they owed $10,000, that was $1,756 interest. Did they owe more than that? His grandfather had been right to set up the trust the way he had. Bowen's parents clearly weren't great at money.

"I could—" Bowen stopped himself before he offered his father a loan. If his dad was feeling like Granddad hadn't considered him capable of handling the estate, a loan from his son, his much more successful son, was only going to make him feel worse. "I could send you pictures of some things around the house. Tegan mentioned you wanted the china bird, but maybe you'd like something else." It was the first thing Bowen had been able to come up with to follow that "I could," but it probably wasn't the best choice.

"I'm fine with the bird. Our place is small. The sheep wouldn't have enough grazing room." Bowen's dad's tone sounded a little strained.

Bowen forced a laugh. Maybe it was time to end this conversation. Everything he said felt wrong. "I guess I'll be seeing you and Mom pretty soon."

"We're looking forward to meeting Alexandra."

He hadn't told them they'd broken up? He was sure he had. It had been almost a year. "We're not together anymore."

"Oh. When did that happen?"

"Not too long ago." Bowen didn't want to admit how long it had actually been. His parents might get their feelings hurt that he hadn't said anything earlier.

"Are you doing okay?"

"I'm fine. We had some good times, but it didn't end up being viable long term."

"'Viable long term,'" his father repeated, as if he weren't familiar with the words.

"We ended on friendly terms." True. Although not friendly enough that they'd seen each other since they had, as Alexandra put it, "uncoupled." They'd exchanged texts a few times, mostly about the logistics of returning belongings and deciding how to divide a few joint purchases.

"You still working those long hours?"

Was his dad thinking the breakup was because Bowen didn't spend enough time with Alexandra? PE had better hours compared to other finance jobs. And Alexandra worked as much as Bowen did, or more. They'd been a good match that way.

But Alexandra had kept at him about not letting her in, by which she meant opening up his guts and displaying the contents. What she'd never accepted was that Bowen wasn't withholding anything from her. He was basically content, which meant not many emotions to "explore" with her. He'd always been there if she wanted to talk about whatever she was feeling, but he couldn't create something that didn't exist.

"The work is paying off. Now that I'm a VP, I think I'll be able to make director on schedule."

"That schedule is something you came up with when you were barely out of high school." They both knew that Bowen hadn't come up with it alone. His grandfather had helped him figure out every step he'd need to take to reach his goals. "It's okay to reevaluate it, you know. Maybe pencil in some time to smell the roses."

Smell the roses. His father was always talking about smelling the roses. "Getting VP is my version of roses." His dad probably couldn't understand that, but it was true. That feeling when he'd knocked a presentation out of the ballpark and gotten the yes—he lived for that. He started feeling itchy. Maybe he should review the numbers he'd need for tomorrow's call one more time. "Speaking of work . . ."

"I'll let you go."

"Sixty is the new forty, that's what the article said." Vic's dad plugged in his laptop and sat down across from her at his tiny kitchen table.

"Does that mean I'm only ten years younger than you?" Vic asked. "Because that would just be weird."

"Since sixty is the new forty, then thirty must be the new—"

Vic held up one hand. "Don't say ten. I can't go through my teen years again."

"*I* can't go through your teen years again," her father joked. "Back to the article. It was saying that just because you're sixty when you get divorced, it doesn't mean you have to be alone forever. Dating after sixty is trendy."

"Nothing more important than being a trend follower." This is not happening, Vic thought. This is not happening. This is not happening. This is *not* happening. She couldn't be helping her dad get set up with online dating because her dad belonged with her mom.

Except her mom had cheated on him.

"First I need to choose which dating site I want to use. I read another article that laid out a bunch of possibilities." Her dad was big on research. He wouldn't make the smallest purchase without reading up on it. She'd seen him read an article comparing toothpastes, which was so the opposite of her mom. His caution made Vic's mother crazy sometimes, but Vic always thought her dad's carefulness was a good balance for her mom's impulsivity. Her dad ended up going places and trying things he probably never would have without Vic's mom. And her dad made sure the bills were paid on time, and that they had a retirement fund.

"Some are just for seniors, others aren't but have a lot of seniors who use them. There's even one called Senior Sizzle if you're not looking for anything serious."

Vic wanted to be supportive. She did. And she would be. Why did Henry have to be holding a meeting over in Greenville though? He should have to be supportive too. "Have you put any thought into what you're looking for?" Please don't say *sizzle*, she thought. Her dad should only use the word *sizzle* if it was in proximity to the word *steak*.

"I'm looking for, I guess I'm looking for someone to talk to."

She'd been so busy keeping her parents' schedules that she hadn't put enough thought into how they were doing emotionally. They both always acted like they were doing fine, at least until her mom practically broke down when she confessed to cheating. But Vic knew acting fine and being fine were very different. She'd acted fine after she broke up with Leo. After Leo broke up with her, she corrected herself. She liked to think of it as something that had been her decision, but it wasn't. It had blindsided her. She'd put all her energy into appearing fine because, if she hadn't, she'd have shattered.

"You can always talk to me, you know. Or come over. Especially now that Henry's living with me. Any night you want, you can come over and eat with us. Unless . . ."

"Unless your mother is over."

"Unless that."

"You have to have your own life, sweetie. But I'm a little lonely sometimes."

Her dad was stoic. Once, he'd ended up in the hospital with a ruptured appendix. He'd been nauseous for days, even throwing up a few times, but he hadn't even called in sick to work. He'd just done what he called "powering through." For him, "a little lonely sometimes" had to mean he was deeply unhappy.

Maybe it would help if he could talk about what happened. "Dad, I know Mom cheated on you. I wasn't going to tell you I found out, but I can't sit here pretending I didn't. It's too much like lying to you."

Her father's face flushed, and he looked down, fiddling with the computer keys. Maybe she'd made a mistake. Maybe she'd just made it worse for him. Maybe he wanted to pretend it never happened.

"That's between your mother and me," he finally said. "It's not something you should— I don't want you to blame her." He sounded defeated and worn-out, and he suddenly looked old to her, shoulders slumped, pouches under his eyes.

"It's okay to be mad at her. Why aren't you mad at her?" Vic burst out. "Because I am. I love her, but I am so mad at her."

"I want to put it behind me. That's why we need the schedule. If I don't see her, I don't have to think about what happened."

Ah, the beauty of denial. Vic had tried denial too. She'd told herself she was fine, fine, fine. But even though she was fine, fine, fine, for months—and months and months—after Leo dumped her, anything would make her cry. She forgot to buy detergent; it made her cry. She slightly singed her grilled cheese sandwich; it made her cry.

Even though she knew denial didn't work, if that's what her dad wanted right now, Vic wasn't going to wreck it. "Okay. Let's go back to what you're looking for."

Her father thought for a moment. "Someone who can tell a joke. Someone who will still laugh when I mess up a joke. Someone who sings all the time, even if she can't sing. Someone who will do anything for her friends and family."

Vic felt like she'd just swallowed an ice cube, cold shooting into her belly. That's Claudette Michaud. He's describing Mom.

Or at least someone almost like Mom who hadn't cheated on him. Someone almost like Mom who hadn't destroyed him.

CHAPTER 9

Another episode of *House* started up. Okay, who would be the patient of the week? Tegan thought, but didn't much care. She'd ripped through four seasons since she got to town, and the repetition was getting to her. House would be a jerk about something, probably wanting to find out something about one of the people on his team, something that was none of his business. The team would come up with a diagnosis for the patient of the week. The POW would get a little better, then get worse, possibly peeing blood or vomiting streams of blood. The new symptom would mean the diagnosis was wrong. The team would toss around some more possibilities. Someone would say Wilson's and someone would say lupus. They'd come up with a new diagnosis. Testing for it would probably involve something risky that no sane doctor would consider, like giving the POW a heart attack. The POW would get close to death. Then House would see some random thing, like a loose button, which would give him the correct diagnosis, and the POW would be saved. Except every once in a while the disease would be untreatable, and the POW would die. 'Cause they had to mix it up a little.

The music over the opening credits began to play, and Tegan realized she'd completely missed the POW reveal. And that she didn't care at all. She clicked off the TV, feeling restless and itchy. Maybe she'd walk into town and get coffee at Shoo Fly's. There was billion-dollar coffee here, even a fancy espresso machine, but she needed to get out. She could drive to Dover-Foxcroft for her just-to-get-out coffee, but she hadn't driven her grandfather's car yet, even though she had the keys. She felt like he wouldn't want her to, which was stupid, because he was dead and didn't have an opinion on anything anymore.

Tegan pulled on her coat, wishing it was heavier, and headed out. She got about halfway down the block, then stopped. Coffee was only going to make the itchy, restless feeling worse. Caffeine was not her friend when she got in this mood. She turned around and walked back toward the house. That's when she saw it. The Fox. Sitting right in the front yard, red coat vivid against the snow. It looked at her, then turned and trotted off. She followed it, and when it darted out of sight, she followed its tracks. Tromping through the snow might help her settle down. She needed more hours at work. Too much free time was also not her friend when she felt like this.

The tracks led her into the field behind the house, and she noticed another pair of tracks, boot tracks, which veered into those left by The Fox, then continued along beside them. Both sets of tracks led her to the Fortress of Solitude. That's what she and Henry had called the tree house they'd built all those years ago.

The wood of the rungs nailed to the tree were definitely new. Was somebody up there right now? The boot tracks ended at the ladder, but she wasn't sure when they'd been made. "Hello?" she called.

"Hello?" Henry pushed aside the strings of keys and jingle bells Tegan had hung for curtains and poked his head out of one of the windows. "Tegan! Hey!"

"I can't believe you're up there!"

"I can't believe you're down there. Come on up. If you want to."

She put her foot on the bottom rung, then started to climb, the motion of her hands and feet still somehow familiar.

"Sit on this side," Henry said when she reached the hatch. "I think the other one is okay, but I've replaced boards over here, so I know it's safe."

"Feeling in need of a Fortress of Solitude?"

"Probably everyone feels the need of one sometimes, but I'm getting this in shape for the girl who's living in the house next door to my parents' place. What used to be my parents' place."

"I was sorry to hear that they split. I couldn't believe it, honestly. They seemed so good together all those times I was over. Is that the wrong thing to say?" She'd seen them fight too, bunches of times. The fights were always loud. Well, half of them. Henry's mother was the loud one. She could be kind of a drama queen. But most of the time before Tegan headed home, they'd be snuggling on the couch. Unlike Tegan's parents, whose fights were in whispers and never seemed to truly end, at least not until they finally got away from Grandfather's house.

"It's been almost a year since they told me and Vic they were planning to get a divorce, and I still can't completely wrap my head around it. I keep thinking, 'But they're my parents.'"

"I get it. I think I only started realizing my parents were actual human beings, in the same way I'm a human being, a couple years ago. One day, I thought, 'Wow, Dad was only a few years older than I am now when he lost his job and we had to move in with my grandfather.' It really made me think more about what it must have been like for him, him and my mom."

Henry nodded. "Things look different when you're a kid. Now I'm looking back, trying to decide if the way I saw my parents back then was completely warped. Maybe there was always an underlying dissatisfaction there, and I just didn't see it."

"If I had to pick which of our parents would still be together back when we were hanging out, I'd absolutely have picked yours." Sometimes his mom and dad would join her and Henry when they were watching *SNL*. His parents would laugh so hard they'd almost fall off the couch. Once they even started a pillow fight with her and Henry. Vic had heard and run in to join the fray. "Mine were constantly fighting back when we lived here. But when we moved away and got away from Grandfather, that really changed."

"I'm glad."

"You got me through it, Henry. I don't know how I'd have survived living here without you."

"That's exactly how I feel about you, Teg," Henry told her, giving her that warm, glow-y feeling. "How crazy is it that we ended up back here at the same time?"

"How crazy is it that my brother invited you out to dinner?"

"You know the reason I said yes?"

Tegan shook her head. "I could hardly believe you did."

"He told me that you'd be there." Henry's gaze was so intense that she had to look away. How must she look to him? Today she was in the "distressed" sneakers, and her sweater wasn't exactly happy, lots of pilling from too many trips though the dryer. She knotted her hands together, hoping he hadn't noticed her gnawed-on nails, although he'd have to have seen them at the dinner.

"What's the story with the neighbor girl?" she asked to get his attention off her.

"Kenzie. I only met her once, but her dad, Samuel, told me she'd been dealing with bullies at her old school. They just moved here a few months ago, and he thinks it might be happening again."

Tegan let out a string of curses, then her face began to burn. He must think she was so crude, using language like that. But Henry repeated every word she'd said, with some creative additions of his own.

"I wish I could talk to her about it, but if she knew her dad was talking about her with me . . . I don't imagine it would go well. And, honestly, I'm not sure what I could say beyond 'I understand.'"

"Knowing someone understands is a lot." That's what she and Henry had been able to give each other. She hadn't been able to do anything about his being bullied. He hadn't been able to do anything about her screwed-up family. But she'd known he was on her side, and that meant everything.

"She's thirteen. I have no idea if she'd even want to come up to the tree house, but it was a sanctuary for me." Henry gave the closest wall a pat.

"For us."

"Remember all those crazy creatures you made out of pine cones, and moss, and twigs, and stuff from the Junk and Disorderly ten-cent table? Those were so amazing. They'd all fallen apart. I wish I'd taken them home before I left for college, especially that gnome. Remember, you used those aluminum muffin tins, and those freakish pot holders."

"With the cat and the tacos in outer space!" Tegan had almost forgotten about that.

"The best part was that Lucite toilet seat with the butterflies and flowers inside. Remember, you used it as a frame?" He could barely get the words out. That's how hard he was laughing. Which made Tegan laugh until her gut ached and tears spilled down her face.

"They really were incredible. You were so talented," he said, when he could talk again.

"I was just messing around." She wiped her face with her sleeve.

"Have you kept up with it, your art?"

And here we go, she thought. The questions about what I've been doing the past dozen years. She'd managed to skate through dinner the other night without having to go there.

"Not too much. You get busy, you know. Speaking of busy, I need to go. I'm working on getting my grandfather's estate organized."

If he talked to his sister, he'd know that wasn't true, but it was the first excuse she thought of. She opened the hatch door.

"Vic has kept up the tradition of Mrs. Libby's ten-cent-Tuesday table," Henry told her before she could start down the ladder. "If you ever feel like messing around again."

The Fox paused to bask in the light from the cord between the two humans. It had been a long time since she'd experienced it, but it was one she'd often sought out in the past, its radiance pleasing to her. As in the past, there was the scent of pain when she was close to these two. In the creatures of her woods, the scent would come with the odor of blood or sickness, but she often smelled pain coming from humans that seemed to be without cause.

Still, despite the unpleasant scent of injury, she lingered in the light of their bond.

CHAPTER 10

Addison came out of the back room wearing a cowboy hat of iridescent snakeskin festooned with pink sequins. "How much for this, Vic?"

Vic shot a glance at Bonnie, who gave a helpless shrug. "It's yours if you want it."

"Great," Addison said, but she didn't sound pleased. Lately, it was like all the animation had been sucked out of her.

"What do you think will happen to a thirteen-year-old girl who wears that to middle school?" Bonnie asked when Addison had returned to the back room. "Because she's going to wear it. She's been wearing the cape every day."

"Maybe it's some crazy trend that we're too old to know about."

"I haven't seen any girls her age wearing anything remotely like it or that whacked-out hat."

"Maybe she's a budding fashionista. Like me." Vic gestured to her flowing striped pants with the wide legs.

"You have fun with your outfits. God knows why, but you do." Bonnie smoothed her already-smoothed hair. "Did it look like Addy was having fun trying on that hat?"

"No. And I gotta say, if I'd dressed the way I do now back in high school, it would've been rough."

"Something's going on with her, but she won't talk to me. Would you try to find out what's going on, Vic? Maybe she'll tell you things she won't tell her mother."

"I don't know, Bon." Vic didn't like the idea of getting Addison to open up, if that was even something Vic could do, then reporting back to Bonnie. "It feels like I'd be betraying her trust."

"You don't have to tell me what she says. It can stay between you two. I just want to know she's okay." Bonnie pressed her hands together, like she was praying for help.

How could Vic say no when it was obvious how worried Bonnie was? "I'll give it a shot."

"Thank you. Something's wrong. I know it."

Vic put down the stuffed Teletubby she'd been about to tag and walked to the back room. She found Addison at the desk, working on an inventory of everything on the bookshelves Vic used for storage. "How's it going?"

"Slow. I'm not even sure what some of this stuff is."

"If you don't know, just describe it as best you can." Vic sat down in the armchair across the desk from Addison, who was frowning at the Fiji mermaid.

"Skeletal thing with a shrunken head and scales," she said as she made an entry on the spreadsheet she'd set up on Vic's laptop.

Vic picked up the iridescent, blinged-out cowboy hat. "What do you have planned for this?"

Addison shrugged. "Just wearing it."

"Okay." Vic considered what to say next, not wanting to hurt Addison's feelings. "You should start a fashion vlog. Show how thrift-store finds can look cool."

"Maybe."

That *maybe* was clearly a *no*.

Addison picked up a portrait of Mister Rogers made entirely out of seeds, studied it, then made an entry.

This fashion tack clearly wasn't working, but Vic had no other ideas, so she stayed with it. "We could set up a corner for you to shoot your vids. You can use anything in the shop. I just got in this biker jacket with spiky rivets and graffiti all over. It might work with the hat." Oops. She shouldn't have said that. Bonnie would kill her if Addy decided to add that jacket to her wardrobe.

Addison laughed. Or that's what Vic thought at first, then she realized the girl's shoulders were shaking because she'd started crying.

Vic scrambled to her feet, circled the desk, then crouched down next to Addison's chair. "Oh, sweetie, what's wrong?"

"Nothing." Addison grabbed a Kleenex and furiously rubbed her face with it.

"Come on. It's not nothing. Tell me. Whatever it is, it will stay between us."

"Everybody hates me," Addison burst out.

Vic could tell Addison that lots of people loved her, including Vic, but she knew that wouldn't help. She decided to go with honesty. "I don't understand."

"Every day, I go to school, and every day, everyone whispers about how weird and gross I am. No one will even sit with me at lunch. I ate in the bathroom once, but somebody climbed up on the toilet in the next stall and took a video of me and texted it to everyone."

Vic felt like someone had reached into her chest and twisted her heart. "Addy, that is beyond horrible. I'm so sorry. How long has this been happening?"

"After Rose left, I usually ate by myself. Everybody already had their own little groups. But it was okay. I'd just read or do homework. People would still talk to me in class. I got invited to Bex's birthday. But then a couple months ago, this new girl started, and, I don't know why, she just immediately hated me, and she got everyone else to hate me too. And I didn't do anything to her. Nothing!" Addison had to wipe away tears again.

"Of course, you didn't." Vic smoothed Addison's hair away from her face. "It's a little like what happened to my brother, Henry, when he was in high school. This group of guys harassed him every day. Girls laughed at him. And he didn't do anything to deserve it." All he'd done was exist, exist in a body they found disgusting.

"Why? Why do they do it?"

Vic had done some reading on bullying. One theory was kids bullied because they were insecure. She flashed on Bowen Gower. That profile didn't fit him. He'd been the most popular kid in school and had always been winning an award for something. In any case, throwing out the insecure theory wouldn't do anything to help Addy.

"I don't know," Vic admitted. "There have always been bullies."

"Why me though? What's wrong with me? I tried to make them like me."

"Absolutely nothing is wrong with you. I think probably it's not about you at all."

Vic considered suggesting that Addy stop wearing the cape to school, but decided against it. She didn't want to say anything that might make it sound like Vic thought Addy brought the bullying on herself.

"It *is* about me. They hate me. I told you."

"What I meant was, if you weren't at that school, the girls would probably be bullying somebody else. It's about them, something in them, not about you. Which doesn't make it any easier, I know." Vic handed Addy another Kleenex. "I think we need a plan."

"For what?"

"For putting a stop to how those girls are treating you. I think a good first step would be to talk to the principal. Maybe she could arrange for a meeting with—"

"No! You said you wouldn't tell anyone!" Addison's voice was high with panic, her breathing coming faster.

"And I won't. I won't. I promise. But things need to change. You can't go through that every day. I'd happily go into your school and punch all of them, but that's probably not the best idea. I'd get arrested. I might go to jail. It would be a whole thing."

Addison smiled a little.

"Are the girls hurting you physically? Do you feel like you're in danger that way?"

"No. They mostly just whisper and text, sometimes they post stuff, like the video of me in the bathroom stall. It got a lot of likes."

Vic suspected that Addy's broken phone wasn't an accident. Addy probably couldn't take seeing one more mean post or text. What was Vic supposed to do now? She couldn't betray Addy's trust. The girl needed a friend, and right now it looked like Vic might be the only one she had.

"I want you to at least think, just think, about talking to your principal or one of your teachers. Or having your mom do it. Something needs to change, Addy."

Addison shook her head. "They'd hate me even more if I told on them."

"Would that matter? They're already making you miserable every single day. If they hated you more, so what, as long as they left you alone."

"They wouldn't leave me alone though. Don't you get that? It's not like they ever do anything right in front of a teacher. I'm just going to ignore them. I tried to get them to like me again, but it didn't work. I changed my hair. I got that sweater—that was so stupid. Like a sweater would change anything. Now I just have to pretend they don't even exist."

That reminded Vic of her dad. Denial wasn't going to work any better for Addison than it was working for him. Addison couldn't go on like this. She couldn't be miserable every single day. She'd end up waking up screaming like Henry used to, used to and still did sometimes. "How can I help?"

"It's okay. It doesn't matter." Addison started typing again, head angled toward the laptop so she wasn't looking at Vic.

Clearly, Vic had been dismissed. She hesitated, then decided to leave it for now. Addison was shutting down. "I'm going to go back up front. Come get me if you need me."

Addison jerked her head up. "Don't tell my mom."

Vic held up both hands. "I won't."

As soon as Vic stepped out of the back room and shut the door, Bonnie hurried over. "Well?"

"She's . . . she's still having a hard time without Rose." Vic thought it was okay to say that much. Bonnie already knew Addison was struggling to find girls to hang out with since Rose moved.

"They were so close. They did everything together. I thought it was great she had a best friend. But now I'm realizing maybe it kept her from forming good connections with other girls in her class."

Vic's thoughts returned to Henry. If he hadn't had Tegan, she didn't even want to think what his life would have been like back in high school.

"Do you think maybe I should push things with Addy? Tell her to invite a couple girls for a sleepover? It's not as if she doesn't know any other kids. She's been in school with most of them since we came to Fox Crossing, and that's been more than three years. I know some of the moms. I could even set it up."

"I think you need to follow Addison's lead on that." The last thing Addison needed was more time with those girls, those horrible girls.

"You think she's okay though?"

"I think she'd going to be okay." Vic was definitely going to talk to Addison again, and soon. She had to convince the girl to open up to her mom. Bonnie said she knew some of the mothers. Maybe talking to them about the bullying would be better than going to the principal. Maybe Vic should just tell Bonnie everything right now. But Vic's gut told her it was better to keep Addison's trust and work on getting her to ask for help.

Vic was still thinking about Addison hours later as she walked from the shop over to Wit's to watch her mother's trivia team battle it out for a spot in the finals of the all-county contest. Vic had been there rooting for her dad's team on Wednesday, which meant she had to give her mom equal time, although, really, Vic could use a night of lots of carby food and bad TV. Also, she didn't especially want to spend hours looking at her mom right now.

At least Vic could still have the carbs. She grabbed a table close to the trivia action, and as soon as Tegan came over, Vic said, "I need french fries. Lots of french fries. French fries, with a side of french fries. Wait, no." Eating wasn't the way to feel better. Well, it might be, for a little while, but she needed to break herself of the habit. "I'll have a turkey sandwich with small fries." There, that was healthy. Healthy-ish. Not Henry-level healthy, but acceptable.

"You okay?" Tegan asked.

"I'm okay. Okay-ish. I'll be okay."

"That's almost exactly how I'd describe myself. Let me go get your order in."

Gavin, the trivia MC, looked like he was gearing up to get started, which meant Vic needed to get over to her mom's table. It wouldn't be a big thing. She'd talked to her mom lots of times since Vic had found out about her cheating.

"Hey, Smarties," Vic called when she reached their table. "Good luck tonight! I'm rooting for you!"

"What are you going to do when you have to decide whether to root for us or the Quizly Bears in the championship?" Honey asked. She'd forgotten to take off the cloth fox ears she always wore when she was working in her shop.

"Probably move to Antarctica."

Vic's mom made an exaggerated pout. She thought she was

being cute. But a sixty-one-year-old acting like she was five? Not so cute.

"The Final Countdown" began to play. "Cell phones off and thinking caps on," Gavin called out. Vic gave the team a wave and returned to her table. Trying not to think of bed and bad TV, she applauded when Buddy got the answer to the first question right, then realized that she'd been applauding for the competition and clasped her hands together, hoping none of the Smarty Pints had noticed.

"Feel like company?"

Vic looked up and saw Bowen standing there, mug in hand. "My mom will get in a snit if she sees me talking to you when I'm supposed to be rooting for her."

"I have exceptional rooting skills."

Vic gestured toward the empty chair. Because, why not? She didn't feel like being alone right now. "My mom, Claudette, is the one in the flowered blouse.

Tegan stopped by the table with Vic's food. "Anything else I can get either of you?"

Vic shook her head.

"I'd like another beer," Bowen said.

"Right back." Tegan hurried off.

Bowen watched her for a moment, then turned to Vic. "I can't believe she's working here."

"I was surprised too. I didn't think she'd be staying long enough to want to get a job."

"She's planning to stay at least a few months. I wonder if I should ask around, see if there's something better. I still know a few people around here."

"She's not happy working at Wit's?" Vic took a bite of her sandwich.

"I don't know."

"Well, maybe you should ask."

"Maybe I should." He corrected himself, "Definitely I

should. Usually, I'm good at figuring out what people want, but not Tegan. We're not like you and Henry. I feel like I'm only starting to get to know her."

Tegan returned with Bowen's drink.

"Teg, how are you liking working here?" Vic asked.

"Banana is the best boss I've ever had. He's such a goofball. Jilly and Ryan are cool too. I gotta get back. Lots more orders coming up."

"My grandfather paid for my college."

That statement came out of nowhere. "Okay," Vic said.

"I never even wondered if he offered to pay for Tegan's. Until right this second, it never even occurred to me." Bowen frowned. "He must have, right?"

"Maybe something else to ask." It was hard for Vic to imagine having a brother who didn't know such basic things about her.

"He didn't pay that much attention to her when we were growing up. It wasn't something I thought much about until Tegan ended up here. I was so focused on—" Bowen shook his head. "My grandfather sat me down before my family moved and said he'd pay for me to go to Wharton, as long as I kept my grades up."

"Just Wharton, no place else?"

"Wharton's the best business school. Part of our agreement was that I'd get my MBA, otherwise, I'd have to pay him back everything."

Hard-core, Vic thought. No room for an eighteen-year-old kid to change his mind about what he wanted to do for the rest of his life. "Did you know you were interested in finance back in high school? I had no idea what I wanted to do when I graduated."

"My grandfather had worked at a private equity firm, so I knew it had great compensation, decent hours, plus interesting work. If I'd had a passion for something else, I might have felt differently. But I didn't know what I wanted, and it sounded like a good deal. A free ride."

Sort of free. Free-ish, Vic thought.

"I think I've been talking too much."

"No, it's fine." It was a nice distraction on a night when Vic needed distraction.

"Fine with you. But there's a woman in fox ears giving me the—" Bowen pointed to his eyes, then at Vic to illustrate. "I think I need to root more, talk less."

Vic knew the woman in the fox ears was Honey, and she knew Honey didn't care that they were talking during trivia. Honey was a lot more interested in what was going on with Vic and Bowen. She gave Honey a wave, and Honey winked. "You're right. We should pay attention to the game," Vic told Bowen. Her mother answered a question correctly, a question about Elvis. Vic dutifully applauded, her thoughts returning to Addy and her Elvis cape and those mean girls at her school.

"Are you okay?" Bowen asked when the trivia match paused so snacks and drinks could be ordered.

"Sure, yes, fine." She thought she'd been doing a good job of looking like a happy trivia fan. "Your sister asked me that too. Do I have a rain cloud over my head?"

"You just seem a little subdued."

"I guess I have a lot on my mind."

"I'm available for consultation."

She realized she wanted to ask him something. "Can you tell me why? Why you did what you did to Henry?"

"I don't think I regret anything more than—"

Vic reached across the table and put her hand on his arm, stopping him. "I wasn't asking you to apologize again." She pulled her hand back. "It's really not about that. I'm just trying to understand. There's a girl who just confided in me that she's being bullied, and I have no idea how to help her." She'd promised to keep Addison's secret, and she had. She hadn't even told

Henry. But now she'd blurted it out to Bowen. She hadn't used names, though. And maybe he could help. "I thought you could give me some insight."

Bowen lowered his head and pinched the bridge of his nose. Finally he looked at her. "I've thought about it, and all I can come up with is that the first time I made some comment about Henry's size, everybody laughed, and I wanted them to keep laughing."

"Why'd you care so much about them laughing?"

"I wanted them to like me."

"Come on. You were the most popular guy in school."

"Not when I got there. I was a junior. I didn't know anyone. It was an easy in."

"'An easy in.' You don't think there was another way?"

"I'm sure there was another way. But I was just going with what got the reaction I wanted." He shook his head. "I guess that doesn't help you much."

"Not really. And the girl, she's making it worse for herself, and I don't understand that either. She's been wearing this crazy Las Vegas Elvis–style cape to school. It's like she's trying to get them to make fun of her." She finished the last bite of her sandwich.

"Maybe she is, in a way. Maybe she's trying to take control of the narrative."

"I'm not sure what you mean."

"Wearing the cape could be a way of choosing what she's bullied about."

That hadn't even occurred to Vic, but it made sense. "Being mocked for wearing the cape would be a lot less painful than being mocked for something more personal."

"It's possible."

"How'd you come up with that idea?" Vic popped one of her french fries into her mouth, then nudged her plate to Bowen. "Have some."

"A lot of my job is figuring people out." He took a fry.

"Seriously? I thought— I don't know what I thought. I don't know anything about what a finance job really entails."

"There's a lot of dealmaking, and that means deciding on the best approach. It's not one-size-fits-all. And sometimes it comes down to making a personal connection."

"I can see you being good at that. The proof is right here. Me sitting with you."

"When a few weeks ago you found me repulsive."

"I'm not going to deny it." She took another fry. "Yet here you are and here I am."

The Fox watched as the female stopped in the snow. Tendrils of new cords stretched between her and other humans of the town, mixed among old cords, stretched but strong. The strongest was the one that shone like starlight. One of The Fox's own cords shone with that same light, the cord that connected her to The Woman. Death was not powerful enough to sever a cord, perhaps because though death could transform, it could not truly end. Life went on in ever changing forms, from cloud to water, sun to tree, rot to growth.

One of the female's new cords bound her to a male The Fox often visited, enjoying the hundreds and hundreds of cords that emanated from him. This new one gave a light that pleased The Fox's senses, giving her another reason to return to the man.

Tegan stopped and stared at the enormous bouquet of plastic flowers on Bucky's grave. Banana had probably put them there himself, but would have some tall tale about how once a year the flowers were left by a man whose life the amazing Bucky had saved.

Smiling, she headed inside. One of her favorite regulars, Maisie, was having lunch at the bar. Could she have left the flowers? She definitely got a kick out of Banana's stories.

"You need anything, Maisie?" Tegan asked. Ryan was taking an order from the one occupied table. The place probably wouldn't start getting busy for another hour or so.

"Not a thing. Except perhaps some conversation."

Tegan was sure Maisie was thinking of conversation with Banana, but since he hadn't yet arrived, Tegan would have to do. "How'd you end up in Fox Crossing? I never asked." Part of being a good bartender was listening.

Maisie took a sip of her drink before she answered. "When your husband dies, they all tell you not to make any big decisions for a year."

"I'm so sorry."

"Thank you," Maisie answered. "After a year and a day, I sold the house, put a few things in storage, then got in the car and drove. Just drove. I liked the feeling of being on the move, being places that we'd never been together. No memories, you know?"

Tegan nodded.

"I ended up here, and for the first time I didn't feel like being on the move anymore. So, I stayed. I rented a little cabin, and I stayed. I suppose at some point I should decide if this is in fact my new home, a place where I want to have the few things that are meaningful to me, like the quilt my great-great-grandmother made for my mom when she was born. She was in her nineties at the time."

"Are you thinking yes, that Fox Crossing is the place?"

"Well, I'm still here. First place I've stayed more than a night since I left home, and that was almost eight months ago."

The door swung open, and Henry came inside. Maisie looked over her shoulder and smiled. "I knew it was him from the expression on your face."

Tegan pressed her hands against her cheeks. "You did?" She was happy to see Henry, but she hadn't thought it would be obvious. Could Henry tell? Did she want him to be able to tell? Her stomach felt a little butterfly-y thinking about it.

"I did." Maisie called to Henry, "Come sit with me."

"Afternoon, ladies." He slide onto the barstool next to Maisie's

"What can I get you?" Tegan tried to get the butterflies to calm down a little.

"She does great beer magic," Maisie told him.

"I love magic, but I'll take an iced tea. I'm meeting up with a couple nurse practitioners in a few."

"You got it." Tegan poured the tea and put it in front of him. The butterflies stilled. It felt like Treehouse Henry and Professional Henry were two different people. Tegan could hang with TH, but PH intimidated her. She didn't understand enough of his project to even know what he'd be talking to the nurse practitioners about, although if she'd been working the night he gave his presentation at the pub, maybe she would. Maybe she should have gone to the meeting. It's not like she'd been doing anything special, probably just continuing to binge *House*. She'd just thought she'd end up feeling stupid.

"Someone has left a most elaborate tribute to Bucky out back," Banana said as he joined Tegan behind the counter.

"I saw that." Tegan couldn't tell if Banana was surprised by the flowers. His comment could be the start of his latest story.

"Hearing about your Bucky has put me in mind of a pet I used to have. Pets, I should say."

Banana put both hands on the bar and leaned toward Maisie. "How many are we talking?"

"Oh, I'd say about a hundred."

"A hundred?" Banana was clearly intrigued.

"A hundred little ants. And I named each and every one of them. There was one who was always floating around at the top of the ant farm. She was Auntie Gravity." Banana gave his *haw-haw-haw*. "There was one who was always marching around with a little sign. She was Auntie Disestablishmentarian. There was one who was always making little doilies. She was—"

"Auntie Macassar," Banana supplied.

Maisie touched her nose and pointed at Banana, one of his usual gestures. "I've never even heard of an antimacassar," Henry said.

Tegan was surprised. She'd thought she was the only one uneducated enough to miss the reference.

"Little doily to keep macassar oil, an old-timey hair product, off the furniture," Banana answered. "That and other grime."

Maisie stood. "I will be back anon." When she returned from the bathroom, she had a rose tucked behind her ear, a plastic rose that looked very much like those on Bucky's grave.

"I need to check on something in the kitchen," Tegan said. "You have to check on something in the kitchen too," she told Banana. As soon as they'd gone through the swinging double doors, Tegan turned to him. "Did you see that rose? Either Maisie is a grave robber, and I think we can both agree she's not, or she's Bucky's secret admirer. And by Bucky's secret admirer, I mean yours. You have to ask her out. I found out she's widowed, and it's been more than a year and a half since her husband died."

Banana crossed his arms, and she thought he was about to refuse. Instead, he said, "I will if you will."

"Me?" It took her a second, then she got it. "Me ask Henry out."

"Bingo."

The butterflies were back. It felt like they'd multiplied and were holding a dance party in her belly. "I can't."

"Sure, you can."

"What's the point?"

"The point is, you like him and he likes you."

Tegan shook her head. "The point is, we're too different. The point is, he's this PhD with a big, fancy job and I'm—I'm here."

"As am I."

"But you own the place."

"Do you really think Henry cares about what you do for a living?"

Tegan hesitated.

"You're not answering because you know the answer is no, he doesn't care. Now, what are you going to do about it?"

CHAPTER 11

Henry trotted down the stairs. He had to be in Greenville in forty-five minutes to go over the possible survey questions with the hospital director, then— His heart gave a kick in his chest. It always did when he saw Tegan. She stood by the ten-cent table, wearing a tiny plastic hand on each finger. "Is it ten cents each or for the set?" she asked Bonnie.

"I would pay you to take them. We've had them on that table for at least six months."

"Inspired, Tegan?" he asked, joining her at the table.

She turned and smiled, and that smile gave him another heart kick, then she waggled her fingers at him. "Who wouldn't be inspired? There's so much incredible stuff!"

"I hope you heard that, Bonnie," Vic called from her spot behind the counter. "You can have the set for a dime, Tegan."

"What have you got planned?" Henry asked.

"I'm not sure. I just know that all this will be part of whatever it is." Tegan pulled off the little hands and added them to the pile she'd started at one corner.

"I can't wait to see what you come up with." He turned to

Vic and Bonnie. "Tegan made the most amazing sculptures out of stuff from this table when Mrs. Libby owned the place." He was so glad she'd followed through on his suggestion to come to the shop and look for things she could use for her art. Tegan wasn't fully Tegan if she wasn't doing something creative.

"Amazing for a high school kid," Tegan mumbled, reminding Henry of the shy girl she used to be.

He could see he'd embarrassed her, so he decided to let the subject of her art drop. He picked up a package with a tiny bright blue harness. "It says this thing is for hamsters. Who thought that was a good idea?"

"Did you notice it's no pull?" Vic asked.

"What I love is that the package says it's perfect for walking or jogging. Jogging." Tegan giggled, not laughed, giggled. It was a beautiful sound.

"There's a dog day-care place in Boston where the dogs go on treadmills." Henry put the little harness down. "I used to see them through the window."

"I lived in Boston for a while," Tegan said.

"You did? I wish I'd known. I went to grad school at BU. We could have hung out." He and Tegan had only lived in the same place for two years, but they'd formed what felt like an unbreakable bond. It's kind of like they were war buddies. He'd have loved to have seen her back then. Who knew what might have happened between them?

"I was only there a few months. I stupidly followed a guy. The wrong guy." Henry wanted to ask questions about the guy and how exactly he was wrong, but it didn't seem like the time, not with Bonnie and Vic listening.

Tegan picked up a squirt gun shaped like a porpoise, turned it over, then put it back down. "I was working at a dollar store. You could have told me about school stuff, and I could have told you what aisle to find the Looped Fruits cereal."

She sounded pissed, and he wasn't sure why. Just a few minutes before, she'd been giggling. "I practically lived on cereal the whole time I was in school." Tegan nodded, keeping her eyes on the stuff on the table, not even glancing up at him. "Well, I guess I better head off," he said after a moment. He had a little more time, but she was clearly done with him. He didn't get it. What had just happened?

"I'm at the animal shelter until six. I was thinking spaghetti for dinner. You in?" Vic called as he started for the door. "I could use the zoodles."

"Sure. Bye, everybody." He left, but had only gone a few steps when he heard Tegan call his name.

"I'm sorry," she said as he turned to face her. "Sometimes my sense of humor isn't funny. Also, sometimes I can be a bitch. I'm sorry."

"It's okay." And it was okay. He just wished he understood what had changed her mood so suddenly.

"I know you probably have a meeting. I don't want to hold you up." Tegan pressed one foot on top of the other. He thought she might be trying to hide the way her sneaker was starting to come apart. "Remember when you asked me if I wanted to go out? If you still want to, I want to."

That gave Henry one more heart kick. "I absolutely want to."

Bowen went over the Feathered Nest presentation one more time. It looked good. It looked very good. He decided to bring a little swag. People always loved free stuff, even people who had a couple mil. He'd bring the assistants gifts too. Assistants greased the wheels. He chose a few pendants and a few bow ties, then considered the options for Liz Kaur. Maybe one of the thin cuffs made with the black-and-white-striped pheasant feathers. He could picture her wearing it. She went for subtle.

Unlike Victoria. He picked up the largest pendant necklace, about four inches at the widest point, and about four inches long. The scale of it said *Victoria* to him. She didn't do anything in a small way. Thinking of her somehow got his phone in his hand. He hit her number.

"How do you feel about peacocks, specifically peacock feathers?" he asked when she answered.

"I'm for them. Why are you thinking about peacocks at eleven o'clock on a Tuesday night?"

It was eleven? He hadn't realized. "I'm pitching investors on a company that makes bow ties and jewelry out of feathers."

"You're still working?"

"I'm about to head out." He just wanted to go over the numbers one more time. "Since you are pro peacock feathers, I'll bring you one of the necklaces this weekend."

"You're bringing me a present?"

He grinned at the excitement in her voice. "I am. I didn't wake you up, did I? I lost track of time."

"Nope. Tonight, I had the surreal experience of helping my dad choose an outfit for a first date. Which is probably why I'm not asleep."

"I recently read an article about how people divorcing in their sixties is on the rise. They called it gray divorce." That probably wasn't the best response. She was talking emotions. He was talking trends.

"Couldn't they just have—? I'm trying to come up with another trend, one that wouldn't have involved blowing up my family, and I've got nothing. My life is a trend-free zone. I don't get out much."

Bowen wanted to say he could remedy that, but his gut told him it was too soon. She'd only recently stopped finding him repulsive. Instead, he asked a question. That was his go-to strategy when he wasn't sure what move to make. People almost always liked talking about themselves. "Was it a shock finding out they wanted to divorce or did you see it coming?"

"Total shock. Then a couple weeks ago—bam—my mom tells me she cheated on my dad. I'm still reeling. I feel like my home has been destroyed." Her voice started to quaver. She cleared her throat, and when she continued, it was steady again. "It's ridiculous to feel that way. I'm an adult, all grown-up. I haven't lived with my parents for more than a decade. I don't know why it hurts so much."

Bowen wondered if it was hitting her so hard because she still lived in the same town as her parents and saw them all the time. "You feel how you feel. Why call it ridiculous?"

"Because nobody died. My mom is still my mom. My dad is still my dad." Bowen could picture Vic twisting her ring or tapping her toes the way she did when she got agitated.

"Maybe it's because you're so close with your family. If I was in your position, it wouldn't hit me as hard because I talk to my parents every few months. If they got divorced, I'd still talk to them every few months, except it would be two calls instead of one."

"I . . . I'm sorry it's like that for you."

"It's fine." He glanced at the time on his computer. "I probably shouldn't keep you. It's getting late."

"Right. Okay. Well, I guess I'll see you this weekend. I should be able to finish assessing everything, then we can talk about which items you want to put in the estate sale, and which you want to auction online. I can also approach collectors directly."

"See you then." Bowen hung up and stared blankly at his laptop for a few moments before he remembered that he wanted to review the Nest numbers one more time.

Vic's kitchen clock did its version of a cuckoo, meaning the proton packs on her *Ghostbusters* clock revved up and shot streams at the Stay-Puft Marshmallow Man. Seven. Fifteen minutes until he needed to leave. Henry picked up Vic's plate and headed to the sink with it, just to have something to occupy him.

"Bring that back!" she demanded.

He looked at the plate and realized it still had an untouched scoop of mashed potatoes on it. Vic always saved her favorite part of each meal until the end.

"Sorry." He put the plate back in front of her and sat down at the table. "I still can't quite believe I'm going out with Tegan Gower."

Vic grinned. "I knew she wouldn't be able to resist you!"

"I thought she'd put me in the friend zone. That fat-friend zone."

"Henry, get up."

"What?"

"Get up."

When he didn't move, Vic stood, grabbed Henry by the arm, tugged him to his feet, and led him to the full-length mirror in her bedroom. "Would you please just look at yourself?"

"I know what I look like!"

"I don't think you do. I think you know what you used to look like. Now, take a real look."

He looked because she wouldn't shut up if he didn't. He looked fine. Face clean. Hair combed. Shirt stain-free.

"And?"

"And I'm not fat anymore. Which I already knew before you dragged me in here." He started to turn away from the mirror, but Vic grabbed him by the shoulders—she had to stand on tiptoe—and held him in place.

"Is that really all you see? The absence of fat?" She gave him a punch on the shoulder before she released him. "Henry, you're gorgeous. Say it. Say, 'I am gorgeous.'"

"Vic, I don't need a pep talk." He walked out of the room.

She followed him. "Obviously, you do, or you wouldn't be surprised that Tegan asked you out."

Henry took his jacket off the octopus coatrack. He was enjoying, mostly enjoying, living with his sister, but sometimes his eyes needed a rest from all her crazy stuff. He'd ditched the comforter on his bed. It looked like it time-traveled to her place from the sixties—orange, with big eyes all over it, some with flowers for eyelashes. Not sleep inducing. He'd replaced it with a plain navy spread.

"I bet she's not even the first woman who's asked you on a date. Am I right?"

He'd told her he didn't need a pep talk. "I'd forgotten how truly annoying you can be."

"Just answer my question and I'll leave you alone."

"Yes, there have been a couple times when a woman has asked me out, okay? I don't walk around thinking I'm repulsive to women. I'm surprised that Tegan asked me out because when I asked her out the first week I was in town, she turned me down." He opened the door. "Don't wait up."

He trotted down the stairs. Vic's shenanigans shouldn't make him late. The drive to the Gowers' only took a few minutes.

It felt strange pulling into the drive, wrong. He'd never gone into the house back in high school. He'd been afraid of seeing Bowen. Tegan always came to his, or they met up in the tree house.

Bowen was far from the only guy who'd bullied Henry, but Bowen had come up with that Titty Committee game, where the guys got points for grabbing his boy boobs. Before that, Henry'd get comments occasionally, but once Bowen started that game, Henry's life had been hell, every day. Not even weekends were safe. If a guy saw him out on the street, it was game on. Even after Bowen left, it was still game on until Henry finally graduated.

Why was he sitting out here thinking about that crap? None of it mattered anymore. Especially now that Tegan had asked him out. Back when they were in high school together, he'd crushed on her hard, but he never let it show. He'd known there was no chance she'd feel the same way about him. But now, he had a second chance.

He got out of the car, and Tegan opened the door of the house before he'd made it all the way up the front walk. She had splotches of silver paint on her shirt and a smudge on one cheek. He wanted to wipe the smudge away with his fingers, just so he'd have a reason to touch her, but hesitated. She'd invited him to dinner, and it seemed as if she'd released him from the friend zone, but he wasn't absolutely sure.

"I'm so sorry. I lost track of time." He felt a little pang as she rubbed the spot of paint of her cheek, taking away that excuse to touch her. "I was working on a new tree-house gnome. I thought I'd only been at it for an hour, then I looked at the clock and realized you'd be here any second. I need to change."

"Show me first?"

Tegan ducked her head and gave that shy smile of hers—heart kick—then led him into the kitchen. She'd spread a sheet over the table and had an array of little items strewn across it. Some he recognized from Vic's ten-cent table. Some looked like they'd been rescued from the trash. He thought she'd done a little shopping at the Mercantile too. "I just finished the face. I decided he should have silver skin. I'm not sure why."

It took Henry a moment to realize that all those tiny hands she'd been wearing on her fingers in Vic's shop had been used to form the gnome's nose. One ear was a seashell. He thought the other one was a made from a gear, possibly from an old alarm clock. The hair was dozens and dozens of pins, the kind with the little colored balls on top. "This is amazing. Even better than the OG, original gnome, although the first guy did have a little bit of a gangster attitude."

"I don't know until I start making the face what the expression will end up being. The way the materials start to come together decides it." Her gaze was a little unfocused as she stared at the gnome. Henry thought she was probably lost in her imagination, envisioning ways the gnome's face might come together.

"This guy looks mellow, like he might have been eating a few mushrooms instead of sleeping under one."

"He kind of does. I'm thinking of using these for his teeth."

She gestured toward a pile of keyboard keys. "I thought maybe they could spell out something. *Mushroom* would be fun, but since it's for the tree house of a thirteen-year-old, I better not."

"You want to order in and hang out here?" They'd planned to go to dinner, but hadn't come up with specifics. "Or we can go out. Anything is good for me. It just looked like you were deep in it with the gnome. I could help with the scut work, if there is any."

"I was going to make the body out of wire coat hangers, then weave some fabric through and have other stuff—I'm not sure what yet—poking out here and there." This was the Tegan he remembered, full of energy and ideas. "You could start unwinding the hook parts of the hangers and get a basic shape going."

"On it. Should we order food now or wait a while?"

Tegan started moving the keyboard keys around. "I'm not that hungry yet. I have a frozen pizza in the freezer and some salad stuff if we want it later."

"Sounds perfect." He'd much rather eat here, just the two of them, than sit across the table from Tegan in a crowded restaurant.

"It's just pepperoni, not roasted pumpkin and chorizo."

Her voice had gotten a bit of an edge, her shoulders hunching a little. Did she think he was too good for frozen pizza? Wait. Did she think he was too good for *her*? He thought back to the day in the shop when she'd gone from giggly to pissed off in seconds. What had they been talking about? Boston. Right. How he'd been going to BU. And she'd been working at the dollar store. It fit. It was crazy, but it fit.

"I had oysters in chorizo-pumpkin sauce for lunch, so pepperoni is perfect." He hoped the goofball comment would remind her he was the same guy he'd always been.

"That's so weird. For lunch, I had roasted pumpkin in oyster-chorizo sauce."

He laughed, and she joined in, then they worked in silence, comfortable silence, for a while, Henry unwinding a few more hangers.

Tegan picked up a blue doll's comb. "Maybe this would work better for the teeth."

Henry gave an exaggerated shudder. "With those teeth, he'd no longer be mellow. They look made for ripping."

"True." Tegan tossed the comb aside. "Maybe something with these." She fingered the petals on a satin rose that was attached to a headband.

"With lips like that, he'd be a lover, not a fighter."

"Not quite the vibe I'm going for." She rooted around in the stuff on the table.

Henry pulled on each end of an untwisted hanger to straighten it out. "Do you want me to cut these into smaller pieces?"

She shook her head. "Do you think you could connect a bunch of them into one long piece, then make a coil?"

"I can try." It took a few attempts, but Henry managed to twist four of the straightened hangers together, giving him one long, thick wire. He bent his arm so it was at a right angle, then, holding the end of the wire in one hand, he looped the rest around his elbow a few times. "About this size?" he asked as he struggled to form the looped wires into a circular shape.

"Keep holding it like that." Tegan grabbed a couple twist ties and bound the loops together in a few places. Her fingers brushed against his, and desire surged through him. Part of him was still fourteen around her, excited by the smallest contact.

Henry got to work on unwrapping another set of hangers. "I'm getting together with Samuel and Kenzie tomorrow night. You want to come with?" Henry hoped it wasn't too soon to ask to get together again.

"I'm working."

Maybe that was a brush-off, but maybe not. "How about if

we come to Wit's, maybe around seven? You could at least hang out for a little on your break."

"You said they were new in town," Tegan said, not answering his question. "How'd they end up here? Did he come for a job?"

"He said he has a cousin in town. We didn't get much further than that. He said he'd gone through an ugly divorce. Seemed like he was looking for a fresh start."

"Like me."

"Like you? Does that mean you're thinking of staying?"

"Maybe. For a while at least." Tegan took the metal ring off the top of a mason jar and snipped a curved section with wire cutters. "Mouth." She plugged in a hot-glue gun.

"Nice." Henry wanted to know more about why she was in need of a fresh start, but he didn't want to push.

Tegan fiddled with the mouth, trying a couple different positions, then squeezed a line of hot glue on one side and pressed the metal against the gnome's face. A section of her hair fell into her eyes, and Henry reached out and tucked it behind her ear, both because her hands were occupied, and because he wanted to touch her so badly.

"Thanks." They locked eyes for a moment, and the air seemed to sizzle, then she looked away. She pulled a leaf off the satin rose and held it up to the gnome's mouth. "What do you think?"

He thought he wanted to touch her again, really touch her, but needed to take it slow. "I like how it looks like he's part plant. A garden gnome partly made out of garden."

"Maybe I'll weave some ivy though the wire of the body. I could use live vines. I could rig up something inside the coil to support a plant and leave a hole so it could be watered."

"It's going to be amazing. You've got to make more than just the one for the tree house."

Tegan pushed the gnome head away from her. "You should

know that I'm a complete screwup. I didn't need to come at all. Bowen's the executor, and he had it covered. I really needed to get away," she said in a rush. "My hours got cut at my crappy job, and I wasn't even making enough to pay for my crappy apartment. Make that the room I rented in someone else's crappy apartment. That's who I am, Henry. You should know that." She sounded almost angry, but he could hear the pain in her voice.

"Getting your hours cut doesn't mean you're a screwup. That could have happened for all kinds of reasons that had nothing to do with you."

"You're talking like it's a onetime thing. It's not. It's my life. Because I'm a screwup." She got to her feet. "Should I put the pizza in? Or do you just want to go? It's okay if you do."

How had they gotten here? When only a few minutes ago, they'd been laughing together. "Where are you getting that? I don't want to go. Sometimes, after I lost the weight, I'd imagine running into you somewhere. You'd see me, and—"

"And?"

"And you'd realize I was a guy, an actual guy. Not just the fat friend."

"I always knew you were a guy."

"You know what I mean."

"I know what you mean. And I always knew you were a guy. I had such a crush on you, but you never seemed—"

He couldn't believe what he was hearing. Before she could finish, Henry was on his feet, kissing her, kissing Tegan. He'd been waiting years for this. Heart kick with steel-toed boots.

CHAPTER 12

"Don't think you're going to get away without giving me details on the date. I'm not expecting, nor do I want, all the details. But I need some," Banana said as soon as Tegan arrived for her shift the next night.

"I will if you will." She could feel the smile stretching across her face as she thought about her night with Henry, the whole mind-blowing, world-exploding night.

Banana gave his *haw-haw-haw*. "Don't bother giving me words. Your face just said enough to make me blush."

Which made Tegan blush.

Which made Banana laugh again. "Told you he didn't care if you served drinks or were the Queen of Sheba."

True. Henry didn't care. He really didn't care. The things he liked about her had nothing to do with what she did to earn money. All day, he'd been texting her things he liked about her—the way she laughed, the way she made him laugh, the three freckles on her big toe, the expression her face got when she was in the art groove, her kind heart . . . He'd sent her at least twenty texts, starting about ten minutes after he left her house this morning.

She realized she was standing there mooning. That was the only word for it, mooning. She was so lost in the mooning that she almost forgot Banana was standing right there. "How about you? How was your date with Maisie?"

"This will tell you everything you need to know. Maisie and I went to karaoke night at Amore, and without consulting one another, we both sang 'Jump." She, the Pointer Sisters. Me, Van Halen. The word *kismet* may apply."

"I think—" Tegan was interrupted by the sound of several dishes hitting the kitchen floor. She rushed through the swinging double doors and saw Big Matt staring at three plates and their contents on the ground. She grabbed the broom and dustpan and got to work. She hesitated as she got ready to dump the trash into the can. Those bits of blue–and-white china . . . she could do something with them. She wasn't sure exactly what, but something.

It was like she'd had all this creativity shoved way down inside her, neglected. Then Henry said she should check out the ten-cent table, the way she used to, and pop! It came springing out of her, like a jack-in-the-box after the last crank. She rinsed the pieces and put them in a sack to take home. Sorry, Dr. House. It might be a while before I get back to you, she thought, then she headed out to the front, ready to do what Maisie had called her beer magic.

A few hours later, a warm shiver went through her, and she knew, just knew, Henry had come in and was looking at her. She turned, and, of course, there he was. Nothing else could have caused that sensation.

"Still okay if I take my half now?" she asked Banana.

"'Go ahead and jump,'" Banana answered, then began to hum, throwing in a few hip swivels. "And make it an hour, on me."

"You're the best." A job that involved Banana time had to be a good job, and she'd felt that way even before he'd gifted her that half an hour. She tossed her apron behind the bar, then hurried over to Henry. She felt like launching herself at him, but this was where she worked, so she settled for a quick kiss.

"I missed you," Henry said.

"I missed you too."

"It's been hours."

"And hours, and hours, and hours," Tegan agreed as they settled into one of the corner booths. "Are you going to tell Kenzie about the tree house tonight?"

"I was thinking of waiting until it's done. I might even be able to finish it up on the weekend."

"I'll have the rug done by then. The gnome might take a little longer. I need to make another stop at the ten-cent-Tuesday table."

"Vic will make an exception and let you do your ten-cent shopping any day of the week. If you catch Bonnie alone, I know she has a few things she'd love to unload free of charge."

The red-haired dad and daughter that Tegan had seen a few times took a seat at the table. Obviously, they were Samuel and Kenzie. "Sorry we're late," Samuel said. Kenzie already had all her attention on the phone.

"No prob," Henry answered, and made the introductions.

Tegan wouldn't have minded if Samuel and Kenzie had been a lot later to give her more one-on-one time with Henry, but he was going to stick around until she got off work. 'Cause he liiiked her.

"I caught Mr. Osborne on my roof with sealant and a putty knife. On my roof. I was thinking ambulance. I was thinking ER. I was thinking all kinds of badness—" Samuel waved his hands around frantically. "I had to go up there. Turned out I had a cracked shingle. He wouldn't come down until he'd showed me how to fix it."

"I didn't even live on Mr. Osborne's street, and sometimes I'd see him out front, hauling trash cans back up to people's houses after the garbage was collected." Tegan took Henry's hand under the table. She couldn't sit this close to him and not touch him.

"Yesterday, I saw him at the Mercantile straightening the cereal section. He's got to be at least forty years older than me. He makes me feel like a complete slacker. He wants to teach Kenz how to snowshoe." Samuel looked at his daughter, who hadn't looked up at the sound of her name. "Right, Kenzie? Mr. Osborne's going to teach you to snowshoe."

Tegan could see that Kenzie had an earbud in on the side her father couldn't see. She was engrossed in a TikTok video, some kind of makeup tutorial.

Samuel reached over and snagged Kenzie's phone, ignoring her yelp of protest. "You can have it back after we eat."

"I love the way you did your eyes." Kenzie had used pale green eyeliner to give herself dramatic cat eyes. "I can never get a smooth line when I try something like that."

"You use tape as a stencil. You have to stick and unstick it to your hand a few times first, otherwise it pulls at the skin around your eyes."

Did it. Got two whole sentences out of the teenager, Tegan thought. "I'll try it. Thanks."

It was probably pressing her luck, but she decided to try to keep the conversation going. "Henry and I met each other when we were about your age. I was over at his house—the house next door to you and your dad—almost every day. He could never come to my place." Tegan hoped Kenzie would ask why.

"How come?"

Hooked her! "My brother was a bastard." Tegan looked at Samuel. "Sorry. Wrong word." She turned back to Kenzie. "But that's what he was."

"What'd he do?"

"He was a bully. He made Henry's life hell." Tegan hoped it would help Kenzie to know she wasn't the only one who'd had to deal with a bully. Henry squeezed her hand. She thought he understood what she was trying to do.

"It got so I hated going to school," Henry said. "Hated going anywhere, actually. You know how it is here, you can't go anywhere without running into people you know, and there were a lot of kids I wanted to avoid."

"You hear that, Kenz?" Samuel asked. "Henry had a hard stretch at school. He—"

Tegan could see Kenzie shutting down. Her dad had pushed it too hard.

"You said I couldn't use the phone when we're eating. But we didn't even order yet. Let me have it." Kenzie put out her hand. Samuel sighed and gave it to her.

Maybe a door had been opened. Maybe Kenzie would remember what Tegan and Henry said if things got bad. If Tegan could get Kenzie interested in decorating the tree house with her, she'd make sure Henry gave them some time alone. That way, if Kenzie wanted to talk, she'd have the chance.

Vic stretched out on the couch. Persephone immediately jumped onto her stomach, Pemberley curled up around her feet, and both started to purr. Bliss. She'd spent longer than she'd expected to at Dwell Dell. It seemed like everyone in the place wanted to shop at the ten-cent table. Bonnie would be happy to know that Vic had sold almost everything.

She reached out one arm and snagged the remote from the coffee table without disturbing either cat. Before she could click the TV on, her phone buzzed. Maybe it was Bowen. He should be getting into town around now. Not that that meant he should call. They already had a time set for tomorrow to continue the work of prepping for the estate sale. She checked the phone, and her stomach cramped. It was the BBQ. Where her father was having his date.

"Vic, you've got to get down here right now," Piper said in a rush, before Vic could even say hello.

"Is Dad okay?"

"Your dad is fine. But your mother is here. And she is not fine. Extremely not fine."

"On my way." The BBQ was only a block and a half from the shop, and Vic ran it.

"I am not leaving!" she heard her mother shout, even before Vic opened the door.

"Once more into the breach," Vic muttered, then stepped inside.

She glanced around the room. Her mom and Piper were on opposite sides of the hostess stand, facing off. Her dad was across the room, standing protectively in front of the woman who had to be his date.

"Mom, hi, can we talk for a minute?" Vic asked as she walked over. "I think you must have the date wrong. This is Dad's night."

"I'm not leaving." Her mother's feet were planted wide and she was gripping the hostess stand with both hands, like she was expecting Vic to try to drag her out of the place.

"How about if you and I go out to eat? How about that fish place you like over in Dover-Foxcroft?" Vic had eaten leftover spaghetti—she loved it cold—before she hit the couch, but she needed to get their mother out of here.

"Don't try to manage me, Vic," her mother snapped.

Vic held up both hands. "That's not it. There are no empty tables here, is all. Why not go somewhere else?"

"That's not necessary. We'll go." Her father ushered his pale, wide-eyed date out the door.

Thankfully, Vic's mom didn't try to stop them. She still gripped the hostess stand, but the fight had gone out of her.

"Mom? What do you want to do?"

"I can get you set up at a table," Piper offered. Maybe not the best idea, the only available table being the one Vic's dad and his date had just vacated.

Her mother looked around, and it seemed as if she'd just

realized other people were in the restaurant. "Can we go to your place?"

"Of course." Vic led the way outside.

"They were only expecting dinner, but they got dinner and a show." Vic's mom rapped on the restaurant's large front window, and when she'd gotten the attention of everyone inside, she dropped into a low curtsy, then started down the sidewalk.

Vic's mom had style. No denying it.

"This afternoon, I went to the Mercantile, and then I drove home, home, to our house, instead of my apartment. It's not the first time, either." Vic's mother took gloves out of her pocket and pulled them on as they walked. "When I was a child, we had a dog, Petunia. We'd had her about three years when we moved to a new house about a half a mile away. Till the day she died, we'd get calls from the people who moved into the old house, saying Petunia was lying in their driveway. She kept getting out and going over there. That's me. I'm Petunia."

Brought it on yourself, Petunia, a little voice inside Vic whispered, but she didn't say it to her mother. Vic could see how much her mother was hurting. When you were hurting because of something you brought on yourself, it made the hurt even worse.

"Are you hungry?" Vic asked when they reached her apartment.

"Do you have ice cream?"

"Sure." Vic led the way into the kitchen and opened the freezer. "Take your pick." She wasn't surprised her mom wanted something sweet. That was the pattern when she was dealing with something painful. Binge out, then spend a couple days eating nothing but Special K and skim milk. Vic and Henry had both picked up some bad food habits there. But they'd gotten lots of good stuff too, like apologizing when you're wrong, like laughing at the same joke fifty times, like treating your family as well as you treated your friends and vice versa.

Vic waited until her mom had scooped out her ice cream and

sat down with Vic at the kitchen table, then asked a question she was pretty sure she already knew the answer to. "Mom? Did you really think tonight was your BBQ night?"

"No. Today, I just sat in the driveway at the house for the longest time, wishing I could go inside and have everything back the way it was, before . . . before everything. I was missing him, I guess, and I knew he would be there, so I just went. Silly."

"Not silly."

"Then when I saw that woman . . ." Her mother shook her head, then took a bite of ice cream. Vic grabbed a spoon and took a bite too. "I wasn't expecting him to be with a woman. It didn't even occur to me. It was like a volcano went off inside me. I saw red."

Saw red. That's how her mother always described it when she completely lost her temper. Maybe now you know how Dad felt, Vic thought.

"I deserve what happened. I know that." Her mother's voice was small. She didn't even look like the same woman who'd been shouting in the BBQ. Back there, her eyes had been blazing, her chin up. Now she looked defeated.

"He wasn't on a date because he thinks you deserve it," Vic said. "He's lonely."

"So am I."

They both took another bite of ice cream.

"They have quite a first-date story. The crazed wife interrupting, making a scene."

"Oh, Mom. I'm sorry it turned out that way."

"I wonder if he likes her."

"Don't go there. You're only going to make yourself feel worse."

"I didn't much like Trevor. He's the one I . . . you know."

Vic nodded. She didn't want to be having this conversation. But her mother clearly needed to talk.

"He made me feel pretty. I knew I wasn't pretty, not anymore. During menopause I gained twelve pounds, twelve pounds, and I couldn't get it off, no matter what I did. But when I was with Trevor, I could pretend I was still pretty."

"Mom, you *are* still pretty." Or she would be if she got her hair cut and colored—Junior Miss Georgia Peach brown to match the bottom or gray to match the top, it didn't matter. That and if she bought some new clothes that fit her right. She wasn't even trying.

"We both know that's not true."

She's punishing herself, Vic realized. How had she not seen that? For her mother, going out in public without her makeup, with bobby pins holding her half-and-half hair out of her face, wearing clothes that were obviously too small, had to be torture. She'd been torturing herself every day for almost a year. The anger that Vic had been trying to shove down started to dissolve. "How about if we go shopping this weekend? I'll even let you pick out an outfit for me." Her mother sometimes called what Vic wore "clown clothes," as in "You'd be beautiful if you stopped wearing those clown clothes."

Her mother gave a smile that wasn't anything like the one she had when she was genuinely happy. "Tempting."

"Let's do it. I should be done working on the Gower estate by five. We could go to Bangor after that. Hit the mall. In addition to allowing you to pick out an outfit for me, I will go to the Lancôme counter and let them do what they will to my face." Lancôme was her mother's favorite. Maybe once she saw all the new colors, she wouldn't be able to resist buying something for herself. She'd done a horrible, hurtful thing, but Vic couldn't stand by and let her keep hurting herself.

"I'm just so tired."

"You can sleep until noon tomorrow."

"Maybe."

Vic had heard that *maybe* a million times as a kid. That was the *maybe* that meant "no way."

"You want to sleep over tonight?" Vic didn't want her mom to be alone. "I'll let you have both cats."

That got an almost-real smile. Her mother loved the cats. "Okay."

Vic thought she'd fall asleep as soon as she got back on the couch. She felt drained, drained but also edgy. She wished Henry was here. They could go out and get a drink or something.

She picked up her cell, then hit Bowen's number, just because it was at the top of her contacts list. They'd spoken that afternoon to set a time for tomorrow. "Did you not promise to bring me a present?" she asked as soon as he said hello.

"I did." He sounded amused.

"Just checking." What was she doing calling Bowen Gower?

"What are you up to tonight, Victoria?"

She'd always liked the nickname Vic, but something about the way he said Victoria . . . "I don't know. I might go to Wit's and I thought you might be thirsty." She thought he might be thirsty. Her mother would not approve of that as an invitation. It hadn't exactly been gracious.

He didn't seem to mind. "I *am* feeling a little parched. I'll see you there."

Vic got up and grabbed her coat, then decided she should make sure she was passably presentable. She'd leaped off the couch and dashed out of the house when her mom called. She should at least brush her hair.

She brushed her hair. She also took a fast shower, then put on her favorite lipstick and some mascara, since she was already standing in front of the mirror. She dabbed on some of her favorite perfume, because it was sitting right there next to the mascara. She threw on a long-sleeved sweater dress with a swingy skirt that was Bonnie approved. She had to change because her jumpsuit—velour, with rainbow stripes on the sleeves, and so comfy—was wrinkled from the lying, and the leaping, and the dashing. Well, maybe not wrinkled exactly. Could velour really wrinkle? But she'd panic-sweated in it, and it probably needed washing.

When she walked into the pub, she saw that the tables had been rearranged to create a small dance floor, something Banana did once in a while when no trivia or other event was going on. She started for the bar since each of the tables and the booths were taken, then realized one of the people at one of the tables was her dad.

"Hi. Okay if I sit for a minute until your date comes back?"

"The hoo-ha at the BBQ was enough excitement for a first date. She went home. It's doubtful I'll see her again." He didn't sound too bothered by the idea.

"It was quite the scene."

"Your mother has always had a temper and a flair for the dramatic. That's why I had to keep buying her wedding rings. But she'd cool down fast, and when she was wrong, she'd say so." He took a swallow of his ale. "I'm sure it was my night to have the BBQ."

"It was. And she knew that. She told me so."

"She did?"

"She misses you." Vic studied her father's face, trying to see how he felt about that.

"I miss her too," he finally said.

"And?"

"And I'll probably always miss her, but I can't go back. I had no idea what was going on, Vic. None. If we tried again, I'd always be wondering if she was lying to me. The lying was almost as bad as the other." He shook his head. "No, the lying was worse."

Vic knew that feeling. It had been the same with her and Leo. She thought they shared everything, and then it came out that he'd been hiding this huge thing, and she'd been completely clueless.

"Do you think your mother is all right?" He smoothed

down his mustache. "For years, even after we were married, she didn't let me see her without makeup. She got it from your grandmother. She did the same thing. And your mother's hair. You know she's always been a little vain."

"I'll make sure and check up on her."

"Are we putting too much on you? It's not just your mother I'm worried about. You're always going. The shelter, Dwell Dell, and now doing all you do for your mom and me."

"I'm fine." She was, even though his question had made her eyes sting with unshed tears. "And Henry's here now. He helps out."

Satisfied, her father finished his drink and stood. "I'm going to head out. You have some fun tonight. You deserve it, Vic."

"Thanks, Daddy." Daddy. She hadn't called him that in years, but it just slipped out. She'd been feeling protective of him, him and Mom, for so long, and realizing that he still felt protective of her, even though she was thirty years old, had been surprising, surprising and touching.

Maybe she should have told him the real reason she'd called off the wedding all those years ago. Well, that's how it had looked. She'd made the announcement, and acted like it was her idea, but the decision had been Leo's. She'd felt like such a failure. She hadn't wanted anyone to know the truth. She hadn't wanted anyone's pity. She hadn't even told Henry the truth. Telling people the wedding was off was hard enough, without going into why.

If Leo had come back months later and said he wanted to try again, would she have said yes? Even though part of her would have wanted to, she didn't think so, because another part, a bigger part, would be too afraid of its happening again. She wouldn't have survived its happening again.

"I'm glad you called."

Vic had been so caught up in her thoughts that she hadn't noticed Bowen coming up to the table. "I'm glad I did, too."

He sat down, pulled a little box out of his jacket pocket, and handed it to her. "Your present."

"Really? For me?" she said with exaggerated surprise. "You shouldn't have!" She opened the box. "It's beautiful." She ran her finger lightly over the necklace. "I don't think I'd have known it was made of feathers if you hadn't told me. The patterns are amazing, and the colors." The Bonnie-approved dress was plain. The necklace would give it some much-needed pizzazz. She couldn't quite get the clasp. She kept losing her grip on the spring ring before she got the chain hooked.

"Let me." He stood and stepped behind her, then moved her hair to one side. His fingers briefly touched the back of her neck, so briefly. She realized she wanted more. Much, much more.

Don't go there, she told herself. You can't be wanting more from Bowen Gower. Doing business with him—fine. Going out to dinner with him—fine. Having a drink with him on occasion—fine. But it couldn't go further than that. Not when he'd almost destroyed her brother.

"How was your week?" she asked as he sat back down. Her voice was a little shaky, but not so much that she thought he would notice.

"Hectic, but good. I prefer being busy."

"Me too." Especially after the wedding that wasn't. The nights had felt so long and lonely. It had been a relief when Miss Violet had suggested, actually more like commanded, Vic volunteer at the animal shelter. Adding in the visits to Dwell Dell had helped too. Vic had had to keep moving, moving, moving, just to survive.

"What have you been busy with this week?"

"The shop. I hit some sales. I volunteer a couple places. I wrangle my parents. I told you how they can't be together. I have this system to keep them apart. Well, tonight, system failure."

"What happened?"

Vic was about to give him the rundown. Then she realized she didn't want to talk about it. She didn't want to think about it. "Would you want to dance with me?" Because dancing with Bowen wasn't so much different from having a drink with him.

"Absolutely." He led her out to the dance floor. Banana had a Pointer Sisters song, one of her mom's faves, blasting on the jukebox. No thinking about Mom, she told herself. And she didn't. She and Bowen danced to one eighties song after the other, until a slow song came on.

They stared at each other for a moment, then Bowen pulled her closer to him, and she wrapped her arms around his neck. She was slow dancing with freaking Bowen Gower.

And it felt good.

CHAPTER 13

"I bought some great stuff at the liquidation sale," Vic announced when she returned to the shop.

"Things I'll like?" Bonnie asked.

"Absolutely. Things people need that we can sell them at a good price, while still making a profit."

Bonnie narrowed her eyes. "Define *need*."

"A pallet of home and kitchen items, like new. I also bought a pallet of thirty air fryers. I know we can't sell that many at the store, but the price was great, and I know we can sell them online."

"Good job!"

Vic laughed. "That should be my line. In case I don't say it enough, good job, Bonnie! Anything interesting happen while I was out?"

"I heard some good gossip from Honey."

"Do tell."

"I heard you and Bowen were slow dancing at Wit's on Friday. How has it taken three days for me to find this out?"

A bolt of heat shot through Vic as she thought about that

dancing. "This is the first day we've worked together since then. I was finishing the last of the assessments at the Gower place on the weekend, and then I had the auction this morning."

"There are phones."

"It wasn't that much of a thing."

"Of course, it was. You haven't gone out on a date in more than a year."

"It wasn't a date. It was a dance. A few dances."

"And dinner Saturday night. Honey is sure The Fox has created another love match."

"Did Honey mention that it was dinner with Tegan and Henry? When I'd finished at the house for the day, we all just decided to go to Flappy's."

"You like him though, don't you?"

Vic had been avoiding asking herself that question, so she avoided answering Bonnie. "He's a lot different than I expected him to be, that's for sure. I didn't think Bowen Gower would have grown up to be anything resembling human."

Bonnie snorted. "He almost doesn't resemble anything human. More like a god. Or at least a demigod."

Vic ignored that, but it was kind of true. "He can be a good listener. And a good dancer. But it's not like anything is going to happen between us. For starters, he lives in New York. I live here."

"True. Which makes him great fling material. And after you have a fling, maybe you'll remember that men can actually be an enjoyable part of life, and you'll at least go out with me once in a while where the enjoyable men might be present."

Vic thought about slow dancing with Bowen, and the way it left her wanting more. Was a fling that much more than a drink or a dance? It wasn't like marrying him and making him a member of the family or anything. "He might not even be interested."

"*Pffft.* Of course, he is. You're pretty as a picture, and I'm not talking about the one you bought at the garage sale last week with the lumpy thing, the mutant baby, and the other lumpy thing." Bonnie pointed an accusing finger at the painting.

Vic had to admit Bonnie's description was somewhat accurate, although the lumpy things were interesting to look at, and wasn't that what art was about?

"And you're sweet. And you're funny. You have atrocious taste in clothes. But with a fling, clothing can and will come off."

Vic caught sight of Addison, resplendent in sparkly cape, shiny cowboy hat, and the newly acquired feather boa. "Cheese it! No more fling talk. The kid approacheth, and I am her role model."

Bonnie's forehead furrowed. "The outfit gets more and more horrible. She wears it every day, too."

In the right setting, Addison would look fabulous, outrageous in the best possible way. Vic could see her dancing at an EDM fest, at least Vic could if she bumped Addy up to college age. But in middle school, she was dressing for social ostracism. Bowen had to be right. Addy had to be taking control in the only way she knew how, choosing what she'd be bullied about.

Addy swung the cape off as soon as she stepped inside the shop.

"How was your day, sweetie?" Bonnie asked.

"Same."

Bonnie's forehead furrows deepened. Addison still hadn't told her mom about the bullying, but Bonnie knew "same" wasn't good.

"Addy, I was thinking today, you could do a new window display. Let's look at possibilities." Vic led the way to the back room. "It's April. Maybe something with April showers?"

Addison picked up a stuffed cat wearing a purple beret with a matching scarf. "Raining cats and dogs?"

"You're brilliant! I have tons of dog and cat stuff. Your

mother will fall down on the floor in relief if you come up with a display that sells this Ren and Stimpy statue." Vic grabbed it off her desk.

Addison took the statue and studied it. "Are those supposed to be cats? Or dogs?"

"One of each. Although the cat looks kind of like a Chihuahua. It's the one sitting on top of the other one."

"I'll look for some other stuff."

"But first, my usual question. How's it going at school?" Vic had instituted daily check-ins on school days, either in person or by text—Bonnie had replaced Addison's phone—since Addy was still adamant about keeping the bullying a secret.

"Like I said, same. Maybe even a tiny bit better. Maybe it's working, and they're getting bored."

Vic had done some research online, and a bunch of the sites had emphasized how important it was not to show an emotional reaction to the bullying. She and Addison had done some role-playing to help Addy keep her face neutral, no matter what the girls said. Boring the bullies into leaving her alone would be great, but it would still leave Addy with no friends at school. It didn't feel like much of a victory.

"I'm glad it seems like it's helping a little." Vic picked up a Hello Kitty toaster that made toast with Hello Kitty's face on it. "Maybe this for the display?" She tried to keep the daily check-ins short, unless Addison seemed to want to talk. Vic didn't want the girl to dread them. "I love your display idea. It's really clever." Vic had read advice that said to build up bullied kids' self-esteem by helping them find things they were good at. She'd make sure Addy had more chances to get creative.

"You can go back out front. You've done your duty."

"Talking to you isn't a duty!" Vic hadn't even thought the check-ins could come off that way. There were so many ways to make a wrong move dealing with a sensitive teen. She didn't know how Bonnie did it. "It's the highlight of my day. Truly."

"Okay." Addy picked up a tapestry of one of the *Dogs Playing Poker* paintings.

"You can take things from the front too."

Vic left her to it. She found Tegan chatting to Bonnie at the counter.

"Look what Tegan made you!" Bonnie called.

"I had a bunch of things left over when I finished with the gnome. I started playing around with putting them together, and they turned into a fox."

"I love it. Those old opera glasses make great eyes."

"Can you imagine how fast we'd sell it during tourist season?" Bonnie gave the fox's head a gentle stroke. "Everyone wants at least one fox souvenir."

"If you want to make more, Bonnie's right, we could absolutely sell them. They wouldn't all have to be fox."

Tegan ducked her head and smiled. "I could do more, but first, I'm going to make Banana a donkey, legs up, like the pub logo."

"You'll just encourage his craziness," Bonnie said, voice warm with affection.

"I hope so. I don't know if he realizes it, but Banana's stories are a big draw. People come in just to hear the latest. I would, if I didn't work there," Tegan answered. "I didn't come by just to drop off the fox. I need to buy a dress, and I don't have a lot of cash."

"You've come to the right place. Despite Vic's outfit, we have lots of nonridiculous clothing." Bonnie plucked at one of Vic's huge puffed sleeves.

Vic was pretty sure they were supposed to be clouds, to go with the airplane-print pattern of the rest of her dress. "Hey, I consider my outfits a draw, same as Banana's stories. People come into J and D, they expect to see snazzy, and Bonnie doesn't deliver. She hardly ever even wears more than one color at a time. While I—" Vic gave a twirl, making the airplanes fly.

"The director of the Greenville Hospital is giving a dinner party next weekend, and I'm supposed to go with Henry. He says it's only for a few people, and he doesn't think anybody will get too dressed up, but the only thing I have that's sort of appropriate is a pair of wool pants that I wear all the time at work." Tegan was talking fast, clearly feeling nervous just thinking about the party.

"Come on. I'll hook you up." Bonnie led Tegan to a large circular rack near the center of the shop.

Tegan and Henry had been together every day—and night— since Tegan asked him out. It made Vic's heart happy. They'd been such great friends back in the day. It felt so right that they were together now.

Unlike Vic and Bowen. No one who knew them in high school would ever think they'd end up a couple. But she wasn't even contemplating coupledom with him. There was no way that was even possible. A fling though. A fling with more dancing, and more more . . . Hmmm.

Bowen took one more look at the Jumbie research he'd pulled together. It was definitely something the firm should be interested in. Tomorrow, he'd circle up with a couple of the directors and lay it out for them. This was the kind of initiative that would get him to director on schedule.

He opened the top drawer of his desk, then slid out the schedule he and his grandfather had made all those years ago. If the firm went ahead with Jumbie, that would be something he'd have told Granddad about. Bowen was going to miss that. He could tell his parents when he'd scored at work. They'd be pleased, but they wouldn't get it.

Bowen looked at the neat check marks that he'd made when he'd reached each step his grandfather had laid out, starting with getting the grades to be awarded summa cum laude when he got his BA.

He returned the schedule to its place in his desk. He hadn't asked Tegan if their grandfather had offered to pay for her college because, once he'd thought about it, he was sure Granddad hadn't. As he remembered it, Tegan had done a semester or two at community college. Granddad had been specific about what kind of education he'd pay for: what school, what major, what graduate degree. To keep his grandfather's financial support, Bowen had been required to show acceptable, meaning near-perfect, grades each semester, and to spend his summers at internships his grandfather arranged. It was nothing Tegan would have wanted, even if she'd had the aptitude.

He wondered what Tegan's reaction would have been if his grandfather—their grandfather, he corrected himself—had come up with a step-by-step plan to get her a job as a . . . What? Art instructor at a university maybe? He wasn't even sure what kind of job would interest her. Vic would say he should ask.

He wondered what Vic was doing. He knew she had a couple volunteer things going, in addition to running the shop. She'd mentioned she went to a lot of locker auctions, estate sales, and garage sales to get merchandise. But by nine, she'd probably be done with all that. Henry was probably with Tegan, so what was Vic doing with her night?

Maybe he should follow Vic's own advice and just ask. The thought made him smile, so he picked up the cell and was about to hit her number when Jana came in and took one of the seats across from his desk.

He checked the level on her gigantic water bottle. "You're ahead of schedule."

"By two hours. That's a personal best."

Jana made everything a competition. It worked for her. If she were following her grandfather's schedule, she'd be a little ahead, while Bowen was a little behind. He'd make up the difference though. He could still make director by thirty-three. "The specs on Jumbie are looking good."

She nodded, but didn't ask any follow-up questions. Had her interest in the company waned? All his research was saying it would be a great opportunity.

"You done for the day?" Bowen asked. Since she hadn't seemed to want to talk about Jumbie, he'd wait for a better time to update her on his findings. Timing was critical.

"Just about." Jana switched her water bottle to her other hand.

"Since you're ahead on your water, do you want to go to Dorrian's for a smash burger?" Jana almost always ordered the smash burger. Bowen made a point of noting the preferences of people he went out with.

"Not tonight." She leaned forward. "There's no easy way to tell you this—"

It felt like every nerve in Bowen's body started firing. Nothing good could come after the words she'd just spoken.

"But we're letting you go. Lund's going to tell you tomorrow, but I didn't want you walking into his office unprepared." Jana took a swallow of her water, then looked him in the eye. The right amount of eye contact was also critical. "How are you feeling about this news?"

How are you feeling about this news? She had to be quoting from some article on how to fire someone.

"I'm feeling surprised." Bowen managed to keep his voice calm, and he mirrored her posture, leaning forward a little. She wasn't the only one who'd studied good communication techniques. "I was promoted four months ago. Has something changed since then? Are there expectations I haven't been meeting?"

He was damn sure there weren't. That's why he was still in the office at nine. He went above and beyond. Always. Above and beyond was his normal.

"It's nothing like that. My feeling is that there's pressure from the top to do some belt-tightening. The firm's going to take on another associate. The thinking is that an associate can do a lot of what a VP does, but with a significantly lower salary." She took another swig of water.

What was Bowen supposed to do with that? She hadn't given him anything to spin. He wasn't going to volunteer to take a $100,000 pay cut, which is what it would take to get him back to an associate's salary. That was ridiculous.

Jana leaned a fraction closer. "How can I help you with this?"

Here was more effective-business-communication speak. It might be helpful if she acted like a human being, one who'd gone out drinking with him numerous times. She was supposed to be his mentor.

"Other than a glowing letter of recommendation, which you know I'll gladly give. Would it be helpful if I made some calls?"

"I'll need to think about that and get back to you." That was the best he could come up with right now. He felt lucky the words had come out in English. He was staggered, dazed, still not quite accepting that he'd just gotten fired.

"Of course." Jana stood. "We'll be in touch." With that she was gone.

Bowen needed to move. He got up and grabbed the gym bag he always kept at the office and walked straight to the gym. He found an empty treadmill, set the incline and speed to his personal best, then bumped them both up a little. He ran until his lungs ached for air, until his legs cramped, but even exhaustion couldn't turn off his brain. He'd gotten fired. He'd gotten fired. He'd gotten fired.

He flashed on the schedule tucked away in the desk that wouldn't be his after tomorrow. He knew as soon as his meeting with Lund was over, security would watch him pack up and then escort him out of the building. Nothing personal, just protocol. His life was destroyed, and somehow it wasn't supposed to be personal.

CHAPTER 14

"We've got trouble, my friend," Vic announced as soon as Henry stepped into the apartment.

Henry shrugged off his coat. "Hit me."

"The Smarty Pints and the Quizly Bears both made it to the finals, which means there is a more than decent possibility that Mom and Dad will have to be in Wit's at the same time, that or one of them will have to quit their team, bringing shame and dishonor down on themselves."

"Shame and dishonor?" Henry sat down on the couch next to Vic. "Do you think you might be being a trifle dramatic?"

"Neither of them will let down their teammates, is what I'm saying. But I don't know what will happen if they have to be in a room together. Well, I know what happened last time, and if you think I'm dramatic, you should have seen Mom. She was screeching like she'd just been stabbed."

"But Dad was with a date. That won't be the case at the pub."

"You should have been there when Dad told me that if he didn't have to see her, then he didn't have to think about what happened. His face. It would have broken your heart."

He could see that it had almost broken Vic's. She'd been dealing with their parents' split by herself for too long. "I'll play referee at the tournament, if it comes to that. You don't even have to be there."

"What's going to happen to them? Maybe Dad will end up with someone else, even though the person he is looking for on the dating sites is a clone of Mom. But our mother? I don't know if she's ever going to stop punishing herself. She's sixty-one. Grandma is ninety and still going strong. Strongish. That means Mom could have thirty years of misery ahead of her."

"Mom should probably see a therapist. Possibly she needs to be on antidepressants, at least short term. It wouldn't hurt Dad to talk to someone either." Henry could, and would, be there for his parents, but they needed more than he or Vic could give them.

"Like that will happen."

Vic picked up one of the sofa's throw pillows and began twisting it in her hands. Usually, she got her anxiety out by twisting her ring. She'd gone into hyperdrive. Henry needed to give her a reality check.

"You need to let some of this go. It's a trivia game that will last a few hours. I get that neither Mom nor Dad would want to let down their teammates, but we can't forget that they have the option of skipping the tournament."

"You're right. I'm being crazy." Vic put the pillow down.

"That's not what I said."

"But it's true. It's a trivia tournament. That's all."

She was saying the words, but Henry could see part of her didn't believe them. She had tears in her eyes. This past year of taking care of their parents, which went way beyond managing their schedules, had left her frayed. Looking at her, he wasn't sure how much more she could take without breaking.

"I'm tagging in. You're off Mom-and-Dad duty, at least for a while. I'll keep the calendar. I'll give Dad dating advice if he asks. I'll try to get Mom to get her hair colored or whatever. I'll also talk mental wellness with both of them.

"I can't—"

"Yes, you can. I'm their kid, same as you, which means I should take as much responsibility as you do."

"You don't even think I should be doing the calendar."

"Eventually, they are going to have to figure out how to live in the same town without us running interference. But I promise I'll keep up with the calendar until you say it's okay to stop. I hate to say it, but if they can't handle running into each other once in a while, one of them might have to move."

"Neither of them can leave Fox Crossing!" Vic exclaimed.

"It would be painful, but not impossible." Right now, Henry's biggest concern was Vic. "Tomorrow, I'll talk to them about how they want to handle the possibility of their teams going head-to-head. Maybe they need to have a breath-holding contest, and the winner stays in and the loser drops out."

He'd hoped she'd laugh. She didn't. "Neither of them is going to agree to drop—"

"I'm going to handle it. You are going to take all those hours you spend managing them and stressing about them and do something fun."

"Fun."

"Yes, fun." Even without wrangling their parents, Vic still had the shop, her hours at the animal shelter, and the visits to the retirement home. She kept herself running, and the strain was showing. "When was the last time you had fun? I want specifics."

"I have fun at the garage sales—"

Henry made a game-show buzzer *beeeep*.

"Okay. Okay, okay, okay." Vic closed her eyes, thinking, then opened them and looked at him. "It actually wasn't that long ago. It was last Friday night after the Mom debacle."

Henry curled his fingers in a gimme gesture.

"The last time I had fun was dancing with Bowen Gower."

Henry waited for the little pop of anger he always got when he thought of the guy, even after all these years, even after the apology. It didn't come. The present-day Bowen had replaced, mostly replaced, the high school Bowen in Henry's mind, and Henry had started to like present-day Bowen. "Then dance with him again."

"Is that okay, though?" She picked up the pillow again.

"Vic, all I care about is you doing something fun, something that makes you happy. If that involves freaking Bowen Gower, whether it's dancing or more than dancing, it's okay with me."

"What are you doing here?" Tegan asked. "That came out wrong. What I meant was, I'm surprised to see you. It's only Thursday."

Bowen sat down his suitcase, a Horizon 55 from *GQ*'s top-luggage list. He'd needed something bigger than the duffel. "It's only a few weeks until the funeral. I wanted to be here to take care of any last-minute details." Underneath everything he said, underneath everything he did, an unending loop of *I got fired, I got fired, I got fired* ran through his brain.

"I'm here. You don't really have to do everything."

"I know. Don't take it personally. I have a bunch of vacation time. I thought I'd use some of it. I've taken a few long week-ends since I started at Garm, but that's it." Because he'd made his job his top priority. He'd given it his all. He'd given it his all, and it hadn't been enough.

"You're due, that's for sure."

"I'm going to go unpack."

"I really want you to let me help with the funeral arrange-ments, or anything else that needs to be done. You delegate at work, right? So delegate. You can give me performance evalua-tions, if that will make you feel better."

"There's nothing to do right now." He didn't need to be

here, but he couldn't be in the city. The city felt like an extension of Garm, every place he usually went—the gym, bars, restaurants—chosen for maximum networking potential.

"Fine. I've got to get ready for work." She walked off.

He'd offended her. Again. Just when things between them had stopped feeling strained. Just when he was getting to know her. He'd make it right later. He needed to unpack. He went upstairs and got everything stowed away, then pulled out his phone. It took him a moment to remember there weren't going to be messages about one of the deals he'd been in the middle of pulling together. He was sure Feathered Nest had already been assigned to someone else, his research into Jumbie put in someone else's hands, his clients already informed of their new contacts.

He glanced at the phone. He could see that there were dozens of texts, all basically asking what the hell happened. The only answer was that he wasn't good enough. If he'd been good enough, Garm would have found the money.

He returned the phone to his pocket. In the near future, he'd need to answer everyone. He needed to make it known that he was looking for a firm where he could take initiative and bring in the companies he knew would turn a profit. He also needed to follow up with Jana about her offer to make calls for him, but even thinking of speaking to her turned up the volume on the *I got fired* loop.

It felt like it had been weeks since Jana gave him the heads-up that he was being let go. It had only been a day and a half. His contacts weren't going to go cold immediately. He could give himself through the weekend, then Monday, he'd get back in there. His new job was looking for a new job, and he was going to work as hard on it as he had on any deal.

He walked out onto the balcony and stared out at the lake. After a moment, he turned back around, sat down at the desk, and powered up his computer. He reviewed the checklist of what needed to be done as executor. He'd done everything he could until the newspaper announcement finished running. He opened the spreadsheet of the house's inventory. Vic had finished the appraisals, and they'd set a date for the estate sale. Nothing needed his attention.

Bowen stood up. He'd go downstairs and get something to eat. Except he'd eaten lunch before his flight, and he wasn't hungry. He looked at the bed. He could take a nap. He'd been running on fumes for weeks, trying to keep all the balls in the air at work. Not that anyone had cared. He felt exhausted, but knew he wouldn't be able to fall asleep.

His grandfather had a large library. Bowen could go find something to read. On vacation with Alexandra two summers ago, he'd read a legal thriller. He'd chosen it because he'd known Paula Hawkins was a fan of the author, and he'd thought it would be good conversation fodder. He'd ended up working the book into a chat in the pre-business part of a business lunch, a successful business lunch. He took out his phone and made a note to touch base with Paula. If there was an opening for a VP anywhere, she'd have it on her radar.

Would he be able to get a VP spot? Or would he have to drop back down to senior associate? No. That wasn't an option. To keep to the schedule, he needed to keep moving forward.

He would definitely dip into another thriller to give him some chitchat options with Paula. But not now. He didn't think he'd retain anything he read. His concentration was shot. Maybe TV was a better option. It didn't take as much focus, and his grandfather had all the streaming services. *WealthTrack* could give him some areas to explore. He wanted to be able to do more than recite his résumé when he started getting back out there. He wanted to have some good picks back-pocketed so he could show he'd be an asset right off the bat. He was going to make sure Garm regretted losing him. He was going to hustle like he'd never before hustled. Maybe he'd make director even faster than his grandfather had.

Bowen realized he didn't have the attention span even for TV right then. He needed to move. If he pushed himself hard enough physically, it would shut down his brain, at least for a little while. He changed into his running gear and headed out. He did a fast walk as a warm up, then started to run when he hit the lake trail, the mud squelching under his sneakers.

He tried to keep all his attention on his form, noting which part of his foot hit the ground first and making adjustments. Keeping his hands loose. Squeezing his shoulder blades together to keep his shoulders from creeping up. Running was the only thing besides work that got him into the zone. No, sex worked too. Work, running, and sex.

As he rounded a curve, he caught sight of a flash of red streaking across the path. He skidded to a stop, startled.

"Was that The Fox?" Victoria Michaud stood about twelve feet from him, and Bowen realized they were in almost exactly the same positions as they'd been back on the first day he'd returned to Fox Crossing, the day she'd looked at him like he was something the dog had thrown up.

Bowen shoved his sweaty hair off his face. "I think it was." His heart was still pounding hard from the run.

"Seeing The Fox twice. Should we go buy lottery tickets?" She closed the distance between them.

"We should fly to Vegas." He was kidding, but how great would it be to go straight to the airport, hop a plane, and spend the weekend in Vegas with Victoria? That might be the one thing that would make him forget about work for a couple of days.

"I didn't think you'd be in town until tomorrow."

"I'm taking a little time off to make sure everything's in place for my grandfather's funeral." Telling the lie to Victoria felt harder than telling it to Tegan. Maybe because the first time the lie just came falling out of his mouth. This time he was more aware that he was consciously lying. Victoria deserved better.

So did Tegan. But he wasn't ready to talk about it. Maybe he'd wait until he had another gig. That way, he could tell people he'd simply changed jobs. Happened all the time. Of course, everyone in finance would know the truth.

"I'm on an enforced vacation. Henry decided I've gotten dangerously stressed-out and has decreed that I take a break from everything. He's going to handle anything that comes up with the parents, Bonnie is going to handle anything that comes up with the shop, and Miss Violet is finding volunteers to cover my hours at the animal shelter. Henry is recruiting Tegan to go to Dwell Dell Tuesday night. I set up a ten-cent-sale table once a week, so people can shop." Victoria threw her arms wide. "So here I am, out on a walk on a Thursday afternoon." She let her arms fall to her sides.

"How does it feel?" For him, having free time on a Thursday afternoon felt shameful.

"I don't like it. All those things—that's my life. I don't need a vacation from my life. But Henry went all big brother, even though, as I've told him repeatedly, he is my *little* brother, so here I am."

"Okay if I join you on your walk?"

"Of course." Her answer showed how much things had changed between them since their last fox sighting.

"Was Henry right? About you being dangerously stressed-out?"

"I love the shop. I love the shelter. I love everybody at the Dwell Dell. I love my parents."

"That wasn't exactly an answer. Is there a *but* in there somewhere that you've left out?"

"But sometimes I want to put on my pajamas at six o'clock, eat popcorn for dinner, find the most mindless TV out there, and veg."

He laughed. "Sounds perfect."

"Liar. There's no way you'd ever want to do that."

True. For him a great night was going out to Dorrian's or the Rabbit, running into a potential investment partner, and pretty much sealing the deal right then. It was a better rush than anything else he'd experienced. But a night on the couch with Victoria . . . that held some appeal.

"The situation with my parents has stressed me out. Not the part where I coordinate their schedules so they don't run into each other. That's easy. That's logistics. But sometimes seeing the pain they are each in . . ." Victoria pressed both hands against her heart.

"Of course," he said, although he had no experience that even came close. He'd never had to deal with the deep pain of another person. Alexandra would have work drama, and that had been easy for him to deal with. He could handle anything about work politics, a part of his being the people guy.

Because he was the people guy, he could tell Victoria was holding something back. If she'd been sitting at the table when he was giving a pitch, he'd have known something was hanging her up, whether it was that the projections looked impossibly optimistic or she was getting a bad vibe from the CEO.

He went for a technique he used in negotiations, rephrasing what she'd said to see if it would lead to new information. "You love them so, it hurts."

"So much. My dad in his little apartment, all alone, breaks my heart. And my mom, I hate seeing what she's doing to herself. She's not wearing makeup. She's not coloring her hair. That probably sounds like nothing, but for the former Junior Miss Peach, that means she's in crisis. I want to fix it. I want to fix all of it, for both of them. But it's impossible. She wants him back, and that's impossible."

There was still something Victoria wasn't saying. Should he push? He'd ask one more question, then let it go. Pushing too hard was counterproductive. "Impossible?"

"She cheated on him. Maybe he could get past the cheating,

but the trust between them is broken. That he can't get past. You can't live with someone you don't trust."

She was still holding back, but he'd pushed enough. "I'm sorry."

"Yeah, me too."

"But right now, you're on vacation."

"Right. Vacation. But even though I'm on vacation, my brain won't shut off. I know there's nothing I can do to change the situation with my parents. I know it, but I can't quite make myself accept it. I keep thinking about it. Going over it in my head again and again. And again, and again, and again. How do I get my brain to go on vacation?"

Bowen wanted his brain to go on vacation too. "I might know a way." He caught her lightly by the arm, turning her toward him, then cupped her face in his hands and kissed her. A quick kiss. A testing-the-waters kind of kiss.

As he lifted his head, she slid her fingers into his hair and pulled his mouth back to hers, and his mind went quiet, all his senses consumed by Victoria.

"To your left!" someone called.

They stumbled apart, then moved out of the center of the path as a guy rode by on a horse.

"Should we continue this someplace else?" Bowen asked.

"Well, the ground is pretty muddy." She sounded breathless, which is how he was feeling.

He kissed her one more time, then they started walking. When they reached the path turnoff that led back to town, they started walking faster. When they reached Victoria's block, she grabbed his hand, and they started to run, laughing.

It had not been long since The Fox last saw the female and the male, but the cord that bound them no longer reminded her of that between hunter and prey.

All around her, the woods were bright with cords that had

formed between new mates, and soon there would be even more new cords as the season of new life began.

Perhaps the change in season explained the change in the cord between the humans. In her world, hunter and prey never transformed into a mated pair, but humans did not follow the same laws.

Vic opened her eyes and found Bowen looking at her. "Hey."

He caught her hand and pressed a kiss into her palm. "Hey."

"We fell asleep."

"We did."

Vic stretched, her leg sliding along his. "What time do you think it is?" From the sunlight streaming through the window, she'd guess two or three.

"Does it matter?"

"Actually, no." Vic let that sink in. "I have absolutely nothing to do for the rest of the day."

"I might be able to help with that." Bowen waggled his eyebrows suggestively.

Vic started laughing and couldn't stop. This situation was surreal. Bowen Gower was in her bed. Her seventeen-year-old self would be horrified. Her thirty-year-old self felt pretty damn good.

"I didn't think it was that funny."

"It's just—" She couldn't get more words out because she was still laughing. She gestured back and forth between him and her.

"And I don't think this"—he repeated the back-and-forth gesture—"is funny at all. I'd say, sensational, thrilling, earth melting, but not funny."

"Not funny, exactly, but surprising, unexpected." Except that she had to admit, since the night they'd danced, her mind had drifted into fantasies that were pretty close to this reality.

"Unexpected? You never thought about the two of us doing

this—" He did the back-and-forth gesture one more time. "Because I'll admit, I thought about it."

She felt her face flush. "Me too."

"And now I'm thinking about it again."

"Me too."

"And as you have absolutely nothing to do for the rest of the day . . ."

CHAPTER 15

"I'd knock before I go in," Bonnie advised Henry. "Knock loudly. Your sister and Bowen Gower came through here a few hours ago, and it looked like they were going to be, let's say, occupied for a while."

"Enough said." It was more than enough when talking about his sister. "I don't need to go up at all. I had a little time between focus-group meetings, and I wanted to see if Vic had already broken down and come into the shop. Guess I have my answer."

"She tried to 'just do a little paperwork' this morning. I had to kick her out. She came back with Bowen."

"I didn't think he'd be in town until tomorrow night."

"He is most definitely here." Bonnie began to work a necklace out of the tangle of costume jewelry she was sorting.

"Then maybe I don't have to worry about her crashing the trivia game tomorrow night. If Dad's team wins, they go on to the championship game. Vic's already freaking out about what will happen if his team and Mom's end up going head-to-head."

"I'm almost hoping it happens. She needs to see the world

won't explode." Bonnie freed the necklace, a tiny red heart on a thin silver chain.

He could see Tegan wearing it. "I'll take this. How much?"

"Vic would never take your money." Bonnie put the necklace in a little bag and handed it to him.

"Would you and Addison be up for breakfast before you have to open up on Sunday? I've been hanging out a little with a guy who's new in town. He has a daughter about Addy's age. Vic told me how Addy's been having a hard time since her best friend moved away. His daughter's struggling to settle in. I thought the two of them might hit it off."

"That would be wonderful. It's definitely worth a try."

"Flappy's at ten?"

"We'll be there."

"Great."

"I was kind of disappointed when Bowen came by for some of his stuff yesterday," Tegan said as they sat down at the biggest table at Flappy's Sunday morning. Flappy's didn't usually take reservations, but Henry convinced Flappy to make an exception. The man would do anything for Vic and, by extension, Vic's brother. "I was picturing your sister finding him a set of clean clothes down in her shop."

Henry laughed. "That would have been epic. I'm seeing plaid pants. I'm seeing a reindeer sweater with a light-up nose."

"I'm seeing that, suede bowling shoes, and a top hat."

"One of those collapsible stunt top hats, that makes a loud pop when it unfolds." Henry noticed his mother coming through the door with Honey and Charlie. He'd been expecting to see her. She was down for Flappy's on today's schedule. He gave her a wave, and she waved back.

"Maybe I should buy my mom a sweater or something." The one she had on was too tight, like all the rest of her clothes. She'd look much better if she had some that fit, but, clearly, looking better wasn't something she wanted. "Maybe having something new would inspire her to take more interest in her appearance and start taking better care of herself."

"Maybe." Tegan sounded dubious.

He waited while Nell filled their coffee cups, then said, "Guess that's me looking for an easy solution. I need to have the conversation with her about therapy. I just don't know how to start. I know when your parents get older, your relationship starts to flip-flop and you start taking care of them, but I wasn't expecting to be here so soon."

"Do you think you could get one of her friends to suggest it? It might be easier to hear from one of them." Tegan poured some cream in her coffee.

"I want to be the one. I need her to know I'm worried about her. That flip-flop hasn't completely happened yet. She won't like the idea of worrying me, and that might motivate her. Although she'll probably just try to convince me that she's fine and that I have nothing to be concerned about."

"At least she's still going out. That's something. When I get depressed, I hole up. I don't go anywhere except for work and food."

"Does it hit you a lot? Depression?" Henry was still trying to get a sense of what her life had been like over the years since high school. He'd filled her in, but she didn't open up.

"Once in a while. Like everyone." Tegan took a sip of coffee, then added a little more cream. "Hey, look. It's Banana and Maisie. You really do see half the town at Flappy's on Sunday." Banana shot Tegan a wink, and she grinned. "They're the perfect couple. Last night at Wit's, the two of them spun out this whole story about a groundhog they claim has a burrow over by Bucky's grave. They kept building on each other's ideas with no pauses. The big finish was the groundhog having a conversation with Bucky's ghost. Everyone sitting at the bar was listening. They loved it." Tegan's eyes were bright with enthusiasm.

"You're really enjoying working there."

"Yeah, I am. I've had other waitressing and bartending gigs, and some of them were okay, but nothing like working at Wit's. I think a lot of it is Banana. He sets the tone. And almost all the regulars are cool."

"I remember Banana telling—"

"Kenzie and Samuel are here," Tegan interrupted. "And she does *not* look happy."

Henry'd had dinner with Samuel and Kenzie a few nights ago. Samuel had insisted she eat with them, even though she'd wanted to take the food to her room. Once she'd been released from the prison of the kitchen table, Samuel had told Henry that it didn't seem like Kenz had made any friends yet. And it hit him that Addy was her age and also in need of a friend. "I hope this wasn't a bad idea."

Tegan gave his knee a squeeze. "Breakfast can only last so long. How bad can it be?"

As soon as they sat down, Samuel held out his hand for Kenzie's phone. She reluctantly gave it to him, then, not bothering with a greeting, she opened the menu, holding it so it blocked her face from sight.

"Sorry," Samuel mouthed.

"Good to almost see you, Kenz," Tegan said, and got no response.

Okay, off to a good start, Henry thought, again wondering if this meetup was a good idea. Maybe Kenzie would talk more once a non-adult was at the table.

Nell swung by, flipped Samuel's coffee cup over, and filled it.

"I want coffee," Kenzie said from behind the menu.

"Fine." Samuel flipped over Kenzie's cup.

Henry suspected he hadn't wanted to launch into another prolonged negotiation, like the one Henry was sure they'd had over phone usage.

Nell filled the cup. One of Kenzie's hands appeared and

pulled the cup closer, then began groping around the table. Henry slid the sugar into its path, and the hand retreated.

"We've been here for dinner a couple times, but not breakfast. What looks good, Kenzie?" Samuel asked.

"The cereal we have at home" came the answer from behind the menu.

Henry couldn't resist teasing her a little. "They have some great homemade muesli."

A twitch of the menu was the only response from Kenzie, but he got another squeeze on the knee from Tegan. When he looked over at her, he could see she was trying not to laugh.

"Hey, everybody, sorry we're a little late," Bonnie called as she hurried toward their table, Addison trailing behind her, looking as thrilled as Kenzie had to be here. Hey, they already had something in common.

"Menu down now, Kenz," Samuel said, voice low. When she didn't obey, he tugged the menu out of her hands.

Addison stopped so suddenly that Nell, coffeepot in hand, nearly ran into her. The girl's face went pale. Eyes on Kenzie, Addison backed up a step, two, then turned and ran, knocking into Banana's chair on the way out.

Bonnie had frozen in the middle of taking a seat at the table. "I don't know what just happened." She straightened up. "We'll be back. I hope." She rushed out the door.

"That girl is so weird," Kenzie said.

"You know her?" Samuel asked.

"Only one middle school."

"Why did she get so upset when she saw you?" Samuel pressed.

"I told you, she's weird." Kenzie picked up the menu again.

Henry had no idea what the hell had just happened. He only knew that getting the girls together had definitely been a bad idea.

*　*　*

Vic opened the door and was hit with a jolt of fear. Bonnie looked shattered. "What's wrong?"

"I'm sorry to bother you," she whispered. "Addy's downstairs, sobbing. We went to Flappy's to meet a friend of Henry's and his daughter. Addy took one look at her and bolted. I don't know why. I don't know what's going on. All I know is that it's bad, and that she won't talk to me. Will you go down?"

"Of course."

"I know it's your vacation. I know—"

"Shut up, Bonnie." Vic opened the door wider. "Bowen's making coffee. Why don't you go inside and have some?"

"Okay." But Bonnie didn't move.

"Go on." Vic gently guided Bonnie inside, then started down the stairs to the back room. She wanted to take the steps three at a time, but she made herself go slowly. She didn't know what was going on. The text from Bonnie hadn't given many details. But no matter what had happened, Vic's acting panicked wasn't going to help.

She found Addy sitting on the floor, leaning against the desk. Vic sat down next to her, so close their shoulders touched. "Want to talk about it? And I say it because I don't really know what happened."

"I had a freak-out at Flappy's. Everyone's going to think I'm a mutant. Which they do already, so what does it matter?" Addy let out a long, shuddering sigh. She wasn't crying anymore, but her face was still wet with tears.

"Can you tell me what made you want to leave so bad? Or we can just sit here if you want. Or I could get the Gooey Louie out of the front and we could play. Nothing cheers me up like picking plastic boogers." Vic hoped that would make Addy smile. It didn't.

"At school I'm prepared. I know girls are going to start saying stuff as soon as they see me, so I go in with my blank face, like we practiced. I should have just done the blank face when I saw her. I don't know why I didn't. I just wasn't ready."

"Henry's friend's daughter is one of the girls who bullies you?"

"She's the one that started the whole thing! Before that, I was kind of friends with everyone. Not friends who hang out after school. But friends who talk to each other in class, who eat with each other sometimes. Then she got there. And she made everyone hate me!"

"I'm sorry this happened. You must have felt ambushed."

"Mom said the girl was new in town. But she's been here for months. I couldn't sit there with her. I couldn't!"

"Of course, you couldn't. Here's what I think we should do. I think we should get your mom, then drive a minimum of two towns away, and have breakfast. And I think while we do, you should tell your mom what you've been dealing with."

Addy shook her head, fresh tears starting to leak from her eyes.

"She knows there's something really wrong and she's frantic with worry. She's not going to be able to let it drop." Vic slid her arm around Addy's shoulders. "I can tell her, if that would be easier."

"I'll do it." Addy's voice was flat. Vic suspected Addy thought things were so horrible that nothing could make them worse.

"I want to tell Henry what's going on. I know he'll want to know if you're all right."

Addy shrugged, and Vic decided to take that as a yes. Henry could work on things from his side, while Vic and Bonnie talked to Addy. They had to find a solution. Addison couldn't go on like this.

"So here it is. The tree house. Tegan and I practically lived up there. We cleaned it up, did some repairs," Henry told Kenzie. "Let me show you." He needed to talk to her alone, and he figured showing her the tree house after breakfast would give them a little time.

Henry started up the ladder. Kenzie didn't follow.

"Go on, Kenz," her dad urged.

"It'll only take a minute."

"We'll wait down here," Tegan said. On the drive over, Henry had filled her in on the few details he'd gotten from Vic.

Henry opened the hatch, and climbed through. Kenzie only came up the ladder far enough to poke her head into the tree house. "Nice." She didn't follow up the *Nice* with a *Can I leave now?*, but Henry knew that's what she was thinking.

"Come up for a minute."

"I can see it all from here."

"You're the reason I fixed this place up. I wanted you to have it. When I was around your age, I really needed it. There was this group of guys who'd yell 'Mooob' every time they saw me. *Mooob* for 'man boob.' I was fat back then. Really fat. They'd moo it from across the street like a cow, from out of car windows, wherever I went, I'd be bracing myself to hear it. Except up here, up here and at home. Those were the only two places that felt safe."

"Okay, I've seen it."

"Your dad told me what it was like for you at your old school. He thought maybe things were getting bad for you here too. That made me think you might need this place, like I needed it."

"I'm going down." But she didn't move. He could see tremors running through her body, but she still had the don't-even-bother-talking-to-me-because-I-don't-want-to-hear-it expression on her face that had been there the whole time they'd been eating.

"Turns out, I should have fixed up this place for Addison. She's the one who needs it."

"I'm going down." But she still didn't move.

"I know what's been going on at school between you two. My sister texted me. She's friends with Addy's mom."

"I barely even know her."

"You know how she's feeling though, don't you? You know because you've felt that way yourself. And that's the part I really don't understand. Other girls might think, 'Oh, we're just joking around. We're just teasing her a little.'" He could hear anger creeping into his voice, and he paused for a moment to get it under control. She was just a kid. "But you know that's not how it feels to Addison."

Henry saw Kenzie's eyes fill with tears, but just for a moment, then she blinked them away. "You fixed this place up for nothing. I don't want it. You didn't even ask me if I wanted it. Just stay out of my life."

"You're right. I should have asked."

She stared at him. Henry didn't think she'd been expecting him to agree with her. "Are you telling my dad?"

"Not as long as you leave Addison alone."

She climbed down the ladder without giving him an answer. He followed, closing the hatch behind him.

The scent of pain pricked The Fox's nostrils as she considered the young one. Another human who smelled of pain without the odor of blood or sickness or death. As long as she'd lived, as deep as her connection to The Woman was, there was much about humans that remained mysterious.

Bowen reached across Vic to the bedside table and snagged his phone without waking her. He quickly scanned the texts that had come in. It had been four days. He hadn't looked at them since he'd seen Vic on the trail the day of the second fox sighting. He'd never gone that long before.

He didn't bother opening any of the texts. He could tell they were more versions of "What the hell happened?" with a few stock alerts mixed in. He clicked on the uValue app. He needed to stay up-to-the-minute if he was going to impress at interviews.

Interviews. Because he'd gotten fired. He heard a rushing in his ears, his blood pumping hard.

He closed the app. He didn't have any interviews yet. It was only Monday. He could take another couple days before he jumped back in. Victoria was still on her vacation through Wednesday. Once she was back, he'd sit down and get in touch with every contact he had. He'd find a place to land.

As he eased the phone back on the nightstand, Vic rolled toward him, looping one of her legs over his hips. "Caught you. You said you were taking vacation days. No checking with work on vacation."

I got fired. I got fired. I got fired. Hearing the word *work* was all it took to start the loop again. Actually, it was always running, but sometimes the volume was turned way down, then something would happen to crank it.

"Moment of weakness." He could tell her this wasn't technically a vacation, but why? He'd tell her he got a new job once he had one. He shifted, bringing his body flush against hers, letting the feel of her skin against his take over his senses, the volume on the loop dropping to a whisper that he could pretty much ignore.

The faint sound of proton packs firing signaled that it was eight. "School's about to start." He could feel tension creep into Victoria's body as she added, "I hope Addison's going to be okay. Henry thinks Kenzie will back off."

"If she doesn't, then her dad will have to be brought in." Bowen wondered what would have happened if his father had been informed he was bullying Henry. Bowen was pretty sure his granddad would have had a boys-will-be-boys attitude. Bowen had pretty much had that attitude himself when his sister first told him that he'd bullied Henry back in the day. Bowen didn't get it. Now he did. At least a little more. He'd never get it the way Henry and Addison did.

"That's the upside to yesterday's debacle. At least Addy finally told her mom what was going on, and Henry put Kenzie in check. I hope."

Vic clearly needed some distraction. At least until she found out how things had gone for Addison at school. "You think we can beat yesterday's in-bed record?" He slid his fingers through her hair.

"I can definitely do better than nineteen out of twenty-four."

"You know me. Win or die trying."

"We should do a kitchen run, get snacks and water, and put them where we can reach them while remaining in contact with the mattress." She didn't make a move to get up.

"That would give us at least a half an hour more bed time." Victoria's bed was the only place he wanted to be.

Vic pulled on her velour jumpsuit, not bothering with underwear. She planned to be pulling the jumpsuit back off shortly.

"You sure you don't want me to go down with you?" Bowen snagged his T-shirt off the floor and put it on.

"No, probably the fewer people the better. The only reason I'm going is because Bonnie asked me to. I'll be back fast, fingers crossed."

"I'll forage for food, then we're back on the clock." He slapped her side of the bed, and she laughed.

She made a quick stop in the bathroom to brush her hair, which definitely looked like she'd been in the middle of a staying-in-bed marathon, then hurried downstairs. Bonnie and Addison stood at the front counter, both looking at the door.

"I don't want to talk to her," Addy told Vic when she joined them.

"It won't be for long," Bonnie promised.

"I don't see why I have to listen to her apologize. It's not really her. She's just doing it because her dad is making her."

Bonnie sighed. "Maybe. But apologizing is the right thing to do. And when someone apologizes, the right thing to do is listen."

"Even when it's fake?"

Vic wrapped her arm around Addy's shoulders. "I'd say we should go out for a triple scoop of ice cream once you get through it, but food is not the way to deal with bad emotions." She gave Addy a squeeze before she released her. "Once Kenzie is out of here, you can pick one thing from the shop on me."

"Because shopping is the way to deal with bad emotions," Bonnie observed.

"Good point." Vic nodded toward the front window. "I'm assuming that's Kenzie and Samuel." Addy crossed her arms, digging her fingers into her skin, all the answer Vic needed. "Would you rather talk to her in the back room or out here?" Vic wasn't sure if Addison would find it worse to be alone with Kenzie or to have three adults, and possibly customers, as an audience. It would probably be easier for Kenzie to apologize without onlookers, but Vic didn't care about what was easier for Kenzie.

"Back."

"We'll be right here if you need us," Bonnie said. "You got this."

Addy hurried off before Samuel and Kenzie could come through the door.

"I'm so sorry I didn't know what was happening between the girls," Samuel said as soon as Kenzie had joined Addison in the back.

"I'm just glad it finally came out." Bonnie had her arms crossed, digging her fingers into her skin, just the way Addy had, and she kept glancing at the door to the back room.

"Obviously, I knew something wasn't right at the restaurant, but I never would have thought— Some girls were bullying Kenzie at her old school. I never would have thought she could do that to anyone else. My brain is just—" Samuel made an explosion sound and threw his hands up.

So many times, Vic had seen Bonnie going through it with

Addy and thought how hard momming was. Dadding was hard too. Samuel was clearly feeling out of his depth, helpless.

"I don't know what's going on with Addison a lot of the time, not anymore. She used to tell me everything, but . . ." Bonnie shook her head.

"Kenzie told me she wasn't feeling well this morning and didn't want to go to school. And me, clueless Dad, just accepted that. When I came home at lunch to check on her, it all came spewing out. That's when I texted you," Samuel told Bonnie. "I know it doesn't help, but she does feel really bad. I tried to get her to explain, to tell me why. She wasn't exactly coherent. Like I said, it came spewing out. It sounded like she was so afraid of it happening again, what happened at her old school, that she made a preemptive strike. Which is no excuse."

"God, growing up is hard." Bonnie gave a wry smile. "Maybe someday I'll get there."

"You and me both."

Vic shouldn't be here. This should be just between the two of them. "I'm going to go and—"

Addison came out of the back room before Vic could finish. Addy didn't head over to them. Instead, she went over to the circular clothes rack and started frantically flipping through the hangers.

Vic exchanged a look with Bonnie, then they both walked over to Addy.

"What happened?" Bonnie asked, voice low enough that only Vic and Addy could hear her.

"She said she'll wear whatever I pick out to school tomorrow. I want the ugliest thing you have." Addy pulled out a sweater with a bejeweled walrus on the front and studied it.

"I don't actually consider anything in here ugly," Vic said as she struggled to come up with a more appropriate response. "It's all just waiting for the right occasion."

"Halloween at the zoo perhaps." Bonnie took the walrus

sweater and replaced it. "Sweetie, I understand wanting revenge. I do, but I'm not sure it's going to make you feel better."

Back when Vic was in high school, getting revenge on Bowen Gower would have felt fantastic. Vic was sure of it. But as Addison's role model, Vic didn't share her thoughts.

"That!" Addison pointed to one of the wig stands along the far wall. It held a fake-fruit-festooned turban that had to be part of someone's Carmen Miranda costume. She strode over and grabbed it.

"Should I let her, do you think?" Bonnie asked softly.

"I would. She's the one who got hurt. It should be her call."

Kenzie was a girl who'd gotten hurt too. But should Addison have to take that into consideration? If Vic had found out that Bowen had been hurting somehow, would that have made her feel differently about him back then? She hoped it would have, but she honestly wasn't sure.

Addison headed for the back with the turban. Then she hesitated. Be the better person, Vic thought. Be you. She smiled as Addy put the turban down on the Barbie Fashion Head; the turban slid so low it covered most of Barbie's face. Addy returned to the rack and started flipping again. Was she looking for something that would be even more humiliating?

"This will look good with her hair." Addy held up a simple green V-neck sweater.

"You have an amazing daughter," Vic told Bonnie after Addison had returned to the back room.

"I do, don't I?"

Bonnie's eyes were wet, and Vic's own eyes were stinging with tears. "Although you have to admit, that turban would be perfection under different circumstances."

CHAPTER 16

"The house is big." Tegan looked up at the hospital director's place. Winnie Sylvester, she reminded herself. Winnie Sylvester, Winnie Sylvester. She knew Henry would introduce them, but she didn't want to forget the woman's name. When Tegan got nervous, things seemed to slide out of her brain.

"Your grandfather's is bigger." Henry parked in front of the double garage.

True. But even after weeks, she still didn't feel comfortable in it. Everything was just so tasteful. So perfect. So spotless, thanks to her grandfather's housekeeper, who Bowen still had come in twice a week. Even Tegan's bedroom felt a little uncomfortable. The only place that felt good was the kitchen, because she'd covered the table in sheets and made it her workstation.

"You ready?"

Tegan realized Henry had his seat belt unbuckled and his hand on the door handle. "Of course." She unfastened her seat belt and climbed out of the car. Her toes immediately started protesting. The shoes she'd found at Vic's shop worked perfectly with the LBD Bonnie had helped her find, but they pinched. She'd bought them anyway because looking good at the dinner was more important than a little discomfort. Vic hadn't even let her pay for them. She'd told Tegan she'd take it out of the profits when Tegan's fox statue sold, and she'd waved away Tegan's protests that it might not sell at all.

Henry walked around the car and wrapped his arm around her shoulders. "What's got you smiling?"

"Just thinking about how nice your sister is."

"The nicest."

"She might be the only person who could make Bowen take a vacation. He said he was back in town to make sure all the details for the funeral were finalized, but that would have taken a day, tops, and the funeral is still more than a week away." Tegan looked up at Henry. "Are you really as okay with the two of them together as you seem?"

"I am. And if I wasn't, looking at Kenzie might have gotten me there. She's just a kid, same as Bowen was a kid back when we were in school."

"But Kenzie had at least some excuse for what she did. Maybe *excuse* isn't the right word. But she had reasons for feeling like she had to protect herself, even if that meant hurting someone else. Bowen had no excuse."

"At this point, what does it matter? It's done. If I couldn't accept that, the only one it would be hurting was me."

"You're a better person than I am."

"Not possible. You ready to go in?" Henry must have felt her shoulders tighten because he said, "You're going to like everybody. They're all really great people."

Yeah. Great people with great houses, great educations, and great jobs. Wait till they found out Tegan was a waitress/bartender, because it was going to come out. Somebody was going to ask the "So, what do you do?" question.

When they reached the front door, it swung open before Henry could ring the bell, and a woman with close-cropped black hair gestured them inside. "I'm so glad to have you here."

She was so sophisticated in a pair of high-waisted navy trousers, with a matching blazer thrown casually over her shoulders. Tegan suddenly felt overdressed and fussy. The feeling intensified when she walked into the living room and saw the other two women. One had a shawl tossed over her shoulders, the other a sweater. Clearly, Tegan should have had some item of clothing casually thrown or tossed.

Get over yourself. Being without a blazer, shawl, or sweater is not make-or-break. Don't turn it into a thing. You're maybe a little overdressed. So what? Better than showing up in sweats and flip-flops. She accepted a glass of wine from Winnie and tried to focus on the conversation. She'd been so deep in her own head that she hadn't even heard what anyone was saying.

Okay, it was just chitchat about some hospital change-up. Way to make her feel included, but whatever, at least she hadn't missed someone asking her a question.

Another glass of wine, a little more chitchat, this time about how it wouldn't be that long before Mr. Winnie—Tegan had missed his name during her internal blazer, shawl, sweater debate—could get the boat out on the lake. She smiled and even murmured something about how beautiful the lake was in the summer. Not scintillating, but better than saying nothing at all.

And, yes, into dinner. She'd made it maybe a quarter of the way through the night. She just had the meal, then maybe a little more convo back in the living room, and she'd be outta here.

She smiled through some discussion of med schools. One of the other couples—why hadn't she been paying attention during the introductions?—had a kid who was trying to decide which one to attend. Nothing Tegan could contribute to that, other than the price of Looped Fruits at the dollar store close to BU. But nobody asked. They could probably see from her lack of blazer, shawl, sweater that she wouldn't have anything useful to add. At least no one asked where she'd gone to school, so there was that.

Deciding that she'd gone too long without speaking, Tegan

complimented the paella. Food was a safe topic for her. Until a debate started on whether Mr. Winnie, who'd done the cooking, had used Bahia, Senia, or Bomba. It took Tegan a few moments to figure out those were kinds of rice, rice from Valencia. One of the people whose name she didn't know said she'd once used short-grain Japanese rice in a pinch, but it hadn't been the same. Tegan had a lot of experience rattling off the specials, but she'd never had to mention the locale of the rice.

It was okay, though, because dessert was up. That meant she'd gotten through maybe two-thirds of the night, maybe a little more. If predinner chat and dinner made up three-fourths, what was the dessert part of dinner plus postdinner chat? Didn't matter. She was definitely well beyond the halfway mark, and she hadn't done anything to embarrass herself, which meant she hadn't done anything to embarrass Henry. Well done, Tegan.

She'd just taken a sip of her coffee when, here it came: the what-do-you-do-Tegan? question. Keep it short, keep it simple, don't apologize, she coached herself. "I'm working over at Wit's Beginning. Almost everyone in Fox Crossing comes through. It's been good to see so many familiar faces from when I lived here."

That answer was about as good as she could do with what she had to work with. But she'd thought the part about familiar faces was a nice touch. Maybe she should have worked in the part about her grandfather being the mayor. Some of these people whose names she couldn't remember might even have known him. One of the couples was from Fox Crossing. She'd managed to register that detail.

"Tegan's an artist," Henry added. "She's been making some incredible found-object art pieces."

Incredible found-object art pieces? Seriously?

He was ashamed of her. That's where the found-object-art-pieces comment came from. He was trying to make her sound important enough to be sitting at a table with his hospital friends.

"I've just placed a few of them at Junk and Disorderly, which is quite exciting. There's an artist, I'm sure you know the one, who got his start selling knickknacks there. From the ten-cent table to the Frick in less than a year. If he can do it, why not me?"

Winnie smiled at her. "Why not, indeed?"

"I don't think I've heard of the artist. Someone who got their start in Fox Crossing?" the woman with the casually tossed shawl said.

"Kidding."

The woman looked puzzled.

"I was kidding."

"Ah." The woman gave a laugh, clearly forced. After a moment of uncomfortable, really uncomfortable, silence, everyone joined in the laughter. Bonus, the uncomfortableness may have sped up the dessert portion of the evening.

Tegan managed to get through the postdinner chitchat portion without causing another round of fake laughter or uncomfortable silence, then, finally, she and Henry were out of there.

Back in the car, she leaned her head against the window, letting the cold from the glass sink into her skin. She still felt hot though, hot and nauseous. Henry was ashamed of her. Which meant this whole thing that had started up between them was pointless.

She thought she'd caused the last uncomfortable silence of the night, but no. Here was another, and it was even more uncomfortable than the one at the dinner table, because this time it was between her and Henry.

"I'm not sure what happened back there," he finally said.

"Nothing."

"It wasn't nothing. It's like you wanted to wreck the night."

She shrugged, staring out the window into the blackness of

the woods that ran along both sides of the road. They drove past the WELCOME TO FOX CROSSING sign at the edge of town. In a few minutes, she'd be home. In a few minutes, this would be over. She'd be able to get away from him.

"That's it? You're not going to say anything?"

"What's there to say? Your friends didn't get my sense of humor."

"I didn't get it either."

Another reason for him to be ashamed to be with her. Not only did she have a crummy job, she couldn't even act like a person for the length of a dinner. She needed to end this now. It wasn't going to last anyway. It couldn't.

"I just . . . Look, I got a text from this guy I was with in El Paso right before we left for dinner. I thought I was over him. I really did. But I realized tonight, I'm not. This thing with us, whatever it is, it's not going to work, Henry. I'm sorry."

Even though they were only a few blocks from the house, Henry pulled over to the curb and stopped the car. "You're going back to El Paso?"

She straightened up and turned toward him. In the dim light from the streetlamps, she could see the pain on his face. Couldn't be helped. Some pain now to prevent even more pain later. "No. It's not like that. He doesn't want to get back together. But I . . . I keep thinking about him. I don't want to, but I can't stop. I'm sorry, Henry."

"We're breaking up then."

Tegan wanted to make sure there was no going back. "We weren't together, not really, right? It's only been a few weeks." She opened the door. "I'll just walk the rest of the way."

"At least let me drive—"

She shut the door before he could finish and started down the sidewalk, hoping he wouldn't come after her.

He didn't.

* * *

Bowen knew he should be making calls, setting up lunches—make that lunches, dinners, and drinks. He'd promised himself he was going to work as hard looking for a job as he'd ever worked at Garm. Then he'd decided he'd wait until after Vic's weeklong vacation was over, because every day they had a new hours-in-bed record to break.

But Vic started back to work at the shop on Wednesday. She was back on parent duty too. He'd gone with her to Friday's trivia game and tried to distract her when her mom's team won, meaning that her parents would have to be at the pub at the same time to compete for the championship. He knew it was a big deal to Vic, so he tried to take it seriously, but the solution was obvious. Can't stand seeing your soon-to-be ex? Skip the game. Recruit a friend to fill your place on the team. Henry or Vic would both be willing to jump in.

The solution to Bowen's situation was obvious too. He'd spent years building up a network of colleagues, bankers, investment partners—both current and potential. Time to make use of them.

He'd lost three days—three days, plus the week he took to be with Vic—that he could have been working those contacts. Then it was the weekend, and he didn't want to reach out to anyone on the weekend. That whiffed of desperation, and desperation stank like failure.

Monday morning, he should have been on it. And he'd . . . he'd checked on funeral arrangements that he knew were already in place. He'd taken Vic to lunch. He'd wondered what the hell was going on with Tegan because she was at maximum surliness. At least he hoped it was maximum. Vic said Tegan had had a falling-out with Henry, but that's all Vic knew, because Henry wouldn't give her details.

Also, Monday morning, people had a lot going. Lots of places had strategy meetings on Monday mornings. Waiting until Tuesday had seemed like a reasonable plan.

But on Tuesday, he'd . . . worked out, but not hard enough to evict the tension from his body. He'd had lunch with Vic, which had helped more than the workout, especially because the lunch had been in her bed.

After that, he'd . . . taken a nap. Probably because he hadn't gotten out of her bed when she'd returned to the shop. That night he'd gone with her to the retirement community and helped with the ten-cent-table sale she did there every week. Much more entertaining than he'd expected, although he should have known that anything involving Vic would be entertaining.

Today, he absolutely should have started making those calls, or at least shooting out some texts. But he'd had breakfast with Vic, a long breakfast, because Bonnie insisted Vic wasn't needed downstairs. Breakfast had gone so long it ran into lunch. And now it was getting close to time to pick up his father from the airport. He'd decided to come in a few days earlier than Bowen's mom. His father hadn't said so, but Bowen got the feeling his mother wanted to spend the shortest time possible in Fox Crossing. She was flying in the night before the funeral, and his parents were scheduled to head home the day after.

Bowen thought he should be able to start reaching out to his contacts tomorrow. He'd need to spend some time with his dad, at the very least making sure he didn't want to reconsider and take something more than the china bird, but there'd be plenty of time to start putting out feelers for a new job.

He heard his sister outside the study. He'd been hoping to catch her before he headed out. She was already pulling on her coat when he reached the foyer.

"I was thinking maybe Dad and I would eat dinner at Wit's. Would that be okay?" It didn't seem like something Bowen would need permission for, but right now, anything could piss Tegan off.

"Sure. Yeah. Let Dad see me slinging grub while you tell him all about your latest trillion-dollar deal."

"It wouldn't be like that."

"Yeah, it will. Unless someone spills a drink. Then he'll also get to see how I wrangle a mop. He'll be so proud." She grabbed the doorknob.

"I got fired."

Tegan turned back to face him, astonished. He hadn't told her before. He hadn't been planning to tell her now. Somehow, the words had come spilling out, which wasn't like him. He almost always thought about what response he was looking for, then decided what to say to make it happen. "I got fired. Which means I won't be telling Dad about my latest trillion-dollar deal."

"What happened?"

The blood began to rush in his ears, making his voice sound far away when he answered, "Basically, I wasn't worth the salary. They thought they could get someone junior to do everything I did while getting paid a lot less money."

"What bastards! What cheap bastards!"

He gave a surprised bark of laughter. She sounded outraged on his behalf. A few weeks ago, he'd probably just have gotten a snide remark about how he might have to hock his duffel bag. "Really cheap. Garm gives bonuses on the anniversary of the day the company was founded, instead of at the end of the year like most places. They booted me about two weeks before I would have gotten mine." Last year his had been more that 150K, but he wasn't going to tell Tegan that.

"Next time you're at Wit's I'll buy you a beer, although with what Granddad left you, I guess you won't be hurting." She said it like it was just an observation. A few weeks ago, there'd definitely have been a lot of anger mixed in. But even though she was hurting, even though almost everything was pissing her off, she was treating him like she cared about him, the way Henry might have treated Vic. "Just don't come tonight," Tegan added. "I know Dad doesn't care, but I'd rather not have him hanging out there while I'm working."

"We can all go out tomorrow. We'll spend some of Grand-dad's money."

"Steak for me then." She turned back toward the door.

"Teg. I basically know the answer to this, but I never asked." She turned to face him again, her expression wary. "What?"

"Did our grandfather offer to pay for you to go to college?"

"No."

"If you want to go, I'll pay."

"Everyone thinks there's something wrong with the way I am." She opened the door.

"It's not that, Tegan. It's righting a wrong."

This time she didn't turn back.

Tegan was still on Bowen's mind when he and his dad set-tled in at a table at the BBQ. Bowen had planned on taking him to the Fiddlehead, which his grandfather had decreed was the best restaurant in Bangor, but his dad had insisted that he was craving one of the pulled-pork sandwiches.

"Tonight, I asked Tegan if Granddad had offered to pay for her to go to college. All these years, and I never ever wondered."

"His view was education was an investment that led to em-ployment with compensation that made the investment worth-while. Nothing Tegan was interested in studying met that standard."

"I don't even know what kinds of classes she was taking when she was in school." The depth of his disinterest in his sister chilled Bowen. "I never even asked. What kind of person doesn't even ask?"

"Your grandfather taught you to focus on your goals to the exclusion of everything else. And I let him do it. I let him." His dad shook his head. "Back when we were living here, I was feel-ing pretty small, living in my father's house, working at a job my father got for me."

Bowen wanted to deny it. But it was true that his father hadn't been able to make it without Granddad's help.

"I should have gotten Tegan out of that house. I should have seen that he was making her feel small every day, same way he did to me. Letting that go on is one of the biggest regrets of my life. No, it is the biggest."

Bowen tried to imagine what his sister would be like if she'd never lived with his grandfather. Had her self-esteem taken such a hit back then that she'd never recovered? Back then. It wasn't just back then. It was still happening, to Tegan and his dad, by the way his grandfather had handled their inheritance.

"I regret that I didn't step in with you too. I didn't feel like I should have an opinion on anything. Who was I to have an opinion? I'd obviously screwed up my life beyond repair. So, I let him teach you what was important in life. That should have been me. That's a big regret too."

"But for me, it worked. I wouldn't be where I am today, if not for him." Bowen knew he could get back to where his grandfather wanted—expected—him to be.

"Are you sure you want to be where you are today? I'm not saying you don't. I just wonder if you ever let yourself think about other possibilities. You were very young when you were put on your path."

Any minute, his father was going to start talking about how Bowen should stop and smell the roses. He'd never understand that Bowen loved his job. He loved figuring out what people wanted, what would get them to yes. And he was good at it. Screw Garm, he was good at it.

Thinking of Garm turned up the loop that was still always running in his head. *I got fired. I got fired. I got fired.*

"He made it clear that you were your achievements. But that's not true. I hope you know that. I hope you don't feel as if you're nothing if you aren't where you should be on that ten-year plan. Because that's how I felt for years. Years."

Bowen got that. And he hated it for his father. But it had been different for Bowen. His grandfather hadn't made him feel small. He'd challenged him. Inspired him. He'd achieved what he had because his grandfather had guided him, and Bowen was never going to apologize for what he'd achieved.

His father cleared his throat. "Back then, I should have made it clear that I loved you whether you won a game or not, because I don't think you got that from him. And if I haven't made it clear now, I love you, and I love Tegan. Period. No qualifications."

Bowen felt blindsided. His family didn't talk like this. They didn't walk around saying, "I love you." He felt like he should say it back. He wanted to say it back, and finally, he did. "I love you too, Dad."

He knew he could tell his dad that he'd gotten fired. But he didn't want his father's sympathy. He wanted to get back out there. He wanted to show that Garm was wrong. He wanted to triumph.

That started with making those calls, sending those emails. He had to get that done.

CHAPTER 17

Every time the door to the pub swung open, Tegan expected Henry to walk in. She knew he'd be here to deal with any fall-out from his parents' being forced to share the space. She didn't want to see him. She'd have called in sick, but she knew Wit's would be packed, and she didn't want to leave Banana short-staffed. Other jobs, other bosses, she would have.

This time it was Cameron coming in, probably just off work from her super-important job. She took a seat at the two-top closest to the bar. Great. Like Tegan didn't already feel crappy enough without the condescension that Cameron would be flinging her way.

It's your job. Suck it up, she told herself, then slapped a smile on her face and headed over. "Wheat beer tonight, or are you switching it up?" She'd only served Cameron one time, but Tegan was good at remembering orders, faces, and names.

"Sure."

"Nachos? It's not our usual bottomless night, but Banana's making them bottomless in honor of the trivia championship."

"Too much for one person." Cameron sighed. "Is there

anything more pathetic than sitting in a bar alone on a Friday night? I shouldn't have come, but I couldn't deal with another night alone in my apartment, and I hate going to movies by myself. And you don't need to hear all this."

Tegan hadn't been expecting that. "This is the perfect place to be. You're never alone at Wit's if you don't want to be. There's an open seat up at the bar. Do you want to move? There's always good conversation going."

"I don't know. Maybe I'll just hide out here. I don't know how I ended up friendless."

"You're not friendless. Last time you were here you were with friends."

"Who I see once a month. Well, we say we'll see each other once a month, which usually turns into six weeks. Around the holidays, two months. I'm the only one who isn't married, and now Manda is pregnant, so I'll be the only one without kids." Cameron gave the coaster a spin. "You better go get me that beer, so I can cry in it."

She was trying to play it off, but Tegan could see Cameron was really hurting. "Come sit at the bar."

Cameron shook her head. "I'm not good company for anyone tonight, including myself."

"Be right back." Tegan hurried behind the bar, pausing in front of her dad. "Need anything?"

"I'm all good."

Tegan had asked her dad to come hang out at the pub. Bowen was going to be coming in with Vic, and Tegan hadn't wanted her dad spending the evening by himself in Grandfather's house. There was no reason to keep him away. He was the last person to be judgy about her job, judgy about anything.

Turned out Cameron wasn't judgy either. She had too much going on in her own life to be judgy about Tegan's.

The door swung open, and Henry walked in. Seeing him, seeing his kind, beautiful face, Tegan was slammed with the realization that Henry hadn't been judgy about her the night of the party. It wasn't in him. It just wasn't.

The person who *was* judgy about Tegan's life? Tegan.

Henry resisted the urge to look for Tegan as he followed Vic and Bowen inside. He was hyperaware she was somewhere in the pub. He didn't want to see her. He was still feeling too raw, even though he kept telling himself he shouldn't because, like she'd said, they'd only been together a few weeks.

The three of them took seats at a table that was close to the middle of the room, the no-man's-land between Quizly Bears and Smarty Pints territories. He allowed himself a quick scan of the place. He didn't want to see her, but he wanted to know where she was. He needed to prepare himself if she'd be coming by the table. Okay, she was behind the bar. Hopefully, she'd stay there.

"What are my rooting duties tonight? Clap for everybody or clap for nobody?" Bowen asked.

"What do you think, Henry?" Vic asked.

"I don't care."

His sister's eyes widened.

"That's not what I meant," Henry said quickly. He wanted Vic to know she had his support, although he wished she'd be able to distance herself, at least a little, from the situation between their parents. "What I meant was, I don't think it really matters what we do tonight. It all comes down to Mom and Dad." Henry was half wondering if his father had decided not to show. He was the only one from either team who hadn't arrived.

Jilly came over to take the table's order. Henry wondered if it was just luck of the draw, or if Tegan had asked her to cover the table because she didn't want to see him any more than he wanted to see her.

"Did you see the story about those Boothbay Harbor fishermen pulling in a woolly mammoth tooth?" Bowen asked.

Vic didn't answer. Her eyes kept flicking to the door. Clearly, she was wondering what was going on with their father too.

"Cool to think of mammoths walking around Maine," Henry answered, appreciating Bowen's effort to get a conversation going.

Vic checked her cell. "Nothing from Dad. Henry, check yours."

"Nothing."

"And the game is supposed to start in fifteen minutes." Vic started with the ring twisting.

"You can get here from any place in Fox Crossing in fifteen minutes," Bowen reminded her.

"For Dad, fifteen minutes early is late," she told him.

"Maybe he decided just to let Mom have the night," Henry offered.

Vic shook her head. "He wouldn't do that to the Quizlies. Even if he did, which he wouldn't, he would have let me know." Now she was twisting her ring so fast that Henry was sure her finger had to be burning. Bowen must have been thinking the same thing because he took her hand and kissed her palm.

Henry looked away, suddenly feeling like an intruder.

"We're embarrassing my brother," Vic said.

"No, not at all." Henry waved a hand. "Carry on." The back of his neck started to prickle and he had the irrational feeling that Tegan was looking at him. He told himself there was no way his body could sense her—

"Here you go." Tegan stepped up to the table with the drinks, even though Jilly had taken the order. "Can I talk to you for a sec, Henry?"

He wanted to say no, but there wasn't a reason to refuse. He now understood why his parents couldn't stand to be at the same place at the same time. He'd thought they were being stubborn and silly, but now he got that it hurt too much. He and Tegan had been together, what felt like together, anyway, for days. His parents had been married for decades.

"Sure." Henry stood and followed Tegan out the back door.

"There's no guy in El Paso. I lied," she said in a rush as soon as they were alone.

"No guy," he repeated, feeling off-balance. "Then why—"

"I wanted to end things between us. No going back. It felt like the easiest way."

"It worked." What was the point of telling him this? She'd wanted it over, it was over. Why drag it out by confessing the reason she'd given was fake?

"Tonight, I had this realization. I'm not a mind reader."

"I'm not following."

"Because you're not a mind reader either." She reached out and touched his arm.

Without thinking, he took a step back.

Tegan jammed her hands in her pockets. "Look, that night, at the dinner party, when you told everyone about the found-object art I was making, I thought you were telling them that to show them that I wasn't just a barmaid. I thought it was because you were ashamed of me. And once I thought that, I went ahead and blew everything up. Because what was the point of our being together if that's how you felt?"

"That's not how I felt."

"I know. That's not you. When we were kids, we were so close. I knew you at the core, same as you knew me. I know, with no reservation, that you are a good, and kind, and decent person. I don't know how I let myself forget all that."

Henry was trying to connect the dots, trying to understand. "You thought I was ashamed of you, so you started being rude to everyone at the party, then made up that old boyfriend?"

"I thought the longer I let it go on, the more it would hurt when it ended."

"Which makes sense, except for the part where it might not have ended."

"It felt like a done deal. But it was based on mind reading, which I guess, somehow, I thought I could do. Although if I could, I should be in Vegas, making millions." She laughed, but tears were in her eyes. "I'm sorry, Henry."

"I'm still not sure how you got to me being ashamed of you."

"I walked into that party feeling ashamed of myself. Everyone there had a better job, a better education, better clothes."

"Clothes? I love my sister, and you've seen what she walks around wearing." As soon as he said it, he realized a joke wasn't the way to make her feel better. "I wish you'd told me beforehand, Teg. We could have skipped it."

"There are going to be lots of parties like that for you. You should be with someone who can fit in. I don't."

"Maybe there are a few people who would look down on you, but I have no interest in being around anyone like that." He scrubbed the back of his neck with one hand. "I do mind reading sometimes myself. Remember the first night at the bar when I asked if you wanted to go out?"

Tegan nodded. "I was so happy to see you, so excited. Then I heard you talking to Banana, and I found out you were heading up the whole community-assessment thing, and I was sure you'd have no interest in someone working at a bar."

"When you said you were busy, I assumed it was because when you looked at me, you still saw the fat kid, and that you'd never be able to think about me any other way."

"Not true. Not at all true." Tegan glanced at the door. "I need to get back in. It's packed. But if you ever think you might want to go out again . . . I completely understand if you don't. But if—"

He'd heard everything he needed to hear and interrupted with a kiss.

"He'll probably be here any minute," Bowen said.

Vic nodded, resisting the urge to check her texts again, since she'd just set her phone down. "I keep thinking tonight might be the last time I see them together. I don't know what we'll do about visiting the grandparents. They moved to Florida at the same time and have condos right next door to each other. Usually, Henry, Mom and Dad, and I meet up there every September. I don't see how that trip can work now. The whole thing makes me sad." Vic ran her fingers though her hair, loosening her sparkly barrette. "I even had to have two birthday parties this year."

Bowen freed the barrette, smoothed back her hair.

He could be so incredibly sweet. "Thank you." She leaned her cheek against his hand. "For my birthday, I bought myself a journal that had a bunch of prompts, which made me realize that self-reflection can kind of suck. But one of the questions it asked was 'What do you need right now?' All I could think of was a doughnut, a doughnut with pink frosting and sprinkles."

"Want me to go get you one? I'll do a county-by-county search."

Vic shook her head. "I was just thinking that this"—she gestured back and forth between them—"is something I really needed. Don't panic," she added quickly. "I don't mean forever. I mean right in this moment, I'm really happy to have you with me."

"I'm happy to be here." He didn't sound freaked-out by what she'd said.

Henry dropped back into his seat. "I thought I might have missed the first question."

"We have about five minutes, but still no Dad." It had taken Vic a moment, but now she realized her brother looked markedly happier than he had when he'd left the table. "Good conversation with Tegan?"

"Very good."

"I'm glad."

In every picture taken of Henry when he was a little boy, he'd had his head tilted to one side, with a smile that seemed almost too big for his face. That's how he looked right now.

Henry hadn't given Vic details, but she'd known whatever had happened between him and Tegan had been devastating. Her heart had hurt for him. Now looking at him was giving her a burst of contact happiness.

"The Final Countdown" began to play. "At tonight's game, we have a substitution," Gavin said as the music faded. "Buddy Dyer will be taking Claude Michaud's place on the Quizly Bears team."

Vic's gut clenched when she heard her father's name. "Something's got to be wrong. Dad would have told us if he wasn't coming," Vic whispered to Henry.

"I'll swing by his place." Henry pulled on his jacket.

"First question. How long is New Zealand's Ninety Mile Beach?" Gavin asked.

"Fifty-five miles!"

There were gasps and cries of protest because the answer hadn't come from anyone on either team. The answer had come from Vic's dad. He stood in the doorway, mud smeared on his hands and face and pants.

"You are correct, sir!" Gavin called. "Correct, but inadmissible."

Vic's mother leaped to her feet. "Buddy is taking your place. You have no reason to be here. Out!" She pointed to the door.

He didn't move.

"I said go!"

He didn't move.

Gavin held up both hands. "Let's take a quick beer break while we sort out the players."

"On me!" Banana called. "Everybody up to the bar."

Nobody moved. People were looking back and forth between Vic's parents like spectators at a tennis match. Vic tried to decide what to do. Jump up and put herself between them?

"I have something to show you." Vic's father started walking toward her mother.

"You're too late. You can't be here. Don't you take one more step!" her mother shrieked.

"Fine." He stopped. "Do you recognize this?" Vic's dad raised his hand.

"Of course, I recognize it. It's a carrot."

What was going on? Had Vic's dad lost it?

"Not just a carrot." He pulled something off the carrot. Something small and metallic. "How about this? Do you recognize this?"

Vic's mother shook her head, and Vic's father threw the little object. Vic strained to see what it was as her mother bent down and picked it up, then wiped it clean with a napkin.

A ring. Vic's breath caught. Not just any ring. A wedding ring.

"I was taking a walk around the lake and ended up behind the cabin where we lived when we first married."

Henry grabbed Vic's hand, and she squeezed it tight. Their mother was trembling, but she didn't protest when their dad took a step closer.

"I saw The Fox out in back, digging, really going at it. When she saw me, she took off. I was curious, so I walked over. The top of a carrot was poking out of the ground, so I pulled it. The ring was around it. The dang carrot must have grown right through the ring. After all these years."

Vic's grip on her brother's hand tightened. Their father took another step. Tears began running down their mother's face. Everyone in the bar remained motionless.

"You threw it, remember? We had that fight about making coffee, and you threw it. We could never find it. I think it must have ended up in the compost heap and made its way into the soil." He shook his head, looking dazed. "I went home, but I couldn't put the carrot down. I realized I needed to bring it to you. The ring is yours. You should have it."

"I can't believe this. Can you believe this? I can't believe this," Vic whispered to Henry.

He didn't answer. His eyes were locked on their parents. Their mom shook her head. "It's not mine, not anymore." "It will always be yours. *I* will always be yours. This past year has shown me that." Tears stung Vic's eyes as she watched her father take the ring from her mother's hand and slide it onto her finger. The bar exploded into cheers when she flung her arms around his neck and kissed him. And kept on kissing him.

Vic felt like she had when she was a little girl and she'd twirl and twirl and twirl until she got so dizzy that she'd fall down. For a few moments, it always felt like the ground was spinning beneath her.

It had been maybe twenty minutes since her parents rushed out the pub door, hand in hand, and Vic still had that dizzy, giddy, unsteady feeling.

Tegan pushed a cold mug into Vic's hand. "Banana's buying everyone in the place a drink."

The trivia game had been rescheduled for the next night, but no one felt like leaving. All around her, Vic could hear people saying her parents' names. No one was talking about anything else.

"It's so crazy how in just a few minutes everything can change completely." Tegan smiled at Henry. "Everything can feel horrible and hopeless, then—boom!—everything turns wonderful." She put her hand on Bowen's shoulder. "That's going to happen for you, Bowen, I know it. You're going to get an even better job."

"Is that even possible? Your grandfather always made it sound like it was the . . ." Vic's words trailed off as she registered the stricken expression on Bowen's face.

"I was going to tell you," he said.

Tegan pressed her fingertips to her mouth. "I thought she knew. You told me, so I thought she knew. I'm so sorry, Bowen."

"Not your fault. You were right to assume I would have told

her." Bowen turned to Vic. "I should have told you. I got fired. A little more than two weeks ago."

"We've been together every day since then. You were lying to me this whole time?" Vic gripped the table with both hands. Her dizziness and unsteadiness increased, but all the giddiness drained out of her.

"Why don't we let you two talk." Henry stood.

"I'm sorry," Tegan said one more time, before she followed Henry over to the bar.

"All that time . . ." All those hours in her bed. Some of it had been rolling around in the sheets. Some of it had been sleeping. But a lot of it had been talking, talking about anything and everything. Except the biggest thing going on in his life. "I don't believe it." Strength surged back into her body, strength and raw fury. "I knew I never should have trusted you. People don't change that much." She got up. "Don't follow me."

"I told you not to follow me," Vic said as soon as he stepped into her shop.

"That was last night. I don't think this qualifies as following."

"Sorry not to be clear. I meant, don't come near me again. Ever."

Not acceptable. Bowan was *not* going to let it end like this. "I'd like to explain. I think you owe me that." As soon as he'd said *owe*, he'd known it was wrong word.

"*Owe?* How do I owe you anything?"

"Wait. Before you answer that, why don't you two move into the back." Bonnie jerked her chin toward a woman who had stopped going through a pile of scarves to stare.

"There's no need to move into the back because he's leaving," Vic told Bonnie.

"I shouldn't have said *owe*. You're right. You don't owe me anything. What I meant was, we've spent a lot of time together these last weeks. I thought—" Bowen stopped to adjust course. "I hoped that because of that time, you'd be willing to listen to an explanation."

She turned and strode into the back room. But she left the door ajar. That felt like, if not an invitation, then an opportunity. He shot a look at Bonnie for confirmation that he'd read the situation correctly.

"Go," she mouthed.

Vic didn't turn to face him when he joined her and shut the door behind him. She continued brushing the tangled hair of perhaps the ugliest doll he'd ever seen, and having been in her shop often, he'd seen a lot of ugly.

Focus, he told himself. He knew he didn't have much time. "When I got fired, I immediately wanted to see you. You and only you." Maybe it wasn't the right strategy, but it was the truth. And truth was vital here. She'd made that clear.

"We barely even know each other." She set the doll down, sighed, and turned to look at him. That was progress. Not a lot, but he'd take what he could get.

"We barely even know each other, but you told me about your mom cheating on your dad. You told me about Bonnie's daughter being bullied."

"Right. I told you those things. And in return? You lied to me!"

Well, he'd left himself open for that response. "I didn't tell you because I didn't want to think about it. And it's almost all I could think about. The only time I could stop thinking about how badly I screwed up was when I was with you."

"Screwed up how? What happened?"

"I wasn't good enough. They decided someone more junior could do my job and save them some money. Basically, they decided I wasn't worth my salary."

"So, you didn't actually screw up anything?"

"If I'd been of enough value, they'd have kept me. It's as

simple as that." Saying the words started acid churning in his belly and cranked the volume on the loop. *I got fired. I got fired. I got fired.* He forced himself to continue. "My grandfather made it to director by the time he was thirty-three. If he could do it, I should be able to, and now . . . Now I'm going to have to find a way to make up the time I've lost, if that's even possible."

"You're not sure you can get another job?"

"Of course, I can get another job. But I had a plan. A timetable. My grandfather and I came up with it before I started college. I was already a few months behind. I should have already gone back to the city. I should be working my contacts. I just—"

"Needed a break?" she asked gently, so gently. He hadn't been expecting that. He didn't deserve that. "After getting fired and losing your grandfather?"

"He wouldn't want me to use him as an excuse. He hated excuses. When I flubbed a play in the homecoming game when I was a junior, he didn't talk to me for a week, even though we still won. Not a word. My sister and my parents don't seem to remember that. All they remember is that I was his favorite. It didn't feel that way when I screwed up. If he'd lived long enough to see me get fired . . ."

"He'd what? Give you the silent treatment like when you were a boy?"

"The silent treatment makes it sound—" Bowen tried to come up with the right word.

"So immature? So petty?" Vic tossed out.

"He was keeping me motivated."

"Sounds like it came with a pretty high price. And I always thought you were loving every second of high school, so popular, Fitzy finalist, Mr. Baseball, prom king."

"Glory days. Didn't always feel like that from the inside."

Vic started twisting her ring. "I shouldn't have come down

on you so hard. I have a thing about lying. But that's not to do with you." Her toes were tapping now too.

"Because of what happened between your parents? The cheating?"

She closed her eyes and shook her head. "I've never told anyone this."

He moved closer and adjusted her barrette. It was about to fall out, as usual. "Told anyone what?"

She looked up at him. "Right before I got married, I found out my fiancé was cheating on me. Which meant that he'd been lying to me for months. I felt so stupid. I should have known. When you're that close to someone, you should know when they're lying."

"And you never told anyone? Not even Henry?"

"I didn't want anyone to know how pathetic I was. I told everyone I broke up with him, when he was the one who didn't want to be with me. I didn't want to . . ." She let out a long breath. "I didn't even want to think about it. And if I talked about it, I'd have to think about it. Like you. With getting fired."

He nodded.

"I'm sorry." She wrapped her arms around his neck.

He held her tight. "I'm sorry too."

"We still have a few days before you go back to New York. You want to stay with me until then?"

"Absolutely. And after then?"

"After then, you're there and I'm here."

True. He'd never expected anything long-term to develop between him and Victoria Michaud. But the idea of only having a few more days was unacceptable. "Is that open to negotiation?"

"I don't see how."

There had to be a way. He'd come up with it. He was an expert at getting to yes.

EPILOGUE

"Here they come!" Vic grabbed Henry's arm and gave it a squeeze as the sleigh pulled by two high-stepping Friesians started down Main Street. Their dad drove the team, and their mom stood in back, her Ms. Senior Fox Fest tiara glinting in the late-afternoon sunlight.

"Mom looks so beautiful." Henry waved to their mom, and she threw kisses back to him, Tegan, Vic, and Bowen.

Her hair was back to its Junior Miss Peach brown, and while she wasn't down to her beauty-pageant 113, she'd told Vic that she wasn't planning to try to lose any weight because Vic's father appreciated what the extra pounds did to her cleavage. Something Vic didn't need to know, although it was so good to have her somewhat-vain mother back.

The next sleigh was bigger, pulled by four horses instead of two. But even though Miss Fox Fest threw as many kisses as Ms. Senior Fox Fest, her smile wasn't quite as bright. Almost, but not quite.

Santa's sleigh came last. Vic caught a piece of the candy he threw, unwrapped it, and popped it into Bowen's mouth.

"Sweet," he said, and Vic was pretty sure he was talking about her, not the candy.

"I've got to get to Wit's. I bet most of the parade crowd is going to be over there in about two minutes," Tegan said.

"I know Wit's doesn't take reservations, but could you help a brother out? Since you're the manager and all." Bowen gave the pom-pom on top of her toboggan a tap.

"I'll save you a table as long as you get there in the next twenty minutes. Best I can do." With a kiss for Henry and a wave to Vic and Bowen, Tegan was off.

"I thought after that last piece of hers sold, she might quit Wit's." Vic looped her arm though Bowen's as they started down the sidewalk. "She can afford to make art full-time."

"She'd miss all her regulars too much. And Banana's crazy stories," Henry said. "I can't wait to hear the new tales he and Maisie come home with after traveling though the Outback."

"I need to stop for a sec at the shop. I want to get a picture of Addy and Kenzie's snow sculpture before it melts."

"I don't think it's in much danger of melting for the next few months." But Bowen pulled out his phone when they reached Junk & Disorderly and took a few pictures. Kenzie and Addy had made two snow foxes, one to each side of the five-foot found-object fox Tegan had made for the shop. They'd entered their work in the snow sculpture contest under the title *Outfoxed*. It had won second place.

Bonnie came outside to join them.

"I told you to close up so you could see the parade," Vic said.

"I had a great view through the front window, great and warm." Bonnie gave the big glittering fox a pat on the head. "I'm going to be eternally grateful to Tegan for this."

"It's definitely going to get a lot of attention when the hikers hit town. I think people will be able to see it all the way from Miss Violet's." Vic gave the fox a pat too.

"But that's not the best part." Bonnie adjusted her scarf,

black, of course, to go with her black sweater and black pants. "The best part is I no longer have to try to sell Barbie, Louie, or the swamel."

Vic grinned. Tegan had worked the swamel's neck or hump—*nemp?*—into the curve of the fox's tail, while Barbie and Louie, still side by side, made up part of the chest. "We're heading over to Wit's. You coming?"

"Can't. Samuel and I promised to take Kenzie and Addy to the movies."

"See you tomorrow, then." Vic gave Bonnie a quick hug, then she, Bowen, and Henry crossed the street, avoiding deposits by the sleigh-pulling horses, and headed into the pub. Tegan waved them to one of the few empty tables.

"I have an announcement." Bowen pulled a thick binder out of his nice leather satchel. Vic had several satchels at the shop she could have given him, but he refused to carry anything that had been touched by a Bedazzler. His loss. "I've come up with a new ten-year plan."

Vic suddenly felt as cold as if she'd been buried in snow. She'd known this was coming. Bowen had been living in town for almost a whole year after deciding to take some time to figure out if his grandfather's ten-year plan was still what Bowen wanted. Vic thought it particularly appropriate that Bowen's inheritance from his grandfather had allowed him to take all those months off.

"Let's hear it," Henry said.

Vic felt like putting her fingers in her ears and going, "La-la-la," but that wouldn't change what Bowen was about to say. She was almost positive that his plan was going to involve moving away from Fox Crossing. Away from her.

"I've decided to start a financial technology company."

"And I'm already confused," Vic admitted.

"Maybe that's because only twenty-one states require high school students to take a personal finance course. My company is going to be for them, combining banking services and financial guidance. I've already found a partner bank that won't charge any fees."

"How's that even possible?" Henry asked. "Don't banks make an insane amount on overdraft fees?"

"Yes, but I made the case that we can charge companies to advertise on the app. I'm also going to get them to post internships. There will be student loan offers, too, since not everyone has a grandfather willing to pay for college."

"Sounds great," Vic said. Because if this is what Bowen wanted, she wanted him to have it. They'd had a good run.

"I'm my own angel, but I've already had some good talks with possible investors about series A funding."

"Now I really don't know what you're talking about." Vic was trying to pay attention, but she kept wondering what this meant. How much longer would she have him with her?

"Basically, I can get the money to make this work because I am very good at getting a yes. Speaking of which . . ."

Suddenly he was down on one knee, pulling a little box out of his pocket, a little box with a ring inside. "Any chance I can get a yes from you?"

Vic laughed. "You want to marry me?"

"Is that such a surprise? We've been pretty much living together."

"I thought you were just taking a break from your real life."

"It started out that way. But the longer I was here, the more I couldn't imagine living anyplace else. Or being with anyone else."

There was a pop, and champagne showered down on them. "I could kind of see where this was going." Tegan put glasses down on the table and began filling them.

"A little premature. I haven't gotten an answer yet." Bowen took her hand in his. "Will you marry me, Victoria? You can wear a patchwork wedding dress covered with sequins. Hell,

I'll wear a patchwork tuxedo covered with sequins if that's what you want."

"Yes. Yes, yes, yes!"

She could hardly believe it. She was going to marry freaking Bowen Gower.

The Fox trotted through the town. The connection cords were especially bright tonight and she wanted to enjoy them. Then she turned for home. From the top of her mountain, the cords of the humans gave the whole town a glow. She was part of that glow because she was connected to each of them. Connected to them, and all the creatures of her woods, and the trees, and the lake, and the clouds, and the moon, and the stars. Connected to those in the past and those yet to come.

She opened her senses, allowing herself to feel each of those connections at the same moment, until the mountain turned as bright as the town, until the whole world glowed.

Keep Reading for a Special Excerpt!

CRAZY LIKE A FOX

Melinda Metz

Return to the charming mountain town of Fox Crossing, Maine—where nature lovers are welcome, the locals are friendly, and a single glimpse of a legendary fox can change your life forever.

Most people think The Fox is just a folktale, designed to lure tourists to the quiet little town on the Appalachian Trail. But kindergarten teacher Lillian Smith is hoping the stories of the white-eared, white-pawed vixen—who brings luck and love to those who see her—are all true. After a chance sighting of the fabled fox, Lillian hopes her hiker boyfriend, Owen, will finally propose. Instead, he publicly dumps her, claiming she's not adventurous enough. Lillian's determined to prove him wrong. But she could sure use some of that foxy magic to win him back. . . .

Luckily, Lillian is not alone. She has her good friend Gavin, the local Boots Camp worker, who agrees to help her reinvent herself—even though he thinks she's fine the way she is. Then there are the townsfolk who also claim to have caught glimpses of The Fox: an offbeat musician with a downbeat career, a not-so-fortunate couple who've forgotten just how lucky they are, and a playwright whose life needs a second act. But if the fox legend is true, things always have a way of working out—for those crazy enough to keep believing. . . .

Look for *Crazy Like a Fox*, on sale now!

CHAPTER 1

"You obviously don't want me to come, so fine. I'm not coming."

Gavin watched as Rebecca yanked her duffle out of the trunk, wincing as he heard the ping of metal hitting metal. The big buckle on her bag had hit his bumper, leaving a small scratch in the Copenhagen Blue paint of his Porsche 944. No big. He could polish it out. Probably wouldn't take more than toothpaste.

Rebecca laughed, pulling Gavin out of his thoughts. "For a second, it actually seemed as if you were bothered that I'm not going with you. But you're more bothered by that." She pointed at the scratch. "And you can hardly even see it." She grabbed the handle of the suitcase that matched the duffle, giving a grunt as she tried to heave it free from the trunk. Gavin took it away from her and lowered it safely to the ground. One of its wheels could have done some serious damage.

"So, that's it. You're just going to help me get my stuff out of your car, and bye-bye?"

What did she want from him? She'd already decided. Or else

she was being dramatic. Rebecca was one of those women who thrived on drama. Look at her, eyes sparkling, cheeks flushed. Kinda unfair that she was extra hot when he wanted to be around her the least. "I never said I didn't want you to come."

"Of course, you didn't. That's not you. You never actually say anything. You just find little ways to push me away." Rebecca slammed the trunk so hard the car jounced. "You're Mr. Passive Aggressive."

"Where does that come from?" It wasn't the first time she'd thrown the accusation at him. It was one of her go-tos whenever they had a fight. And every time it sounded like made-up psychobabble crap.

Rebecca laughed again. Sometimes he hated the sound of her laugh. "Where? So many places. Like when my friend Sofia was in town. My oldest friend. I could tell you didn't want to meet her, not that you said so. Of course, like always, you pretended everything was fine, then you showed up late and said you'd already eaten. You didn't even order an appetizer, just sat there pouting."

That was unfair on a multitude of levels. "That was more than two months ago, Rebecca." It was like she kept a database of every wrong move he'd made. Everything she *considered* a wrong move. Most of them weren't anything. Including this one. "And, like I explained at the time, my study group ran late, because Dom showed up without the notes. I couldn't leave until we'd gone over all the material, or I wouldn't have passed the final."

He half expected her to jump on him for still being in school at twenty-seven, one of her usual fight moves. Even though, what did it matter? So he'd taken a few semesters off, changed his major a couple times. He was almost finished now, just a few more credits left. Since she didn't start with the school stuff, he kept going. "And, like I told you, somebody got hungry, so we ordered pizza, which is why I was late and didn't feel like eating. But I got there. Who cares if I ate or not? And it's not like the two of you didn't have plenty to talk about before I got there." He'd already explained this to her easily twenty times, but it was like she didn't even hear him. "If you're being honest, I bet you were even glad to have some time without me around. I'm sure Sofia had stuff she wanted to say to you that she didn't want to talk about in front of a stranger."

"That's not the point. The point is—passive aggressive. Like now. You don't want me to come with you. But instead of saying so, you start doing all the things you know make me crazy, like playing your video game so late that I went to bed without you on Saturday, and then yesterday, I wanted to make us a nice dinner for our last night in the apartment, so I decided to make the marinara from scratch. And what do you do? You kept sneaking in red pepper flakes until it was so spicy, I knew if I ate it, we'd have to stop at every gas station between here and Maine. So I had to have Cheerios."

"You eat lots of spicy food. You—"

She held up one hand like she was directing traffic and wanted him to stop. So, he stopped. Even though that hand was as bad as interrupting, and she always got on his case for interrupting her.

"I can eat some spicy food, just not spicy food that also has tomatoes, which I know that you know. And you've been acting like a jerk for weeks in all kinds of ways, just so I'd get mad enough to tell you to go by yourself. Well, it worked. Go by yourself. I'm done. We're done."

"Because I put in a few too many red pepper flakes?" Unbelievable.

"No. That's not what I'm saying. I'm saying you've been pushing me away in all kinds of little ways, nothing too big, nothing you couldn't dismiss as me being crazy."

Gavin couldn't stop a sigh. "You *are* being crazy, Bec. Why wouldn't I want you to come? Are you PMSing or what?" He should have known that was the wrong thing to say. The expected explosion came fast and hard.

"See? And now you want to make it my fault. Because that's you. You never accept the blame for anything." She pulled out her phone. "If you had just been upfront and said you wanted to break up, I wouldn't be standing here calling an Uber to go to my sister's because I sublet our place, without your help, thank you very much, and I did it because . . . because I don't know. I should have seen this coming a mile away. You've been acting like a jerk for the past month. You've probably been freaking out because I kept giving you more chances instead of kicking you to the curb."

Her voice was getting that quaver, and he could tell she was moments away from crying, and he didn't even know why. Nothing she'd said was any big thing. One night when he went to bed after her. Or maybe a few nights, because he'd had that tournament. And a few too many pepper flakes? And the thing with her friend? It wasn't like he blew it off. He'd been a little late, yeah, and yeah, he hadn't ordered anything, which made no difference whatsoever. He had been there, what did it matter if he ate or not? And it was freaking months ago. But he couldn't say any of that, because now she was crying.

He pulled in a deep breath and gave it one more try. "Rebecca, we just moved in together a few months ago. Why would I have agreed to that if I didn't want to be with you?"

"You agreed to it. You *agreed* to it," she said again, her voice getting higher and more quavery. "Like you were doing me some kind of favor?"

"No. That's not what— Do you have to analyze every word? I just talk, you know. I just . . . talk. What I meant was, we just moved in together. Why would we have moved in together if I didn't want to be with you all the time?"

"I don't know. Maybe that's something you should do some

thinking about. Although, what does it matter now? We're over."

Should he try to change her mind? She sounded absolutely definite. "Well, okay, this is good-bye then." She didn't look up, even though he was sure she'd finished putting the address in.

He got in the car. When he glanced in the rearview mirror as he pulled away from the curb, Rebecca's head was still lowered toward her phone. Gavin got some Nick Cave going. Rebecca used to complain about the less-than-pure sound quality that came out of the Porsche's stereo when he used the FM transmitter and his phone, but it made Cave sound even better, especially the old stuff. Gavin tilted the sunroof and cranked the music as loud as it would go, until he could feel it in his bones. With every mile down I-95, he felt the Rebecca-induced stress sliding out of his body. He gave all his focus to the music and the feel of the car, the tightness of the hydraulic power steering, the sound of the exhaust and the occasional rattle, the precision of the shifter.

About three and a half hours out of Newark, he got himself a Hot Mess sub, emphasis on the hot, at Cowabunga, a place he'd discovered road-trippin' it a few years before. Definitely not something Miss Rebecca would want to put in her delicate tum-tum. He took it down to the beach and kicked off his shoes so he could dig his toes in the sand while he ate. Warm sun. Good eats. Salt air. Life was good.

Back in the car he got some Limp Bizkit going, a move Rebecca would probably call passive-aggressive if she was with him. She always said it was angry music, and that he should have grown out of it. But, hell, his father hadn't been a teenager when he and Gavin were listening together. It brought up great memories of hanging out with his dad, and it was perfect driving music, although it did feel kinda out of place once he was off the highway on a dirt road with pines rising up on either side, like green walls.

He cut the music, and, a few seconds later, he spotted a sign up ahead that read "Welcome to Fox Crossing, Maine. Founded 1805," and smiled. This was what he needed. A real, old-school summer vacation. He deserved it. He'd busted his butt this semester and had worked almost full-time at his barista gig. And that was another thing Rebecca had disapproved of. His lack of a real job. But that's why he was in school, to get the marketing degree to get a real job. And, anyway, the tip money was prime. So yeah. He deserved some vacay. He'd be working, yeah, but mostly outside as an instructor getting hikers prepped for hiking the Appalachian Trail. Not exactly hard labor. It would—

Gavin slammed on the brakes hard enough for the Porsche to fishtail. "Please, you go first," he muttered as a fox trotted across the road in front of the car, taking her time, unfazed by the sound of him screeching to a stop to keep from mowing her down. Strange-looking fox. The tip of the tail was black instead of white, and one sock was white instead of black.

Guess I should have taken that sign more literally, he thought as he watched the fox make her way under the Fox Crossing sign and disappear between a couple blueberry bushes. He did a quick check of both sides of the road to make sure there were no more critters headed his way, then put on the gas, eager to see the town again. He'd only spent a night there back when he had been hiking this end of the AT, so it would be mostly new. Gavin loved new. Maybe he'd meet someone. Have a nice, fun summer fling to go along with the summer vacation. Yeah, this summer in Fox Crossing was going to be exactly what he needed.

"A charm of foxes," Lillian Smith murmured, her gaze traveling around the cozy shop, taking in the fox kites flying near the ceiling, the string of cute little copper fox bells tied to the doorknob, fox socks waving from the clothesline stretched across the bay window, the fox pillows on the window seat beneath, the fox—

"I almost called the shop that." Lillian turned toward the voice and saw a petite woman, maybe in her seventies, with a pair of cloth fox ears perched on top of her head. "But I ended up going with Vixen's. I own the place, and I thought the name suited me as well as the store. Not in the ill-tempered sense. I'm as sweet as Honey, which is my name or at least what everyone calls me. My actual name is Ruth Allis, and I'm a vixen, in the sexually attractive sense." She winked at Lillian, and gave her skirt, a fifties-style poodle number, but with a fox where the poodle would usually be, a flirty swish-swish. "I've still got it."

"I can see that." But an endless number of coffee dates from a slew of dating apps had proven that she didn't have even a smidge. Her mother said all Lillian had to do was get herself out there, so she'd gotten herself out there. Over and over and over again. It wasn't that she didn't have the, well, the assets, but she didn't have the attitude. She couldn't flirt. At all. It made her feel squirmy and embarrassed, so squirmy and embarrassed that most of the time all she'd wanted was to put in enough time that she could leave. Usually, it seemed like the guy, whatever guy, had felt the same way.

Her stomach tensed as the negative thoughts threatened to take her over. She pictured them as little rat-like things with dozens and dozens of pointy yellow teeth. You know how to deal with them, she told herself. She imagined herself holding a glittery wand with a star on top. She flicked her wand at the rats—zing!—turning them into beautiful dappled gray horses that then galloped away.

Why did she still let those thoughts get to her? She didn't have to know how to flirt, not anymore. Not since Owen. Somehow, he'd had the patience to get through her squirmy and embarrassed, not to mention her awkward and shy, to see, well, what she thought of as the real her. And now, she was almost, pretty sure almost, about to be engaged to him. To be married to him. There had been a time when it had seemed there was no chance she'd be married before she was thirty, but then she had met Owen.

Honey chuckled. "I was just about to start telling you about how every single girl needs a little something foxy, but then I saw that smile come out. You've got the smile of a girl who's already lucky in love. Just nod if I'm right."

Lillian nodded once, then followed it up with five or six fast head bobs. "My boyfriend's doing a section hike. Last year he did Springer to Harpers Ferry. This year, Katahdin to Harpers. We're both teachers, me kindergarten, him sixth grade, and that's how we'll be spending this summer. I just dropped him off at Baxter State Park." Wow. She was talking a lot. And fast. She was just nervous. Excited. Nervous-excited. "He had me make a reservation at the Quarryman Inn the night he plans to arrive in Fox Crossing. I think, maybe, he might, maybe . . ." Lillian couldn't quite bring herself to say it. She might jinx it. That's where all the nervous-excited was coming from.

"Might pop the question?" Honey finished for her.

Lillian managed to keep it to one nod this time, her cheeks warming. "We're going to be able to spend the whole summer together. Well, in bits. Any time he gets to a town, I'll be there. And he hinted that maybe we'd kick off the summer by getting engaged. He showed me some rings in a window and asked which one I liked."

"It sounds like a done deal to me, then. A man doesn't show a woman engagement rings unless he's serious. But even though you don't need any fox luck on that front, you have to see the panties we carry." Honey winked. "I'm sure your man would like to see them—on you. There are some with little foxes all over, but my favorites are the ones with the fox face, just over the— Well, I'll let you see for yourself."

Lillian followed Honey deeper into the store, even though she liked her matching beige bra-and-panty sets. They worked with everything. Smooth lines, nothing to show through her clothes. Not that her clothes were see-through-able. She'd tried sexier lingerie a few times, but it gave her that same feeling trying to flirt did, just a squirmy sensation, and Owen seemed happy with her usual practical things.

"I have to know the story of your charm of foxes. There has to be a story, and I love stories," Lillian said as she looked at the undies display. Not for her, but she definitely wanted to buy something, a keepsake to remember the cute little town, especially if Owen ended up proposing to her here.

"Of course, there's a story, the story of how Fox Crossing came to be." Honey straightened her fox ears, then fluffed her blond curls. "It started with a fox, of course, and my husband's great-great-great-grandmother, Annabelle Hatherley. She'd recently been widowed, left with a little baby. The people of the settlement did what they could to help her, but they didn't have much to give. The community was one bad winter away from annihilation, and that winter was closing in. And even with all her sorrow, wondering how she and her child would survive, when she saw a fox with her leg caught in a trap, Annabelle saved it. My theory is that she couldn't stand the thought of even one more death, no matter how small. She took it home and some say—"

Honey leaned closer and lowered her voice. "Some say she nursed it with the same milk she used to feed her little boy, the milk from her own breast. The Fox survived, and so did the settlement. It wasn't too long after that that one of the settlers, Celyn Hanmer, discovered slate on Annabelle Hatherley's land, and that was the start of the Fox Crossing Mine Company. That company turned the settlement into a thriving town. Some say it never would have happened if Annabelle hadn't saved The Fox, and the mine and the town and my store were named after the vixen."

Honey adjusted the position of a ceramic fox on the shelf of a nearby curio cabinet. She was clearly waiting for Lillian to beg her to go on, and Lillian was happy to oblige. "I'm missing the connection. How did The Fox play a part in Celyn's finding the slate?" The way Honey said "The Fox," made it sound like it should be capitalized for extra importance, so that's how Lillian saw it in her mind, and she gave it the same emphasis when she said the words.

Honey made a second adjustment to the ceramic fox, then continued. "It so happened that a fox, The Fox, Annabelle Hatherley's fox, caused Celyn's horse to shy and dump Celyn on his butt. He had to go after the animal, and, when he did, he saw something sparkling in a cliffside. He knew it was mica. He'd done mining back in Wales before he immigrated, so he knew that where there's mica, there's usually slate. He had the knowhow, and Annabelle had the land. They teamed up on the mine. Some say that fox is still with us and that whoever sees it shares its luck. I'm one of them. I know—"

The shop door opened with a bang, setting the fox bells tinkling, and a little girl, brown hair pulled back with easily a dozen multicolored barrettes, maybe about eight years old, raced over to Honey and flung her arms around her waist. Honey took a step back to absorb the impact, then hugged the girl tight. "This is Evie," she told Lillian. "My great-niece," she added in a whisper.

The girl let Honey go. "She doesn't like the 'great' part. She thinks it makes her sound old. I'm staying here with Honey for the whole summer! Honey always comes to visit us, but, finally, I get to see Fox Crossing." She pulled a business card cut into the shape of a magnifying glass out of the bright blue purse she carried and handed it to Lillian. It read:

Evie Hendricks
P.I. (Private Investigator)
with the P.I. (Powerful Intelligence) to solve your
P.I. (Pressing Inquiries)
555-542-1743

"If you need my services, call the number. It's my sister Kristina's phone. My parents won't let me have one, even though I've explained that it's essential for my detective work and that if I got a special number that spelled out 'Call Evie P.I.,' I would earn more than enough money for a cell and the fees. I explained it would be a P.I., Priceless Investment, and they still said no. But Kristina will take a message if I'm not with her."

Lillian carefully slid the card into her wallet. "I'll only be here for about a week and a half, but you'll be the first person I call if I come across a mystery."

"Or it can just be if there's something you want me to find out for you. My mother says no secret is safe from me. For example, I know that you work at a preschool, that you have a boyfriend, and that although most visitors to this town are hikers, you are not."

"I was just telling Honey I'm a kindergarten teacher, so very, very close. But how did you know?"

"Your purse has a child's fingerprint on it in what I suspect is finger paint. She touched the small orange oval, which Lillian hadn't noticed. "Some might have thought that meant you had a young child, but I observed that you are wearing a silk blouse. My mom says she hasn't worn anything that isn't machine washable since my sister was born, so I deduced you work with little kids. Your tote says 'Miss Violet's Boardinghouse for Trail Widows,' and you aren't wearing a wedding ring, so I deduced you have a boyfriend, one who is out hiking. And if you were a hiker, you'd be with him; also, you wouldn't be nearly as clean or smell so nice."

The little girl had only looked at Lillian for about ten seconds before she'd made all those deductions. "Wow. I'm so impressed! Or should I say that I admire your"—Lillian paused for a moment, thinking—"Preternatural Insights?"

Evie grinned. "I don't actually know what that first word means, but it sounds good."

"Preternatural means extraordinary. A lot of times people use it to mean psychic."

"Thanks! I'm adding that to my list of *p* words. I'm not psychic, though, just observant. I know pretty much everything about everyone I meet," Evie bragged. "Like I knew there was some secret about my sister, Kristina. My parents knew something was wrong. I heard them talking about it. But they didn't know what. I investigated and found out she was being bullied by—"

Honey placed one hand over Evie's mouth. "She's bubbly. She gets that from me." She kissed the top of Evie's head. "Let's let Kristina talk about Kristina. I want to hear about you." She slid her hand away, and Evie immediately started talking again.

"Me? My Field Day team came in first in the Mummy Relay. I was the mummy. Everybody had to take toilet paper and—"

The fox bells on the door jingled, and a girl around fourteen, presumably Kristina, walked in, followed by a tall, white-haired man.

"Kristina! Get yourself over here!" Honey threw open her arms. The girl hugged her great-aunt as tightly as her little sister had. Lillian turned and picked up a fox paperweight from the curio and turned it over in her hands, trying to ease herself away from the family reunion.

Honey put her hand on Lillian's arm, pulling her into the group. "This is my gorgeous great-niece Kristina." She said "great-niece" in a whisper. "She gets the gorgeous from me."

Lillian didn't quite see how a great-aunt had passed down traits to her great-nieces, but Honey sounded certain that she deserved the credit. "And that's my gorgeous husband Charlie."

"He just had a birthday," Evie volunteered. "He's seventy-four years old and—"

"I'm much younger than he is," Honey cut in.

"She's actually—" Evie began.

"One more word, and it's the last you'll ever utter," Charlie warned. "I love you, but I will not be able to stop your Honey from plucking out your tongue." He wrapped his arm around Evie's shoulders. "Come on. We just got in an order of gummy fox candy, and they need a taste tester." He guided her through a curtain, fox print, of course, that must lead to the back room.

"I'm related to them. They have to think I'm gorgeous," Kristina muttered to Lillian, not quite meeting Lillian's gaze.

Lillian disagreed. Maybe Kristina wasn't *gorgeous* gorgeous, but she had lovely skin, her light brown hair was glossy, and her brown eyes were large and striking, flecked with gold. Lillian didn't try to tell Kristina that, knowing it would make her even more uncomfortable than she already seemed.

"We think you're gorgeous because you're gorgeous," Honey insisted.

"Honey was just telling me how Fox Crossing got its name." Lillian thought the girl could use a subject change.

Kristina smiled, a dimple appearing in one cheek. "I love that story. Start over, Honey."

Honey took off her fox ears and put them on Kristina's head. "You know it by heart. I tell it every time I come to visit. You tell . . ." She looked at Lillian. "We didn't get to names, at least not yours."

"Lillian Smith."

"You tell Lillian the rest. I was just saying how some of us believe The Fox is still with us."

Kristina shook her head. "No, you go. You tell it better."

"Somebody please tell me," Lillian begged. "The Fox would have to be more than two hundred years old! Or did you mean people see a ghost fox? Or feel The Fox's spirit?"

"Not the spirit, the actual fox!" Evie called. Her voice sounded like it had to make its way through a mouthful of those gummy foxes. A second later, she popped back through the curtain. She swallowed hard, then continued, "It's still living in the woods. Last year, my cousin Annie saw it, and if she hadn't, her boyfriend, well, he's her boyfriend now, would have died. He'd fallen into a river and gotten hypothermia, and The Fox got her to him just in time. She saved his life, but she wouldn't have if it weren't for The Fox. And the two of them never would have gotten together. Kristina is hoping she'll see it, now that we're finally getting to visit, because she—"

"How do people know it's the same fox?" Lillian asked. She didn't like to interrupt, and she hated the possibility of ruining the story with such a mundane question, but she had the feeling Evie had been about to say something that would mortify her sister.

"Evie, you still have a few more flavors to try," Charlie called, and Evie returned to the back room, throwing a wave over her shoulder.

"We know it's the same fox because Annabelle Hatherley wrote about it in her diary," Kristina explained. "She said it had one ear that was almost white, and that it had white on one leg where most foxes have black. And the tip of its tail is black, and ordinary foxes have white tips, not black."

"And everybody who has seen it has good luck. Everyone!" Evie yelled from the back, her words again sounding like they were pushing their way through gummy candy.

Lillian was enchanted. The story felt like a beautiful fairy tale, but with no poison apples or treacherous wolves. "That is the best story. Thank you for sharing. I think I want this." She plucked a necklace with a delicate silver chain from the jewelry holder on the curio. The small silver fox charm was beautifully detailed. "You can never have too much luck, right?"

"Right," Honey and Kristina answered in unison.

A few minutes later, Lillian was walking back toward Miss Violet's Boardinghouse, the fox charm resting lightly at the base of her throat. She pressed her fingers against it, and her heart gave a little flip. It was definitely going to happen. When Owen got to town, they'd have dinner at the inn, and he'd propose. She had the luck of The Fox on her side.

Not that she believed the story. Now back when she was Evie's age, she would have believed with her whole heart. She'd believed in wishing on the evening star, birthday candles, and dandelion fluff, and she'd had a collection of lucky pennies she'd found that she saved for use in wishing wells. Actually, she still made wishes, but she was a grown-up now and knew wishes didn't have any actual power. She'd loved hearing the tale, but she didn't actually believe it either.

Still, since she had a few days in Fox Crossing, maybe she'd take a few walks in the woods. She'd been wanting to get a closer look at the lake anyway. And if she happened to see a fox with unusual markings . . . Well, it would be the product of some genetic mutation that had gotten passed on through the years, but it would be fun to get a glimpse of the town's local legend. Especially before Owen arrived in Fox Crossing.

Gavin grinned as he stepped into Wit's Beginning, his friend's pub. Banana stood on the bar, taking a bow. Gavin joined in the applause. When he had stopped to get gas a few towns back, he'd seen a tweet from Banana announcing that Banana had finally earned his damn mug.

Banana gave anyone who hiked the entire Appalachian Trail a special mug, and a mug full of their drink of choice every day for life. No one who wasn't a 2,000-miler was allowed one, and, until earlier today, that had included Banana. He'd hiked everything but the 100-Mile Wilderness, which started outside Fox Crossing, multiple times, but something had always stopped him from getting through that hundred-mile stretch, a couple times injuries, a couple times helping other people who got injured, a freak hailstorm once, and an assortment of other types of bad luck. That's how he and Gavin had met. Three years ago, Gavin and his then-girlfriend, Niri, had spotted Banana doing first aid on a hiker who'd fallen off an embankment and busted a leg. They'd stopped to help, and Gavin and Banana had been in touch on and off since then. It was Banana who'd hooked Gavin up with the summer gig teaching hikers what they needed to make it through the Wilderness—and the rest of the trail.

"Gavin! Welcome, my friend!" Banana scrambled off the bar and started toward him, pausing again and again for handshakes, back slaps, and hugs. "You made it," he said, when he reached Gavin, then gave him a hug, enveloping him with a cloud of just-off-the-trail stank. Brought back good memories. He looked good. He had to be sixty-something now, but his frame was still wiry, without the paunch a lot of guys his age sported.

"No, *you* made it. You made it through the Wilderness." As soon as the words were out of his mouth, the old Madonna song started playing in Gavin's brain, and he couldn't resist. He planted his hands on Banana's shoulders and started to sing in his best falsetto, which was pretty damn good, if he did say so himself. Heads immediately started to turn, and Gavin gestured for the crowd to join in. A few minutes later, he had everybody, except for a few clueless and/or inhibited ones, serenading Banana with "Like a Virgin." When Banana managed to stop laughing, he started singing too, then took another bow, get ting even more applause.

"You're as crazy as ever," he told Gavin. "How'd you even know all the lyrics anyway? You weren't even born when Madonna put on the veil."

"I had a part-time gig hosting a karaoke night for a while. Heard it many, many times."

"Come on. Let me introduce you to Annie and Nick. They co-own the Boots Camp." Banana led the way through the crowd, getting stopped every few feet for more love. Banana was one of those guys who turned acquaintances into friends within minutes.

Gavin was sure there were a ton of locals in the place tonight, but he bet there were some who'd just met Banana and that they'd been applauding as hard as the people who'd known him for years. Gavin knew the power of the Banana. He'd made lots of buddies on the trail, but Banana was almost the only one he kept up with. He'd instabonded with the guy. Probably partly because they'd teamed up to get that hiker to the hospital, which involved swimming across a lake while towing him. But only partly. The rest was just Banana.

"Here's your new instructor," Banana announced as he came to a stop in front of a booth where a man and a woman, both around Gavin's age, clearly a couple, were sitting. The guy got to his feet and stuck out his hand. "I'm Nick. And this is Annie. Have a seat."

"Good to have you here." Annie reached across Nick so she could shake Gavin's hand too. "We only have a few courses going right now, but we're ramping up for the summer. Next Wednesday, we start the Boots Camp, the six-week intensive training course."

"Looking forward to it."

"Got your mug?" Banana asked.

"Would I walk into this place without my mug?" Gavin pulled it out of his backpack, and Banana took it from him.

"Spirited Banana?"

"Of course." The Spirited Banana was one of Banana's specialty microbrews.

Banana took a few steps toward the bar, then turned back. "Where's Psychick?" he asked, using the trail name of Gavin's old girlfriend. Well, former fiancée. Gavin didn't usually think of Niri that way, because she'd only been his fiancée for about two months. She'd also helped with the trail rescue. He hadn't told Banana they'd broken up? He could have sworn he had.

"Uh. We're not together anymore." Maybe he'd just leave it at that. He didn't need to get into how he'd started up a relationship with someone new—and then broken up with her too. With a couple more things, nothing serious, in between.

Banana sat down across from Gavin. "What happened?"

What had happened with Niri? He hadn't thought about it in a while. There wasn't one big thing that had led to his breakup. It wasn't like she'd cheated on him—or that he'd cheated on her—nothing like that. "I guess, I don't know, maybe we were on different timetables. I'd, let's say, taken a break from college, and was always working a couple jobs, which meant some nights and weekends. She'd just started working as a budget analyst and was all about the career." Gavin shrugged. Banana looked at him for a long moment, then stood back up. "I'll go get that drink."

Hopefully, when Banana got back, he'd wouldn't try to find out more about the breakup. Banana had a talent for getting people to spill their guts. Maybe it was a bartender thing. And Gavin preferred to keep his guts in place. "So, Banana said that you just started Boots last summer?" he asked. He definitely didn't want to do anymore talking about his relationship history with his new bosses.

"Yeah, Nick decided to try to put me out of business." Annie gave Nick's knee a squeeze.

"Actually, I wanted to team up with Hatherley's Outfitters,

which has been in Annie's family since before the town was even a town, but she refused."

"Because he decided to start a business practically overnight. It might have been two nights. And I had no desire to team up with someone who was so impulsive. I didn't think he'd even make it through the summer." Annie took a swig of her beer. "And then he starts making money. And just because he gave good customer service, while my Yelp reviews said I was, among other appellations, surly."

"Surly? Really?" Gavin wasn't getting any of that vibe from her, although she'd shot him an assessing glance when he'd been telling Banana about Niri. He'd probably sounded like a slacker, with the college break and low-ambition jobs. Not something a boss wanted in an employee. But, come on, none of that mattered when you were a hiking instructor. What mattered was time on the trail, and Gavin had that.

"If Annie thought you were ready to take on the Wilderness, she'd be sweet as sugar. If not, well, watch out." Nick smiled at Annie, and Gavin could see he was a goner, totally in love. "She has an incredibly big heart. She doesn't want anyone to get hurt. Sometimes that concern came out as—"

"Surly," Annie and Nick finished together.

"Which is why being an instructor at Boots is a much better fit for her than retail," Nick continued. "You'll need to put in some hours in the barn on the Boots grounds. We sell stuff there, and Annie and her family still have the Outfitters in town."

"Which is doing nicely, now that I'm no longer on the premises," Annie added.

Which didn't seem to bother her at all, Gavin thought. Good for her. Gotta play to your strengths. "I've been told that I'm charming." One of his strengths. "I've never done sales, not exactly, but I made a lot of tips serving up lattes, and I think that's because I gave good customer service. Not just making the drinks right. Remembering names, remembering all the little details they'd tell me about their lives. And I'm definitely familiar with pretty much all the hiking gear out there."

Nick pushed his horn-rimmed glasses—what Rebecca would have called geek chic—higher on his nose. "I'll get you on the schedule."

Gavin nodded, mind still on Rebecca. They'd had some good times together. He pulled out his cell, planning to shoot her a quick text, tell her how much she'd love it here. Maybe she'd decide to come out, and give him—them—another shot. Then he saw a barmaid with a laden tray weaving her way through the crowd, black hair, short skirt showing off long legs, smattering of freckles. He loved freckles, and wondered if she had them all over. Playing connect-the-dots on soft skin was one of his favorite activities. He put the phone away. He had been right when he'd pulled into town. It was time for a summer of fun with someone new. He caught the barmaid's eye and smiled, and got a smile back.

Old friend. Cool job. A smile from a cutie. What else did he need? Life was good.

"How'd you like your place? Does it have everything you need?" Annie asked.

Banana had set Gavin up with a summer sublet from a guy who was out on the trail. "Great. Great view of the lake. And more kitchen stuff than I know what to do with. Seriously, there was one thing, a metal cylinder with another cylinder on top that had a zigzaggy top. I have no idea what it does."

Nick laughed. "That would be a corn stripper, takes corn off the cob."

"Which seems kind of pointless when it's so easy to eat when it's on."

"I would have had no idea what it was either," Annie admitted. "Nick does all the cooking. Except breakfast. I pour a mean bowl of cereal. But most mornings we eat at Flappy

Jacks. If you're not into cooking, it's right on Main Street. Good food, good prices."

"I remember it. I hit it for one of those massive breakfasts before I started into the Wilderness. I'm sure I'll be a regular," Gavin answered as Banana sat back down and passed Gavin his beer.

"Looks like that fox luck is still with you. Congrats on earning the mug, man," a guy said to Banana as he passed by the booth.

Gavin had almost forgotten about the legend of the town fox, but Banana had been obsessed with seeing it. He'd gotten convinced a sighting was the only way he'd finally get through the Wilderness. "You really, honestly believe that some varmint has magical powers? Or is it just one of the tales you like to spin?" Banana had an endless supply of tall tales, one of the things that made him such entertaining company on the trail.

"Everything that passes my lips is the honest-to-heaven truth." Banana tried to look deeply offended as Nick, Annie, and Gavin laughed in his face.

"I can't vouch for the rest of what comes out of his mouth, but I will say The Fox saved my life," Nick answered.

"Actually, I saved his life," Annie said. "If I hadn't found him and dragged his frozen ass to the hospital, he'd have died of hypothermia."

"But she wouldn't have known she needed to find me, if she hadn't seen The Fox. She pulled out her phone to take a picture—and then she decided to check the tracker app to see how I was doing."

"Because I knew he wasn't ready for the Wilderness. For one thing, his calves, while very nice, did not have the circumference of those of someone who'd done the necessary conditioning."

"And because she saw The Fox and then checked the tracker when she had the phone out, she knew I was in trouble. She could tell I had been swept into the river, although it wasn't the actual me, it was my backpack with the tracker in it."

"So, you can take that as The Fox bringing him the luck he needed to survive. Or you can take that as me making sure he had a tracker before he left my store."

"I say a little of both," Banana told them, then turned to Nick. "And last year, I saw The Fox right before I got the call from my daughter asking if I'd take care of my granddaughter, Jordan, over the summer. Changed my life."

That was one of the things that Gavin and Banana had talked about when Gavin was avoiding talking about his relationship. He knew how much it meant that Banana had gotten close to both his granddaughter and his daughter after years with nothing but polite exchanges of Christmas and birthday gifts.

"I thought seeing it meant I'd finally get those last miles in, but what The Fox luck brought me was something much better."

"You know what? I think I saw The Fox on my way in."

Banana slammed his mug down on the table. "What?"

"It had weird markings. Your fox has weird markings, right?" The story Banana had told Gavin on the trail was coming back. "Mostly white ear, a white sock."

"Black tail tip." Banana ran his hand over his bald head. "You saw it?"

"Right as I was heading into town."

"Well, hold on to your butt, son, because, somehow, someway, your life is about to change."

CHAPTER 2

Lillian smiled as she heard Miss Violet reaching for one of the high notes in the Queen of the Night aria—and missing by quite a bit. She was giving it her all though, her voice charged with wrath and the desire for vengeance. Lillian realized she missed opera. She and another teacher and the teacher's husband used to have season tickets to the Asheville Light Opera, but she'd let her subscription slide around three years ago. She hadn't wanted to waste any Saturday nights, when she could be spending them with Owen.

Miss Violet hit, almost hit, another high note with gusto. The proprietress of the Boardinghouse for Trail Widows always sang when she made breakfast, which meant it was time to head downstairs. But first—Lillian pulled up the tracker app on her cell and checked on Owen. He was making good progress. He should make it into Fox Crossing about five and a half days from now, with time for a nap and a shower before their dinner reservation at the Quarryman Inn. She gave her fox pendant a tap for luck, the way she did every time she thought of their reunion dinner.

She started toward the door, then paused as she caught a glimpse of herself in the cheval mirror, a beautiful piece with a frame of cherry wood. A lock of her long, curly blond hair had escaped from her ponytail, and she tucked it back into place, then she pulled in a long, deep breath. She didn't have anything to feel anxious about, but tell her stomach that. It wasn't in knots, but it was tight. She'd been the only guest at the boardinghouse the first three nights, but last night, two other women—Ginger and Bailey—had checked in. Sometimes Lillian had a hard time talking to new people.

She took another step toward the door, then turned back to the mirror. Maybe she should change. The sky-blue T-shirt was one of her favorites, but it was slim cut. Was it too tight? She could never decide. Sometimes having big breasts was great, but sometimes . . . not so much. She got more than her share of embarrassing comments—some of them yelled from across the street. She wished Owen were there. He always told her if he thought she was wearing something that didn't make her look her best.

Should she change? She'd found sky-blue nail polish at the town mercantile that was an exact match to the shirt, and she'd used it to paint her toenails. On impulse, she'd bought a little package of tiny stick-on rhinestones and put them on her toenails too. They made her think of stars in a sunny summer sky, which wasn't possible, because stars and the sun weren't out at the same time, but which would be beautiful if it were possible. Owen only liked nail polish that was red or pink, but she'd have plenty of time to repaint her toes before he got to town, and it had amused her to paint them blue while she was hanging out in the room last night.

She wouldn't change, she decided. But then she thought of the two women downstairs. She'd been wearing a baggy shirt last night when she'd briefly chatted with them over tea and cookies in Miss Violet's parlor. Would they sneak looks at her chest? Because it wasn't only guys who looked. She was never sure if women were doing a comparison, and maybe wishing theirs were more like hers, or if they were thinking that she was somehow slutty.

Wand time, she told herself. She imagined zinging all the crazy, negative rat-thoughts, turning them into beautiful horses, and watching them gallop away. Other people had their own lives. Nobody was spending that much time thinking about her. Lillian was always reminding herself of that. But so many times when she'd been out with her mother, her mother would make these snide little comments about the women around them. That one had on too much makeup. No man wanted a woman with that much gunk smeared on. That one didn't wear any. Who thought they looked good with no makeup?

With a growl of frustration, Lillian grabbed a button-down from the dresser and pulled it on. Left unbuttoned it made her breasts less obvious. There. Now she was ready to go downstairs. It would be fine. No, it should be better than fine. Pleasant. It would be pleasant. Bailey and Ginger were both perfectly nice. Sitting at a table with them for breakfast should be fine. Pleasant.

So, get down there, she told herself. After one more deep breath and one last look in the mirror, she left the room and followed the sounds of Miss Violet's warblings to the kitchen. Ginger and Bailey were already seated at the big kitchen table.

Lillian did a quick mental review of what she'd learned about the two women the night before. Ginger's boyfriend, a college professor, had just started a SoBo hike, and would go as far as he could before he had to go back to school. Bailey's husband was just hiking to Chairback Gap and back, so she'd only be in town a few more days.

Lillian's mother would say Bailey, with gray streaking her brown hair and an extra twenty pounds, was all but asking her husband to cheat on her. Lillian's mom had no patience for women who, in her opinion, had let themselves go once they got married. In her mother's opinion, a woman had to work as hard to keep a man as she did to get him in the first place. Not that keeping her hair colored and her weight the same as when she was a high school cheerleader had stopped Lillian's dad from cheating. Cheating, then leaving, back when Lillian was little. There were times Lillian was so tempted to remind her mom of that, but she never did. It would hurt her mom too much.

Ginger, on the other hand, would get full points from Mom, her hair falling in perfect waves, nails newly manicured, and a fresh, no-makeup look that Lillian knew from experience took a half an hour in front of the mirror to achieve.

"Morning," Lillian said, taking what, after only three days, had become her usual seat. She gave herself a mental reminder not to slouch. She had a tendency to hunch her shoulders, a bad habit Owen had helped her break. Miss Violet, still singing, headed for the table carrying a platter of scrambled eggs and home fries fresh from the skillet. She began to set them down, then froze, the platter a few inches from its destination. Her song petered out.

"Are you all right, Miss Violet?" Ginger exclaimed.

"Miss Violet!" Bailey cried.

Lillian gently tugged the platter away and set it down. "Miss Violet?" The woman's eyes were glassy. "This happens some-times when she gets an idea," she explained to the other women. "She's a writer." Lillian gave Miss Violet's arm a light pat.

Miss Violet blinked once, twice, three times, then smiled. "I apologize, sweeties. I'm working on the end-of-summer play, and sometimes I get lost in my imagination. I thought I just had an idea that would work, but no." She gave a dramatic sigh. Everything about Miss Lillian was dramatic.

"What's the play about?" Bailey asked, spooning some eggs onto her plate.

"It's about—I'm not sure what it's about. Nothing feels right, so I keep starting again. It's vexing. Usually by now I'd have the whole thing done. I don't understand it. I never have writer's block."

"I'm sure it will come to you." Lillian gave Miss Violet's arm another pat.

"Of course, it will, my sweet." Miss Violet whirled around, setting her long lavender scarf flying, returned to the stove and pulled a baking sheet full of enormous cinnamon rolls out of the oven. She began to hum as she used a spatula to transfer the buns onto another serving platter. The humming turned to singing as she put the platter on the table, and the singing grew in pitch and enthusiasm as she wandered out of the room.

Lillian didn't know what her mother would make of Miss Violet. Probably she'd think it was pathetic of a woman who was pushing sixty—hard—to try to attract so much attention to herself, with those purple python-print wedge heels and the couldn't-be-natural red hair. By "trying to attract attention," Lillian's mother would mean trying to attract male attention, but Lillian got the sense that Miss Violet dressed to please herself and no one else, and that her style was part of what she'd heard Miss Violet describe as her "creative spirit."

"I think Miss V just got another new idea." Ginger picked up one of the rolls and dropped it on her plate, then waved her fingers. "Maybe wait a minute before you touch those."

"She reminds me of Jo March," Bailey commented.

Lillian smiled. Bailey and Ginger were both being so nice and normal. No side-eye. No hint of attitude. "Genius burns."

"Exactly." Bailey took a sip of pineapple juice. On her first day, Miss Violet had said every meal needed some flair, and Lillian thought the juice—served with little purple parasols—was this breakfast's.

"I don't get it." Ginger used one finger to test the temperature of the cinnamon roll.

"You know, *Little Women*," Bailey said. "That's what Jo's sisters would ask when she was frantically scribbling away on one of her stories or plays. 'Does genius burn, Jo?'"

Ginger shrugged. "I watched part of the movie, the one with what's her name from that movie where her father trained her to be an assassin since she was practically a baby."

"Saoirse Ronan," Bailey and Lillian said together.

"Sounds right. But I fell asleep. I'm horrible about falling asleep in movies. I fell asleep in all three parts of *Lord of the Rings*. Bryan was ready to dump me. He wrote his dissertation on some connection between Germanic heroes and the heroes in that movie—book. It had something to do with Beowulf. He's a Tolkiendil. I've learned not to say Tolkienite, unless I want to watch his head explode, which every once in a while, I admit I find amusing." Ginger laughed, then popped a piece of the roll into her mouth. "Still a little too hot, but worth the slight tongue damage," she said once she'd had a long swallow of her juice.

"I'm the opposite of you," Bailey told Ginger. "I live for movies. I like to sit right up front, so the screen fills my whole field of vision. The best part is, I know for those two hours—I go to the theater; I don't like watching at home—the phone won't ring and the text won't ping. If there's nothing I want to see, sometimes I'll go anyway, just for that. Sometimes, I'll treat myself to a triple feature, if I really need that down time."

She was talking like she didn't even have a husband. "Didn't that cut into Stan's conditioning time?" Lillian asked. A triple feature had to be six hours minimum, but probably more than that with time between shows and meal breaks. That meant pretty much a whole day off, and when you were prepping to hike even part of the Wilderness, you didn't take days off.

"Pfft." Bailey gave a dismissive hand wave. "I go by myself. Stan can't sit still for even one movie. He used to make me nuts wriggling around, then making trip after trip back to the lobby for a soda, then popcorn, then bathroom. And then he'd act like it was my fault that he got off his training regimen by eating junk. Our relationship got much better when we agreed to spend our Saturdays apart. He does his hiking thing. I do my movies, swim, hang with friends, and he hikes. Then Sunday is couple day. He gets in a short hike, but he makes sure he starts at dawn and is home and out of the shower in time to take me to brunch."

Lillian couldn't imagine going to the movies by herself, even if she were willing to give up the Owen time she got as they drove to and from whatever trail he'd chosen to tackle. She'd feel like everyone was looking at her, at the pathetic woman who obviously couldn't get someone to go to the movies with her.

"I hike with Bryan some, but only day hikes." Ginger pinched off another piece of her cinnamon roll and popped it into her mouth. "I spent one night in one of the shelters, and I'm never doing it again. A mouse ran right across my face, and one of the hikers was emitting baked-bean-and-beer farts all night long. Dis-gus-ting. What about you, Lillian?"

"I don't walk fast enough to do day hikes with Owen. Sometimes I'll do a little stroll on my own, then find a nice rock where I can sit and read in the sun. Or I go back to the car if the weather's icky," Lillian answered. "Speaking of Owen, I'm going to head out to the Boots Barn after breakfast to set up a food drop. You want to come, Bailey? Bryan will probably be needing fresh supplies before he gets through the Wilderness."

"He should have enough to make it from Katahdin to town. He prides himself on his ability to hike miles on one stick of jerky." Bailey shrugged. "I've stopped trying to understand it."

"Owen could definitely carry in everything he needed." Lillian somehow felt the need to defend him. "But I like to get him some little extras. A drop for Bryan could be a fun surprise, let him know you're thinking of him."

"He'd just get annoyed. I'd be messing up his man-against-wilderness thing, although it's not like he doesn't bring in multiple pouches of beef stroganoff. It's not exactly living off the land." Ginger shook her head, smiling fondly. "There are lots of things I don't get about him. And same goes for him about me. He is baffled by my desire to soak in the tub for two or three hours. He thinks of it as marinating in dirty water, although I've explained to him that I don't get all that dirty in a day of HR drama. On the important stuff, we're in sync, though. That's what matters. I'm going to go check out Junk and Disorderly. There's a local carpenter who makes beautiful things, and he sells them through the shop. Either of you want to come with? It's almost around the corner from here."

"Me." Bailey raised her hand like a schoolgirl.

"Mmmm." Lillian was tempted. She loved searching for treasure in junk stores. "Better not. I want to make sure I get the order in in time for it to be at White House Landing when Owen gets there."

"We should do dinner together," Ginger said.

Lillian had planned on making a quick dinner in Miss Violet's kitchen. Breakfast was the only meal served at the boardinghouse. That's what Lillian had done the last few nights, because she didn't want to sit in a restaurant by herself. But Ginger and Bailey were friendly. And the few times she'd gone out with Owen and his work friends, he had complained she didn't talk enough. This would give her some practice. "I'd like that."

Day four working at the Boots Barn, and Gavin had broken his sales record every day. Wasn't hard. The merchandise was high quality, and the prices were fair. Gavin stretched out in one of the hammocks displayed toward the back of the barn, along with some tents, and used one foot to get a gentle rocking motion going. Excellent breakfast in his belly. Some hammock time. Satisfaction of a job well done. Life was good.

"See, I told Nick you were industrious and hardworking," Banana called as he came through the big double doors.

Gavin grinned and kept swinging. "Inventory done. Shelf straightening done. New sign for sock sale done. Just waitin' until it's time to open up."

Banana walked over to the new display, where Gavin had strung a bunch of socks from fishing line over a sign that said "These'll Blow Your (Old) Socks Off!" Banana nodded his approval. "You been over to Flappy Jacks yet?"

"Yeah, including this morning. That omelet with the blueberries? I'm now addicted."

"Next time, sit in the last booth on the right."

"How come?"

"That would be telling."

"And you love to tell, so tell."

Banana grinned. "Actually, I can do better." He pulled his cell out of his pocket, tapped the screen a few times, then walked over and held it in front of Gavin.

"Wow." Gavin climbed out of the hammock and held out his hand for the phone so he could get a closer look. Banana handed it over, and Gavin stared down at the pic of the booth's tabletop—and the dozens of pictures of hikers under the glass. Including one of him and Niri, looking grungy as hell. Happy as hell too. "Blast from the past," he muttered.

"Three years ago."

"Feels like ten, and like a couple months ago at the same time." Gavin took a last look at Niri's smiling face. They'd burned hot for a while. Hot enough to get engaged. But . . . He gave a mental shrug and handed Banana back his phone.

Banana looked at the picture for a moment before he put the phone back in his pocket. "And, you said you split up because of timetables being out of sync? I didn't want to call bullshit on you in front of Nick and Annie that first night, but, I call bullshit. You two were good together. So, what really happened?"

Crap. "Honestly?"

"Otherwise, what's the point?"

"Honestly, I don't even know." Banana just stared at him. "I'm serious. I can't really remember. We just fizzled."

"I'm missing something. You were together when we talked about you two coming up here for the summer, and you're saying you can't remember why you split. It should still be raw."

Gavin had been hoping he wouldn't have to explain, but he wasn't going to lie to Banana's face. "The girl I was with when we talked, that wasn't Niri."

"You broke up with Psychick, got together with another woman, broke up with her, and you never said anything." Gavin thought Banana would start hitting him with questions, but he didn't say anything. "And you two were together how long?"

"Me and Niri?" Banana nodded. "A little more than a year. We didn't last that long after we finished the hike. It was one of those trail things. You know how things get really intense out there."

"Yeah." Banana drew the word out, sounding dubious. "But you two were engaged before you started the hike. Or do I have it wrong?"

"No. You're right." Gavin really didn't want to be having this conversation. The whole Niri thing, ancient history. No point in picking it apart. But Banana kept looking at him, not asking anything, but looking with that Banana stop-bullshitting-me face. "I gotta straighten up the maps before we open." Gavin turned and started for the display. The one he'd straightened as soon as he came in. He only made it about three steps, then he couldn't take being that guy, the guy who couldn't give a friend a straight answer.

He turned around. "Okay. You're right. Things were serious between Niri and me before we hit the trail. We were hiking the Wilderness partly to celebrate getting engaged. When we got back, we even started looking at houses. Her parents were going to help us with the down payment." His chest was feeling tight. This is why he didn't like looking back. And what was the point? It wasn't like it changed anything. "And . . . and I know I should have some big reason we split. You don't just break an engagement over nothing. But, I swear to you, there wasn't anything I can point to and say, yeah, that's what ended it. Maybe it's just because I was twenty-four. I had no business thinking of getting married."

Gavin tried to put himself back there, back to the day they broke it off. They'd been looking at houses. And . . ." Dang, it was fuzzy. It should be something that stuck in his memory. "I remember that I didn't like one of the houses we were looking at," he said slowly, trying to pull it up in his mind's eye. "She got pissed. Really pissed. Way out of proportion. And then I said something like, 'if we can't even agree on where to live, maybe we shouldn't be doing this.' Then she said maybe we shouldn't. And that was it. We just stared at each other. She started crying. . . ." Gavin shook his head. "She pulled off the ring. I took it. And that was it."

"You didn't talk about it again, after you'd both had a chance to cool off? Making a big purchase like a house, it can make anybody a little nuts."

"We didn't." Had she tried to call? Left him a message? He didn't think so. "And the more days that went by, the harder it felt, until it basically felt impossible. And that's it. That's the story of the end of Gavin and Niri."

"That's rough. If we were at the bar, I'd buy you a drink. So, you're owed a drink."

"I'll take it." Relief washed through Gavin. Banana wasn't going to try to suck more details out of him and analyze it all. Because Banana was a dude, for starters. "Although, it was probably a good thing. I'm not ready for marriage now, forget about three years ago. "

Banana rubbed the corner of one eye. "I was just reading that the brain isn't fully developed until age twenty-seven. So maybe now that you're firing on all cylinders that will change."

Gavin laughed. "Maybe. But I'm not looking for anything serious or long-term right now. I want some down time, no fights and craziness."

"Who wouldn't want a break from that? You know there are actually some relationships where fights and craziness aren't the norm."

"I was thinking we should get in more of a variety of Fox Crossing merch."

Banana held up both hands. "Okay, hint taken. No more relationship talk."

"I'm serious. Those socks with the LL Bean logo on them sell like crazy. All I have to do is point them out, tell them the mountain on the logo is Katahdin, and—sold. Hikers love this town. If we got in some—"

The door swung open, interrupting him. The woman standing there was like something from a fifties pin-up calendar, all curves, though she'd done a decent job disguising them under that shirt she wore on top of her tee. Had to be at least a couple sizes too big. "Are you open? Or am I too early?" she asked.

"We're open, and if we weren't, I'd open up just for you." He heard Banana give a snort, but ignored him. Yeah, what he'd said had been a little cheesy, but who cared? The important thing was he hadn't just stood there gawping at her.

"I'm interested in setting up a food drop at White House Landing. It needs to be there by Tuesday night."

"Sure. I can hook you up. You just need to choose the food." Gavin walked over to the wall with all the packets, protein bars, and other trail food and gestured for her to join him. "Is it for you . . ."

"Me? No. I'd never make it. I'm a walking through the park type."

He wasn't surprised. She looked soft. Not that that was a bad thing. But there was a look hikers got, men and women, and she didn't have it. Those cute little toes of hers, the nails painted sky blue with little sparkly bits stuck on, had clearly not spent time in a pair of hiking boots. For starters, all the nails were intact. No abrasions or bunions. No pieces of Leukotape covering blisters.

The toes on her left foot gave a little wiggle, and Gavin realized he'd been staring. At her feet. Like a freak. "So, you're looking for about five days' worth of supplies, I'm guessing. That right, Twinkle Toes?"

She gave a startled laugh. "You clearly haven't seen me dance."

"I betcha got some moves. But I was thinkin' more like twinkle, twinkle little star." He nodded toward her feet.

"If they were stars, they'd have to be on dark blue, right?"

"But stars in the sky on a summer day? I like it. And I think there's such a thing as too much reality."

"I completely agree." They locked eyes for a moment, and Gavin felt a rush of heat, then she blinked and turned away, reaching for a pack of tortillas. "Owen, my boyfriend, that's who the supplies are for, is getting sick of tortillas, but I know bread doesn't last well in a pack."

Boyfriend. Of course, boyfriend. A woman didn't walk around with the curves, and that curly blond hair—wasted, pulled back in a pony, but still—and those cute little toes, and not have a boyfriend. Oh, well. Couldn't win them all, so back to work. "You could go with bagels. Not as delicate as bread," Gavin suggested. "Or you could do crackers. I always tied some to my pack with a bandana."

"I think he'd like crackers. I'll send a bandana too."

"Maybe some pork rinds? They take a little more room, but

if he's sick of tortillas, he might like something with a little crunch. They're crammed with protein."

"I find them disgusting, but, good idea. I know he'll need more salmon packets and noodles and instant potatoes and nuts. He'll need more Greenbelly Meals. And seaweed. Because if he's eating pork rinds, he should also be eating something green, whether he likes it or not."

Gavin loaded her picks into a basket. "You know your stuff. Your guy couldn't ask for a better trail angel." He hoped the boyfriend appreciated her. She was really looking out for him.

"Thanks." She was blushing. There was something about a blushing woman. Always got him thinking about sex. He bet she got a full-body glow going when she— Not what he should be thinkin' about. He was working here. He wanted to break his sales record again today. And he thought she'd just asked him something.

"Sorry. What was that?" He didn't offer an explanation for zoning out. It wasn't like he could tell her the truth.

"Can I put other things beside food in the drop? I wanted to send some socks."

"Clean, dry socks. Doesn't get much better than that on the trail." Gavin led her over to the display he'd made. She laughed when she saw the "These'll Blow Your (Old) Socks Off" sign. Gavin loved making a woman laugh, and her laugh was an especially good one, throaty and full. And somehow, he was thinking about sex again. "If you want to really spoil your guy, get him a silk bag liner," he said, after she'd added a few pairs of socks to the basket.

"Already did. Present for him starting this summer's section of the hike."

"How about one of these little massage rollers. Only three inches around, but it really kneads out the muscles, and if he's getting plantar fasciitis pain, like most hikers do, this thing really helps."

"I'll take it. Hopefully, he won't toss it and complain that it was a waste of space. I usually do pretty well choosing things, but there have been some that he handed off or trashed immediately."

She didn't sound put out about it. If Rebecca had bought him— He shoved the thought away. They were over. Why waste time thinking about her?

"I guess I shouldn't get anything else. Too much weight. Unless you can think of anything vital I'm forgetting."

Every ounce counted out on the trail, and Gavin wasn't going to load her order with stuff that would just end up getting tossed. Making sales was one thing. Wasting someone's money, that was something else. "Not unless you want something for yourself. We have some killer chocolate. My fave is a milk chocolate bar with nuts and dried cranberries covered with a dark chocolate shell."

"Sounds amazing. I'll take one." She pulled the edges of that loose button-down she wore closer together. Had he been staring again? He turned away and headed for the cash register— and the display of chocolate beside it.

"Would it be okay if I add in something for the drop that I didn't buy here?" she asked. "I know some places don't allow that."

"That's not a problem."

"Oh, good." She dug around in her bag and pulled out a pale green envelope. The name *Owen* was written on the front in penmanship that looked like it belonged on a fancy invitation. "Nice handwriting," Gavin commented as he took it from her.

"Thanks. I perfected it writing the name of my crush on all my notebooks back in the seventh grade." And there was the blush again. "And I can't believe I just said that."

"I wish a girl like you had had a crush on me back when I was in the seventh grade. Although, I probably couldn't have worked a girlfriend into my packed schedule of smoking pot and Legend of Zelda marathons. Got turned on to that one by my dad. Actually, the pot too. Him and my mom. They gave me a bong on my thirteenth birthday."

"What?"

He'd shocked her. To him, his parents were just his parents, and he'd always found them pretty dang cool. But they weren't exactly conventional. "They were of the do-it-at-home-where-we-can-keep-an-eye-on-you school of thought." Sort of. They also just really liked to party. "So, what happened with this crush of yours?"

"Nothing. I'm not sure he even knew my name. If he'd ever spoken to me, I'd probably have had to race straight to the bathroom." He raised his eyebrows. "I always have to pee when I get nervous, and talking to him, talking to any boy back then, would have made me extremely nervous. And I *really* can't believe I just said that."

"If it'll make you feel better, I'll tell something embarrassing about myself. Okay, I told you I played Zelda, but I played tons of other stuff too, and I unlocked the Snake Beater achievement in Metal Gear Solid 2. Which means nothing to you." He used his fingers to rake his hair away from his face. "Okay. Uh, in Metal Gear you play this character called Snake, and at one point Snake's looking through some lockers. In one there's a poster of a woman wearing not so much of anything. I, as Snake, took a good long look, and, uh, not at her face." She started laughing. Loved that laugh. "And that's how I unlocked the achievement. What can I say? I was, like, eleven. I was curious. Now that's way more embarrassing than getting so nervous you have to pee, right?"

It took her a few seconds to stop laughing enough to speak. "Thank you for that glimpse into male adolescence. I didn't have any brothers, so . . ."

"Sisters?"

"An only."

"Me too. Always wished I had a bro." His parents let him do pretty much whatever he wanted, but staying up till two on a school night probably would have been more fun with a brother. Although, there were lots of nights his dad kept him company. Together they'd unlocked the Horde of Hoofbeats achievement in WoW, and that would never be embarrassing.

"Might have been nice having a sibling." She slid her card into the reader, and he realized in a few seconds she'd be leaving.

"So, what are you going to be doing while you wait for your boyfriend to make it into town?" What was he doing? It wasn't like he could ask her out.

"So far, I've just been looking around the town. I met a couple other trail widows. We're getting together for dinner tonight."

"Sounds good." Because what else was he supposed to say. He handed her the bag with her chocolate bar and her receipt. "We'll make sure all this will be waiting for him at White House."

"Perfect. Well . . . bye."

"Bye." She headed out of the barn, and he let himself enjoy the view for a moment, then started transferring her purchases from the basket to one of the Boots Camp drop buckets. He hesitated with the pale green envelope in his hand. It wasn't sealed. The flap was just tucked in. He carefully pulled it free and removed a sheet of matching paper.

"You're not thinking of reading that," Banana called from over by the coffee maker, "without letting me see it too." He joined Gavin at the register and looked over his shoulder as Gavin read:

> Dearest Owen,
> I love you. I love you. I love you. I love you. I love you. I love you. That's one for every day I haven't been able to say those words to you. I'm counting the days,

hours, minutes until you arrive here in Fox Crossing. My arms ache for you. My lips burn for you.

I think about you almost every moment of every day, at least those moments I'm awake, and even some when I'm asleep, because I dream about you almost every night. I love imagining you out there in the Maine woods, making your dream come true.

I want you to know how proud I am of you. When you get here, you'll be through the hardest stretch of the entire trail. Not many people have the mental and physical strength that you do. I know exactly how hard you've worked. I'm honored to have a small part in helping you reach your goal.

I love you! (I had to say it one more time!) So, so much!

Your Lillian

Gavin folded the letter and replaced it in the envelope.

"Nice letter," Banana said.

Gavin wondered if any woman had ever felt that way about him, had cared so much about his dreams. Although, he couldn't think about a dream that felt big enough, at least right now. He'd hiked the Wilderness with Niri, and done all the rest in sections, by himself sometimes, sometimes with friends. But if he hadn't gotten in every mile, he didn't think he'd care all that much. It had been fun, but he wasn't one of those hikers who saw it as some kind of quest or life test. Was there something other than hiking the AT that he felt that way about? Not getting a specific job, or going to a particular place, or anything that he could think of. Maybe just 'cause he'd always been able to find what he needed to be happy wherever he was.

"Nice letter," Banana repeated.

"Yeah." Gavin put the letter on top of the supply bucket. "Wonder if he knows how good he's got it."

Banana laughed. "Jealous? It seemed like you were liking what you saw."

"Come on. What man wouldn't? It's not like I was going to do anything about it." Gavin put the top on the bucket and wrote Owen's name and the delivery date on the side. "You ever have someone write you a letter like that?"

Banana scratched the salt-and-pepper scruff on his chin. "Letter? No. But Lea felt that way about me once. When I wanted to open the bar with a friend, she was behind me a hundred percent. She was up for moving to Fox Crossing, even though there was only one other black family here, and she worked as many hours as I did when we were getting the place up and running. She really did make my dream her dream. Then it went south. But for a while, yeah I had that."

"Must be nice." Gavin heard a strain of bitterness in his voice, which he hadn't been quite aware he was feeling.

"It was. But maybe that's why it went south with me and Lea. Maybe it wasn't good for her to be so focused on a dream that wasn't hers. She wanted the bar for me. But maybe we should have found something we both wanted. Or at least found a place where she could have something she wanted as much as I wanted the bar."

Gavin hadn't thought about that part of it, the downside for the person who was supporting the person with the dream. "You think that woman, Lillian, feels that way?"

"Didn't sound like it. It's different when it's for the short haul. It's not like she has to give up her life to be his trail angel."

"Yeah, just some months of it. Hey, I was wondering, does that barmaid, the one with the freckles, does she have a boyfriend?"

Banana gave his haw-haw-haw of a laugh. "Tell me again. How long ago did you split with your girlfriend?"

"Don't make it sound so— I'm not looking for a replacement girlfriend. I'm new in town, okay? I just thought maybe she'd want to have dinner with me some night." And possibly also have a little summer fun with him, but he wasn't sure Banana would want to hear that.

"As far as I know, Erin is unattached. She's just home for the summer. So you know, she's still in college."

"Hey, so am I. Are we talking freshman or senior?"

"Going into her senior year. But she worked full-time at the bar for a year before she started."

"And you're saying you think she's too young for dinner?"

"For— None of my business. But she breaks things when she gets mad. She worked for me last summer too, and she almost bankrupted me when she was going through a breakup. That happens this year, and I'll be sending you the bill."

"I'm not planning on breaking any hearts, so I won't be paying for any dishes." The last thing he wanted was drama. Light and easy summer fun. That's all he was looking for.